Praise fo

'One of the most important voices to emerge from the People's Republic in years . . . Startling.'

Daily Express

'Achieves something we haven't seen in Chinese fiction for a while – a refreshingly non-verbose, verb-driven, first-person narrative of taut tension . . . [the] writing is pared back, short, driven by pace, and very to the point . . . a rollercoaster read, so grip the seat, hang on, and be prepared only to relax when you've got to the end of the ride.'

Los Angeles Review of Books

'An unlikely page-turner [that] provides a chilling insight into the mind of a psychopath.'

Irish News

'Shimmering sentences and jolts of original thinking . . . break through the taut, descriptive prose like shafts of sunshine in a strip-lit room.'

Big Issue

'A Yi's isolated narrator is equal parts calculating monster and forsaken victim: deserted, neglected, and ignored, he finds that his only means of feeling alive is to engender death. This austere English PEN Award winner offers an exponentially more chilling alternative to the plethora of dystopic titles; fans of Mo Yan, Yu Hua, Fuminori Nakamura, and even Keigo Higashino will surely find resonating, realistic terror here.'

Library Journa'

'Disturbingly convincing.'

The Complete Review

'Yi, a former police officer, is slowly rising to prominence on the literary scene in China, where this novel was published in 2011. *A Perfect Crime* is a commentary on both the culture and on the amorality and emotional detachment of one individual in it.'

Booklist

'Doused in blood and gushing with ethical conundrums, A Yi's *A Perfect Crime* is a disconcerting medley of misanthropy, escapism, and media monstrosities . . . Where Anthony Burgess sought to conjure a world of abstract flair and inexplicable cruelty in *A Clockwork Orange*, Yi strikes a far deeper chord, delving into the mind of a youth whose lethal motivations are abundantly and undeniably troubling.'

World Literature Today

'Tightly crafted . . . less a traditional catch-him-if-you-can crime caper and more a psychological probe into a pathological mind.'

Wall Street Journal

WAKE ME UP AT NINE IN THE MORNING

by

A Yi

Translated by Nicky Harman

ONEWORLD

A Oneworld Book

First published in the United Kingdom, United States and Australia
by Oneworld Publications, 2022

Copyright © 2018, 2022 by A Yi (Ai Guozhu)
Original title: Wake Me Up at Nine (早上九点叫醒我)
This translation published by agreement with Metropoli d'Asia srl,
Milano, working in conjunction with Anna Spadolini Agency

English translation copyright © 2022 by Nicky Harman

ISBN 978-1-78607-665-6
eISBN 978-1-78607-666-3

Printed and bound in Great Britain by Clays Ltd, Elcograf S.p.A

Oneworld Publications
10 Bloomsbury Street
London WC1B 3SR
England

Stay up to date with the latest books,
special offers, and exclusive content from
Oneworld with our newsletter

Sign up on our website
oneworld-publications.com

MIX
Paper from
responsible sources
FSC® C018072

Character list

In rural China, families with the same surname often live in the same village. In Aiwan, the Ai clan predominate.

Chinese names consist of a surname (Ai, for example) plus given names (such as Hongyang). The first character of the given name is the generational name (Hong, in Hongyang's case). This is shared by all males of the same generation. Thus, the names of the men in Ai Hongyang's generation all start with 'Ai Hong'.

The male generation senior to Ai Hongyang have the generational name Zheng, so their names start with 'Ai Zheng', while the male generation junior to Ai Hongyang have the name Shi. Their names all start 'Ai Shi'.

Ai Hongyang: Formidable outlaw and leader of Fan township's criminal underworld. From Aiwan village (Fan township) in Jiangxi province.

Ai Muxiang: Ai Hongyang's only sister.

Shuizhi: Ai Hongyang's ex-wife.

Jin Yan: Ai Hongyang's lover.

Zhou Haihua: Another lover of Ai Hongyang.

Ai Hongbin: Hongyang's cousin, and his closest friend and associate.

Ai Shiren and **Ai Shiyi**: Hongbin's nephews (sons of his older brother Ai Hongshan).

Chen: Ai Shiren's wife.

Ai Shi'en and **Ai Shide**: Hongbin's sons. Hongyang and Shuizhi had no children, so Shide stands in as chief mourner at the funeral.

Ai Shiguang and **Ai Shiming**: Sons of Ai Hongqi.

Zhou Ping: Ai Shiming's wife.

Ai Hongliang: Hongyang's cousin, a local teacher in Aiwan. He shares Hongyang's story with his nephew, Xu Yousheng, for much of the novel.

Ai Hongxing: Hongliang's elder brother. He has been missing – presumed dead – for eight years.

Xu Yousheng: Ai Hongliang's nephew.

Yilian: The woman Ai Hongliang is in love with.

Daoist priest: Officiates at the funeral ceremony.

The Eight Immortals (the eight men carrying the coffin): Ai Shiren, Ai Shi'en, Ai Shiguang, Ai Shitang, Ai Shizhong, Ai Shishan, Ai Shigang, Ai Shican.

Fuzhong: A village mute, under Hongyang's protection.

Shu Shuang: Childhood friend of Xu Yousheng; takes over as leader of Fan township's criminal underworld after Hongyang's death.

Li Jun: Shu Shuang's cousin and subordinate.

Di Wendong: A policeman from Fan township's police station, later transferred.

Yuan Qihai: Chief of Fan township's police station, later promoted to deputy director of the County Justice Bureau.

Zhao Zhongnan: A policeman at Fan township police station, later promoted to deputy chief and instructor at the police station. A friend of Ai Hongliang's from their schooldays.

Hu Yan: Deputy director of Niujiaolong Reform through Education camp.

Boss Ho: A businessman from Fan township.

Ho Yamin: Boss Ho's son.

Ho Dongming: Deputy mayor, Fan township .

Squint: Real name Hou Fei, from Qichun, Hubei province. A friend of Hongyang's from the Reform through Education camp.

Hook-Pinch: real name Yu, sixteen years old, Squint's girlfriend.

Pickle-Face: Hook-Pinch's classmate and friend.

Wolfdog: Hongyang and Squint's enemy from the Reform through Education camp.

Chen Wangkai: Hongyang's uncle.

PART I

AIWAN, PRESENT DAY

1

Xu Yousheng was to hear a lot more about Jin Yan when he arrived in Aiwan.

Jin Yan glanced up at the blue sky. It appeared ominously clear and calm. Tufts of white clouds drifted by, white horses blanketing the mountaintops and covering the sky all the way to Mongolia, their tails rising and falling. She was shocked by the sky's placid indifference. Around her, everything was permeated with the vile, nauseating smell of slops and sour wine, reminding her of last night's orgy of food and drink in the village.

Every time she caught sight of someone, she would mechanically repeat: 'He's not dead, he's not dead.' She kept saying the same old thing – 'I saw him plain as day, propped against the door, ordering me to get him a cup of water. He can't be dead' – in a vain attempt to distance herself from the appalling fact of Hongyang's death.

The corpse was still being prepared for burial. Every so often, the door into the inner room was pushed open by Hongyang's only sister, Muxiang, as she carried in a basin of clean water, bent over and out of breath, a dry towel gripped between her teeth. Or she pulled it open as she came back out, and stood with one hand pressed to her back as she pointed at the basin, its water scummy with flakes of pale skin, the wet towel hanging over its edge, until a young woman who had been waiting outside deftly removed it.

At her parents' funeral, Muxiang had been distraught. Tears had rolled down her cheeks and she had fainted a couple of times. But now her little brother was dead and she did not say a word. She was on her own from now on: death could do what it liked with her. She looked for comfort from no one, and gave none to others, just bestowed caresses on this hand or that. In no more than the time it takes to cook a meal she had left Yuehua, where she had gone as a young wife so long ago, and come back to Aiwan. As swarms of the family's relatives followed in her wake, this little village of no more than two rows of houses clinging to the mountainside received them as if they were bringing tribute to the imperial capital. No one stipulated who could or could not enter the room of the deceased, but everyone understood that those last private moments belonged only to those who had lived with him or earned his trust. His ex-wife Shuizhi, Wife Number One, had lived alone outside the village for the last ten years or so in a little place called Ruanjiayan, where she had a house and a paddy field, grew her own food and looked after herself. She had a face like potting compost and a heart grey as ashes, and turned up only occasionally at night at the shop in Aiwan when she needed salt, fuel or soap.

The night Hongyang died, Shuizhi told them, she'd had strange palpitations, as if a rabbit was trying desperately to scrabble its way out from inside her, leaving behind a great emptiness in her body. She cried a little, more out of self-pity than because she intended to do anything about this strange feeling.

When Muxiang turned up, the melancholy look in her eyes was enough to communicate her sad news. She addressed Shuizhi gravely as 'Younger Brother's Wife', and it was only then that Shuizhi learned of her husband's death and slumped to the floor in shock, mumbling: 'So that's why!' Then she set off for the home she had left so long before, hands trembling, anxiety leaving her unsteady on her feet.

They'd rebuilt it in the meantime, and it all looked so different that she almost fell over the threshold. Her headscarf slid off and everyone saw the hair hidden underneath, which was a dirty grey flecked with white. She shrieked and wailed before the silent corpse, her shrill cries asserting rights she had lost a very long time before. Shuizhi was now officially a widow, no longer the 'free' person the law had decreed her to be after their divorce. She pushed open the door and went in to help her sister-in-law Muxiang wash the body, from the hair of its head to its scrotum, foreskin, anus and between the toes, professionally, conscientiously, but with the same roughness she'd use to scrub a wooden floor or kitchen table. Then she tried to dress him in his funeral garb and discovered that his strong round arms had grown thin and frail and dangled uselessly at his side. His head lolled like that of a sleeping infant. 'You sit up!' she muttered, her resentful tone telling them all that she was not just the abandoned wife, that she and she alone was his nearest and dearest and always would be: spouse, sister, mother, all women, rolled into one. 'You were such a big mouth all those years, now you sit up properly for me!'

Meanwhile, Jin Yan continued to declare the same thing to anyone she saw: 'He just went to sleep, he can't be dead.' The previous night, after he'd said goodbye and seen his friends off, Hongyang had climbed on top of her. It had taken all her strength to deal with his colossal weight, and her legs had gone limp and she'd yelled: 'You're squashing me, you swine! You'll be the death of me! Why don't you drink yourself to death?' She kept up a stream of curses until finally, early in the morning, she let out a terrible scream. People came running to their room, but he had long ago stopped breathing. They stood silently around the corpse, heads bent. Only Jin Yan beat her breast and tore her hair like a soap opera heroine, shaking him over and over, screeching, 'Husband, you can't die, you can't die, my husband can't be dead!' And he lay there, his body icy-cold and still reeking of drink, his head flopping to one side no matter how hard she shook him. Some of them shot her a stern glance and whispered, 'He's gone.' And eventually she stopped her cries of 'My husband!' It occurred to her that any moment now she might be tried for his murder.

She imagined them asking: What did you feed him? How did he die? You tell us that! Did you poison him? Or, at the very least: A woman like you with such a good opinion of yourself, who knows all about dressing up and having a good time, how come you can't even look after a man? Excuse us, have you got a bed cover to put over him?

Actually, no one wanted him alive more than Jin Yan did. With her husband alive, people from all over had flattered her, doffed their hats at her, made way for her. She could act like the provincial capital official on a village visit, at leisure all day, doing whatever she pleased, enjoying the local scenery with no reason to roll up her trousers and get to work in the paddy fields. She had always regarded these people as friends – peasants were so easy to get close to – but after last night, she sensed that behind their good nature there was a fair degree of cynicism. It was the cynicism of the hunter towards the hunted, of humans towards animals. And mixed in with this was another kind of cynicism, a sort of confident superiority that seemed to whisper: You're nothing but a hooker.

She was afraid of their anger too, afraid they might investigate the cause of death. Sudden death demanded an explanation, you couldn't say that his brothers, nephews, father or neighbours had killed him, or that he'd killed himself. It could only be her, she imagined them saying. It didn't matter that the evidence proved she had nothing to do with it, it would be enough for everyone to grunt 'Uh-huh, uh-huh' in unison and she would be criminalised. After all, she was a woman, an outsider from Hubei province, a female outsider who couldn't sleep unless she had a man's dick to rest on. A dangerous woman, a bad woman.

'Get a doctor to have a look at him,' she said. Their voices rose an octave with annoyance and they almost threw her out, but she crouched at the door and insisted that he'd only been drunk, until Hongbin yelled: 'Get out of here!' As she left, she felt a sudden lightness, and laughter bubbled up inside her until she was seized with the fear that being ejected and stripped of her status meant that she was about to become the chief culprit. She kept looking up at the indigo-blue sky, so blue it seemed on the brink of shattering to pieces, so gloriously blue it made her weep.

Jin Yan didn't know if she had permission to leave the village. To the east was Back Ridge, a narrow concrete road only four li long that joined the Jiu Fan highway at Zhao Hollow. It was almost deserted, had been for the last hundred years, not like the road heading out towards the west, which was lined with the homesteads of Aiwan folks' relatives. There birds twittered under the baking sun, a mountain stream trickled under the bridge between moss-covered pebbles, its banks covered with the spreading branches of cotoneaster, and the breeze ruffled a nearby clump of bamboo.

At the roadside, light and shadows gently quivered. Old Man Hongshu was there, waving his dead right hand with his left and dragging his paralysed right leg behind him. He stomped along all morning with an air of blind determination, though he could hardly walk. His head was like a skull, only its eyeballs alive, shooting looks of furious resentment as he muttered, 'One hundred and twelve,' 'One hundred and thirteen,' counting the number of times he had waved his right hand. When he brushed past Jin Yan, he did not look at her. She walked on another ten metres and then came to a halt because she heard voices from the bamboo. 'Get a move on, quick!' they urged her.

'No, it's a trap.' Old Man Hongshu couldn't yell at her or grab her, he could only stand where he was, waving that huge crippled right hand, shaking his healthy left leg and forcing sounds from his mouth. But he would certainly make it his duty as an Aiwan man to attract the villagers' attention, and even if he didn't, it wouldn't take long for the rest of them to realise she'd gone and then they'd bring ropes and sticks and take her captive. See, she's got a guilty conscience, they'd say.

And as they had the night before, her legs went limp and the backs of her knees shook and shook and shook some more, as if they could not hold her up any longer, and she sobbed inwardly: Dad! If you still remember your daughter, get here – fast!

She heard footsteps from the stream, and when she turned to look, she saw a woman approaching with a bucket of dirty washing. There was nothing for it but to go back with her tail between her legs. Jin Yan comforted herself that even though she could leave, it wasn't the right time to go, with the corpse scarcely cold, and she kept encouraging herself silently: Shut your eyes, and this difficult day will be like so many others, it will vanish like ripples on the surface of the stream. She tried to imagine herself standing at some point in the future, casually recalling this long-ago moment. I nearly wet myself with fear, she might say.

In the end things were settled by Shiren, a nephew of Hongyang's. 'Of course he's dead,' Shiren said through gritted teeth as he gave Jin Yan a stinging slap across the face. Even though she felt the salty tang of blood as it spurted from the corner of her mouth, she found herself smiling. But a short moment later she felt a fierce rush of air, like a door slamming against her cheek, and she got another slap. 'If you weren't his mistress, I'd have got rid of you a long time ago,' Shiren said as he whacked her.

She felt a huge sense of relief as she repeated this silently: 'If you weren't his mistress' means 'If you weren't my relative.' Her relief was tinged with gratitude. No one was bothering with her, they were all much too busy forming an assembly line and doing their bit so that everything would be ready to bury the corpse: tomorrow was an auspicious day, and by the next day the body would stink if the burial was put off.

It was true that some of them were angry, but for now they had only an overriding contempt for Jin Yan. The punishment could wait. She did not understand what was going on, just wandered around wanting this, wanting that, bringing more blows on herself. Feeling she hadn't been cuffed enough, she went on provoking Shiren, winding him up like a clockwork toy. It was only by goading him that she could test the length and breadth of the punishment, only when the blows hurt that she could truly appreciate their magnanimity. She had spent years as an actress, using the stage name Shenzhen A. Fang, and now she put those skills to good use, weeping and laughing, throwing fits and shrieking, clinging to Shiren's calves and spinning like a top on the floor.

After this had been going on some time, Shiren squinted down at her with his cigarette dangling from his lips. He bent down and grabbed her chest, pinching her slack breasts between his fingers, then hauled her upright in his arms and delivered another hard slap across the face.

'What way is this to behave? He's still your man regardless, even though he's dead, even if you're not his woman, so now you can get the hell out of here. The further the better,' he pronounced.

And she went, sobbing and sniffling.

'Colgate!' Shiren shouted after her retreating figure. 'Without Colgate toothpaste, he wouldn't get out of bed in the morning. He used to send someone to buy tubes of it in our store, not any old brand, not even Crest, it had to be Colgate, as recommended by National Caries Prevention, or he'd go on hunger strike.' Eventually Shi'en, Shiren's cousin, pedalled off to Fan township to get him some.

2

Well, that's how people are, thought Xu Yousheng as he prepared to leave Fan township. He'd started by thinking that he absolutely must do something, at the very least shout out the news that someone had died. But it produced not even a frisson of interest in the little town. It was as if everyone had already heard it and just gone on with what they were doing. A large lorry braked with a dull snort, the flies dive-bombed a desiccated corpse-like fried breadstick that had lain unsold since the morning in a greasy basket, the earth turned on its axis, and a man who had pissed and shat on their heads for more than a dozen years was dead. It was as insignificant to them as a bamboo stake propped against a wall ten thousand li away quietly sliding to the ground, or a shell shifting a centimetre along the ocean floor. They were indifferent.

Hongyang should have known that the death of someone of his rank would have only a limited effect. So said Zhu the schoolteacher. Zhu licked his finger and flicked the pages of a blue-bound accounts book as thick as a dictionary, which listed the quantities and prices of goods bought and sold and the names of those who bought on credit. After a short pause, he made a note to the effect that Xu Yousheng had said his uncle Hongbin would drop by and pay what was owed. When he got to the pages where some funeral couplets had been copied out, Zhu seemed to feel they were bad luck. He held the book at arm's length and craned back his neck as far as he could. 'Nothing suitable,' he said. But then he did write out on a sheet of cut green paper the words:

Some have enjoyed what I began,
But sadly, all will end with me.

General Wang Jingwei had written and personally presented this couplet to Zhu, and he was passing it on to Xu Yousheng. As he saw Xu Yousheng come out of his shop – the shop was right by the gate to the public health clinic, with a huge signboard reading *Burial Clothes and Wreaths*, which often upset patients out for a stroll so much that they were reduced to tears – he clapped Xu Yousheng on the shoulder and followed up with a 'Well, that's what people are like.' Xu Yousheng reckoned he was depressed all morning for precisely the reason that he himself would die one day.

The speeding moped made him bold as the roadside bushes flew by and were left behind and the cement road rushed away in front of him and the wind poured into his shirt, making it swell like a sail. Man and machine flashed along in almost complete silence, mere shadows cast on the sunlit wall, so that Xu Yousheng felt like he was wearing an invisibility cloak. He yelled imperiously at the hoe-toting peasants who stood in the middle of the road. He, after all, was doing business for the dead. 'Out of my way! Out of my way!' he shouted, as if he was charged with an imperial edict that gave him the right to ride full tilt through their paddy fields, trampling the rice seedlings under his horse's hooves. In reality, the message he carried was only a pretext, the key thing being to reiterate that he had the right to trample the seedlings as his horse's hooves sank a hole in the mud, toppled fresh plants and sprayed mud in all directions.

His enthusiasm faded when he reached the lower slopes of Tieling Ridge, and he began to regret not having come on a bicycle. The road dropped from the peak, steep and winding. In the years since Liberation, a total of twenty-seven vehicles had plummeted head first into the lake halfway down the mountain. One of them had been a three-wheeled cab with sixteen passengers and an electric motor nowhere near powerful enough to get up the mountain road.

Xu Yousheng stopped to smoke a cigarette. His load of funeral goods attracted the unwanted attention of some kids from Laowuzengjia village, though not the one with the squint. They gawped at the goods and then smiled ingratiatingly at him as they tried to figure out from the changes in his expression what was going on, but he yelled: 'Get the fuck out of here!' and they scattered. These were good children, unlike Hongyang, who had looked daggers at you, even as a little kid. A person like that was born once in a generation, he thought.

Zhou Haihua sat on a plastic stool, rubbing soap into the clothes while the washing machine in the corner hummed away at its work. She carried on handwashing because she wasn't convinced the washing machine got the clothes clean, and hard manual labour was women's *raison d'être*, a path to self-esteem. Her husband – home from the county community middle school where he taught because it was the summer holidays – sat with one leg draped over the other, his chair tipped back and his head resting against the wall, his eyes reduced to narrow slits by the angle of his head. This was something out of the ordinary, this house, with its sumptuous glazed roof, ceramic wall tiles, aluminium alloy window frames and roller shutter doors. Hongyang had stumped up the money for it, though he could not say so outright, nor could Haihua. Her lawful wedded husband could not mention it either. He had found that very difficult to accept at the beginning, but gradually realised that he had no power to fight back, or, to put it more accurately, to refute it. She keeps things to herself, she isn't one to talk to outsiders about family stuff, he comforted himself by thinking. Although such thoughts often made him feel worse, hell, the gloom always passed eventually, didn't it?

With today's news of Hongyang's death he felt a stab of anguish again, though, like when he had been asked to leave the house once before so that those inside could get together in a huddle to have a good gossip in which he figured prominently. Well, that would be the last time he'd be troubled by that stuff. No, no, surely it wouldn't be the last time, the schoolteacher thought. Some people die, but *he* would live on. On people's lips, in their expressions and in their hearts, Hongyang would be immortal, and he was destined forever to be the sad bit-part player in that man's drama.

The husband looked at his wife now, at the damp hair clinging to her temples and the beads of sweat on her forehead, neck and cleavage, no doubt thinking the same way as Xu Yousheng: how it must have softened Hongyang, it must have emptied him out completely, the delicacy of this woman's appearance, only slightly marred by a touch of sweat. When Hongyang pressed Zhou Haihua's buttocks against himself, making her shriek for help, and the ground rose and fell beneath her feet, her forehead no doubt must have grown damp, sticking her hair to her temples just like now. She is as beautiful as a fox demon. She has no need for make-up or flirting, no need to throw herself at a man, she only has to sit her plump white body by the roadside for men's imaginations to run wild. Her buttocks, perched on the stool now, are broad and firm, and her tight trousers emphasise their full curves. With her back turned to that man's cock, well, it had to happen, he thought.

Sometimes Hongyang would drop in and have sex with Zhou Haihua after he had set out from Aiwan, or when he was on his way back home from Fan township. Many years ago, this homestead in its narrow pass had been a nightmare for Jiuyuan travellers – outrageously expensive and full of crooks looking to make easy money out of hapless outsiders. More recently, however, it had simply been a tea and relay station for Hongyang, an imperial lodge, you might call it.

Her husband watched her silently as she rubbed the garments, lifting and dropping them with a rhythmic splashing. She remained quite unaware of his cold and relentless gaze. But she must already know; how could she not? The news had been going around since morning and must have arrived at the county town, especially now so many people had mobile phones. Her silence was probably because she was waiting for him to process his feelings. When he'd thought it through, he'd probably get to his feet and come over and say: He's dead. She would drop her head even lower. He would go on: He's dead now. She would begin to weep, and before she'd finished, she'd throw her arms around his legs, soaking his trouser legs with soap suds, and his legs would go rigid as he bit the insides of his cheeks.

He had to act resolutely. The trouble was that he was such a simple soul. No one was gentler than him. He had an underbite and his lower teeth stuck out a couple of centimetres, which created the impression that everything he did was a bit of a joke.

Once Xu Yousheng topped the first rise and stopped for a smoke, he could see the husband sitting with his elbows propped on his knees and his fists jammed against his teeth, staring earnestly at his wife. She was still rubbing the clothes, lifting and dropping them, as if she could hide behind that rhythmic splashing.

Xu Yousheng would stop once more before he reached the pass, from where the road sped on downwards. The buffer strip at the bottom was called Zhao Hollow, and was the perfect spot for him to pause and have a quick smoke on the way down. To the east of the hollow was a dug-out cliff face where the layers of rock had crumbled. To the west, there was a narrow concrete road – that was Back Ridge – at the end of which was Aiwan, Xu Yousheng's destination.

The rain had stopped, replaced now with bright sunlight. Everything looked crystal clear, the bare tree branches glistening with an almost oily sheen as a raven whooshed overhead towards Aiwan. The enormous bird tucked in its wings and glided down until its belly almost grazed the ground, then gently opened them again and soared into the sky, rising, falling, flying, gliding, like the spirit of some ancient prophet.

Jin Yan had come from that direction too. Three years ago, when she had arrived in Fan township, the man who brought her said they were doing location filming here and that he knew the director. When she got out of the car she looked like an actress with her long permed hair, her red dress, her nails painted royal blue. In her hand she clutched a knock-off, dung-coloured Louis Vuitton bag, a long, thin Esse cigarette held tightly between her fingers. With each drag her bosom swelled, the blue-grey smoke streaming from her scarlet lips like motorbike exhaust. She leaned up against the car door, swinging one high-heeled sandal from her big toe.

The driver had also brought a man he introduced as Boss Ho. The man had a long hair growing from his nostril and appeared as frantic as a donkey torn between two bundles of grass, not knowing whether to look first at her face or her bosom. All the while his penis stood up inside his trousers, which you could see had been left partially unbuttoned. He grasped her small, icy hand with his sweaty paw. She went with him, mincing along like a model on the catwalk, into the Fan Township Hotel for a 'bit of business'. Once inside the room, Boss Ho stripped down to his underpants and said the business was no more than a quick poke, and she looked up at the ceiling and imagined the clouds five thousand feet above them.

At that exact instant, the gates to Hollywood slammed shut. There were grains of coal dust on Boss Ho's slack belly. Jin Yan almost cried as she looked down, like someone who's just received a text telling them they've won a prize and then had a follow-up message reminding them that there's no such thing as a free lunch. This was what she did, after all. A minute later, Boss Ho ejaculated.

She had spent three years slinking around the township, and some of the high-school girls had even modelled themselves on her. And now Hongyang was dead and she was back where she'd started. Her legs permanently akimbo, she waddled like a penguin. She had been squashed so thoroughly she was almost as flat as a pancake. Xu Yousheng even imagined that when Hongyang lay on top of her, her legs and arms automatically sprang upwards. By now, she bore the scars of the years she had spent here: hair matted with dust, scabs at the corner of her lips, a bruise under one eye socket. 'You just wait, you sons of bitches,' she muttered to herself, and happily imagined a bunch of men with drills rushing house-to-house poking them all, right down to the family hens.

Jin Yan felt gloriously spiteful; she was not leaving of her own accord but being driven away by hatred. She did not know where she was or where she was heading. Her subconscious seemed to be in control. She knew she should be waiting by the roadside for the minibus that would take her to Fan township and the county town, from where she could catch the Beijing to Hong Kong train and be back home before the day was out. Instead she trudged blindly on, and even at this pace she wouldn't be in Fan township before dark. She was in the grip of intense emotion. She had wanted to punish herself – without punishment she would feel guilty her whole life – but now it had come, she felt aggrieved. The very thought made her chew her lip and tremble with fury.

Xu Yousheng was the first familiar face she saw after leaving the village, and her tears erupted like Coca-Cola fizzing from a freshly shaken bottle. To his bewilderment, she threw herself upon his chest.

'He won't come back to life, you'd better accept it.'

'Don't say anything.'

When she'd caught sight of Xu Yousheng, he had been sitting sideways on the bike, one leg draped over the other, staring blankly as she approached. He had a half-smoked cigarette hanging from his lips, a long finger of ash trembling at its tip, poised to fall off. He's loyal to me, she thought. Even the way he's avoiding me betrays how much he loves me.

This was how she figured it: A woman knows perfectly well which man really loves her. Other men only love her cunt, but this one loves the person she is – her personality, her temperament, her life experience and her destiny – and to him she's not just a sex object. Even if he doesn't meet her eyes, he's always present, full of sympathy. And it's not the sympathy of a master but that of an elder brother: the helpless, anxious sympathy of someone who feels impelled to protect her. Over the last three years, every time Xu Yousheng had looked at her his expression was melancholy, his eyes a deep lake.

Or maybe that was what she needed to feel.

He put his arms around her gently and his penis stiffened. Jin Yan ranted and raved about everyone from Aiwan while he listened earnestly but took in little. She tugged at him and, still talking, they took the gravel track down to the riverbank at the bottom of the hollow, Xu Yousheng pulling his bike behind him. In the dappled sunlight, the pebbles were hot underfoot. His head started to spin, and as the smell intensified all around, so too did his desire.

'Why did they beat me?' she was saying.

'Who beat you?'

'Shiren and Hongbin.'

'Right, I'll get them for that.'

'You give them a beating, for me.'

'I'll remember they beat you.'

'You've got to give them a beating.'

'Uh-huh.'

'Beat them to death.'

'Uh-huh. Beat them to death.'

'Swear it.'

'I swear.'

She giggled. Then she kissed him hard on the cheek. 'Do you love me?' she asked.

He nodded.

'Naughty boy. Poor boy.' And she snuggled into his arms.

He caressed her breasts, so soft it felt like they were stuffed with cotton padding, and his heart was suddenly weightless. She closed her eyes, but he glanced up from time to time through the clumps of silver grass that blocked the view of the road. Then she sat on the bike seat and he pulled at her knickers and she bent her legs before stretching them so he could pull off the knickers more quickly. All the while she was saying 'Don't do that.' She put both hands behind her and held on to the handlebars – no mean feat – and spread her legs to expose her private parts, out of bounds to him until now.

Mountain streams, wet stones, piles of hay: anywhere surrounded by peace and silence somehow sent a chill down your spine when thinking of the terrible consequences. And all the while she was still saying 'Don't do that.'

Xu Yousheng felt that the real test was the act of sex itself. It was cruel to pit a man who was new to it against an experienced woman. Inside himself he was shrinking away, but his body was driving him on, and when he saw her narrow entrance he felt sorrow. 'It's difficult like this,' he said. Finally, he gave her luminous white thighs a few slaps and turned and went down to the riverbank, where half a dozen glistening green water-drop Bodhisattva plants were growing, leaves broad as palm fans. He plucked six leaves and poured water over them, then laid them in three rows of two on the ground.

'I can see you know what you're doing,' said Jin Yan, crawling onto them. She positioned herself on her front, each elbow, knee and foot resting on a leaf. Her golden buttocks stuck up like a horse's rump as she quietly waited for Xu Yousheng.

Xu Yousheng was playing for time and inserted two fingers into her vagina, which was dripping wet, so wet that he had to withdraw his fingers and flick the drops off, flick, flick, like a doctor shaking down a thermometer. 'Don't, don't,' she groaned. Finally he penetrated her with a penis so stiff that it trembled, and gritted his teeth (according to a medical journal he had read, fifteen thrusts were enough for it not to count as premature ejaculation) before being swept away by ecstasy.

He had entered the body he had desired for so long, the body of a woman, the body of the Virgin Mary and the Guanyin Goddess of Mercy, the body of the celebrated widow who had belonged to Hongyang. His corpse was barely cold in the ground, but Xu Yousheng and she had become one. 'I didn't let him walk all over me, I made use of him too, a good many times,' she said. The truth was that she was little more than a mistress or a hooker, though.

Two and a half years earlier, when Hongyang had first become aware of her existence, he had walked into a nightclub and said to the pimp, a man from a different province who also happened to be her boyfriend, 'I'm going to set her free.' The man took out his knife and Hongyang snatched it and plunged it into the tabletop. 'I'm going to set her free,' Hongyang repeated, gripping the pimp's scrawny arm. The pimp screwed up his face and yelled, 'Mate, I've invested so much in her, spent so much on her, shed so much blood for her, and now I'll never make it back.'

'Did you bring her up? Has she got the looks she has because you've spent money on her? How much have you spent on her board and lodging? What gives you the right to earn money from her? Are you her dad?'

It was more than he would normally say in an entire day. Hongyang tended to think of talking as being rather undignified. He thought it over, figured he had nothing else to relieve his loneliness, then gave his opponent a good beating.

'Get the hell out of Fan township,' he said. And the pimp did just that, and a few of her clients followed too and lay low for a bit, worried that she might let on about their wretched performance in bed – she always had shot her mouth off.

'I'm setting you free,' Hongyang told her. She nodded, and followed him to the township Cooperative and later to Aiwan village.

Now there was a clock ticking loudly in Xu Yousheng's head, to sixty seconds, and then from the first minute to a full five minutes (no one could accuse him of premature ejaculation if he could last five minutes). Stretching endlessly before him, time was a huge basket that he would never fill no matter how hard he tried, so he attempted to eke out his thrusts and avoid anything that might overexcite him by alternating little movements, a word or two, a caress.

'I haven't done it for a long time, otherwise . . .' he said.

'Don't say anything – this is how I like it. The point of life isn't to arrive, it's to follow the road and look at the landscape,' she said.

His confidence boosted by this lyrical language, Xu Yousheng took hold of her chin and asked: 'Does it feel good?'

'Why do all men ask that question?' she said. That made him feel disheartened, but at the same time he got his first peek into the great man's shameful secret: Hongyang had always charged into the fray and ejaculated after a couple of thrusts.

Xu Yousheng said tenderly: 'I want us to spend the rest of our lives together!' The words were no sooner out of his mouth than he wondered what the Fan township folk would make of it once they knew. His words sounded phoney even to his own ears, and he wished he could unsay them. When she said she was planning a trip home to see her family, he felt immensely relieved, then full of regret.

'Will you come back?' he asked.

'Hard to say.'

'Look me up if you come back.'

'If I come back, of course I'll look you up. Or you can come and see me.'

'I'm going to miss you.' He looked at the time on his mobile. 'You could get the bus – it would take two hours. If you hadn't met me, you'd be nearly there by now. Don't keep on walking, it'll take you forever.'

'Give me a ride on the bike.'

'I'd like to, but I can't right now.'

'Why can't you? Give me a ride on the bike.'

'I really can't.'

He embraced her again and again, then pushed the bike back to the concrete road.

Jin Yan pinched his cheek. 'I was only joking.' She walked on alone, then as she reached Zhao Hollow, she came back and put her arms around him again. 'I like you so much.'

'I feel the same way.'

Xu Yousheng followed her with his eyes as she went to stand on the main road. She winked at him, and he felt for a moment as if all he could see was a shadow wavering in the warm air, the way we're used to seeing our shadows in running water. A moment later, the bus from Zhangjiaba roared up, belching exhaust fumes, and the driver went down to the stream at the bottom of the hollow to get some water. He noticed that someone had left a mystery message there, in the form of six leaves lined up, two by two, in three rows.

Jin Yan sashayed to the bus door. It had soldering marks all over the bodywork, like scars on human skin, and the cracks were crammed with mud. The windows had either had their glass knocked out or shattered into a cobweb design of thin white cracks. She looked at her reflection, then backed away and looked around to see a fuzzy image of her buttocks in the broken glass.

When the driver came back, she finally boarded. She spent a bit of time hunting for a seat, took out a paper towel and wiped it clean, to mark herself out as different from the rest of them. Then she looked through the window, they waved at each other, and the bus belched more grey-blue smoke, toiled up the hill and disappeared from sight.

Xu Yousheng turned the bike around and headed back to Aiwan. The once-brilliant day seemed to have grown dark, a common feeling when someone was gone, as if the light was decaying and growing patches of mould. He felt that he was travelling to the end of time: night time. And to the end of the world: the United Nations, China, Jiangxi province, Jiujiang city, Ruichang county town, Fan township, Yuanjiuyuan administrative area, Xiayuan village, Aiwan hamlet. And she was taking herself off in the opposite direction. He already missed her terribly, felt completely gutted, as if they were parting forever, even though he was only going to stay a day and a night in Aiwan.

At the bamboo thicket, Xu Yousheng got off the moped out of respect. The potholes in the road had been full of water, so the concrete bridge was covered in track marks of different shapes and sizes, and he could tell which cars had sped past towards the village, the drivers probably hooting the horn loudly because they lacked even the slightest respect for the dead.

PART II

HONGLIANG'S TALE

3

Just yesterday they had all been tiptoeing around Hongyang because he was so sensitive to noise. They would never forget the time the shopkeeper next door had failed to understand that he had to pull down his shutters very quietly. Hongyang had swung at his aluminium alloy doors with a hammer and caved them in.

'If you think about it, Hongyang has only ever admitted he was wrong once in his life,' Uncle Hongliang said. Hongliang wore a haughty expression that made him appear older than his twenty-six years. His only brother Hongxing, who had disappeared eight years ago, would have been forty-three.

Hongliang was the product of elderly parents and had been a lonely, bored child. Every time a kid his own age clapped him on the shoulder, he would duck away in fear. But it meant that he had talked to Hongyang, who was eighteen years older than him, as confidently as if they were the same age. Hongliang's mother, Xu Yousheng's maternal grandmother, had ordered him to wash up a stack of dirty dishes soaking in the pink plastic bowl, left over from last night's big feast. Tomorrow they would be covered in grease again. 'You eat, you shit, you shit, you eat, you die,' he groused. The old woman took no notice, apart from coming over every now and then to turn off extra lights. He waited until evening until he washed them.

Hongliang began to tell a story to Xu Yousheng.

It was the first and final time Hongyang had been so humiliated. They hoisted his arms up high as he trotted along with his head on one side, whinging that they were treating him like some petty thief. There were two rake-thin police officers, and Hongyang, who was built like a bear. They escorted him to Back Ridge. Back then the concrete road wasn't built yet, so the jeep couldn't get any further than Zhao Hollow. We were upset, not because one of our own had been taken away, but because he was so useless; year after year we'd swallowed his insults and waited on him hand and foot, and it turned out he was a complete coward. A coward! What I'm saying, Yousheng, is that you have to get a bit more streetwise, grow a thick skin, put up with a certain amount of humiliation. All the same, though, what you absolutely mustn't do is grovel like a Pekinese dog. You can't act completely spineless, right?

He didn't even wave an arm in protest, he seemed perfectly happy to go along with them, and off he trotted like a good boy. When he got to the bend in the road, he shouted that there was a wild boar. Taking advantage of the guards' surprise, he shook himself free and took off up the mountain. He thought he could use the brief distraction, grab that golden opportunity to flee, but one of the policemen shouted at him: 'Don't move or I'll fire!' and Hongyang stopped and stood there, his legs trembling, until he slowly turned round and saw that the cop was just pointing his finger, an impressive-looking finger. Then he took to his heels again.

When he got back to the village, he was very pleased with himself, told everyone about it, then got together some food and went and took refuge on the mountain. We thought good riddance, and never gave him a second thought. But they came back in force, the two cops and two members of the Public Security Bureau's team, and a driver, and a heavy-duty four-battery torch too – that was what they later used to hit Shuizhi on the collarbone when she was resisting arrest. That was a bad blunder, although at the time there didn't seem to be any other way, because if they returned empty-handed, they might be asked: 'And where's the person we sent you to pick up?' Worse still, they would feel the locals' eyes on them. They wouldn't say it out loud, but there would be silent criticisms about how the police had messed up again. The local police could not bear to lose face, and besides, it made the whole country look bad. Their police badges were embroidered with the five-pointed star, the ear of wheat and the Great Wall, they had to re-establish their authority, they must not betray any weaknesses.

At their wits' end, they decided to take Shuizhi away in the hopes that this would persuade Hongyang to give himself up. But then they were criticised for their action by the Public Security Bureau. Any other time and they wouldn't have acted like that, but just this once they felt a fierce sense of dignity. They wanted to piss on someone who'd made them doff their caps in the past. At the same time, they thought picking up a woman would be as simple as grabbing hold of a chicken. How could they know she'd be so hard to move?

First, Shuizhi flung herself to the ground to make herself heavier, then she grabbed and bit their calves. Whenever she came up against some large object, she clung to it, even going so far as to hook her legs around it too. Women were such a pain in the neck. To try and make it go a bit more smoothly, one of the Public Security team members raised the torch and banged it down on her collarbone. And that was it. She foamed at the mouth, gabbled wildly, and gasped for breath as if she was about to expire. They knew by now that she was of no value in herself, but it was just their bad luck that they couldn't let her go. If they did so, they'd be a laughing stock. It was like a certain General said about the proverbial plot of desert land: Although it has no military value, you can't *not* conquer it, because army morale depends on it.

So they dragged Shuizhi off to the threshing ground. That ostrich, Hongyang, skulking on the mountain, had a bird's-eye view. If he'd gone, we'd have put a stop to what they were doing to Shuizhi, but he was crouched down in a low bush, and right here . . .

Xu Yousheng's thoughts began to wander. Jin Yan must have left Fan township by now. He shoved his phone back into his pocket. A moment before, he had washed a bowl, washed his hands in a bucket and dried them on the seat of his trousers, then taken out his phone to sneak a look and see if there were any messages, but there was only a spam message from an online magazine, which read: *Everything's wrong about a place a woman's abandoned, things will never go well there.*

Hongliang continued.

Shuizhi's legs left two trails in the dirt, and she wailed piteously. Then, in the interests of dramatic authenticity, she went quite rigid before apparently coming to her senses again, though afterwards she would say that this rigidity was a last rush of vitality before she expired. Her eyes were dull and she groaned over and over: 'I'm . . . going . . . to . . . die, I'm . . . going . . . to . . . die.' She tried everything.

As soon as they got to the deserted surroundings of Back Ridge, they could stop pretending to care what happened to her. They carried her along by the arms and feet, as if she was merely a stretcher – after all, she only weighed seventy or eighty jin – though she had put up an incredible struggle up till now. She was as dried-up as a crack in the rock that nothing could grow out of, she hadn't been able to bear children, and she was nothing to look at. As long as she was still herself, though, so long as a finger of hers was still alive, so long as her groans floated in the air and people still spoke of her, then she would continue to taunt Hongyang, a reminder of his failings as a man.

We heard a rustling from up behind the village. As he ran down the track brushing against the tree branches, his teeth knocking together as if he was being kicked along the hard road surface until his skull nearly cracked open, he caught up with the officers. Sounding more like the police than the police themselves, he commanded: 'Let her go.'

'We thought you weren't coming!'

Their words sounded strange and uncertain. The whole object of the exercise had been to force Hongyang out into the open, but now that he was here, they had to try their utmost to convince themselves that they were in control of the situation. By now Hongyang was a whirlwind of excitement, a jumble of words rushed from his mouth like a swarm of bees. Finally, he pulled himself together and forced himself to speak slowly.

'You . . . can beat and . . . abuse me a thousand . . . ten thousand times . . . but you cannot . . . touch my woman . . . once . . . understand?' He was so confident that he was in the right that he grabbed the collar of one of the Public Security team who in turn had hold of Shuizhi by the collar, and demanded: 'Tell me, why are you beating her? Why? Why?'

And that was when they realised they hadn't prepared themselves. There was no time to think up a plausible excuse now, so after a feeble attempt to fob him off, they finally retorted: 'We beat her, so what?'

A bowl spun through the air and dropped into the bucket with a dull thud, and Hongliang demonstrated the beating by pretending to slap Xu Yousheng's face a few times with a soapy hand, as Xu Yousheng backed away.

*   *   *

'What's all this about, eh?' Hongyang slapped the officer, first across the right cheek, then the left, back and forth, back and forth, bam, bam, bam, a total of eighteen smacks, as if smacking away his own weakness and inferiority.

The officers grabbed Hongyang. Then all those old people in the village who had lived too long and were bored out of their minds came running. They started swiping at the officers' legs with their brooms and walking sticks, until the officers finally understood that you could not lay a finger on the old and the young and the women. They lowered their heads and tried to break through the wall of people that hemmed them in. We stood stock-still, not stopping them but not letting them through either. We formed a sort of human wall – as you know, there's nothing illegal about that.

Finally they found an opening and slipped through. One of the officers, the gangly one with sloping shoulders and a very big head, even went as far as to ask us: 'Excuse me, please let us through.' He was definitely the most courteous of the lot. I wouldn't be surprised if it was his first police operation. He was very fair-skinned and didn't act like a countryman. And that was how the whole thing concluded, oddly enough. They were supposed to pick up Hongyang but didn't, and Hongyang's woman got a severe beating.

We waited in the end-of-performance silence, both sides having abruptly called it quits, wondering quite where the sound and the fury had disappeared to, why calm had descended so quickly, until they exchanged looks and made off, leaving us open-mouthed. They put all their energy and determination into their legs, as if they were mime artists, and disappeared in a cloud of dust. Only Gangly walked at a more sedate pace. He must have been tempted to fly along with them, because he peered after them, although he only walked a little faster. Even though he was no doubt aware of our eyes fixed on his retreating figure, he kept a tight grip on himself. I suppose he imagined he could leave safely this way, but I bet he was also thinking how you can't just scuttle away like a frightened rat when you're in a uniform.

Then the other Public Security team officer, the one with the Stalin moustache, landed him in the shit. When he was a safe distance away, he brandished a kitchen knife and yelled: 'You Aiwan folk, don't do anything stupid, I've got criminal evidence here.' We started shouting and yelling then, especially the man who realised he'd lost his kitchen knife. He'd been waving it in the air, making chopping motions with the back of the blade, and somehow it ended up being stolen from him. He thought the knife might get him convicted or, worse still, executed, so he set off in pursuit, followed by a dozen others.

The police scattered, one of them running up the mountain. Only Gangly was still walking, though he sped up so much he nearly fell over his feet. As we surged forwards, it looked like he was one of us – he reminded me of a defeated soldier trying to pass himself off as an ordinary civilian in a crowd. We never did catch them up, we were upset about that, and scared too, though all we wanted to do was to get hold of the evidence, and on our way back, the sight of Gangly made us even more upset. He was red-faced with annoyance as he tried to blend in, and for a while it looked as if he would get away, until someone gave a loud laugh and it dawned on us that here we had a hostage.

We lifted him into the air, yelling crazily: 'We got him! We can do what we like with him!', as if we were going to carry him off on an ox cart heaped with resin-soaked firewood and put him to death. Afterwards I heard he'd resigned from the police and had gone off travelling. I don't know if that's true, but maybe he's looking down from the heavens on us tiny-as-silkworm-egg mortals right now.

*　　*　　*

Xu Yousheng looked up at a plank on the ceiling, which was yellow and glowing like a pine torch though it must have been white and covered in whiskers to start with. A chandelier dangled from it, and some cured meat and countless dust tendrils; the outside layer of fat was wrinkled and hard, like human hams that had had to be cured, not thrown out, because they'd been cut off the body. We live in a vertical society, Xu Yousheng thought as he looked at his uncle, and we're at the bottom of the heap.

Gangly's tears spilled from the corners of his eyes, as if someone had knocked over a water jug, and he prayed 'Merciful Bodhisattva!' in a reedy voice. We flung him to the ground. Then Hongyang got hold of him by his collar and pulled him up.

'Why did you arrest my woman? Why did you beat her? What crime did she ever commit?'

But the man wasn't making any meaningful sounds by then, just whining. In the end, he signed a document certifying that firstly, we had never harmed the police with that knife or any other weapon, secondly, Shuizhi had been arrested without any cause and had been seriously hurt, and thirdly, the police would foot the bill for all the medical treatment of Shuizhi and any other injured villagers.

As he pressed his fingerprint on it, we clustered around him like a flock of vultures, and without being asked, he silently took out all his money. Someone suggested that he should carry Shuizhi on his back to the local hospital, and had started to make a stretcher with split bamboo woven across two straight pieces of wood, when someone else said to him, 'You dickhead, you're walking straight into a trap!' And anyway, we had no idea what our next move should be and we let him go.

Down in Zhao Hollow, Gangly met twelve colleagues from three local police posts. They were armed with two pistols, each ready to fight their way back to Aiwan, when a motorbike sped up and the rider shouted at them to stay where they were. The Bureau chief had been dispatched by the mayor, who in turn had been phoned by Zhang Gongti. Zhang Gongti worked on the provincial government planning committee, his aunt was from Aiwan, and it was he who put a stop to this business, saying that each side had suffered losses, and that they should call it quits. It was only Shuizhi who carried on whispering so convincingly that anyone listening to her for the first time might believe that she had been critically injured. She was a good woman, and she knew that by whispering she could mount up the evidence for Hongyang and all the villagers, and if and when there was a settling-up, she would be able to say: I nearly died, you know, I was in bed a whole week and I actually nearly died.

The chandelier looked like an anchor. The lamp base had been forged, bent, welded and spray-painted to look like it belonged in a European country house. It was lit by six coffee-shop-style bulbs, each emitting a warm golden glow like everlasting candles, and Hongliang often raised his tall, amber-stemmed glass to the chandelier and sipped his brandy, to the accompaniment of Fleetwood Mac on the sound system. The vocals were low and gravelly, gradually eclipsed during the song as the instrumental took over, making you feel weightless, as if suspended over a waterfall.

Hongliang used to listen to one particular ballad over and over as he sat under the chandelier, writing love letters he'd never send. Until, one day, he received a response. She came back, by buses and trains, from Xiushui county town. After his three years of teacher training college, their relationship seemed to retain a hallowed ambiguity: every day as the sun went down, he waited by the basketball court to see her come out of an alley to fetch boiling water and go back the same way. They would sneak glances at one another, unless she was uninterested that day. If that was the case then she wouldn't look at him, but if she was interested she'd flaunt herself, and he'd waste a lot of time feeling upset about it.

Now she came swinging along wearing a long sleeveless jumper, a short denim skirt and black leggings, and he didn't know what to do. Her long legs, encased tightly in black nylon, nicely rounded and well proportioned, tempted his lustful eyes upwards to roam over her perfect body. She was brand new, had not had time to go to rack and ruin, he observed surreptitiously, and for many days afterwards, those long legs – especially when she wore the white ballet flats that made walking difficult and encased her dancer's feet – would trample on his heart like a watchful deer in a forest, making him double over to relieve the piercing pain of having loved and lost her. He had the urge to push up her leggings to reveal those long smooth legs. Her scent seemed to speak to him, making him feel as if his insides were full of soft fur. This was the only visit the goddess paid him.

The day after that, Hongliang's mother grew frantic. She kept saying that she couldn't see any more, until the chandelier's six candle bulbs were swapped for a fluorescent tube. This calmed her down, and she stuck her portrait of the Bodhisattva, goddess of mercy, back on the wall once more.

She moved her meditation mat to a position with better light, and here she peeled the yam vine stalks that poor people ate in season but rich people fed to the pigs – though one day they might get sick of rich meat dishes and appreciate the crisp freshness of these greens for one day – and she liked to get Hongliang to wash everything because ever since she'd given birth to him, she'd been phobic of water.

*   *   *

As Hongliang and his nephew sat washing the dishes, the moths were drawn to the fluorescent tube like iron filings to a magnet. Its brightness was dazzling. Even though a shade would have helped, every peasant's home had a light that glared like this. As the poem in Hongliang's schoolbook went:

> The more clamorous the cicadas,
> the quieter the woods,
> the louder the birds,
> the more serene the mountains.

The poem speaks of irredeemable poverty. Xu Yousheng watched the moths hurling themselves against the chandelier, then looked at his uncle and thought: He always told my dad he was Napoleon, Marshal Tian Peng, descendant of emperors, but he's stuck here studying clan histories, county annals, teahouse dramas and folk tales, to pass the time.

If only Hongxing had not disappeared, then Hongliang might have been able to leave home. But then there was the day Hongxing lost contact with his family and was never heard of again, dead or alive, and the family elders went to the Gaoquan coal mine to berate the mine owners, and Boss Ho found witnesses who swore that Hongxing had gone off with a bunch of others leaving only a rusty enamel cup and an empty ashtray in his room, and they had found no trace of him down in the mine. 'Our wages were too low for him, he went off to Hubei to make money,' said Boss Ho.

So they went to Yangxin county in Hubei, but they had no luck there either.

The day after Hongliang first began to tell Hongyang's story to Xu Yousheng, Hongliang's mother saw Hongxing: the funeral procession ran for cover as the sky filled with roiling black clouds, as if countless black tanks were advancing overhead. Lightning burst through the sky like a camera flashgun that gave everything a halo: the millet leaves, withered from a mere half day's sunshine; a shallow trickle of water, flowing slowly in the ditch. Ants stood in the cracked clods of earth with one leg raised as if in meditation, and shiny plastic bags took flight in the wind. This dramatic scene was followed by pitch darkness, the same darkness that comes when the fire goes out. After that there was light again, a light that exploded like heavenly cymbals banging. The mourners had never seen things so clearly, but they did not see what Hongliang's mother did: dozens of inky black corpses floating on hills, streams, fields and roads.

She saw Aiwan's dead from the past twenty years, heads and arms dangling, shoulders upright as if suspended – even those who had been paralysed in life were like that, their stick-like legs wobbling slightly – with trickles of blood oozing from the corners of their mouths, distorted expressions and clothes so shabby they looked like they'd been flogged. Their eyes were open but unseeing, like imbeciles, and they held sticks with which they beat the grass in front of them. They were so immersed in their pain that they'd lost their wits, their feelings and their memory. The slightest breath of wind made them instinctively huddle together, then creep forward between one lightning flash and the next.

Hongxing was still wearing his blue uniform from the Finance Office. It was covered in handfuls, or rather shovelfuls, of coal slag, from the top of his head, over his shoulders and down to the toes of his shoes. He did not look at his mother, or at the village, as he opened his crusty, grimy mouth and attempted to let out a groan of pain.

'Son, son, son, son, son, son, son,' the wretched old woman cried as she tried desperately to reach him. 'My son, my son!'

Great rolls of thunder rang out, and the rain pelted down in torrents as if the heavens were exploding. After this the skies brightened, and the scenery was covered in a gorgeous film of pearlescent water droplets on the leaves of the bent branches. The newly varnished coffin gleamed even more brightly now as the water buffalo prepared to heave itself to its feet, wrestling its rear quarters out of the slurry and pushing up on its front legs.

The hordes of dead had disappeared without a trace, and Hongliang's mother was soaked through. Her pockets, her old-fashioned cloth shoes and her tangled hair, even her eye sockets were full of water. She was drenched in the very liquid she was so intensely afraid of, and she stood in the fields wailing piti-fully: 'I saw him, I really did! He must have died in a coal shaft, far from home.'

Two months later, Hongliang was taken away, and there was not a single person in Aiwan willing to lift a finger to stop them. No one, that is, except for his mother, who gave the police ciga-rettes and demanded that they teach him a good lesson, as if she was consigning him to their care.

From Aiwan he was taken to the county town, which he had once thought so alluring. On one occasion he had spent three nights outside the residence of the chief of the Education Bureau, although he never did get to present him with the gifts of spirits and cigarettes he had brought with him. He ended up consuming them himself, until he was thoroughly intoxicated. What's more, he never did get the transfer, not even to Fan township. But at least he managed to score a historic hundred on the county town's only snooker table. Hongliang had dragged his bow-tied opponent's reputation through the dirt, so that now the townsfolk watched with some curiosity as Hongliang was taken out of the police jeep, his hair chopped short with a few passes of the scissors, and the victims' families stood at the gate of the city hall holding banners denouncing the government department for being too lenient with this bad apple among the teachers' ranks, this 'engineer of the human spirit' accused of molesting large numbers of his female pupils, though what seemed to outrage the villagers more than anything was that he had infected them with genital warts.

By the time Xu Yousheng finally received permission to visit him in prison, Hongliang had gone grey at the temples. He sat, head bowed and wordless, for two whole hours. Xu Yousheng had begrudgingly come to respect Hongliang, shaking off the contempt he had previously felt towards this village uncle. He thought this respect probably arose out of sympathy for the man, who was pretty much the same age as him, and who was, after all, his mother's little brother. He knew that Hongliang would not be coming home for a very long time, and would be stepping into his coffin as soon as he did. So Xu Yousheng pulled out all the stops, as if he was visiting someone acutely ill. He dredged up everything he had seen and heard to share with his uncle, enthusiastically at first but soon running out of steam as he scoured his memories, afraid to pause for breath until the prison guard who had let him in with a nod and a wink announced the end of his shift. Xu Yousheng and Hongliang got to their feet at the same moment, and Hongliang gave his nephew a look. Poor man, thought Xu Yousheng, he'll never get over this.

Now, though, the day before the funeral, Hongliang still had respect and status, or rather he *thought* he still had respect and status. He was wearing a threadbare pink shirt, the uniform at his teacher-training college. He was desperately clinging on to shreds of dignity as he strode back and forth, barking: 'Wei? Wei? Hello? Hello?' into his mobile phone. He ended up in an argument with the stonemason about the characters that made up Hongyang's name. 'So much to do,' he said, turning to Xu Yousheng. 'The feng shui's been done and the only auspicious day in the next couple of weeks is tomorrow. But the slab hasn't been carved yet, and I'm always the one who has to sort these things out.'

His shadow fell on the two stacks of rice bowls that he had pulled out. They were wobbling, and Xu Yousheng re-stacked them into six piles. Hongliang offered him a cigarette that cost thirty-five cents. Xu Yousheng had brought his own, best-quality Jinsheng at twenty-three yuan per pack, but had not dared take them out for fear of offending the other man, so he abstained and lit his uncle's cigarette for him.

'Why aren't you smoking?' asked Hongliang.

'I will in a bit.'

Hongliang picked up the story of Hongyang once more.

Just two months, and Hongyang changed from being a coward under arrest to a man who marched up to the local police station and challenged them.

It's hard to explain this change. We all know that every event has one outcome but many causes. Take my story, for instance. I came home to teach at Jiuyuan Central Primary School because graduates have to go back to the place where they're registered, and because your granny wanted me back after your elder uncle had disappeared. But it was also because I was fed up with city life – the way people constantly interfere there, the way officials are always using you. You know that I'm pretty easy-going, and maybe also a little proud, so when I figured out that the Rangxi Community Middle School was only offering a temporary position, I turned it down.

Plus you don't know how to give gifts, thought Xu Yousheng, who had seen his uncle making a present of knock-off spirits.

You paid forty yuan more than the asking price for a bottle of fake Langjiu, and anyone who drank it could tell straight away.

Who knows why Hongyang went to the station to challenge the police? Maybe he felt beholden to the village elders, or maybe he was the kind of person who liked repaying a debt. In fact, he was desperate to repay the debt: he never liked to owe people a favour because it bruised his pride, never mind that Shiren was just a kid and it was he who had stepped forward when Shuizhi was taken away. But I think the main reason was that he was ashamed that after the last incident the general impression had been that the local police had lost and he, Hongyang, was the winner. If you think more carefully, though, victory really belonged to a fearless bunch of old folks from the village, and to Zhang Gongti, who was a thousand li away. Hongyang simply benefited from his association with them. He was just a weak man keen to protect himself – he wasn't even arrested and he started yelling blue murder, while his wife was dragged out of the village with two welts down her face like great scars so that everyone, kids included, who had felt kindly towards him now felt entitled to criticise him as much as they liked.

He found himself unable to explain why he had let one opportunity slip, then a second, then a third, and by the time he realised, things were settled, it was too late to mount a punitive expedition, and all he could do was nurse a heap of grievances. Cries of 'Ai-ya! Ai-ya! Ai-ya! Ai-ya!' buzzed around like bluebottles. Even though he brushed them off, before long they circled around and flew right back again, repeating the circle and returning a thousand, then thousands of times. He tossed and turned all night, blaming himself for messing up that day, until finally he saw only one way to even things up, thinking: You all invaded my territory and humiliated my woman, so I'm

going to invade your territory and put you in your place in front
of the whole township. You just try living that down! In the end
he waited, then Shiren had his mishap. It wasn't a big deal, but
Hongyang wanted to move quickly after that.

'Didn't he slap someone from the Public Security team?' asked
Xu Yousheng.
    'When?'
    'When they took Auntie Shuizhi away.'
    'It was Hongyang who got the slap.'
    'Didn't you say he slapped the Public Security officer who
was taking Auntie Shuizhi away?'
    'The Public Security officer did grab Shuizhi, that's true, but
I never said Hongyang hit him.'
    'Shit.' Xu Yousheng rubbed his cheeks dry and took the ciga-
rette his uncle had offered. 'I must have misremembered. Let
me think now . . . I did remember it wrong.' The pair fell silent,
a ballooning silence that felt oppressive. Hongliang took off his
glasses, which he wore for show: they had no lenses. There was
a sheen of sweat on the tip of his nose. Finally, he raised his
buttocks off the chair and lit his nephew's cigarette with the
ingratiating air of a Chinese puppet army officer addressing his
Japanese superior.
    'You're pretty bright, Yousheng.'
    'Don't talk rubbish, Uncle.'
    'I've heard it said you fucked a whole lot of hookers in Fan
township.'
    'What?!'
    'Nothing wrong with fucking!'
    'I never did. My mum and dad keep a close eye on me.'
    'Hah!' Hongliang slapped him on the back. 'Your gran always
says to me: "Your nephew's about to get married, but you
haven't yet, and once he does, and has a child, you'll be a

great-uncle." That upset me a lot, because when I was born my great-uncle was bald as a coot.'

'That's how old people think.'

'The problem is, I want to get married, but I can't bring myself to do it. I've got a mental block. Actually, there's only one thing I can't figure out. I never could, I still can't, and I never will be able to, probably not even when I'm at death's door.'

'What thing?'

'The stuff about what's between the two poles of yin and yang.'

'What do you mean?'

'Well, magnetic polarities repel each other, and opposite polarities attract, don't they? How's that supposed to work?'

'I'm still not sure I understand.'

'How men and women get it together, that stuff. I can't figure it out. How come other people can take that step but I can't? Not even when there's obvious interest on both sides. You've got more experience in that than I do, you must have some tips you could pass on to me.'

'I really don't.'

Xu Yousheng was getting whiffs of camel dung from his cigarette, so he didn't dare breathe in too deeply, but nor did he dare stub it out. Hongliang got to his feet and paced back and forth, head raised, hands clasped behind his back like an old-time scholar. As he paced, he muttered 'Very mysterious' to himself.

The younger man thought of Hu Yang, who had returned from Beijing the previous month. The two of them had been at school together and had known each other since they were both toddlers in open-crotch trousers. Hu Yang had been as bulky as ever, but now he dressed completely differently in his Gitman Bros shirts, Acne jeans, Gucci brown and white leather shoes, Louis Vuitton belt, Lindberg ultra-light titanium-framed glasses and a Calvin Klein wristwatch. He had neatly trimmed whiskers with a hint of dark stubble, and carried a brand-new iPad in one hand and the latest model of iPhone in the other. He acted as if he was only having a meal with Xu Yousheng out of a sense of obligation. Xu Yousheng had chatted politely, but Hu Yang was bent over his phone, pretending he hadn't heard – Of course he'd heard, thought Xu Yousheng – or, if he wasn't doing that, he was holding up his iPad and taking a photo of Xu Yousheng. When he received a text it pinged, and when he sent one it chimed. Only a hi-tech gadget could deliver prompt reminders in such quiet tones. He doesn't have anything to say to me, Xu Yousheng had thought, feeling that his former classmate talked as if he was angry and impatient with him for wasting his precious time. Hu Yang's blustering final statement was intended both to bring things to an end as quickly as possible and to stoke his own indignation, and Xu Yousheng had felt dispirited in the face of such scorn.

But Xu Yousheng's disappointment didn't stop him doing an impression of Hu Yang for his uncle's benefit now: 'Why do you think women put on make-up every day? It takes them anything from twenty minutes to two hours. They paint their fingernails and their toenails too, usually red, sometimes green or purple, though, sometimes even nude, so all you see is the shine. And their clothes! Have you ever watched them deciding between seven, eight, even ten outfits, weighing up how to make the best of their figures, how best to dress for the weather? Then there's the question of what other women will be wearing too. They want to stand out from the crowd in a subtle way, they don't want people to think they're freaks. They're continuously making comparisons, interrogating themselves, making sure they look their best. That's the reason women are always late, sometimes by as much as two hours. It's not that they're lazy – sometimes they plan to leave in the morning – but it's not until noon that they get out of the door, umbrella held aloft even when there's no hint of rain.

'And why do you think they take such pains to get themselves looking nice, spending four times as long on the preparations as on the job they're going out to do, sometimes spending a whole week getting ready for a dance that'll only last an hour? Because they're virtuous? To make sure people show them respect? To encourage the rest of society to be law-abiding? Because moral respect is important to them? No! It's obviously because they crave attention. That's their sole objective: praise from men. Other women are their rivals. As a man, your mission is to respond to that need. Even if the expression in your eyes is as dumb and greedy as an animal's, even if your words sound blatantly pompous, hypocritical, corny, it doesn't matter. They've spent so long getting ready, and you've got to acknowledge that.

'Imagine they've prepared a fancy dinner for you: you'll reach out with your chopsticks and eat it. They'll ask you: "Do you really mean it? Am I really that good-looking?" and you've got to swear a solemn oath before God, with your hand on your heart and without a second's hesitation, that of course she is. A woman sometimes wants you to confirm your big talk, and in that case, forget about your conscience: you've got to swear on the honour of generations of your forebears that you're being absolutely sincere. That will be the happiest moment in her day, and she's willing to pay any price for it: her body, her soul, she'll even steal from her work or her parents to achieve that high. Just one sentence of praise costs you nothing, comrade, remember, you just need to open your mouth. In the past, that was what you could never manage. I wonder if you still can't . . . When they walk out got up all gorgeously, you withdraw into your shell, you freeze up and go rigid. You think they'll thank you for having good manners? You're not even as good as a mirror – mirrors don't talk, but at least they're loyal enough to look back at them. You take one look at them and run, and they find that humiliating, get it? Have some guts, mate, have some guts.

'If every idiot behaved like you, women would start letting their standards slip, wouldn't they? Whatever happens, you've got to respond, your eyes have got to widen in amazement and you've got to stare like you're seeing Niagara Falls, like she's the most beautiful woman you've ever seen, even if she's nothing much to look at. That's how you'll get somewhere with women.'

Hongliang ignored the spittle flying from Xu Yousheng's lips, so concentrated was he on committing all these words of wisdom to memory. 'That's marvellous,' he exclaimed, his face radiant. His happiness lasted up until the moment when Xu Yousheng's scorn became more refined and barbed. His nephew, a township man, was playing at being from Beijing, passing judgement on a country cousin in a Beijinger's tones, and that worried Hongliang.

Xu Yousheng planned to clap Hongliang on the shoulder, like Hu Yang had done to him, and to add the following by way of a parting shot: Young man, in theory, the woman who can't be won doesn't exist! He wanted his storming performance to end on a happy note so his uncle wouldn't feel humiliated.

Hongliang looked comically anxious, though. 'That's great, but you're talking about high-class women. You must know the saying that any woman who comes to this village is bound to run away again.'

'Right, Uncle . . .' Xu Yousheng didn't say any more, just looked up at the craggy landscape around them and allowed his thoughts to wander: We're pretty much alike, me and my uncle, both of us are despicable. Although Beijing's the peak of the map, it's a peak we'll never scale, a place where Ferraris roar like angry lions because they're stuck in traffic. Meanwhile, here in the back of beyond, even if a lorry stalls in the middle of the road the driver has plenty of time to fire up his engine again. To folks round here, Jiujiang city is heaven and there are lots of people who work their whole lives to buy themselves a room on the outskirts of town. But in a street like Wangfujing in Beijing, even if you come from cities like Nanchang, Changsha or Wuhan, they look down on you as a bumpkin. In Beijing, wherever you stop, you're in the centre: the city's so huge, it's like the universe exploding outwards.

Xu Yousheng's thoughts continued: There are forests of skyscrapers, the shadows of helicopters brushing their glass walls, the lobbies of office blocks stretch for acres, and they're all lit up even in daytime, and office staff and executives with blue folders in their hands sit at their computers or wander over the carpeted floors, doing business with every country in the world while blue-collar workers are relegated to the goods lifts. Look at us, holding our wicker basket shiny with dirt as Uncle crams it full of all the rice bowls. Tomorrow those bowls will be full to the brim with chunks of fish and pork, and dried tofu strips. Plus there's an ancient plough in the corner, as well as a hoe, and behind the bedroom door is a bucket for pissing in that you could make with a dozen wooden slats and wire hoops or bamboo splints, made watertight with several coats of tung oil inside. It's an enormous engineering project to build a proper indoor bathroom, after all. In Aiwan, Hongyang is the only person who has one, and even then the toilet's always broken and no one can fix it. A piss bucket can hold a month's worth of piss, but if you can't be bothered to empty it, it gives off a choking smell of fertiliser and flakes like psoriasis stick to the side of the bucket. And then there are the unrelenting insects, which for some reason are everywhere. They cover every inch of the countryside, and even if you never see them, you can always hear the noise they make, weaving a blanket of sound to smother the earth. City folk have no idea, just like they don't know there are ghosts that you can see on moonless nights, the ghosts of eight generations of ancestors with sneers on their faces entangled in the trees, waiting for us to pull away twigs so they can float free.

Hongliang had poured the tea and was droning on about Hongyang's life, his voice an irritating buzz. He was endlessly garrulous, like a machine that makes such a racket that you want to smash it. Xu Yousheng tuned him out.

Hongyang's nothing compared to Beijing, he thought. Jin Yan is probably on the road there right now. She's no different from other women – animals, the lot of them – but why is she the only one who gets me going? She's dug a great hole in my heart, she's dug out my flesh and blood and there's a great gale blowing now through the hole, and I'm empty and desolate, no more tears left to cry, I'm sure I'm in love with you, a prostitute, I fell in love with you today, in this village that still holds your breath. I miss you so much. You and the disgraceful thing we did together.

4

Hongliang continued.

That day Hongyang left very early, while the rest of them were still flat out, sleeping like the dead: their flesh slack, their body temperature low, passive, motionless, peaceful and beautiful. Humans spend around one-third of their lives asleep. It's completely different from their waking state, when they're constantly on alert, wary, suspicious, fearful, but as soon as they're asleep they drop their guard, just like that. Yousheng, you remember those murders at the Leshan forestry station in the 1960s, when all the forest rangers had their throats cut? It happened because the murderer went inside for a scoop of water to drink. In his statement, he admits that he counted one, two, three, four, five: all five guards asleep, and it was as if they were asking to be murdered.

Hongyang had been waiting up since eleven that night. Early in the morning he pulled open the door and went out to wander up and down the silent village street. When dawn glimmered in the east, he figured it was time, and went to rap on one of the windows:

'Shiren's banged up in the police station,' he said.

'I know.'

'But Zhang Lei was allowed to stay in the clinic,' Hongyang stressed. He seemed about to say more but stopped himself. He didn't say: You'd be inhuman if you didn't go, or: They beat up Shiren and you never said anything. You wait and see if anyone speaks up for you when they come for you. In any case, the sleepers simply moved the electric fan back into position, pointing it towards themselves, shook out the blankets and dozed off again. Hongyang thought they'd only stir themselves when it was Zhang Lei who was getting beaten up. And he left. What he should have said was: You reckon Shiren hasn't been beaten up? He didn't say anything, though, he just went on his own. I reckon that he'd planned it all when he was waiting up all night. He'd already made the decision.

Those five cops can't have forgotten the way they'd been humiliated: they'd gone to arrest Hongyang for an unpaid fine of four hundred yuan, and ended up surrounded by the old folk and kids of the village, who chased them away. Anyway, Hongyang must have been truly fired up to go and knock on their door in person. I remember a township guy doing something similar – he had no money and no position, in fact he was in trouble with the police himself, but when his mate was arrested, he upped and went straight to the Criminal Investigation team and handed out cigarettes to everyone, right down to the prisoner who was sweeping the floor. Everyone thought he was being ridiculous, because to plead someone's case, you have to be at least a deputy head of section, or at least know someone who is, and this man was inviting everyone to a meal at the Suting Hotel and handing out boxes of best-quality Jinsheng cigarettes.

'It was my mate Shu Shuang,' Xu Yousheng interjected.

Anyway, he wined and dined them for three days, held his mate's hand through the fence and talked to him like a lover, until he himself was arrested. It was in the *Ruichang News*, and the whole article took the piss out of him for his 'foolish code of brotherhood'. They might as well have said outright that he was a dumb brute with a low IQ. That's the way a hero behaves, right? Hongyang just had to take the first step towards Fan township and he became some sort of god. As he was leaving for Zhao Hollow, though, there was only one person in Aiwan who realised that this was a historic moment, thinking: Dammit, no one's doing anything, and today's the day. It was Hongbin, who liked to stick his nose into the community's business, and he went out banging a gong and shouting at everyone to get out of bed. It made me think how Aiwan has been united at times. Only when things have happened in our village, mind you – when bad things happen to fellow villagers who've left, we've never stuck out our necks for them. But that day, for the first time, Aiwan folk were going into battle. We got on our bicycles, motorbikes, in our carts and vans, and we caught up with Hongyang at a place called Laowuzengjia. He looked neither happy nor disappointed to see us, he simply carried on going. Some kids on bikes rode in circles in front of him, giving him respectful looks, and a van stopped beside him. Hongbin, who was in the passenger seat, said: 'Get in, Hongyang.' He didn't answer. Hongbin jumped down and said: 'Hongyang, come and sit in the van, forget the walking.' And then Hongyang got in and sat there, bolt upright, looking straight ahead.

From then on, he was our leader. He always wore an enig-matic expression on his face, one that you could read either way. That was to let us know that we were to take our orders from him alone, otherwise they weren't legit, but he wasn't prepared to tell us any more than that. That day, he got the van to stop on the west side of Fan township, and walked down the tarmac road to the town centre on his own, casting a long shadow behind him that we were scared to step on. It was a day to be proud of – we were all so proud we stared straight ahead, not looking left or right. We had to let the township folk get a good look at us, not the other way round. All the same, we were aware of every movement they made, almost like actors looking at the audience looking at the actors. They looked as if they'd only seen stuff like this in their dreams – Aiwan folk were well known for their timidity. We were the little guys compared to any of the township families, and we shocked them by arriving in town looking so ferocious that they fled, leaving chickens trailing red strings, fish flapping in tubs, straw hats, fast-melting ice and half-uttered sentences behind them. The lad who did the meals at the local police station turned up, gave us a look and scarpered. 'They're here, they're here,' he yelled, bolting the gate and locking the two doors to the back yard. We moved like a herd of migrating water buffalo, stamping our hooves in the road and bellowing. We certainly were proud of ourselves.

Hongyang wasn't the first to saunter into the township this way. Gangster types always made a performance of it, with their designer sunglasses, gold chains, Lion motorbikes, camouflage trousers, all-over tattoos, Mongolian knives and knife scars. Then there was always one waving a pair of scissors, his thumb and middle finger poking through the finger holes. The scissors were always the export, inspection-exempt kind, and came from the East China Knives and Scissors factory in the county town. Only Hongyang had come empty-handed, just a sleeveless vest slung over his shoulder that permanently threatened to slip off. The sun shining on his pectorals made them look like two slabs of limestone, oozing a sheen of sweat. His neck looked thicker than his head, as if his skull was a block of metal cast on top of it, as he strode into town towards the place he was to have long-term dealings with. At the top of the hill stood a rectangular two-storey building made of brick and cement, the morning sunlight making it look like it was a lofty temple casting a pitch-black shadow deep as a pond on the tarmac road. The local police station, the infamous 'black hole', awaited him.

'Did they beat him up?' Xu Yousheng asked.

'No.'

Xu Yousheng decided to take one last look at his mobile phone. If there was no text, then he'd turn it off. There was no need to check, actually. He always knew if a call or a message had come through, even though he'd set it to silent. Even if you are a goddess, you're infuriating – not answering, not messaging, Xu Yousheng thought resentfully.

At that moment, his uncle's voice reached his ears.

'Are you listening?'

Hongliang continued.

That morning the police station never opened its doors. Hongyang walked up the twelve concrete steps.

'Why do you think police stations and law courts and buildings like that are all built at the top of such high steps, Yousheng, have you thought of that? Why don't they have just three or four steps, like the farm machinery depot? The police station used to be the credit union building, and back then there were only eight steps, but after it was converted, they added four more. Why? So that as you climb up, the important business you came for goes out of your head and you begin to think about your position in relation to the police station. Country folk use the importance of their business as a crutch, it allows them to lose their inhibitions and become recklessly aggressive. The bleak, towering building seems to say: You be careful, I'm your master, not a servant you send on errands, you better get that straight. The building strikes some people with such fear that they even drop their complaint then and there just because they're worried it'll cost them more or it'll get them into more trouble than if they hadn't raised it.'

Hongyang's knock on the door at the top of the steps was irresolute. He wanted everyone to understand that he meant business.

This was just his softly-softly approach, but we all knew he was flustered. That's natural, isn't it? He couldn't help gulping audibly, and even expelling breaths through pursed lips. He stared despondently at the printed note stuck to the left of the main door on the pebble-dash walls, as if help might come from there. There was no going back now, though: a growing crowd of onlookers had gathered and they were waiting expectantly for the performance to begin. The silence from within encouraged him. He pounded on the door until his fists swelled up, and then he used his feet. But the door was thick and deadened the volley of kicks. 'Open up! Open up!' he yelled. Then he picked up his hoe and beat the door with it. The sun-scorched paint began to flake off, and the door, like a beast startled from its slumber, reacted with the dull sound of a bolt under pressure or a cellulose fibre breaking. Hongyang flew into a rage. He looked like someone had murdered his father and his eyes flamed red, scaring even us. Eventually, Hongbin came up the steps and restrained him, saying, 'That's enough, Hongyang, that's enough . . .'

'Did the police not respond at all?' asked Xu Yousheng.

Someone did respond. Young Di pushed open an upstairs window and asked: 'What's up?'
Hongyang pointed at him. 'I've got something to say to you.'
'What?'
'I'm saying I've got something to tell you.'
'Who are you?'
'Hongyang, from Aiwan.'
'You've come at the right time.' We heard the curtains being swished across. When someone's in a hurry it takes several goes to get his leg into his army trousers. In those days, fatigues were still khaki green, and the keys that hung from his belt loops jangled as they shook. Then he stepped into his shoes and

stamped his feet a few times. He opened a drawer and took out his truncheon, banging it experimentally on the tabletop a few times, then slammed the door shut. Even though we were expecting it, the ferocious bang made us flinch. He was the only fierce character at the station in those days.

'Did he open up?' asked Xu Yousheng.

'No. We could hear him trotting along the corridor and clip-clopping down the stairs, we could hear everything when he was moving around the room before, too. But the door stayed shut.'

'Doesn't sound very fierce,' said Xu Yousheng.

'Let me finish and then you'll see.'

A little while later, the upstairs window opened again and the deputy political instructor poked his head out. He was only thirty, but his face was all lined and his waxy bald scalp had a comb-over of a dozen strands of hair. These were marks left on his body by years of hard scheming. He was a smooth talker with a heart of stone: thoroughly vicious. The conversation went like this:

'Hongyang,' he said. 'What's your beef? Tell me all about it.'

'If the fight was between the two of them, why did only Shiren get banged up?' said Hongyang.

'Ah, well, that's because Zhang Lei was no match for your Shiren, right? Zhang Lei's injuries were pretty serious. After we took everything into consideration, we got him into the clinic. I mean, we didn't know how to stop the bleeding, did we? And they said he'd be released from there.'

'They should have been banged up together, or released together.'

'I've already told you our reasoning. There was no way we could have him die on us at the police station. He was bleeding, that's why we did it, that's how we always do things, right?'

'No. You should have released them both together. You hurry up and let Shiren go. When Zhang Lei's brought to trial, I'll bring Shiren right back to you. I guarantee it.'

'Hongyang, old man, you're right, of course you are. I've told you, Zhang Lei will be back in no time at all. If it's this afternoon, then you can take Shiren home this afternoon. We don't want to make things more difficult than they need to be. Listen to me, I guarantee that Zhang Lei will be up in court within twenty-four hours. A minute longer and you can hold me to account. Is that all right?'

'No.'

'You don't believe me?'

'It's nothing to do with whether I believe you.' Hongyang must have felt that all this beating around the bush wasn't doing his reputation as a tough guy any good, and immediately followed up with: 'Just tell me straight, are you letting him go or not?'

The deputy political instructor gave him a long look, and finally nodded. 'Just wait a minute, I'll go and ask the chief.' He withdrew his head, carefully shut the window and shot the bolt. The smile on his face instantly faded. He gritted his teeth. He had done what had to be done, resolved what he could, and what he couldn't resolve didn't matter. In any case, this wasn't his police station, he thought. He went and appealed to his boss: 'This lot . . .' He said no more, just shook his head.

The station chief sat back down on the sofa, his face flushed red as he heaved the weary sigh of a man in a dilemma. 'Let me think.' He leaned forward, his head in his hands.

The boss's career had long been in the doldrums. He had no hopes of promotion, the only question now being whether he could hang onto his job at all. The Political Commissar, his direct superior, was due to retire any day now, so he had been put into the police station as deputy chief. He had arrived from the county town in his jeep, descending on Fan township as if he were a senior official – only to be faced with a mountain of unpaid bills from shops, restaurants and garages, as well as IOUs from employees. The county-level police were responsible for the entirety of the Public Security team's wages and those of the drivers, and part of the wages of the township police. The latter should have been paid out of the local government's budget, but the local government were demanding that the county government give back to the township the amount they took in local fines and that that sum be used for their wages, thus effectively making the county police responsible.

And starting any job also required funds for fuel oil, maintenance services, business trips, accommodation and food. To get this machine in motion, the station chief levied fines on small fry like petty thieves, gamblers, prostitutes and their clients, unlicensed taxis, and even people who illicitly felled trees or smuggled tobacco, all basically people of good character. There were several crackdowns. The trouble was that in the view of the township police, this was killing the goose that laid the golden egg. The township became such a law-abiding place that there was no one else to crack down on and thus no more income-generating opportunities for the police. There was nothing for it but to go further afield on night patrols, in search of anyone who had slipped through the net. This was hard work. It was also annoying and potentially dangerous.

No one wanted to go on these patrols, with the exception of young Di. Di had been assigned to the station after he graduated from the provincial police college, and as a fledgling enforcer of the law, with his newly acquired handcuffs, truncheon and custody cell keys, he was greedy for a chance to inflict punishment the way the newly married were greedy for sex. As the older police officers saw it, his enthusiasm just showed what a rookie he was. As he put it, 'A day without beating someone and I get itchy fists.' He beat up any detainees he came across, even if they weren't his, simply by virtue of the fact they had come into the police station. 'Fess up!' he would yell at them. In some cases, even those who had confessed everything still got a few slaps from him. The station chief knew Di was a time bomb, that one day he would overstep the mark and his career would go up in a puff of smoke, but there was no one else to use – what other choice did he have?

'In the station you listen to me, but outside, you listen to Di,' the chief used to say. He created an irregular police patrol, to be led by young Di. He deliberately put the deputy political instructor in it, under Di's command. The man hated Di, whom he regarded as a hyena, waiting to pounce and take his job as soon as he made the slightest mistake. Sometimes the station chief would join the patrol too, in an attempt to back up Di's authority. 'You don't joke around in the army. Di's in charge, even I have to follow his orders,' he said.

Di was a remarkable hunter, with a nose for sniffing out any kind of shady business. Sometimes he could tell that there was unlicensed gambling going on or estimate how many people were at an illegal party just by seeing the lights on in a house one li away. He made a point of asking at restaurants and shops the names of people who'd been flashing their money about, because anyone with money invariably gambled. He always went around with dog food – cowardly gamblers left guard dogs at the entrance to the village, or at least to their houses – as the treats gave him a way of silencing the beasts.

He strictly enforced the rule against wearing leather shoes: number one, you couldn't run so well in them, and number two, they made a noise on gravel. If it hadn't been for the need to arrest people, he wouldn't have employed a jeep on operations: its headlights were a giveaway, so he used to order the driver to park up several li away from their destination.

Returning empty-handed left him feeling guilty about the fuel they had used. You could use up the strength of employees and mules, but fuel was an expense, and he considered himself entrusted with the running of the police station. Effectively its second-in-command, he always put himself on the front line, running up to flimsy doors, kicking them open and personally dragging gamblers out. He would appear in the village as if by magic. In time he became the chief bogeyman, and parents used to say to their children: 'Stop your bawling, or Policeman Di will get you!' until Hongyang arrived on the scene and shared that honour. Whenever rumours reached Di's ears that people were out to get him, he would thump his chest, saying: 'I'm not afraid. Let them come whenever, any place, I'll be waiting for them!' He waited and waited, and was almost disappointed when no one came forward to challenge him.

What he did not know was that his enemies had bypassed the township and gone straight to the county town police, petitioners' office, disciplinary committee, and even the Party Secretary and the mayor, to put in their complaints. Those who could, hitched a ride to Jiujiang and the provincial capital.

These complainants were the ones without local connections. The ones who had connections went and complained to the relatives of local officials. They all said the same: 'The state can fine me but it has no right to beat me.' Every complaint had a file opened for it, and every time something happened that was connected to the complaint, it went into the file. The police officers sent a thick file of papers off to their superiors, where it became so well known that they would groan 'Not him again!' Because of this, the Party Secretary and the mayor were not fond of the Public Security Bureau chief, while the PSB chief despised the local police.

The PSB chief was unwilling to kick Di out of his job just because he wasn't his man, but he also felt he couldn't be expected to keep taking the rap. Three times the township station chief went in fearful and trembling to the county town, and every time he returned ashen-faced, looked at young Di, then found he couldn't quite put into words what he needed to say. Instead he put his arm around his junior's shoulders and made a few reassuring noises in the hopes that the young man would get the message. That particular leopard was never going to change his spots, though. And when the chief tried putting it more strongly, young Di grew furious and refused to work. After a few days of stalemate, it was clear that the police station was losing money, and that the chief was going to have to try and persuade him back to work.

That day, however, young Di had done nothing wrong: he was merely bringing in Shiren and Zhang Lei. Arresting people during a punch-up was perfectly normal, that was what the rules and regulations laid down. Hongyang's 'demand for an explanation' was only his attempt to play tough, but his posturing was, to the station chief, the straw that threatened to break the camel's back. A cesspit yawned before him, covered by only the thinnest layer of paper. He, the station chief, had to get across it, or else he'd literally land in the shit. He rubbed his face with his palms, pondering the ultimatum the PSB chief had sent down – 'I've said all that needs to be said, you figure it out for yourself' – but he couldn't think of a way out, so he kept repeating to Di: 'Just give me a moment to think.'

'How much more time do you need?' asked Di.

'I've told you time and again, why didn't you listen to me?'

'Was I supposed to let them break in?'

'I'm not talking about that.'

'Then what?'

'Just think of the consequences.'

'If we let people break into the station, isn't that "consequences"?'

'Why are you the only person I can't get through to?'

'I can't sit around here while you're thinking about how to get through to me.'

'You stay right where you are!' the chief snapped. 'It's precisely because you never keep a cool head, and you're always making trouble, that we're in this mess now! I've told you over and over to keep a cool head, and what do you do?'

'What have I done?'

'You've made a heap of trouble with the higher-ups, do you see? It's one thing after another. I keep having to wipe your arse and it's still not clean.'

'That must be hard for you, sir.'

'I'm telling you, next time there's a problem, you're going to take responsibility, go and say you were wrong, and get it docked from your pay.'

'Of course.'

Di smirked and repeated his formulaic apology – he was sorry he'd hurt the feelings of his brothers and sisters, the common masses – and strode off to reception. Part of the room was separated off by a silver-painted grille where loans and savings had been dealt with when the building was a credit cooperative, and where now people waited to register their hukou residence permits. Sometimes when people were brought in they were handcuffed to the grille. Di strode over and smacked Shiren's head against the bars three times, then undid the handcuffs and sent him out of the back door. The kid in charge of the kitchen stove threw him a fearful look, which Di responded to with a rough kick that brought tears to the boy's eyes.

'You little squirt, who told you to lock the main gate?' said Di.

Shiren went around to the main road, shaking the circulation back into his wrists, and walked over to his supporters as if he were Gandhi, Mandela or Castro. We applauded, then escorted him and Hongyang home. We left dense clusters of footprints and gobs of spittle in the dust and the new, spongy surface of the asphalt. The township market resumed its predictable daily rhythm, bustling in the early morning then quietening down as the shoppers dispersed, laden with purchases. But the clamour of public opinion went on for several days.

The police station never did open its doors that day. The station chief held a staff meeting and lectured them again on keeping the public satisfied, stressing that in the final analysis what was important were their working practices. Everybody did the usual criticism and self-criticism, the deputy instructor nodded from time to time, and young Di left halfway through. He got on his motorbike, sped out of Fan township and rode forty li to his family home, where he went fishing.

In the meantime, Hongyang's footprints, and the dents made by his hoe, stayed on the police station door. The awe the police station had inspired for so many years vanished in the space of a single morning. The chief was transferred to the hukou registration department. Finally, one day he banged on the desk of the PSB chief and shouted: 'You want us to fleece the public and at the same time you want us to keep them happy. Do you take them for fools? You sit here in your office day in, day out and they come and complain to you about us, and you say: "Don't you worry, brothers and sisters, I'll sort things out for you." Of course they're satisfied with you, but what about us? Do you have any idea how difficult it is for us?' These were the very same words that Di had shouted at him and the very words that the PSB chief used when he shouted at the Party Secretary and the mayor.

No one ever mentioned Hongyang's pleas for mercy again. Sometimes people would imitate his cries of 'Ai-ya! Ai-ya!', although that was just by way of background to the story of

how he challenged authority, to explain his strategy. But the
thing is, Yousheng, there was much more to come. There was
another chapter. A week later, when all of Aiwan's inhabitants
were still slightly intoxicated, young Di roared into the village
on his blue Jialing motorbike, churning up the dust. That
motorbike was the best in the whole of the police station, and
looked gorgeous as he slammed on the brakes and screeched to
a halt. Di revved the engine until the exhaust smoke covered
the threshing floor.

'Get that damned Hongyang out here,' he yelled.

His legs clenching the seat, he rocked from side to side,
checked the fuel gauge and, seeing that it was getting low, paddled
the bike with his feet over to the petrol can at Hongzhi's gate.

'Gimme some.' He rested the bike on its stand and stared
fixedly at Shiren, who was wiping his hands with a small towel.
Shiren stood where he was, half-bent over. Di unscrewed the
petrol cap and repeated himself: 'I said, gimme some.' Shiren
took the petrol cap from him and put it on the stool, then stuck
the hose into the can and sucked the other end, pushing it into
the fuel tank when he had the petrol running. With his arms
around the can, which was sitting on two stools, he clicked his
fingers at a nearby group of kids. 'Come here and take this,' he
ordered them. They came over and held the can at an angle.

Young Di's dark skin gleamed and his teeth shone white
between fleshy lips, testament to the fifteen minutes he spent
brushing them three times a day. He was an educated man and
that was what he expected of himself, even though he was terribly buck-toothed and his gums were an unattractive shade of
burgundy. It was very hot, but he stuck his hands in his trouser
pockets and paced back and forth, watching with an anxious air.
Cautiously, we drew closer, then stopped at an appropriate
distance. He glanced at the bamboo broom leaning against the
wall of Hongzhi's house, and one of the kids brought it to him.

Then he swept the chicken shit, leaves and sharp pebbles off the threshing floor.

According to clan records, the tamped-earth threshing floor, with the stone-lined gutter around it, had been rebuilt two hundred years ago by the family as a status symbol. Apparently Chinese characters inlaid in the stone had once read *The Ai Clan Looks after Itself*. But any trace of these words was long gone.

As the bamboo tips of the broom tickled the ground, it made them think of the salon girls in town who scratched their clients' heads with their scary fingernails when they washed their hair, sometimes raising bumps on their scalps. Then young Di took the edge of a grass mat between finger and thumb and tipped off the sweet potato strips laid out to dry, smacked the dust off his hands and surveyed the battlefield. Hongyang arrived on the threshing floor, unsure what was going on, and looked hard at Di. They each searched the other's eyes as if to plumb the depths of their opponent's soul. You can tell a lot about people by what's in their eyes.

'And there was me thinking you were some sort of big shot,' Di said with a smirk as he beckoned to Hongyang. In martial arts competitions at police college he'd been third in his year group, and could have come top in the year group below, but he claimed he didn't want to 'take advantage'. Most of the time, he would only punch once and his opponent would be spitting blood. They put in complaints, whinging that although they'd had strong bones Di had kicked and broken them. 'Our bones snapped, boss!' they would wail as they coughed up blood.

'What's this about?' asked Hongyang.

'A fight, what else?' said Di, taking off his uniform jacket and showing his toned muscles. His pectorals swelled as if he had been bitten on the chest by poisonous insects.

'If I win, I'm taking Shiren back with me. If you win, I'll never have anything to do with Aiwan again.'

Hongyang thought for a long time. 'OK,' he finally said.

'A free fight, till one of us is defeated. It's in the lap of the gods,' said young Di.

Hongyang took off his jacket too, and his cloth shoes, thinking that those were the rules.

One of the onlookers called out: 'If he tells you to eat shit, would you do that too?'

Hongyang glared at the speaker, who promptly fell silent. This was between Hongyang and Di and no one else. This was a battle between two factions, two countries and two camps, yes, but it was also a battle between two individual heroes.

'How do we begin?' he asked.

'Just say the word,' said Di.

'Begin,' said Hongyang, entering the arena warily. Di rested his weight first on one foot then the other, before starting to jump around him, stopping every now and then to stand, head bowed, rotating his fists together at his chest as if they were propellers. Hongyang watched. It was a ritual he had never seen before. Then he reached up with his left fist and held his right fist at shoulder-height, repeating 'Begin!'

Di leapt up and down and then, with lightning speed, stooped and made a grab for Hongyang's legs. Hongyang recoiled swiftly, but still Di got hold of one ankle and ran around to the left, dragging his opponent with him. Hongyang hopped after him and Di changed direction, ducking to the right. Hongyang again hopped after him. Finally Di tired of this game and dropped Hongyang's leg. He beckoned again to Hongyang, who was purple in the face, and began to advance like the supreme fighter that he was. Poor, wretched Hongyang faced him, his whole attention focused on avoiding the blows that rained down on his chest, ears, Adam's apple, chin and eye socket. Luckily for Hongyang, his height was an advantage, and he could let his opponent hit him.

That was a wise decision. After just one bout it was clear that he was incapable of striking back, though the rest of us bystanders were convinced he had a chance so long as he didn't fall down. He watched Di's moves closely, analysing them rapidly to think up new tactics. He began to understand when Di was striking for real and which blows were feints and parries. He ran back and forth around his opponent, who danced like a butterfly. He waited for Di to declare the fight over, or for the opportunity to finish it himself. He thought he should carry on a little longer before surrendering, to show he'd pulled out all the stops for Shiren.

Then something interrupted the sequence of events. Di was getting cocky at having the advantage and took a moment to wipe the sweat from his brow. For an instant, his hand covered his right eye while his left arm hung limp at his side. He never said: Wait a moment! or: Time out!

Right then and there, we whispered to Hongyang: 'Kick him! Go on, kick him!' Our whispers were filled with secret excitement and urgent concern – it was now or never, there was no time to lose.

The fight that had gone out of Hongyang seemed to return. He lifted his leg. His upper body was still on the defensive, but that leg stayed high in the air. In that split second, he knew he'd got it wrong. Young Di launched himself forward, unseeing yet accurate, and grabbed him not by the lifted leg but by the one Hongyang was standing on, hefted him upwards with his shoulder and tipped him to the ground. At five foot eight, Hongyang was a tall man, and he landed with a dull thud, like a great felled tree. We all heard his wretched groan. Luckily, he had been battered as a boy so had learned a trick or two, and as he was slammed into the ground he instinctively grabbed Di's head and took his opponent down with him. They grappled. There was deadlock for a while until, as if by mutual agreement, they pulled apart. The next instant, they were tangled up once again: Di crouched down, struggling to free his thigh, while Hongyang pounced on Di's back and pressed him to the ground. Finally the Xiayuan village committee chairman clapped his hands and announced: 'That's enough!' And Shiren, who had quivered with fear throughout the fight, added: 'Grandpa Hongyang, I'll go with him, it's fine.'

But Hongyang, whose head was pressed to Di's buttocks, grunted desperately: 'Get the hell out of here, all of you.' More time passed. The sun was going down in the west, the air growing cool as darkness crept across the land like black mould. As far as the host was concerned this was no problem, but it was disastrous for the visitor. A whole day had gone by, and still he had not settled the matter. So when it became imperative that the fight come to an end, Di made a feint then threw himself into a fresh attack, scooping up Hongyang's legs like a leaping fish. Hongyang took a breath and bounced frantically backwards. Just as he was about to land on his rump, we onlookers managed to catch him. Di flung himself to the ground and crawled forward like an army scout, his right hand held out rigidly like a crab's claw. He seemed completely consumed by fury at his failed move. He forgot the bargain he had made with his opponent. And in the fading light, Hongyang strode over to him, lifted his leg and prepared to finish him off with a kick to the head. We shut our eyes and looked away, almost weeping. Half a second or a second later, we expected to see Di's round head shattered, his nose broken, his tongue ripped out and his dangling eyeballs spilling into what was left of his mouth, those two once-ferocious front teeth lying in the dust as if they were planks ripped from the door. Some of the onlookers were already bent over, retching in anticipation of this horrendous sight.

The expected shriek never came. Instead, we heard a dull thud. Hongyang had caught Di a glancing blow.

'Caught him a glancing blow?'

Xu Yousheng wasn't so much querying it as demonstrating that he was still paying proper attention. Of course it would have been a glancing blow. Hongyang had only just died (and he drank himself to death); it is obvious he never inflicted serious injury on the policeman Di Wendong. There was no mystery about it. Uncle, he thought, you carry on making up stories, take your time, take it easy. You may be stuck in a poor village in the back of beyond, in your hermitage, as you put it, but Hongyang has given you clout with the outside world, so you can shoot your mouth off. And everyone wants something to be proud of. Townsfolk have their office blocks and their factories, you have Hongyang.

Xu Yousheng wanted to piss, and squeezed his bum cheeks together. He felt himself grow hot as he remembered how, just today, he and Jin Yan had lain in the sunshine and she had taken his penis into her wet vagina as if she were gently massaging him. His penis still had some of her secretions on it, though the warmth had gone.

That's right, Hongyang caught him a glancing blow, and it was Hongyang who was injured: his foot bounced back when it struck the ground, and it clearly hurt like hell. He grimaced, gasped, and hopped on the other foot, apparently unable to put his damaged leg on the ground. Then he looked up again, and it seemed to us that he had a crick in his neck, though afterwards we discovered that one of his eyeballs had swollen badly. He looked foolish yet managed to spit the words out one by one: 'No winner, no loser. Neither of us won or lost.' His face was covered in tears, and they mixed with sweat and dust till they turned to mud. He must have felt relieved and happy with the outcome. The alternative, killing a public servant, would have incurred the ultimate penalty, but in the last fraction of a second, reason had kicked in and he had restrained his impulse. Instead, his great foot grazed young Di's ear. They say you could see the imprint on Di's face for days after, but that was an exaggeration. Di crawled to his feet and cupped his hands together in a courteous acknowledgement that Hongyang had handed victory to him. You have to admit that Di was a hell of a guy. He collected his jacket, put his shoes on, mounted his motorbike, and was off like the wind.

'You going without stopping for something to eat?' asked the village committee chairman.

'That's right,' said Di. There was blood all over the ground. People were still wobbling up on their bicycles, heedless of those who shouted at them that it was all over. Hongyang's legs were trembling like leaves. He stared vacantly at Di's departing figure until the black dot vanished from view. Then, and only then, did he turn to go.

5

Hongliang noticed the time, picked up his plastic bag and told his nephew: 'Let's go to Hongyang's house.' Tucked away in the bag was the hairpin that his mother had worn for so many years, always insisting it was made of silver; a pack of fancy Qunyinghui cigarettes; and a photograph of him in his elder brother's arms when Hongliang was a little boy. As a youth, his big brother had always had a scowl on his face, which people said was a sign that he would die young.

'Take the letter with you,' the old lady had said.

'What letter?'

'This one.'

'Who do I give it to?'

'Hongyang.'

'What?'

'Put it in when you seal the coffin. Tell him to ask your elder brother where his remains are.'

'How's he supposed to write back?'

'He'll find a way.'

Hongliang plodded along, his shoes slapping against the ground with every step. Walking so slowly gave him an opportunity to chew things over. He was going so slowly he was getting in Xu Yousheng's way. The latter walked first on his uncle's right side, then on his left, but he did not dare walk ahead. The sky was heavy and dark as if roofed over with an awning of steel hawsers and bearings; a pungent smell like that of lake water wafted over them, scraps of paper fluttered in the air, and there was a mood of desolation, like when all the shops have shut up for the night. Hongliang sniffed. 'It'll rain tomorrow.'

Xu Yousheng said nothing, and Hongliang went on: 'It doesn't matter if it does. Tomorrow's still the best day for the funeral.'

'Who's the master of ceremonies?'

'Hongbin.'

The village children whirled past them; the Daoist priest, emissary of the city that never sleeps, had arrived. He was banging his cymbals in a desultory fashion while the suona player spat on his reed in an attempt to get rid of the dust that clung to it. Then, he put the instrument to his lips and began to play. A ribbon of sound full of warmth and grace curled up into the air and drifted away. Today was a rare holiday for this sleepy backwater, and everyone was in a state of excitement. Everyone, that is, except for Hongliang, the only one to display the gravitas of a village elder. He continued his tale.

One day just before the New Year, Boss Ho turned up in Aiwan, driving the most battered of his three cars. He stuttered and stammered miserably until finally he managed to get his words out: 'I'm completely useless. I've let my friend down.'

This was not unexpected. Boss Ho had been only too delighted to invite Hongyang to invest some money with him, at first. Ho pounded his chest and assured him that profits were there for the taking, no trouble at all. They had all reminded Hongyang that he needed to get his head around finance and contracts, but Hongyang had said if he did, he'd get taken for a ride. He took out two hundred thousand yuan and didn't even ask for a receipt. Boss Ho pulled fifty thousand out of his wallet, then opened it some more to show him that there was not a cent more in there. He hung his head in shame, then looked up at Hongyang and said simply: 'You were owed forty thousand, and I topped it up with another ten thousand from my own pocket.'

To stop Hongyang taking issue with that, he talked about all the disasters that could strike if you ran a coal mine. Flooding, pit collapses, gas explosions, extortion, blackmail, expenses like gifts and sponsoring events, thefts, being reported to the authorities, and a string of accidents with his coal lorries. They'd all driven up his costs hugely. Such bad luck, he said, you'd never imagine some of the terrible things that happen, but they just keep happening. He wiped his eyes with hands that were smutty with coal dust. 'This fifty thousand yuan, I had to move heaven and earth to get that amount together.'

Everyone knows, though, that a new mine is a machine for printing money, you print whatever you need each day. While he was in the car, Boss Ho had prepared another twenty thousand yuan and another ten thousand, in case he needed to placate Hongyang with more. In the world of business, the first offer doesn't count. But Hongyang had accepted the fifty thousand yuan. Boss Ho was secretly delighted. He declined the offer of dinner and made off while the going was good. Although bouncing along the potholed road shook a lot of spare parts loose in the car, Boss Ho bounced his way home.

Later, when Hongbin heard what had happened, he hurried over to see Hongyang. Holding up four fingers, he said: 'This is what Ho made on that.'

'Forty thousand?' asked Hongyang.

'Four million, at the very least.'

We all thought that Hongyang would try and get even with Ho, but he just said: 'Never mind how much Ho made, you've got to see it from my point of view. I made a cool fifty thousand sitting at home without lifting a finger. What could be better than that?' This sounded like just another way of saving face. Then again, that's the kind of man he was. No principles at all, except when others had none and it suited him to sound principled. As Hongyang grew older, though, he gradually learned the art of patience. If he hadn't died, he would definitely have got his hands on the Ho family's assets.

Xu Yousheng followed his uncle to Hongyang's house. The entrance was now spick and span. A light bulb had replaced the old flush-mounted ceiling light under the tiled porch, and the moths fluttered around it.

The house was four storeys high and stood out like a sentry tower in the village. Before the third and fourth floors had been added, it was obvious that there would be no use for them, but Hongyang liked to splash his money around. Right now, it was splendidly decked out, ready to serve as the backdrop for a sumptuous funeral feast. By this evening, no doubt it would have reverted to a deserted temple of no interest to anyone. Maybe Shuizhi would come and live here, though that would probably do no more than speed up its rate of decay. Couplets on green paper had been pasted up, delivered earlier by Xu Yousheng before he went to do his uncle's washing-up. He had propped the electric bike under the jujube tree at the gate and Hongbin had taken the couplets from Xu Yousheng, reading aloud as he unrolled them: ' "Sadly, all will end with me . . ." Is that a dig at Hongyang for having no children?' he asked.

'I don't know.'

'And then there's the horizontal scroll: "You can laugh or you can cry . . ." What does that mean?'

'I don't know. Zhu the teacher said it comes from an elegy General Wang Jingwei wrote on his deathbed.'

Hongbin had looked extremely annoyed. Xu Yousheng could see he was tempted to tear them up, and instead of donning his white funeral overshoes, he had hurried over to his Uncle Hongliang's house.

However, by now the couplets had been pasted in place. Around the gate, crowds of children were on their knees grubbing through the red and white streamers left over from the firecrackers in search of unlit fuses, which they squabbled over.

Xu Yousheng and his uncle went in through the unlatched door. You could work out what was there with your eyes shut: the smells of a freshly extinguished candle giving off a wisp of acrid black smoke; russet-coloured jute sacks filled with chaff; disinfectant used in the toilet last night; trousers that smelled of piss, because their owners had leaked drops of urine into their crotches like water dripping from a rusty tap; pork shoulder cooked in the pot; stir-fried peanuts being served to the guests, crunchy and crisp; alcohol that drifted through the veins of the dead and the living alike; Diao brand soap, which Shuizhi and Muxiang had used up a bar of when they washed the corpse; all sorts of tobacco; the coffin, freshly varnished so it looked like it was wearing new clothes. People squeezed their way in and out, buoyed by the kind of lively excitement only permitted on festive occasions. Of course, when they came face to face with the bereaved family, they assumed a serious expression and murmured: 'To die like that, all alone . . . How could he up and leave us . . .' But they did not sound the least bit grief-stricken. From inside the room where Hongyang had met his end, they could hear the clatter of mah-jong tiles, like the pitter-patter of a rainstorm on a roof that soon eased off to a final drip-drop. A group of women were deftly dealing and playing. There was an air of triumph as if they had just conquered a fortress, and the once-clean room was thick with smoke.

Xu Yousheng looked at the portrait of the deceased on the offerings table. It was the picture he had brought with him.

'Did he have crap in his trousers?' Hongbin asked Shuizhi as he took it. Shuizhi squeezed out a tear, like squeezing pus from a spot, then shook her head.

'They don't all crap themselves,' she said indifferently. 'And besides, he vomited such a lot that night.' Hongbin gripped the silver gilt frame in both hands and looked down at it. Then he held it up in front of him.

'You're a great man, Hongyang, a really great man.'

They clustered around, mesmerised by the magic of the photograph, their expressions exactly as Xu Yousheng had expected: foolish, mouths agape, fingers holding half-smoked cigarettes from which wisps of smoke curled upwards. They stared at the dead man, and the dead man stared back at them, and they were filled with painful memories. Only yesterday he'd ruled the locals with a rod of iron, even driven them away. Now, they stood shoulder to shoulder, muttering, 'Hey, he's really dead.' They had to keep repeating it to themselves, to be sure the great man was dead, properly dead, not like one old man from the Zhao family who had died three times, returned on each occasion, and still wasn't dead.

Shuizhi got out a greaseproof paper bag, licked her fingers a few times and pulled out a bundle of small notes secured with a rubber band, which she gave to Xu Yousheng. Then she opened his hand again to check he had it before bringing him a plate of cookies, her lips pressed tightly together like a ventriloquist's as she muttered, 'Have a snack.' Xu Yousheng promptly declined and Shuizhi walked away. As she passed Hongyang's corpse, she stopped, knelt, threw her arms around his legs and burst out crying, wetting the ground around her with her tears. The other women rushed over, and she allowed herself to be helped limply to her feet. But she soon got into her stride again, greeting her guests with a 'Welcome! Sit down and take the weight off your feet!' like the capable village woman she was.

Xu Yousheng ran a photographic studio in the township. It had tall French windows, and was furnished grandly with American-style long birch dining tables, a conference room for dignitaries, a huge oak table. It seemed criminal to him that the township

government had used it for official meetings and hung a traditional Chinese scroll in there just because it looked like a meeting room. There was a piano, a bar, a large fireplace – the works.
The studio gave him the social status he lacked because he had
no proper office job. Once the decoration had been finished,
the landlord upped the rent considerably, but his parents
accepted that this was a form of amusement that would keep
him safe and sound at home. It was better than having him
roam the streets, after all. Still, his mother often grumbled that
all of this cost thousands. He could not afford a car or a motorbike as well. She told him: 'Earn a bit of money if you want
them, otherwise you'll have to wait until I die.' They had forked
out to send him to Jiujiang Vocational Technical College, but he
had dropped out of the course.

Although the photographic studio and the guest house
were the township's most elegant buildings, the trouble was
that his clients were a disappointment. They trailed mud in
with them, marking the parquet floors and annoying him so
much that it wasn't unknown for him to throw them out. He
never managed to explain how to pose naturally, while they –
with their deer heads, rats' eyes, swarthy faces and swanlike
shapes, three parts human, seven parts demon – tried vainly to
transform themselves into gentlemen, film stars or fairy-tale
heroes. Or else they looked at themselves in the mirror, trembling, their eyes bulging with terror like toads no matter how
hard he tried to reassure them. They would never become
models, and he would never fulfil his dream of becoming a
photographer. 'That's right, cross your legs, and don't put
your hands behind your legs, you don't want to look like a
strutting frog, stick them in your trouser pockets, but not all
the way in, you're not a beggar, you don't need to keep root-
ing around for small change, leave your thumb out, that's
right, one thumb,' he said. 'That's right, good, *good*' – said in

English – 'show your teeth, it looks more natural. You're damned useless, do your mum and dad know that? Try, try and relax, that's right, good' – said in English – 'sit up straight, look over here, here, look at my finger on the button, right, waan ... twoo ... ta-ree ... Good, and another one ... good ...' Xu Yousheng felt like he was a megaphone, always shouting the same thing, starting and finishing at fixed times since they were all programmed to commit the same mistakes, damned idiots they were, idiots to beat all idiots. The sole exception was Hongyang. His only success. And still today the picture of the dead man gazes aloof from the pages of *Photographic Portraits* magazine.

The day it was taken, Hongyang had walked into his studio full of curiosity. He looked around at all these new things with a sneer intended to hide a faint sense of inferiority. 'Fucking hi-tech!' he said. But as soon as he sat he seemed to take over, as if he were an old-fashioned host accustomed to pushing his clients around, an overbearing host determined to keep his guests on his toes. He was the first client Xu Yousheng had had who sat perfectly at ease. And so the perfect portrait appeared before Xu Yousheng's eyes: ferocious, calm, bloodthirsty, disagreeable. You could not tell from his face what he was thinking, but his eyes made it clear he was in complete control of you. He looked you straight in the eyes, and forced you to meet his gaze. You could not tell if he was about to attack and kill you. The embodiment of evil. A totem.

Fine. Xu Yousheng hurriedly focused the camera and tested the flashgun. The pop of the flash made Hongyang turn his head away and Xu Yousheng was worried that he might have missed his opportunity, but luckily Hongyang faced forwards again and stared straight at the camera lens. Everything was perfect, and all Xu Yousheng needed to do was press the shutter.

Just at that moment, one of Hongyang's cronies burst in. He whispered a few words into Hongyang's ear, and to Xu Yousheng's distress, his subject got up to leave.

'Wait for me,' Hongyang said.

In the recreation room of the Cooperative building, Boss Ho's son, Yamin, was sitting with his legs resting on the mah-jong table, one draped over the other. 'I'll wait here, you go and get him,' he had said, flicking ash from his cigarette to the floor. Three days before, he had driven into the township in his Buick, with all the arrogance of a man from the county town, and stated brusquely that he'd killed a man and wanted to hole up for a few days. A knife was embedded in the mah-jong table. After a morning's play, he reckoned his opponents were cheating and started swearing, finally flinging his money to the floor, saying: 'Pick it up if you want it. And keep the change.' When Hongyang arrived, he was holding a toy gun: he pulled the trigger, a flame spurted out and he lit another cigarette, then waved it in the air till the flame went out. 'Did you throw that money down?' asked Hongyang. Ho cocked his head, squinted at Hongyang, sizing him up, and said: 'Yes.'

'Who's your dad?'

'You should ask who I am.'

'You got away with it today,' said Hongyang, picking up the money and asking: 'Whose is this?' One of the men took it from him. 'Count it to see if it's all there,' said Hongyang.

'That doesn't happen,' said Ho Yamin.

'What doesn't happen?'

'Getting away with it.'

Ho Yamin put his legs to the floor and stubbed out his cigarette on the green baize table. Then he walked over to Hongyang, looked up at him and pulled out his knife. He was irritatingly brash and had the face of a raw youth, with greasy skin covered in pus-filled pimples and a body that sometimes quivered slightly. He opened his mouth to speak, but before he could do so, Hongyang raised his fist and broke Ho's nose, punching it so hard it was a wonder he didn't leave a fist-shaped hole in his face. Then he wiped his bloody fist on the boy's temple, opened both arms wide and guffawed hysterically.

'That's not right. The boss man shouldn't pick up the money for the customer, should he?'

Ho Yamin thudded to the floor as if felled by a thunderbolt, letting go of the knife as he did so. 'Fuck.' He sounded petty rather than abusive. With an aggrieved air, he reached for his knife, as if he was merely taking back what was his.

Hongyang watched attentively and, as the boy was about to grip the knife, seized his hand and gave it a fierce tug, pulling him to his feet.

'Fuck off!' The tears spilled out.

'Again!'

'Fuck off!' came the howl.

Hongyang led Ho by the hand, paced in a circle a few times, then pulled the hand towards him and examined it admiringly, the way a carpenter might admire a stick he had just whittled.

'What a pity me and your old man have been friends all our lives.'

There was a crack like a piece of firewood snapping, and Hongyang forced Ho's elbow joint backwards, using so much force that he almost lost his balance and keeled over. The poor boy let out a scream like an artillery shell hitting the ceiling and burst into wails of 'Mummy, Mummy, Mummy, Mummy, Mummy, Mummy, Mummy, Mummy!' He tried to run, but he didn't get far before he fell to the ground, still crying out for his mummy.

'My friendship with your dad is worth millions,' said Hongyang, finally letting go of the boy's elbow. Everyone stepped back. Boss Ho's son, still twitching, tried to scramble to his feet. He was covered in dust from head to foot, and when he saw his arm dangling, he was terrified.

Hongyang clapped his hands and ordered: 'Take him up to Hongling Ridge and leave him by the roadside.' Then he strode out.

Back at the studio, he said to Xu Yousheng: 'Let's carry on.' And he sat down on the sofa in his chosen pose. His greying hair was tousled, his forehead impressively broad and his deep-set eyes gleamed menacingly, casting an alarming shadow slightly to the left of the bridge of his nose. His breathing gradually steadied, but his displeasure at the incident had pulled his lips downward until they were as taut as a wire bow. The collar of his black greatcoat stood up, his arms were like tree trunks, and his abdomen had an imposing bulge. His splayed fingers rested on his knees and the last drops of blood dripped from his dust-covered fingertips.

'Right, right.' Xu Yousheng pressed the shutter urgently. In the photo, Hongyang looked like a tiger that had just devoured its meal, lying sated on the mountain, its whiskers still blood-stained, fixing you with a tranquil gaze and apparently wondering whether it could be bothered to rip you apart too.

Today, Hongyang was laid out in the rattan chair, flecks of soap still visible on his hair and face. He wore a clean set of clothes and looked as if he was fresh out of his bath and taking a nap. His face was covered by a sheet of yellow paper held down by a wine cup resting on his forehead that rose as the electric fan blew over him to reveal the deathly white skin underneath. His lips were ashen. Only his thickset frame was recognisable, and even then it kept sliding down the chair like silt, forcing someone to run in, grip the body under the armpits and pull it up again. People walked back and forth feeling perfectly safe; children mischievously lifted the paper and pulled faces at him, one even tried to stick a cigarette up his nostril; newcomers, who had come to pay their respects, peered silently at the corpse the way they might peer at a recently captured wild beast. Hongyang had become extremely soft and gentle.

Hongbin had a cigarette stuck behind his ear and looked impatient as his bent figure patrolled the room. Hongliang, his hands stuck in his trouser pockets, watched him scornfully. Hongbin asked: 'Is the slab ready?'

'When you get to Screwturn tomorrow, it'll be there for sure.'

'Good.'

Hongbin was still suspicious, though. He had learned the hard way that his uncle could never get things done, though he was oblivious to the fact that his uncle felt exactly the same about him. Hongliang carried on roaming around the house, his nephew at his heels.

6

They spent a long time wandering around this space where past and present were entangled, finally ending up on the second floor. Hongliang sat down on a pink-upholstered sofa, lounging on it the way only someone with power and influence could, one leg draped high over the other. Xu Yousheng sat on a pouffe looking at his reflection in a giant LCD screen that shone black like ice at night. 'This is the difference between East and West,' came the voice from the sofa. 'In the West, everything is subject to regulations, while in the East, we let nature take its course. So here, objects come in all shapes and sizes, while over there electrical appliances, guns and patrol boats are all produced to the same standards. This LCD screen looks like a black rock that Westerners have bequeathed us.'

The speakers, made of real wood, sat squarely on the TV cabinet. Their deep bass notes were not intended to imitate the sounds of the ordinary world; no, they were designed to filter, transform and process normal sounds, creating something more beautiful and more impressive in the process, just as HDTV showed images that were clearer than anything in real life and transported people to another world. A two-door drinks cabinet stood in the corner, the water left untouched, the cool box below stocked with dark beer, coffee and vodka. The only object that looked out of place was the safe that had been fixed to the wall when the room was built, its four legs cemented to the floor. The green paint was peeling off it, showing flakes of rust underneath.

'That's the cause of this disgraceful business,' said Hongliang.

Downstairs, the widow was still weeping. She sat on the floor in a mess of funeral paper, cigarette butts and indignant spittle, an overturned incense burner and a broken cup. The recliner had been shifted so the corpse was now facing the wall. The room looked like a battleground. Shuizhi clung to Hongyang's leg, moaning his name over and over until the syllables blurred and began to sound like 'Wengweng . . . my wengweng . . .', like a signature that has become so familiar it dissolves into a lazy squiggle. Outside the room, Hongliang strained his ears and concluded that there were still some women with her, though they were silent because they had not managed to console Shuizhi, who was determined to keep on crying. She would never have wept so unrestrainedly had they not been there. She had a point to prove.

'Do you think she's crying like that because this is all such a nasty business?' asked Hongliang. 'No children, husband just died and not even buried yet, and now she's under attack . . . It's not surprising she's in pieces, don't you think?'

'Right. But it's not all that. Maybe she's finding things too complicated so she's hiding behind her tears. Like a pheasant, hiding its head in the snow and thinking its tail is invisible too. She knows she's stupid, she knows that normally she can't get a single logical sentence out. She's never seen so much money. Even though she deserves it, it's still a scary prospect. She's terrified that people will wonder how she came by this amount of money legally, and reckons people will say she's not fit to inherit. Even if most people condemn views like that, she's still very afraid. A huge pot of money is exactly what she thinks will come her way, though it's the thing she's most afraid of too. It's like she's sitting alone in a temple on a stormy night, listening to the galloping of a horse's hooves. You don't know where the horse is coming from or when it will appear, and it's enough to turn you into a bag of nerves. She's just an ex-wife, and all she has to protect her is a bit of paper she can't read. Muxiang's used her wisdom, or rather, her diehard determination, to settle the arguments, but Shuizhi is in a panic. All she can do is cry, and play the suffering widow—'

Muxiang used her sleeve to wipe a bit of soap off the corpse's neck below his ear and cried: 'Brother! Can you hear me?'

After a moment or two, as if convinced there wasn't going to be a response, she turned away and spoke in the exhausted, resigned tones of a cancer sufferer: 'Anyone who wants money, come and get it. I don't want a cent. But don't you think of bothering Shuizhi or Hongbin again, that's my one condition. Just take what you want while I'm here.' And she pulled four bank passbooks from an inside pocket and threw them on the floor.

It looked for a moment as if the young woman Zhou was going to pick them up. Muxiang, meanwhile, gave a piercing shriek: 'Brother! Brother! I'm coming!' And, forcing herself into a jerky run, she hobbled furiously towards the wall. It was only at the last moment that someone grabbed hold of her to stop her thumping her head against it.

'Auntie Muxiang really was trying to bash her brains out,' said Xu Yousheng.

'Well, it was just Hongyang's earnings. Muxiang is a good woman at heart – she promised that all the male cousins with the generation name Hong would receive ten thousand yuan. Ten thousand yuan, that's real money, and out of the blue too! Although Hongyang raked it in these last few years, he spent a lot too. He never planned to save up. He did later, but not at the start. And now he's dead. The cash is all that's left. And they got ten thousand each. You can blame him for not giving you more when he was alive, for being mean. Hongyang didn't plan on leaving you anything, though. Hongbin got the most, a hundred thousand, but he could have taken two hundred and twenty thousand. Hongbin was with Hongyang the longest, nearly twenty years of his life. He never achieved much or did anything like hard work, but he's had to make all the funeral arrangements, and someone will have to uphold Aiwan's interests from now on. They might even have to go to prison for it, and there's no one willing to do that except Hongbin. I've never had much respect for your Uncle Hongbin, he's a dope, but he's the only one prepared to do things properly.'

Hongliang began to tell the story of Hongyang's money.

Muxiang and Shuizhi wanted to do things the right way too, because when they went to look for the strongbox key, they made Hongbin go with them. They went through his wardrobe and chest of drawers, they looked under the bed and even in the toilet cistern, but they couldn't find it. Hongbin kept firing questions at them: Where did he put his valuables? When did he last open it? What does the key look like? Stuff like that. They couldn't agree on their answers. Finally, when pressed further, Shuizhi said she didn't know if it meant anything, but one night, five or six years earlier, Hongyang had been walking home, drunk as a skunk, when he passed her lonely house in Ruanjiayan. He yelled: 'Shuizhi, come out!' and she came out. Then he yelled, 'Stand right where you are!' And she stood right where she was. Then he burst into tears and said drunkenly: 'Shuizhi, whatever they say, and whatever I've done to you, forget all that. If anything happens to me, you move back into the house and give the fourth floor a good sort-out.' She heard him say 'Scram, you bitch!', before she turned and went back into the house.

During all the time they were getting together and breaking up, over and over again, he could not conceal his loathing for her. Thinking about it now, it seemed that he'd had a premonition of his own death as long ago as that, although he probably envisaged getting banged up for life, or getting the death sentence. He loathed Shuizhi the way we often loathe our close family, but when faced with disaster he also knew she was the only one whom he could trust.

The three of them climbed three flights of stairs and looked up at the hole that led to the fourth floor. Hongbin brought over the ladder and Muxiang and Shuizhi climbed up. The concrete floor was more or less even, and the dust was at least an inch thick. Apart from a few steel reinforcing bars protruding out of the floor, there was absolutely nothing else to be seen. They went over it with a fine-tooth comb but could find nothing. As they came back down, Muxiang said: 'Shuizhi, there's something under your shoe.' And when they looked, they found a chunk of dirt sticking to her sole. There was something with a rubber band around it which, when they knocked off the dirt, turned out to be a key. When they opened up the strongbox, they found ten credit union and agricultural bank passbooks and a slip of paper. Hongyang had laboriously noted down instructions, getting some of the characters wrong: *Give the passbooks with Shuizhi's name on to Shuizhi. Give the passbooks with Muxiang's name on to Muxiang. The passwords are their dates of birth in the lunar calendar. Give the other two to Hongbin – the password is my date of birth in the lunar calendar. Any problems, contact Ho Dongming in Fan township. Wherever I die, bury my body at Screwturn.*

When they looked again at the passbooks, they realised that Hongyang must have been planning this for a while. He'd saved virtually nothing for himself, but he had put aside a fixed amount for each of them. Every time he withdrew money using the passbooks, he topped it up to the original amount afterwards, and then saved quite a bit more besides.

The three of them shed tears as they divided up the passbooks. Hongbin only wanted to take eighty thousand for

himself, he said he'd distribute the remaining hundred and
forty among his male cousins. Muxiang said *she* wanted to give
them money. And after much toing and froing, they resolved it
like this: they would give another twenty-one distant male
cousins ten thousand each, with Hongbin paying out a hundred
and twenty thousand and Muxiang, ninety thousand, and
Shuizhi was not to pay anything at all. It would be a great day
in the village when the money was distributed. Imagine how
happy everyone would be. But Hongbin was always capable of
messing up a good deed. He could have sent Shiren, Shiyi,
Shi'en or Shide, all of whom were reliable, to Fan township to
collect the money, but instead he promised to distribute it only
after the funeral. You don't do things like that when someone
dies. The longer you string out the business, the more everyone thinks there's something shameful about it. That's what
money does – although everyone thinks you're lovely when
you've got it, it's a real headache too. Hongbin always said you
couldn't trust anyone else to get things done, yet he was the
worst of the lot.

At this point in his story, Hongliang got to his feet. 'You wait
here,' he said and went indoors. He looked everywhere for a
pen and paper but couldn't find one, so he used lipstick to draw
a diagram for Xu Yousheng on the coffee table, which squeaked
as he drew.

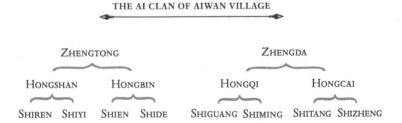

THE AI CLAN OF AIWAN VILLAGE

ZHENGTONG   ZHENGDA

HONGSHAN   HONGBIN   HONGQI   HONGCAI

SHIREN SHIYI   SHI'EN SHIDE   SHIGUANG SHIMING   SHITANG SHIZHENG

'That looks balanced, doesn't it?' said Hongliang. 'Opposing forces equally matched.'

You might be forgiven for thinking that this business is down to one woman making a scene, which happens plenty at mahjong, and that it's all the fault of Zhou, Shiming's wife. There are plenty of devious people like her around, always ready to kick up a fuss. But how could one person have such an impact? How could things get so out of control? Well, she was just the touchpaper that lit the conflict between all three generations of the two branches of the Ai clan, the Zheng brothers. They had never come to blows before, they were always polite, but under the surface they always had it in for the other branch. They've loathed each other for eighty years. And they made sure they brought up their children feeling the same way. For generations, they've been talking about a theft at a building in Puting township, De'an county, a jewel of an old house that's still standing, although they've never been there to explore it. Having eliminated the possibility of burglars from elsewhere, for all that time they've arbitrarily blamed the other branch of the family for pulling an inside job. They're all arguing about the exact same guest room, and they agree about its description: it was under the roof, the outside wall was like a sheer rock face, the only window was jammed shut, and although the windows were covered by nothing more than sheets of paper – they couldn't afford glass – they were intact. There were no signs of an intruder, the door was bolted shut from the inside, and at daybreak it was still bolted shut. There were no gaps in the walls of the room: it was sealed completely airtight.

Still they can't agree on what happened. Each generation passes this message down to the children: The building was burglar-proof, so the theft must have been an inside job. The Zhengda branch think the Zhengtong branch stole it, and vice versa. Before the money went, Zhengda and Zhengtong were the closest of brothers, setting off together in the teeth of a spring snowstorm, each carrying the same amount of money on their backs. Before they left, their father impressed the following on them: 'That money is the cornerstone of the families you're each going to found, the capital for each of you to bequeath to your descendants.' They spent the night in the guest room, but the very next morning, Zhengtong's bundle of money was still tucked under his head, and Zhengda's had vanished from his hiding place inside his jacket. Although both men searched for it frantically, imagining all sorts of possibilities, none of them seemed plausible.

When Zhengda's suspicions finally fell on his own brother, the absolute faith the pair had in one another took a serious knock. Zhengtong, with his usual arrogance, refused to answer his brother's questions, and Zhengda made oblique accusations. They never trusted each other again. When they got themselves wives, they finally had someone to pour it all out to: 'He's shameless! He suspects his own elder brother!' Or: 'He's actually robbed the brother born of the same mother!' Or: 'I bet Zhengda's used the money to pay off his huge gambling debts. If he doesn't clear his debts, he'll be hunted down and killed. And if he does use this money to clear them, our dad'll drown him in the water butt!' Or: 'All Zhengda's family get meat to eat nowadays, and it's our portion they're eating. If we starve, he'll be responsible.'

Zhengtong and Zhengda were the only ones who knew the facts, and when the brothers died, the answer to the riddle died with them. The one certainty is that on that night, one of the brothers must have got up and taken the bundle of money, buried it somewhere, then come back to the house and gone back to sleep. Each patriarch, Zhengtong and Zhengda, left behind him only a solemn vow that he personally had been completely honest and above board, that he had done nothing wrong. But without a shadow of a doubt, Zhengda's descendants were angrier than Zhengtong's. Although the passing of the years had smoothed out differences in their economic circumstances, whenever anything untoward happened, Zhengda's descendants always decided that Old Man Zhengtong had had a hand in it: once a rat, always a rat, as they say. His descendants were as shameless as their granddad. One branch of the family reckoned the other branch were all a bunch of thieves, while the latter thought the former were all rabid dogs that would bite you given half a chance. To show their contempt for their cousins, each branch built houses further and further away from the other, until they weren't neighbours any more.

There are feuds within every clan, human society has always been like that, and the message is handed down from the woman of the family to daughters-in-law and infants: 'Beware of the ones who have demonstrated a bad character . . .'

'Right,' said Xu Yousheng. 'My mum was always warning me about Ho Dongming, but you all treat him like a god!'

'Of all the people in Aiwan, no other families have divisions as deep or as obscure as they do. The two branches of the clan are always shooting their mouths off, embellishing the story, but they say it's conclusive proof of their confidence in themselves, and that they're only doing it to remind the next generation that honest people should always keep a respectful distance from bad characters. They're not going to martyr themselves in defence of the family honour, they figure they don't need to because the family's reputation is unassailable. And even though they're estranged, they'll still get together if they're short of players at a mah-jong game or if something's going on in the village, and they'll be more polite to each other than people who get on well.

'Until now, that is. It's that young woman, Zhou, who's evil. She tried to hide her own bad behaviour by dragging in age-old disagreements. And all of a sudden, both sides of the family are at each other's throats again, saying what they really think about the other side. All these years, each branch has regarded themselves as the magnanimous peacekeepers in the relationship. They never had any idea that the other side had such low opinions of them. They overrated human nature. Now they're up in arms, and they've hurled themselves into the fray. At first I thought the brawl had been staged, that they were just waiting for someone to step in and calm things down. But then I discovered that the enmity runs much deeper than I ever imagined. They were going all out to try and knock the other side out with stools, they wanted to scratch each other's eyes out, they were gasping like they were going to suffocate. And I had a sudden vision of Zhengtong and Zhengda rolling out of the grave they'd been forced to share, and hurling stones at the other side.

'At the time, you said it loud and clear: "If something was said in the past, then only one person should feel shame, but now all of you, on both sides, should feel shame," ' said Xu Yousheng, looking at his uncle as he fiddled with the DVD player and amplifier. 'Dammit, it's been wired up wrong. We've got a good machine and we can't even use it. Things kicked off between the younger generation on both sides, you got knocked to the ground, your glasses slid down to the tip of your nose and confusion was written all over your face.'

Downstairs, Zhou was still bouncing up and down, shrieking: 'This is a vicious attack, you're all vicious! Don't bring other people into this, you're the bullies!' Actually, she had no real reason to accuse anyone of anything, as all she had to go on were loud but baseless accusations. She was convinced that her man, Shiming, and his brothers and cousins, Shiguang, Shitang and Shizhong, had taken up the cudgels on her behalf because she'd been humiliated, though all they were doing was fighting over an old family grievance. As Hongliang had put it just before, they were fighting over the whereabouts of a bundle that disappeared eighty years ago. In time, Zhou would understand that. Like any coward, when she did find a reason to attack her opponent, she revelled in self-righteousness. She saw herself as spearheading their denunciation of old man Zhengtong.

'How could you?! How could your family behave like that?' She grabbed the hair of Shiren's wife, Chen, who had never been in a fight in her entire life, poor woman. Zhou picked her up off the ground, elbowed her in the head, considered her for a moment and then spat 'Come on!' at her before hauling her away by the hair. Chen's body stumbled along after her hair. Zhou banged the young woman's head against the door. 'You've got sticky fingers, all of you, and then you go accusing other people of thieving,' said Zhou, giving her a slap.

When the battle first broke out, she had been completely engrossed in her mah-jong game, anxious to destroy the evidence. Only she would do something like that. She was capable of slapping someone's face in front of everyone, then feigning innocence and asking: 'Where's the proof I slapped you? Who saw me do it?'

When Chen and the other women demanded to look at her tiles, she grabbed them and held them clasped to her chest, as if those pieces, half the length of her thumb, were children she was shielding from harm. 'Hand them over!' cried the women. Zhou was a blatant cheat: she used to mess around with the tiles that were out of play, the ones that had to be put back into play. Sometimes she flicked her fingers across the table, ostensibly to see what tiles she or others had in their hand but actually to swap over some of the tiles. Although generally people were only concerned about their own tiles, Zhou got hold of so many that the others started to suspect something peculiar was going on. And when it came to working out the money, she put down a fake fifty-yuan note.

Chen thought there was something not right, though she wasn't quite sure what it was. When Zhou counted the points, she paid close attention, and even when the score should have been obvious, she ended up with a different figure. But she sounded so reasonable that Chen was tempted to believe her, and ended up in a real muddle. When it came to shuffling the tiles, Chen picked up the money at the gate and her heart skipped a beat. Although she used to run a shop, she'd never seen a banknote as shiny as this one. Still, she felt awkward. She didn't want to pick it up and wasn't comfortable palming it off on other people, so she looked for an opportunity to give it back to Zhou. Instead, Zhou flicked the note aside and said: 'Isn't there some small change?'

'I played three tiles of seventy thousand, Wuniang played one. Don't move.' And Chen finally caught hold of Zhou's hand.

'Those are mine!' said Zhou.

'Is that so? Wuniang, you remember, you played one, I played three, right?' said Chen.

'I remember, and then you said: "What bad luck, you got three tiles of seventy thousand,"' said Wuniang.

'Let us see them, maybe we've done you an injustice,' said Chen.

'You can't look at other people's tiles when you're playing a game,' said Zhou.

'It's stupid to swap tiles like this. Maybe once is OK, no more. We may be poor, but we've got our standards, don't you think?' said Chen.

'When did I swap the tiles on the table?' said Zhou.

'Look, look! She said it. I never said you swapped the tiles on the table. You did,' said Chen.

'You're a troublemaker,' said Zhou. 'I've never seen a trouble-maker like you.'

'We'll see if I'm a troublemaker when you show us your tiles,' said Chen.

The three women clustered around, Zhou still hugging the tiles close to her chest. They were only putting on a show of force, but Zhou was panting for breath, scarlet in the face and mulish, like she was going to bolt for the door. Sounding injured, she said: 'When did I swap the tiles?' a couple of times. The other three could scarcely believe that someone so immoral set such store by her reputation. 'Where the hell's it all going to end?' she finally yelled.

As the shrill cry reached his ears, Shiming threw down the nail he'd been hammering and came in.

'She says we deserve to be poor our whole lives,' Zhou said, pointing at Chen.

'What?' said Shiming.

'When did I say that?' said Chen, indignant.

'You said that even if you're poor, it's no excuse for having a bad character,' Zhou turned to the other two women players. 'She said that, didn't she?'

The women were speechless.

'She said we're scum and deserve to be poor till we die,' Zhou finished.

'Bullshit!' exclaimed Shiming and flung his claw hammer at the wall, where it made a dent and knocked off flakes of white paint.

'You make her show us her tiles,' Chen said to him. 'Make her give us a look.'

'Bullshit!' Shiming repeated.

As if each of them had sensed something odd at the very same moment, Shiren, Shiyi, Shi'en, Shide, Shiguang, Shitang and Shizheng all came running in. Eighty years after the event, the most powerful forces of Aiwan village were massed around Hongyang's corpse, armed to the teeth like warrior heroes of old, ready to strike.

'Damn you! What right have you to tell us that we've got to listen to reason? It was *your* grandfather stole our inheritance, and now you're grabbing hundreds of thousands more yuan, cent by cent,' Shiming said to Shi'en. 'What the hell gives you the right to talk to me like that?'

'What are you talking about?' Shi'en shot back, giving Shiming a shove.

Eighty years of accumulated silence, the silence of refined and gentle courtesy, the accumulated weight of words unspoken, and of umbrage taken, prevented them from listening to what the other sides were saying. Eighty years of simmering, murderous resentments inculcated in the family burst all at once into a conflagration that was to consume everyone within its reach. Every bit of scandal attached to either branch of the family was broadcast in public – it was all most enlightening for the bystanders. Each side heaped abuse on the other, as if they were setting up a ladder for their opponents to step on in order to hurl down even more abuse on themselves. They said things that made sense, they said things that were utter nonsense. It was like they had opened Pandora's box.

Uncle Hongbin took an unlocked bike from Tianjiapu, where he had been discussing the funeral arrangements with the village committee, and hurried home. He appeared deeply concerned and ready to administer justice.

'Stop right there, all of you!' he shouted.

'Stop?' Shiming said. 'You rip-off merchant, what right have you to tell us to stop?'

'What have I ripped off?'

'You've ripped off Granddad Hongyang's money.'

'He left it to me! Left it to me, understand? It's down in black and white. If he left it to me, what business is it of yours?'

At this point, Hongbin felt he was tumbling into a vortex, and indignation welled up inside him. If I'd known, he thought, I wouldn't have given any of you so much as ten thousand. I did it with the best of intentions, and look at the terrible results. He shouted at them angrily, but they roared back even louder. For an instant, he had seen himself as the head of the entire family, and wanted to be regarded that way, and here he was, being sucked into the vortex and forcibly interrogated. As Hongliang had said, he lacked the ability to deal with situations like this.

The others completely ignored him. It was only when his son took a thump that he was able to establish his position as the boy's father, and threw himself into the fray. The ensuing brawl was like a playground fight, a tornado buffeting every corner of the room. Anything they could move served as a weapon; even the corpse only narrowly escaped being drawn in.

Shuizhi could do nothing. She found herself being pushed around by the others, and fell over a few times. 'Apparently it doesn't matter who you are. Anyone who gets in the way is going to be pushed over,' she wailed loudly, but no one paid her any attention.

Outside the door, angry arguments could be heard. Inside, Shitang charged around, while Shiyi attempted to shield himself with the corpse. Shitang lunged several times over the dead man's head and was about to poke the mourning staff right past his ear, when he jerked and nearly landed on the corpse's chest. Very embarrassed, he kowtowed to beg Hongyang's pardon.

The way Shitang told it afterwards, the corners of Hongyang's mouth twitched fleetingly. 'When I looked again, though,' he added, 'he was back to looking like a dead man.'

It was Muxiang who finally put an end to the fighting. She came back from Han You, the village barefoot doctor, with some painkillers, and fell to her knees in the middle of the maelstrom. She was so overweight and frail, heaven knows how she slipped into the room so quietly.

'I'm kneeling before you,' she began, kowtowing over and over. 'Ladies and gentlemen, I'm kneeling before you.'

Those on the fringes of the crowd pushed forward, anxious to understand what was going on. The feuding cousins were physically restrained, but they carried on lashing out so fiercely that they were in danger of falling over and they had to be pulled even further apart.

Muxiang, the cancer sufferer, the dead man's elder sister, the respected elder, then got to her feet. 'If any of you have something to say, then speak up and say it.'

'So this is what I've got to say,' said Shiming. 'I reckon *you're* entitled to divvy up the money, but what gives Hongbin the right?'

'I think it's old Ma Shuizhi who isn't entitled. Get it out and divide it equally,' his wife put in.

'The portions for Hongbin, Shuizhi and me were all stipulated by Hongyang, and that's that,' said Muxiang.

'Then Granddad Hongyang can get out of his coffin and carry it himself,' said Shiming.

'Each of the Hong cousins gets ten thousand, that's what Shuizhi, Hongbin and I decided. And that's perfectly reasonable. And I need you to carry the coffin too.'

Muxiang went to the corpse. Behind her, the descendants of Zhengda were arguing furiously. She bent down and wiped a flake of soap from below his ear and whispered his name as if he were still alive.

Xu Yousheng was getting bored with his uncle's story, and got up to stretch his legs. He became aware that his footsteps were a clever way of controlling the vocal cords of the woman downstairs. When he got to the top of the stairs, the sound of weeping floated up; when he went back to his uncle, the sound faded away. Finally, when he started to walk down the stairs and Shuizhi peeped through her fingers and spotted him, the weeping rose to a crescendo. Muxiang was sitting beside the corpse, one of his hands gripped in hers, her eyes closed. A few other women were lolling against the wall, holding serviettes. The floor was in a wretched state.

'Don't cry, Auntie,' said Hongliang.

'You're educated, you understand what's right,' said Shuizhi.

'Of course I do, and no one's going to fight you over your entitlement. There are no other heirs.'

'That's not what I meant.'

'Don't cry, you've got to look after your health.'

7

This was when Hongbin came back.

'He was always going to come back. He's the only one in Aiwan with this obsessive sense of responsibility, he's always fretting,' Hongliang said to his nephew, looking with an aggrieved air at the hand-painted scroll hanging from the wall. A pine tree spreading its dark branches, a bright sun in the distance, the mist billowing in from the mountains. 'Hongyang, you've departed for the land of the immortals and left me to sort out this terrible mess,' he muttered to himself as he put his cigarette to his lips.

Muxiang woke up, opened those bovine eyes that made everyone feel sorry for her, shuffled her feet into her shoes and reached out a hand to Hongbin.

'If only they hadn't been swindled on their investment last year . . .' he said. 'If they'd just gone along with Hongyang instead of doing their own thing.'

'Don't get het up about stuff like that, Hongbin,' said Muxiang.

'I'm not getting het up. With people like that, what's the point? The Eight Immortals are supposed to be family members, that's always been the rule. But if they refuse to come, there's nothing we can do. The ancestors have always said we shouldn't go begging for help either. If Shiguang and Shitang don't come, I'll make up the numbers with Shiyi and Shiliang. There's no shortage of people. And then let's see if they have the nerve to come and ask for their ten thousand yuan.'

With Hongbin back and in charge, Shuizhi got her broom and began to sweep up. The tear streaks had gone from the swarthy old woman's face. She always seemed to be hiding behind something, either tears or work. Then she asked: 'When will the coffin be sealed?'

He glanced at his Shanghai-brand watch, which was nearly twenty years old now. 'Soon. The Daoist priest is having his meal as we speak, and he's got to have enough to eat and drink to give him the qi energy to perform the ceremony.'

Hongbin went to the side room to look at the coffin. He was surprised to see the varnisher still there. He wasn't varnishing the coffin, however, but was walking round and round it. 'OK, that's enough,' said Hongbin. The varnisher looked meekly up at him. He had his brush in one hand, the can of varnish in the other, so he could only stand there and allow Hongbin to stuff a packet of cigarettes into his trouser pocket, a gesture that felt humiliatingly like bribery yet cheered him up nonetheless.

He so badly wants it to be him in there that he can't bear to leave, thought Xu Yousheng, who had come in with his uncle.

The four men each picked up one end of the coffin from where it had been resting upon two benches, lifted it to their shoulders, and carried it out through the immense glass doors.

'I thought it would be much heavier,' said Xu Yousheng.

'How heavy can it be?' said Hongliang. 'It's not very big, the coffin planks are only a few inches thick . . . Hongyang deserved better.'

'Well, that can't be helped. It's all been such a hurry,' said Hongbin.

'But it shouldn't have been such a hurry,' said Hongliang.

'What could we do? This is the only propitious day for a couple of weeks. Are you saying we should have waited until the corpse started to stink?' said Hongbin.

What kind of an almanac tells you there are no propitious days for a couple of weeks? Hongliang wanted to ask. But he kept his thoughts to himself, and he and Xu Yousheng busied themselves with arranging the corpse in a sitting position facing south, so Hongyang would be able to face the front door of the house he had built. Then he fetched the offerings table, replaced the portrait on it, along with the pig's head, the cockerel, the carp, cakes, pastries, fruit, wine, wine cups, chopsticks and bowls, and ghost money, and positioned a terracotta basin on the ground in which to burn the ghost money. The head of the corpse flopped to one side; Hongliang grasped it between both hands like a melon and leaned it against the back of the chair. 'His flesh is still soft,' he said.

Hongbin held his finger under Hongyang's nose. 'He's well and truly dead. We may as well not bother to cover his face with funeral paper.'

From the east side of the village came the ear-splitting explosions of firecrackers.

'Who could that be so late? It sounds like it's coming from Fan township,' said Hongbin.

'How should I know?' asked Xu Yousheng.

'Someone's spent a lot of money on those firecrackers. I wonder who it is,' said Hongliang.

Xu Yousheng shrugged indifferently. 'Search me,' he replied.

'It could be the young folk, but I thought they weren't going to come,' said Hongbin.

They sat on the threshold smoking one cigarette after another as they waited for the new arrivals. The lamp under the porch tiles beamed out a vast circle of light, outside which the darkness was a pool, like the billowing waters of a lake.

No one came for a long time. Maybe they were all enjoying themselves in the village.

Eventually, the four men nodded off. Half an hour later, they were startled awake by rustling noises, and a young man in an ill-fitting shirt emerged from the darkness on his knees. His eyes fixed on the ground, he took three paces, knelt and kowtowed, hands spread in front of him, then repeated the sequence. A woman followed behind, carrying a shoulder pole laden with two large baskets of gifts: Coca-Cola, Fanta, Sprite, Minute Maid orange juice, coconut milk, Red Bull, cans of cold tea – milk, green and herbal – mineral water and plain drinking water, beer, red wine, Huadiao rice wine, Fenggang spirits, Gujingxian spirits, fresh milk, calcium-enriched milk, Deluxe milk, breakfast biscuits, filled biscuits, crackers, jianbing pancakes, xuebing pancakes, chocolate, Snickers, custard tarts, blueberry tarts, baguettes, plaited bread loaves, beef jerky, dried pork floss, dried fish slices, shredded squid, raisins, hawthorn berries, candied jujubes, tree peony bark, red dates, walnuts, sunflower seeds, melon seeds, buttered peanuts, crisp-fried peanuts, pistachios, pine nuts, almonds, hundred-year-old eggs, dried bean curd, chicken wings and chicken feet, preserved sausages, rolled oats, orange juice, black sesame paste, milk tea, powdered milk, soya milk, instant noodles, brown sugar, rock candy, white sugar, 'Thirteen Flavours of Wang Fuyi' seasonings, Zhenjiang vinegar, Arawana sesame oil, soya sauce, rice, mung beans, more jujubes, wood-ear fungus, shiitake mushrooms, bean vermicelli, pickled mustard greens, fermented bean curd, mandarin oranges, tins of pineapples, peaches in syrup, tins of eight-treasure rice pudding, honey and a carton of Yuxi cigarettes. On top of all this, there was a Gold Shield-label Mao suit hanging from the shoulder pole, an outfit Hongyang had liked to wear at autumn and winter festivals.

Hongbin hurriedly fell to his knees on the sacking at the foot of the steps. There were more firecrackers, loud as machine-gun fire and lasting more than quarter of an hour. The new arrival made his way through a haze of blue cigarette smoke and helped Hongbin to his feet.

'Good of you to come,' said Hongbin.

'Uh.'

'Very courteous of you.'

'Uh, uh.'

The man hurried over to the corpse and embraced one of the legs, shaking it back and forth and letting out a low whimper. He sounded more like a wolf cub than a human being as the mucus from his nose dripped onto the corpse's shoes.

Hongbin and Hongliang were so affected that when they came over to help the stranger to his feet, they too burst into tears. What a good thing this fool had turned up to remind them that they were not simply dealing with a corpse but a flesh-and-blood man who was worth remembering, whom they had all grown up with, they thought. Those shared years had been glorious ones – and now Hongyang had left them!

The woman put down her shoulder pole, took out a posy of flowers and, imitating the way her parents had taught her so many times, stuck it in the lapel of the corpse's jacket. The black ribbon had four characters embroidered on it: 再生父母, *zai sheng fu mu*, which meant 'great benefactor'. When she tried to speak, her words were hard to understand. The men concluded that she wasn't quite right in the head. Other than this, however, she seemed entirely normal, and last year she'd even had a baby. Under the excellent care of this woman's mother, the infant had already learned to say 'Mama' and 'Papa', two words more than its own father and mother would ever be able to pronounce.

The man's name was Fuzhong, although no one knew his age or where he came from. He had been born disabled and never learned to speak. One day he had been found abandoned on the streets of Fan township, and had simply lived there ever since. Every time the urban hygiene unit cleared him off the street and put him on one of the pig trucks going out of town with instructions to drop him off a good distance away, he always doggedly made his way back again. He roamed around, finding shelter at first in cowsheds, haystacks and under bridges or carts. Later on, he made himself a more permanent home by building a rudimentary lean-to against the perimeter wall of a construction site using concrete slabs and plastic. He wore a padded jacket pullulating with lice, bedbugs and germs. The coat kept him warm in winter, but he continued to wrap it tightly round himself even in the height of summer, so that no one would steal it off him. He was encrusted with dirt from head to toe, as if he had come out of a mineshaft, with only his two eyes gleaming white beneath the grime. He spent his days sitting by the roadside that the farmers used on their way into town, his hand outstretched, begging for food. There was no shortage of people who took pity on him, especially in the village, where the inhabitants were charitable folk who kept him supplied with titbits and leftovers.

Nothing lasts forever, though, and eventually there was a common consensus that while everyone had done their best, if they continued to help him they would merely prolong his suffering. Death was perhaps the most humane way out for him. Even then, however, he managed to survive on scraps that he scavenged from slop pails, until the day came when Hongyang arrived to lord it over the township.

That day, Hongyang saw him and rifled through his wallet. Finding no small change in it, he casually threw down a hundred-yuan note. And so a pattern was set: Hongyang kept giving Fuzhong one hundred yuan, sometimes turning back to throw the note down even after he had already passed the beggar.

Fuzhong had no idea what to do with the money. He was often seen stupidly thumbing through the wad he had accumulated, like a child counting its pocket money, wondering what to do with it. In the past, when people had given him one-yuan notes, he would throw them away when he was bored of playing with them, or otherwise use them to wipe his bum. Now he was getting a hundred-yuan note a day – more than three thousand a month, more than a bank clerk earned. But people did not dare take the money off him, because Hongyang was a thoroughly disagreeable character and you didn't want to get on his bad side. He had given it to the beggar, and woe betide anyone who took it off him.

'Where's the money, Fuzhong?' The regularity with which busybodies asked him this question finally made Fuzhong realise that he had something of value. It was not that they were worried he might lose it, they just didn't want anyone else getting their hands on it before they had a chance to do so. It was a long and painful thought process, but once light had dawned it took him barely an afternoon to learn to guard the money with his life.

Fuzhong observed the magical process in which people did deals with each other: you handed over a bit of paper with a man's head on, and you got things back that you needed. He surmised that the significance of human life lay mainly in those bits of paper. An even greater miracle was that when Hongyang threw down the fifty-first banknote, Fuzhong vigorously shook his head, refusing to accept it. His hair and beard were matted and tangled and his jacket was as filthy as ever, the sleeves shiny and thickly coated with grease, worse than a rag used to wipe a restaurant cooker with. But despite all this, the mud streaks were gone from what you could see of his skin. He appeared to have been given a new lease of life, and from then on he often took a dip in the river's icy waters to wash himself. People imagined that the water downstream from Fuzhong's bathing spot turned black with dirt whenever he entered the water.

He gestured energetically at Hongyang, trying to make him understand what he wanted to say: I've come here to wait for you, to tell you my plans. His passionate devotion to Hongyang was clear; he was like a child finally reunited with a much-loved and respected teacher. He managed to convey, wordlessly: 'Someone's usefulness lies in the fact that they can sell their strength and skill and the products thereof. Now I know how to make money.' Hongyang patted him on the shoulder and handed him a cigarette by way of welcoming him to human society. And promptly forgot him.

Fuzhong filled the gap left by the cobbler and set up his own repair business, mending punctures and pumping up tyres as a sideline. Although he still stank and was as dirty as ever, he was working hard. His intellectual abilities improved, although even in a small community like Fan township he still lagged behind. But in certain key respects he demonstrated an intelligence and directness that exceeded any of his neighbours. Zhu the village teacher taught him the basics of business and wrote out for him the words that were the key to success in making money: technical competence, friendly service, giving his client a stool, bowing to his client in farewell. Zhu explained all this to Fuzhong in mime.

To everyone's surprise, Fuzhong's business did better even than Zhu's own. He might not have been able to speak, but he wasn't shy about using his voice. The streets rang with his cheerful cries. Customers, in particular female customers, sometimes came to buy from him just to see his beaming smile. When he took the payment they bestowed on him, his fingers trembled and there was a gleam of genuine gratitude in his eyes, which made you feel like you were doing him an enormous favour. He liked counting his money, which seemed to grow as if by magic every time he counted. He lived a frugal life, limiting himself to one meal a day, and aimed not to spend a cent on anything except in the direst necessity. When a bunch of swindlers swooped on the village with their silver dollars, Peruvian sols, lottery scratch cards, competitions on beer cans, fake seeds and contracts for miniature pigs, few escaped their scams unscathed. Except Fuzhong, the only one who got hold of them and insisted on mending their shoes.

There was a family in Dongshan village who had a fool of a daughter for whom they could not find a husband. After watching Fuzhong for several weeks, they commissioned a matchmaker. The couple were duly married, and Fuzhong now had a wife, on top of his successful business. The one thing his parents-in-law were unable to make him understand, even after dropping every kind of hint, was that they wanted his money. When eventually they managed to make this clear, he was unconcerned and handed it all over to them to look after.

The amount exceeded their wildest dreams. On his behalf, they bought the newlyweds a single-storey home and thought they might as well move in with them – after all, their only son was a deputy company commander in the army. After their grandchild was born, they finally left their misery behind them and embraced this new source of joy, proudly showing off the baby to the townsfolk.

They finally had something to look forward to in life. The infant was fair-skinned and had a broad forehead that shone with intelligence. He was adorable. Perhaps one day he might even be like his uncle. He could become president, a bureau chief or a professor: someone of importance in this world. Fuzhong also earned a bit of money for the township's Party Secretary, who wrote about him, attributing his wealth to the government's 'Sunny Skies for All' project. His picture appeared in the *Xunyang Evening News*, and its pages were plastered all over the township walls. Fuzhong might have been illiterate, but he wasn't going to miss out on the opportunity to show off his new-found fame to his customers.

Now Fuzhong's face was streaked with tears. As the Daoist priest approached through the darkness, Fuzhong's nostrils and jaws twitched in time to the banging of the priest's cymbals. He gazed at the corpse as if entranced, unable to believe that this was his benefactor who, just yesterday, had flown around as if on winged feet. When anyone came over to try and to raise him to standing, he clung to them with cries of 'Ah! Ah! Yesterday he was still alive, why was he so determined to leave us?! Why didn't you wait for me, my benefactor, why didn't you wait?' At least that was what they assumed he was trying to say. When the priest indicated that he was taking charge, Fuzhong was pushed back out of the way. He stood with his arms around his smiling wife, a sharp sob escaping him every now and then. She kissed him as an expression of benign goodwill.

So devoted, thought Xu Yousheng. Loyalty like that is rare nowadays.

The priest was clearly confident that he could deal with both the human and the spirit worlds, and that both needed his aid. Assuming the aloof demeanour of a public personage, he solemnly approached the coffin. Just now, he had agreed to dine at Hongsha's house. They – that is, Hongsha and his younger brothers, Hongqi and Hongran – were concerned not about the food – they barely touched the spread of delicacies laid out on the table – but about the music. With the passionate fervour of Aristotle and his pupils, they discussed rhythm, arias and pitch, concepts about which the villagers were both ignorant and indifferent.

Today, the brothers had received the opportunity to make a public appearance. Unlike their father, the musician Zhengxun, who would stand in the fields playing his instrument whenever he felt like it, they had always kept the instruments they'd inherited locked up. Although making music should not be done in private, the way you played with your money or valuables, they had inherited from their mother's side of the family a deep-seated reticence about showing their skills on any occasion except for a big celebration or memorial service, in the same way as they felt that jogging through the village streets in one's shorts was inappropriate. They said to the priest, 'If you had not come, sir, we wouldn't even have remembered we had these instruments at home. Now let us take on the onerous task of playing them for you.'

All this gave the priest goosebumps. It wasn't like they admired or respected him, they just wanted to embrace him as a kindred spirit, whether he liked it or not. The main thing was that they would have a chance to show their musicianship in public, and it was the priest who was going to offer them this opportunity.

The priest, however, could have asked any ignoramus to bang the cymbals or the drum to accompany him. After all, it required nothing more than the most basic training. He might even have dispensed with this supporting role altogether, and cogitated for a long time before slowly nodding.

You can imagine how the brothers' eyes sparked the way a piece of firewood catches alight. With a smile and more nodding the priest allowed them to ask him in what order they should play the music, how to keep in time, when to take breaks, how to bring the music to an end. To ensure that the entire performance would be perfectly harmonious, they asked him to settle on a secret signal. The priest did so. He knew that once this funeral was over, they would be waiting for the next time, for him to turn up again along with the ravens that foretold a death.

Right now, each of them was secretly desperate to be the one who got to play the suona, while making a show of modestly declining that honour. 'This is what I propose: the eldest brother this time, the second brother next time,' declared the priest, though he knew perfectly well that next time it would be the eldest too. The priest lifted the spirit tablet in his hands and placed it on the offerings table. It read:

*This tablet is dedicated by his grieving son Shide to the inestima-
ble Hongyang of Aiwan
Who came into this world the eighth day of the seventh month,
1968
And departed this life the ninth day of the seventh month, 2012*

He lit three sticks of incense, blew out the flame and, clutching the smoking sticks in his hand, began to mutter prayers, at
intervals bowing, hands respectfully clasped, towards the
corpse. More and more people clustered round and followed
suit, bowing to the corpse with their hands clasped in front of
them. The three brothers struck up with their instruments.
Then the priest invited the 'grieving sons', Shide and all the
cousins with the generation name Shi, to step forward and pay
their respects individually to the dead man, like you toasted
the guests one by one at a dinner. The priest privately thought
that not including the Hong cousins in this part of the ritual
would cut the ceremony a bit short. But as he moistened his
fingers in the water bowl and flicked the droplets into the air,
Hongbin came over and whispered 'That's enough now' into
his ear.

'Enough?'

'We're economising.' Hongbin turned to Shuizhi. 'Sister-in-
law, what do you think?'

'Whatever you say,' said Shuizhi.

'It's fine,' said the priest.

'We'll settle up with you, then.'

'As you wish,' said the priest. 'We'll close the coffin.'

Hongliang took Xu Yousheng into the dead man's bedroom
and, not wanting to be sent out on any more errands, quietly
pushed the door shut. The disconsolate priest gave the agreed
signal, swiping through the air with the fingers of one hand as if
trying to catch a mosquito, and the three brothers struck up

– bang-clackety-bang-clackety-bang-clackety-bang-clackety-bang-
clackety-bang-clackety-bang-clackety-bang-clackety-bang-clack-
ety-bang-clackety-bang-clackety – until finally they placed their
hands over the gong and stilled its roiling, quivering sounds.

'If I were the priest, I'd leave,' said Hongliang. 'Your Uncle
Hongbin is not very good at organising these occasions. He
reckons a Daoist priest is a service worker, that he snaps his
fingers and the man does what he says. I agree that the priest is
a service worker, but when he's trying to serve you as well as he
can, you don't start attacking him like that.'

As laid down by the ancestors, the Eight Immortals were to
be selected only from the eldest sons of the same generation of
the same clan, unlike other clans, who customarily brought in
their neighbours to perform the chore. The following were
settled on: Shiren, Shi'en, Shiguang (his place to be taken by
Shiyi), Shitang (his place to be taken by Shiliang), Shizhong,
Shishan, Shigang and Shican. They were led by Shide, who was
wearing the long mourning robe tied around the waist with a
rough hemp rope and carrying the mourning staff in his hand.
He knelt before each of the eight ritual gifts in turn, pronounc-
ing: 'Thank you for your trouble!'

The eight men tied towels around their arms and lined up,
and Hongbin inspected their ranks as if he were a senior officer,
straightening their collars and nodding gravely. They each stood
tall and straight and gazed resolutely back at him.

As Hongbin took his hand away, they silently moved into
action. The plan was to open the coffin and spread inside a layer
of ash mixed from lime and kitchen ash, filtered through a fine
bamboo sieve. Then they would lay a white cloth on top and
scatter ghost money over it, a ritual which, in this instance, was
rich in metaphorical meaning, before lifting the corpse into the
coffin and adding more ash, and also the dead man's most treas-
ured possessions. The burial quilt would be laid on top and then

the coffin would be sealed. However, since none of them had been assigned to specific tasks – 'This was just what your Uncle Hongbin was incapable of organising!' Hongliang exclaimed at this point, jumping up angrily – they all fell over each other's feet as they scrambled to lift the coffin lid, shovel in the ash, carry the offerings table into position and collect the offerings together.

'Here, here. No, here!' They exchanged anxious glances. One hand grabbed a candlestick that was in danger of toppling, while another hand held the coffin lid; one man had the spirit tablet tucked under his arm, the ghost money between his teeth and a bucket of ash in each hand; another hurriedly reached out one leg and attempted to kick one of the apples about to roll onto the floor back into position with the tip of his shoe, caus-ing the apples to roll down one by one and bump around the room, which was dim and murky because of all the ash floating in the air. A cockerel, its legs tied together with string, flew out of the kitchen, and one man tried to stun it with a smart martial arts move, the adamantine fist, but the cockerel flew right back in again. One man rubbed his eyes with ashy fingers and then grimaced, fell to the floor and rolled around in agony, though without uttering a sound.

'No one but these Aiwan boys could create such appalling chaos and confusion,' Hongliang muttered to his nephew.

'So chaotic yet so quiet,' agreed Xu Yousheng. 'I've never seen anything like it. They're sneaking around like thieves afraid they're going to get caught.'

'You're quite right. I'm tempted to go and tell them that no one's rushing them,' said Hongliang.

Finally, the Eight Immortals succeeded in doing what they had to do. Four of them placed the corpse on a white sheet on the ground, and the other four each lifted a corner of the sheet, as if they were hunters carrying a boar they had just killed. The corpse rested once more on its buttocks on the tautly stretched sheet, but it was so heavy that the four had to keep changing hands, and the tips of the corpse's shoes stuck up so much that they were in danger of brushing someone's nose. The head flopped to one side, and one arm flopped out of the sheet and ended up dangling, the fingertips dragging on the floor, until Hongbin rushed over to tuck it back in. They pulled this way and that, before Hongbin gestured to them to spread out a bit so that corpse lay slightly more extended.

When they got to the coffin, they grunted with exertion as they raised the corners of the sheet and heaved the corpse aloft, their hands trembling violently. 'Damn, the pillow's not here,' Hongbin said, and hurried into the bedroom. He pushed open the door, causing uncle and nephew to leap from their chairs. 'What are you two doing?' he asked disapprovingly. The pair turned red with embarrassment, but Hongbin hurriedly snatched up the pillow without waiting for an answer, rushed back to the coffin, and threw it inside.

Finally, the bearers slid Hongyang into the coffin on his quilt. Hongbin tied his legs together with cotton thread and began to place the funeral offerings in with him, gently at first, then more haphazardly, until eventually they were simply tossing them inside. Hongliang put in a plastic bag too, with the words: 'Brother Hongyang, the road ahead will be hard, but you absolutely must take this letter to my elder brother Hongxing, and ask him where he is.'

'Ah! Ah! My . . .' There were incoherent noises from the side room. Shuizhi came bursting into the room as if fleeing a flash flood descending from the mountains. 'Stop her!' commanded Hongbin. The Eight Immortals lined up in a human wall as Shuizhi slammed into them, but no matter how hard she punched she could not break through. Eventually she was forced to sit down on the ground, whereupon she grasped their legs and began to bite.

'Ah! Ah! That heartless . . . ah! Ah!' She stopped biting and started to slap the ground. Hongbin flung in two bags of ash and then covered the coffin, hammering the lid shut with a wooden mallet until he was sure the tenons were snug in the mortises. Then he waved people back.

Shuizhi crawled over to the coffin and banged on the lid. Muxiang got very slowly to her feet, steadying herself before making her way shakily over to the coffin. Her fragility and carefulness lent her gait a certain grace. She put her cheek to the coffin, its lid still wet with varnish, and crooned: 'Little brother, little brother, can you hear me?'

The other women rushed over to the grief-stricken pair. 'You'll do yourselves an injury carrying on like that,' they said, even as they all fought to say goodbye to their beloved in this way. The onlookers and the Eight Immortals, the latter of whom were washing their hands in baijiu spirit, stood gazing at the inscription on the gleaming dark wood of the coffin:

A man we knew
Better than anyone else
Left us in this house
It seems like he walked into the coffin himself
And waved goodbye with the words: I'm going now.

Gradually, a feeling of loneliness stole over the assembled mourners. It was partly because Hongyang had gone, or rather because he had abandoned them. They solemnly absorbed the fact that there was one fewer man in this world, that this had made the world a bigger, bleaker place.

The Daoist priest pinched the burial quilt between his fingers and smiled sarcastically. 'You want the great man to die of cold in the next world?' He banged his cymbals again to show that he was taking charge, and sang out: 'The grieving son has invited me to begin the event. Will it be a short or a long one? A short one will last two or three hours, a long one will go on until daybreak. If you ask me, I'll tell you the long one is the best.' He led Hongbin and Shide's branch of the family in walking around the coffin, making them kneel and rest their heads on the bottom of the man in front every few steps as he sang the gentle, long-drawn-out notes in a voice that was pitch-perfect, rounded and vigorous. He sang for nearly twenty minutes. There was no doubt he could have gone on all night.

When, midway through, there was a break, Hongbin and his relatives sat rubbing their knees. It was as if they had been kneeling on stones, and they grimaced in pain with the slightest move. They looked dull and exhausted, as imbecilic as labourers after a day's work, mute and unwilling even to lift a finger. The endless repetitions of 'Stand up–kneel down–stand up–kneel down' had stupefied them, and their only wish was to get it over with, drink a cup of tea and have a good sleep.

'One of you should nail down the lid,' said Hongbin. But no one moved. The silence of each person seemed intended to warn the others: Don't look at me. I'm too tired to move. The mute Fuzhong seemed to be supervising, and everyone looked at him. Finally, when it was clear that no one wanted to perform this task, Fuzhong went over and looked up at Hongbin, saying, 'Ah, ah.'

Hongbin looked at him and picked out some nails. He put his hands on the claw hammer Shiming had rejected as unsuitable, then found one a little bit bigger. 'Normally you should drill a hole before banging in the nail, but there are lots of things we don't have time for now, and luckily the coffin wood is thin, though by rights we should have given Hongyang a pricier coffin,' he muttered hoarsely.

Before he began work, Fuzhong closed his eyes and lightly stroked the wood of the coffin, the way a musician strokes the cloth cover of her guqin. No one piece of wood is ever exactly the same as another, just as no two trees are ever exactly identical. Fuzhong began feeling for a hole into which he could drive the nail. He knew the unusually long one he held between finger and thumb wouldn't stand much hard hammering. Every now and then, he crooked his middle finger and tapped on the coffin lid. Then he would listen carefully. He would detect either a rising tone of fright, or perhaps mockery, or a falling tone, almost as if a raconteur were telling a story or answering a question. The latter was disquieting, reminding him of the sensation of meeting someone who is always smiling and apparently laid-back but also extremely strong-willed.

Fuzhong pressed a particular spot with his fingertip, held the nail to it, and considered for a long moment before wielding the hammer. In the dim lamplight, half the room was in shadow, and his movements had a certain epic solemnity to them. He tilted his head to the right, which meant he was unable to see what his left hand was doing. But he had a good feeling about this. He hammered lightly on the head of the nail, stopping if he found that it didn't feel right, and tapping out another spot on the coffin lid, like a billiards player prodding the ball with his cue. Finally, he sensed that he had found the right spot and prepared to increase the force of his blows little by little. He stroked the nail and gauged its direction to make sure it entered perfectly straight, then continued tapping. When it was in halfway and still standing proud, he moved around so he could inspect it, and then went back to give three more blows – bang, bang, bang. In an instant, he had tapped it home so that only the nail head was visible on the surface. Still not satisfied with his handiwork, he retrieved a screwdriver, placed it on the nail head, and banged it with the hammer until the nail was countersunk. Although the coffin and its lid had already been a close fit, the nails ensured that they fitted even more tightly. He could never repay Hongyang's generosity to him in full, but he did his best, nailing down the six hinges on his own initiative too.

When he was positive that not so much as a needle, not a splash of water, not an earthworm or an ant, or even any sound, could get in anywhere, he finally stopped and let out a long cry. The Daoist priest applied flour paste to the hinges, performed one circumambulation, and impressed his seal on the coffin.

8

Fuzhong threw the hammer into the store cupboard and banged the door shut. The frightful noises, like the sluggish trickling of a stream, rang in Hongliang's and Xu Yousheng's ears even though they had left the room some time before. In the side room, Hongbin and his family were still falling to their knees every couple of minutes like wind-up toys as the Daoist priest recited his prayers. They alternated between kneeling upright, resting with their palms spread on the floor, and huddling on all fours with their bottoms stuck up in the air, dull-eyed like castrated animals, as if uttering one last sentence – 'I'm doing my duty for the dead man' – before turning once more into dumb, unresisting beasts. From time to time, they clapped their palms together like cymbals. Their circumambulations of the coffin continued until daybreak, their sporadic clapping helping to kill the mosquitoes that emerged at nightfall. But those in charge of errand boys never get tired; the Daoist priest led the little procession, hopping on one leg and lifting the other, then changing around, muttering his prayers, until at daybreak his chants rose in pitch like a kettle of water coming to the boil. Hongsha and his two brothers accompanied him in their wrinkled suits, sweat raining down their foreheads even as their fervour remained undimmed.

Hongliang lay on the rickety camp bed with a copy of Ovid's *Art of Love* open at his side. In the city, the bed would normally have been used only to accommodate impecunious students, the sick or the widowed. But for now the iron mesh bed still counted as furniture befitting a town house. He had stopped rubbing the creased corner of the pink envelope, and it lay inside the book. He dozed. The book and letter smelled as if they had just been delivered in the mail. Xu Yousheng imagined the writer of the letter smoking it over sandalwood, as if she were casting a spell. The same smell lingered in the ink, too. She must have a refined lifestyle, and he imagined that in her fairy-tale cottage, a butterfly fluttered around, attracted by the smell of new wood that clung to her body.

In the first letter, she had written:

I haven't told Mother about our affair, because I honestly don't know how to broach it with her. I want her to accept it as completely as possible. I've been desperate to find the right moment and the right way, but at the last moment I've always backed out. I need to summon my courage. Please give me a bit more time.

In the second letter, she continued:

If you don't have it yet, you can't say you've lost it.

There was a noise from the bed, and Hongliang spoke: 'I can't sleep, what about you?' He could recite the contents of the letters word for word.

'Me neither,' said Xu Yousheng, and clicked his phone on. He gave it a bit of time to start up, the way someone going to buy cigarettes allowed the old geezer behind the till a little time to awaken from his snooze and hobble over to the counter to serve him. But there was nothing. Why did he always think that if he turned off his phone and turned it back on again, there might be a message from her? Maybe he'd got the number wrong? Then he reminded himself that last time he'd definitely keyed in the number she'd given him and she hadn't hung up until she'd heard the ringtone. Bitch, bitch, motherfucking bitch, he thought.

Xu Yousheng looked up at his uncle, who was starting a new story about Hongyang.

Before the new chief walked into the local police station, he scuffed his cigarette butts underfoot till they turned to dust. He was wearing the sort of high-top leather shoes once beloved of street gangs. The shoes initially looked comical on a man of his age, but after a little while we grew used to them.

A few days later, his suitcases arrived in a military jeep, along with stories about his background. He was from Liuzhuang village and had served seven or eight years in the army, though no one knew exactly where. His parents would tell no one where he was stationed, until one day he was spotted by someone at a public execution and they realised he had been working in a nearby city all along. He had been waving the flag and ordering the execution squad to put on their masks – though his own mask was stuffed into his trouser pocket – and fire at the kneeling prisoner from behind, after which a white-coated doctor went to certify the death. When they turned the prisoner over, he was still twitching, so the police officer gave him a ferocious kick in the crotch with the stiff, reinforced toe of one of his high-top shoes. The man went rigid and died, lying there like a bag of cement.

There were more stories about his prowess at shooting those prisoners who tried to escape. As soon as the pursuit squad were armed, the dangers of running away multiplied: after all, shooting dead the runaways was sanctioned. Even when he had retired from those duties and completed several stints in local police stations, controversy still surrounded him. Some said he had received his award because the higher-ups wanted to conceal the fact that he shot runaways in cold blood and had fabricated stories about escapees on the rampage resisting arrest and endangering the security of locals, especially of schoolchildren.

Once he joined the police, he always asked to be seconded to remote mountain areas and border regions, because he hated being cooped up in an office. In Hongyi, it was alleged that when a cattle thief heard who was coming after him, he fell to his knees, hands clasped behind his head like something out of a TV crime series, and polished one of the stones beside him to help the marksman aim accurately, so certain was he that his capture was imminent.

This policeman arrived in the township soon after the Spring Festival. Not that there was much of spring in the air; winter appeared to have concentrated all its deadly firepower on the world. The sky was leaden grey and the earth was covered in frost, plunging humans into despair and making birds reluctant to take wing, so that they sat for hours at a stretch on branches or power cables, like dozens of dark blobs of cow dung.

After some days of closed meetings from which young Di and other community cops were mostly excluded in view of several recent complaints against them, the new boss threw open the local police station gate, took out his pistol and started taking potshots at the trees. Bullets flew left and right amid wisps of blue-grey smoke, but it took a while before those damned birds flapped their wings and attempted to take off into the sky before plummeting to earth instead. It was a very long time since the people of Fan township had seen anyone firing a gun. It sounded like popcorn exploding.

Just then, Hongyang roared into town in the passenger seat of a Longma pickup, ostentatious as always, as if he was on a tour of inspection. The ecology of the township was changing; there was less thieving, cheating, brawling, boozing and extortion. The traders under Hongyang's protection took care to conceal their illegal firecrackers, contraband tobacco and raw pork. Hongyang walked into the store run by his son-in-law Yushui and sat down to a game of chess with Hongbin, his 'chief lieutenant'. The latter had long made it his mission to sit there, ready to personally take on any officials who came to make trouble for local shopkeepers. With a touch of arrogance, he encouraged them to recite the rehearsed answers they'd give if they were questioned: 'I know this isn't the right way to do things, but I'm doing it on Hongyang's say-so. Why don't you go and talk to him? He's playing chess over there.'

Hongyang tried to see them right; he had taken their money, after all. He allowed a lot of businesses that couldn't get official approval to function under his watch. If he said it was OK, then it was. He could invalidate official permits. And right now he still believed he was protecting these shopkeepers. Every day at dusk, he got in his pickup and went back to Aiwan, to return the next morning with the punctuality of a peasant to see to his affairs.

The local police station tried to stop his operations. They stuck a floor-to-ceiling notice on their bulletin board, just one at first, and then more appeared, spreading like wildfire around the township to warn the locals: *We're cracking down; We're hitting hard and fast; Better turn yourselves in.* The voice of the female announcer echoing from the force's propaganda vans with the same message was clearer, more resonant, more pitiless than any man's, enough to give you butterflies in your stomach.

Some people handed themselves in and confessed to trivial misdemeanours, while others packed their bags and took themselves as far away as possible, comforting themselves that they were passing the police station under cover of darkness. Peace reigned once more. Even Hongbin had to face the likelihood that the police were going to pull down Hongyang's flag, though Hongyang himself ignored what was going on and continued to turn up every morning, his face deadpan as always, before he departed at the end of the day without a trace of anxiety. He simply asked Hongbin: 'How do you expect me to run away?' Hongyang considered making himself scarce for a while, but that would have been truly humiliating. No way did he want to become an object of pity and mockery again. The numbers of followers who rode into town behind his pickup gradually dropped off, though, until he told them to stay home, that he'd go on his own. And there was no longer much 'business' for him to do when he got there. He would have done anything to keep his dignity, but he did not know when the authorities would make their move, or how. It was all getting him down, and he was even reduced to passing the time of day with people he had once spurned, people who, arms crossed over their chests, spent all day propped against the railings at their doors, unmistakably mournful expressions in their eyes. You could almost hear their nervous thoughts: You can't have two tigers on one mountain, or: This is going to be a hell of a fight. Yet there was also the whispered hope that good would triumph over evil.

The day it happened, the sky was gloomy and overcast, and it felt more like evening as Hongyang drove into the township. As he followed the road that wound its way for three and a half li around Tieling Ridge, skid marks from cars braking were evident on the slippery surface. Even on the flat, he found himself zigzagging.

That morning, he was completely focused on handling the pickup. It wasn't the first time he had driven himself, but he didn't have much experience at the wheel.

'And the Santana and the Buick he drove after that ended up as write-offs too,' added Xu Yousheng.

He ought to have stuck to the Longma pickup – better a hoe-toting peasant in the State Council than a man in a fancy suit. But Hongyang had a stubborn streak to him, a rough-hewn quality that still shone through on occasion, even as it was gradually eroded by wealth and success until eventually he lost that lovable naivety and there was no distinction between him and a

Party Secretary, or a mega-rich businessman. Thanks to him, cheap cigarettes had enjoyed a revival, with all the lads in the township smoking Daqianmens. After this, he switched to the pricier, soft-packet Zhonghuas instead, because he thought they made him look good.

Anyway, getting back to what I was saying, that day, right up until the moment six firearms appeared in front of him, forcing the pickup to stop, Hongyang was still fiddling with the controls, trying to work out how to switch the headlights between full beam and dipped. At the roadblock, he applied the handbrake with the aplomb of a chauffeur and asked: 'What have I done wrong?'

'You come to the police station, then you'll find out,' they said.

Hongyang had rehearsed this scenario numerous times, but he was still flustered when it happened. He swallowed and his voice changed pitch as he pretended a calm he did not feel. Then he casually held out both wrists, just like in a film. The police, however, had no intention of cuffing him. They made him walk ahead of them. He drew himself up, looked skyward and obeyed, waving his arms, telling them: 'I can walk perfectly well by myself.'

Actually, the police had no intention of urging him on, nor of holding him by the arms, but Hongyang wanted the people lurking at their front gates or behind their windows to understand that he hadn't given up yet. Onlookers like these were always greedy for a glimpse of someone whose life, reputation or dignity had taken a fatal hit. They lived for stories of some poor sod being killed, crippled in an accident or caught lying, being diagnosed with an illness, raped, turned in or arrested. He knew they would creep forward, drinking in every detail. What a way to end up! they might sigh, or they might give a little sob. Pure *Schadenfreude*. Their scrutiny stung Hongyang, causing him real pain. Several times he was almost at screaming point.

It occurred to me one day, Yousheng, that when martyrs go to their execution shouting slogans, it's not like you read about in books. They're not shouting because they're calmly convinced of the righteousness of their cause, but rather to salvage their pride before they're shot. There's nothing more shaming than being dragged to one's execution under the public gaze like a beast to the slaughter. Executioners deprive their victims of the image they've built up so painstakingly throughout their life, because the way you manage your whole life is part of your image, isn't it? They display their victim like an animal, covered in its own piss and shit. And so people turn passionate and vehement, in a futile attempt to persuade us that depriving them of dignity means nothing. Hongyang asked his captors one by one: 'What's your name?' and when they smiled and did not answer, he added: 'Wait a moment!' In the past, he had used to be able to quell people for days with just a look. Now, though, as he rolled up his sleeves ready for combat, all he got in response were knowing smiles that settled silently on the street like snowflakes. They slung their rifles over their shoulders and, as Hongyang made a show of strutting fearlessly, unconcernedly, up the steps of the police station, Zhao Zhongnan propelled him inside with a kick up the arse.

They dealt with this whole business behind closed doors, I believe, to add an air of seriousness to their work. They never drove away the people who turned up to peer inside, and when finally it was jam-packed outside the entrance, Zhao Zhongnan finally pushed open the door a crack and asked the crowd: 'What are you looking at? There's nothing to see here.' But he didn't stop them looking past him either, and that meant that the police were happy for people to get a look-see.

The next day they hung a placard around Hongyang's neck and escorted him into the middle school as part of their law education lesson, telling the pupils, 'Children, if you want a classic, living example of what not to do, this is it.' Obviously they wanted those kids to go home at the weekend and tell their parents all about it, so the news would get spread throughout the township and surrounding villages.

And if it were not for the fact that they were not yet confident that the judgment against Hongyang and his evil deeds – the cruelty of his methods, his vile actions, the serious consequences for his victims, the extreme wickedness and great danger he posed to people – would go their way, they would surely have put in a request to the Politics and Law Committee to have the verdict delivered publicly. It was at their instigation that a band of volunteers assembled to beat drums and gongs, to line the street and let off firecrackers, and to carry an embroidered banner aloft to the police station. It was as noisy as a public holiday in the township with people lining the streets to watch Hongyang being bundled into the prison van and taken away for a stint of Reform through Education. This showed the gulf between the mighty and the fallen, was how people saw it. Hongyang was being crushed under the heel of the new police station chief, like one of his fag ends.

The chief then took the phone from a subordinate who had dialled the number for him. He spoke with the confidence and patience of one who expects the whole world to do his bidding. Few in the township had met someone so nearly approaching his godlike status, his every gesture embodying the magisterial manner and boldness of a frontier general of ancient times.

He spoke into the phone: 'Zhang Gongti?' Then: 'I've got a name, you know. Yuan Qihai. That's the surname Yuan, as in General Yuan Shikai. And my personal names are Qi, meaning inspiration, and Hai, meaning ocean. Chief of Fan Township

Police. Deputy Section grade. I'm formally reporting today as someone senior to you in years, and asking you to stop interfering in the work of the local police station. Today we arrested a man called Ai Hongyang, and tomorrow we may arrest some other kinsman of yours. Let me be clear: if you interfere again, then I'll raise with your superiors the matter of whether Communist Party cadres should turn a blind eye to the outrages committed by family members or not. Mark my words. Leave it alone.' And with that, he put down the phone.

I've heard it said that at that moment, those present felt as if a torrent of water was rushing through them, making them literally stagger, and almost burst out crying. Some led a round of applause which thundered around the entire township, while others wiped away tears of emotion. When it was all over, they reflected that Hongyang really was not irredeemably criminal, and that Zhang Gongti was a source of pride to his fellow villagers. But at the time they were carried away by this joyous celebration of moral righteousness.

I always felt that while Yuan Qihai gave the impression of being impulsive by nature, he was actually extremely shrewd and knew exactly how to use a political label to his advantage. Hongyang's class definition was now a 'princeling' – son of rich parents – although his kinship with the wealthy Zhang Gongti was tenuous; Zhang Gongti was the son of the sister of the husband of the niece of his uncle's great-grandfather.

In fact, Hongyang was a peasant living off the land, but the iniquitous label 'princeling' stuck and lost him all popular support – the masses always want to see justice done, isn't that right? Hongyang got an all-day beating at the police station, and even though there was insufficient evidence, he was sentenced to a year of Reform through Education, on the grounds that he had 'sabotaged production and the social order'.

The day of the beating, the only remedy Hongyang had was to fight to protect his knees from damage, the way a family whose home has been razed to the ground by officialdom fights to save the tablet mounted over the front door. He had nothing else to defend. When he realised that his knees were his strength and he could use them to really annoy the authorities, he made even more of an effort to protect them. You remember the old spirit-breaking beatings on the legs and buttocks, Yousheng? A new arrival was always given thirty strokes of extra punishment by the prison guards, not to cripple him but to make sure he reflected properly as he moaned and cried on the ruthless might of those in charge. Nowadays, it's changed – instead of standing up for a beating, they're made to kneel. They mostly haven't been in an interrogation room, so they don't know what to expect. They look around at how the room's set up, its walls painted green to waist-level, the newspaper rack coated in dust, red desks with documents on them, the same as any other office. They rub their hands together and look enquiringly at the officer, like a cook or a worker who's been hanging around anxiously awaiting instructions. At that point, they still think they're human, and they wait respectfully – they might even get a cup of tea – until suddenly they hear a fierce voice: 'Kneel!' The relationship between the officer and prisoner is instantly changed into that of dictator and subject. The prisoner is left for a little while, and then the officers come back in and check up on them. 'Kneel properly! Straighten your back!' That's how they begin the interrogation, and only once you're properly doing what they have asked do they start in with the questions: surname, given name, age, sex, nationality, birthplace, residence, family members, previous convictions.

They dragged Hongyang into the interrogation room, and the empty corridors echoed with running footsteps as everyone scrambled into the back courtyard for a glimpse, milling around the steamed-up window. They could see nothing inside but blurred shadows; even the sounds were muffled. Still, they managed to conjure up every detail of the punishment in their minds. Speculating and imagining what was happening made it all the more terrifying.

'Kneel down!' came the order. When pressing him down by the shoulders and kicking him in the back of the knees had no effect, someone hurried off to get a weapon.

'Now let's see you try to stay standing!' A long nail-studded cudgel described a wide arc and slammed into Hongyang's knees. Hongyang's shadow abruptly elongated, then he appeared to bounce upright again.

'Will you kneel!' One of the officers began to box his ears, not on one side then the other in quick succession, but slapping one side of the face, again and again and again, as if his face was a tinder they were trying to raise a spark from. Those outside imagined his nose beginning to bleed and the blood dripping onto the floor, the splash spreading, vivid as flower petals. They imagined Hongyang glaring at his opponents with eyes full of hatred as they grabbed a hank of his hair and slammed his head against the wall. If they go on, he'll be beaten senseless, he'll suffer a horrific death, those outside thought.

Fuzhong paced back and forth in mute anxiety, a pack of cigarettes clutched in his hand. When the back gate opened and the boy in charge of the cook-fire came out with a pail, Fuzhong smiled ingratiatingly and offered him one, but the lad ignored him and strolled over to the well. Fuzhong ran away, and the boy went back inside with the water.

It was getting towards dinner time, and this whole business would soon be over. People began to disperse, but stopped instantly when cries of alarm rang out of the window, causing those standing nearest to leap backwards. A large patch of white fog appeared on the glass and then, before it had time to clear, another patch materialised and the windows shook. Inside, Hongyang was shaking the rusty iron window bars, gasping desperately. Behind him, Yuan Qihai threw cold water at his naked back, then resumed lashing him with a maroon leather belt.

'I'm not insisting that you kneel, you can lie on your belly today,' said Yuan Qihai. Soon enough, Hongyang slithered to the floor like a loach.

Did this count as surrendering? Maybe, maybe not. But he ended up cooperating. Whatever they said, he responded: 'If that's what you say, then so it is.' It wasn't that he didn't care about their questions, it was simply that he was tired. He had taken a chill and coughed so much that they sent the boy to make him some ginger tea.

As soon as you give in, they turn as warm and friendly as a spring day. No doubt they felt a huge sense of pride in their achievement and hitched up their trouser belts as they snorted to themselves, like a herdsman who's succeeded in breaking in the most untameable of wild horses. Hey, Yousheng, these kinds of harsh tests – to kneel or not, to give in or not – are something all fine fellows have had to undergo down the ages. If you kneel down, you realise how nice and warm the earth is. If you surrender, or accept an amnesty, you realise your mortal enemy is like a father to you. But once your aloofness and pride have flown away, that's you gelded, right?

Hongyang was dragged towards the police jeep, the toes of his shoes bouncing over the ground like a hoe. They opened the jeep door and made him stand for a bit. He looked a little lost, as if he was leaving on a long journey. The police chief got inside with him, exhorted him repeatedly to behave himself, then got out again. The prison van hooted madly and careered along the road out of the township like a circus pickup. It took a good few days for the locals to get used to the fact that Hongyang was no longer around. Yet when he returned a year later, they had almost forgotten him.

Midway through his sentence, we went to visit him in the Niujiaolong Reform through Education camp, and he spoke like a businessman who's seen the light: 'There are some things you can't change, you just have to adapt to them.' His head was shaven and he had lost a little weight, though he looked stronger, pared down, you might say. He seemed relaxed and well rested.

He pointed to a photograph pinned to the police's public noticeboard. It showed a bald man who had lost his eyebrows, as if he'd had chemo. His face was bloated, the skin translucent, the eyes small and dull. The corners of his lips, by contrast, were upturned scornfully, as if he might bare his teeth at any moment. 'It took me a long time to learn how to deal with this man,' Hongyang told us.

I'm telling you, Yousheng, this deputy camp commander – his name was Hu Yan – used to roast a handful of peanuts over his coal briquette stove and warm himself some wine as he dreamed up new ways of using all the many powers he'd accumulated in his years in the job to while away the time as he entered a lonely old age. He dressed like an old-style police officer, his collar always done up to the neck with hooks and eyes, belt fastened, hat tightly tied under the chin. That was unusual by then; most of his colleagues only wore their hats when they went to see the head of the provincial department. He took himself very seriously, and yet he also wore a bright yellow toy trumpet pinned to his chest. He'd bought one for his grandson, thinking to himself that it reminded him of his army days. It was like an old-fashioned military bugle. The thing filled him with divine inspiration; he was sure he could imbue it with magic powers.

And he did. From then on, the comically hoarse toots it emitted, rather like the quacking of a goose waddling to the pond edge, became a source of helpless terror and indignation for the detainees. When they least expected it, it would make them flinch in pain. They tried to prepare themselves for it, sometimes keeping watch for a whole morning outside their dormitory as he paced back and forth outside the fence with the toy trumpet raised. He'd look back at them, baring his few remaining yellowed teeth in a smile, sometimes even waving a greeting. Then he would give them a blast just when they reckoned that it was impossible, when the car came to fetch him for a city break, for example, and he had already got in and banged the door shut as the car sped out of the gate.

It was like treading on hot coals. They would leap into the air and rush to the drill ground without stopping to tie their shoelaces, or to wipe the toothpaste from their mouths or the smell of spunk – not unlike disinfectant – from their palms. They were terrified of arriving after the sound had ceased, because that meant having to stand outside the canteen and not getting any food for a day. Often, it was only because of these people's ill luck that the rest of them appreciated that they were getting along fine. 'Very good,' Hu Yan would say, looking at the lines of men approvingly. 'Very good, very good.' Memories of his army days, when he had been battalion commander, almost moved him to tears.

He had had five hundred men under him, and grunted happily as he counted them, squad by squad: 'One Squad, very good. Two Squad, very good.'

Then suddenly he turned fierce and shouted: 'Ten-shun!'

They shuddered to a halt, as if electrocuted.

'Stand at ease!'

They stood at ease.

'Ten-shun!'

They stood to attention again.

'Number off!'

They flung their heads back and jerked their number to the right, one after another.

Then it was: 'Mark time, one two one, one two one . . . Ten-shun!' 'Right turn, at the double . . . Ten-shun!' 'Left turn, first row, march! . . . Ten-shun! Second row . . . Ten-shun! Third row . . . Ten-shun! Fourth row . . . Ten-shun!' 'About turn, forward, three steps right . . . Ten-shun!' And so on and so forth. They would spend a whole day trudging from one corner of the drill ground to the other, or wheeling round and round an axis point like a compass, or marching back and forth in rectangular formation. It reminded me of something that Ryūnosuke Akutagawa, the Japanese writer, said: There's no worse punishment than pointless, repetitive exercise. He, of course, was talking about putting two iron balls weighing about twenty pounds on two platforms about eight feet apart and forcing prisoners to carry them back and forth.

One day they were drilling in the rain, and the rain drummed down on the brown plastic roof of the viewing platform, like applause as the curtain comes down. They were soaked right through to their goose-pimpled skin. The rain made them hate Hu Yan more than ever. They watched as, clad in raincoat and rubber boots, he trampled through the mud and his boots solemnly splashed their trouser legs. Sometimes they exchanged looks that meant: Everyone together now! But they could not bring themselves to do it, just waited there. It was as if a loved one had them tightly round the waist or was gripping their arm to stop them being foolish, reminding them to let someone else take the flak: there are so many others. That was human selfishness. People like that did not deserve salvation. Finally, encouraged – or incited – by the rest of them, Hongyang protested. Although his voice was scarcely louder than the rain, they heard it, and by tacit agreement they stood motionless.

'Don't move,' was what Hongyang said.

'Quick march,' ordered the old commander, wondering if he had not spoken clearly enough.

'Don't move,' Hongyang repeated.

They held their heads high, letting the rain wash down their expressionless faces. The commander was becoming impatient and made his way towards them.

'Right turn, stand at ease, stand to attention,' he ordered someone.

The recipient of the orders made a half-hearted effort. Stood at ease when ordered to stand to attention and stood to attention when ordered to stand at ease, that kind of thing.

'Don't listen to the old git,' Hongyang ordered the man, whereupon the latter ceased to follow Hu Yan's commands.

The old man trembled with rage. He was apoplectic! His hands shook uncontrollably, as if he was wretchedly hungry, and he could not get a word out. This was the biggest shock of his life, and his panic was obvious. But he got a grip on himself soon enough. Uttering vile curses about their mothers' cunts being black, stinking and unwashed, he lowered his head like a wild horned beast about to charge and plunged into their ranks, abandoning his usual controlled demeanour to make it even more obvious how much contempt he had for them. Jabbing one man in the armpit with a teacher's pointer – yes, really, he had a light green pointer – he said sarcastically: 'What did you just say?'

'It wasn't me,' said the man, only to receive a savage blow in response. This happened a few more times, until Hongyang said: 'It was me.'

'Very good,' said the old man, ambling over and tapping Hongyang on the forehead with the pointer. Then he dismissed everyone, except for Hongyang. The men dispersed, looking sympathetic as only bystanders can.

The old man crouched as he waited for them all to be gone, smoking a cigarette. The calm before the storm. Bound by the camp rules, the men had to go back to their dormitory. Only one, a man from Qichun county nicknamed Squint, came over, gave Hongyang a hug and whispered something in his ear.

'What?' asked Hongyang, who by now was feeling desperately betrayed, afraid and furious.

'I said: submit, mate,' Squint repeated with emphasis before the old guy could come over and lash him on the back. As he went, he kept turning and nodding repeatedly at Hongyang as if to remind him of the importance of his words. To Hongyang it sounded like *Schadenfreude*. He shut his eyes in distress. The battle was about to begin, and he clenched his fists and braced himself.

But the flogging did not begin immediately; the old guy went back to the viewing platform some distance off, opened his folding stool and sat down. He delivered the orders lazily: 'Quick march, stand to attention, at ease.' Hongyang stood in a puddle, his cloth shoes sodden with rain, the cracks between his toes filled with mud that would give him a nice case of toenail fungus. The rain slanted down and his clothes stuck to his body as if they were dissolving.

'Only you could do this,' said the old commander, and Hongyang trembled all over with rage. One chopstick's easily broken, whereas ten chopsticks are as hard as iron. He had known things were going to turn out like this, and was furious with himself for joining a group that had then flooded heartlessly past him, leaving him standing there like a stone pillar as soon as the old man gave the order. They were finished with him, had left him entirely alone. Now he had plenty of time to contemplate the harsh punishment that he alone was facing and that they had foreseen when they were preparing to resist. They were all sneering at him now, the same way the old guy was, as if to say the following: We could have told you so, mate, you didn't need to do it.

When the bell rang to announce the end of that day's shift, the policemen all flocked over to watch. Once they were assembled, the old guy got up and, with the enthusiasm of an orchestra conductor, put Hongyang through a series of difficult manoeuvres. One of the officers carried a bundle of keys, the longest of which was to the confinement cell. He made a point of walking over and looking Hongyang over with apparently genuine concern, playing the good cop, amiable, reasonable. But his keys told a different story: a dark reminder that he could just as easily lock you up. The windowless solitary cell was like a blind shaft, its walls scored with bloody marks. Terrible cries could sometimes be heard from within, a chilling call to the detainees to keep themselves in check. The shrieks and moans suggested to them that the prisoner was being chased in small circles by wolves or ghosts, his ribs being scratched by filthy, sharp claws.

Stories were passed down from one generation of prisoners to the next of people who had died a miserable death in the confinement cell. Stories were told of men who had fainted simply when they heard the key being put into the lock, of others who wept wordlessly when they were released because the open spaces outside were too wide and the light was too bright.

'Do what you're told,' said the jailer, keys in hand, coming over to peer meaningfully into Hongyang's eyes, and with him came a moustachioed colleague, who had two nicknames. The first was 'Ball-breaker', because he used to like grabbing and messing with the men's balls, the way old guys rotate shiny metal balls this way and that between their fingers to build up their strength. His other nickname was 'Ironhand'.

The old guy sitting on the viewing platform had only one task, and that was to issue Hongyang with his marching orders.

'There's no such thing as a bad order, only an order badly executed' was an oft-repeated catchphrase of his.

'Stand to attention,' he commanded. 'About turn, march, and back again!' Back and forth, for nearly an hour. Hongyang heartily wished that the old guy would come down from his perch and give him a quick beating, a furious beating, because at least then there would be a clear end in sight, not like this, where he was a leaky boat adrift on a boundless ocean. You couldn't tell when the old guy would take it into his head to call things to a halt.

The thought might have been in his head from the start, or might not even have occurred to him. He had no rules, no effective experience, to go on. At one point, the old guy got to his feet, walked to the concrete edge of the platform and raised his right hand. Hongyang watched with impatience, even gratitude. But the right hand was gradually withdrawn and Hu Yan went back to his stool. He was like a farm wife holding up a bunch of millet stalks for the hens clustered around her to see, then walking away without scattering them. The hens, kept alive only by their own willpower, would suddenly be plunged into starvation.

'Hey, hey, hey, carry on,' ordered the old man, lighting himself a cigarette.

'Sadist,' commented Xu Yousheng.

That's right: more than a pervert. Time after time, a little kernel of hope sprouted in Hongyang. He might start counting in the hope that by the time he got to five hundred it would all be over. But when he got to five hundred, he discovered that nothing had finished; everything was a dream, everything was wishful thinking. Hu Yan and the punishment that came from him could not be altered through Hongyang's willpower; in fact, he had no power at all to curtail it. Hope could only bring with it even greater pain. Without hope, though, there was no way he could lift his legs, which felt now like sodden sandbags.

When the off-duty officers turned up, bringing the old guy his dinner and a fresh bottle of wine, Hongyang felt the knife being twisted in the wound. Up until now, Hongyang had been watching the wine in the bottle gradually going down, and waiting for the old guy to throw it away in case a drop or two remained.

Now, though, the horizon grew darker. The sky had been growing gloomier all day, with gigantic clouds looming seemingly close enough to touch. You could hardly tell if it was night or day, but when night finally fell it seemed to everyone as if a tiny chink of light remained. In that twilight time between day and night, Hongyang's will finally broke and he almost threw himself on Hu Yan and throttled him. That's what he said, Yousheng, he said he'd gone crazy. Hu Yan was still on the viewing platform, tinkering now with the electrical circuit box. After a while, he clicked on the lights.

'Fuck . . . fuck,' sobbed Hongyang, and when the officers had all gone, he spat: 'Fuck your mother.'

'Who are you swearing at?' Hu Yan got to his feet.

'At myself.'

'Then do it again.'

'Fuck your mother.'

'Whose mother?'

'My mother.'

'Then say it properly.'

'Fuck my mother.'

'Go on.'

'Fuck Ai Hongyang's mother.'

'No, no, I meant march on.'

Yousheng, if Hongyang had been on death row, the old guy wouldn't have dared treat him like that. Even if Hongyang had attacked the man and shoved a sharp stake up his arse, he couldn't have touched him because Hongyang could only die once and he'd already been sentenced to death.

The old guy knew what went on in these detainees' minds. They were generally shut up in a Reform through Education camp for between one and three years – though only one, in Hongyang's case – and for the duration of their stint, he could and would abuse them at will. Sometimes he would come up to them, pretending to be all matey, and say: 'If you're not feeling any pain at all, then we should find some other way of reform-ing you.' He was like a hyena at the roadside, constantly attack-ing, harassing, provoking his prey, acting as if he was going to tear you limb from limb. Once you felt agitation, and loathing, and then anger, then he had achieved his aim. He wanted to see your fury destroy you, destroy your life, your ideals, your goals and all your plans, so that you were left with nothing. One way or another, we're always meeting people like this in our lives, Yousheng, and you have to learn to rub along with them.

Once Hongyang had fallen apart, he saw the raindrops bounding like a shoal of silver fish under the lamplight, and for some reason it made him think of Squint. Squint's suggestion had been so preposterous, so comical, it might have come from some travelling con man with the mantra 'Satisfaction guaran-teed'. But he had looked as if he genuinely meant it. Hongyang reran the scene in his mind a few times, and still felt that this complete stranger had been genuine. He decided to try it out. As Hu Yan carefully manoeuvred himself down the slippery wet steps of the viewing platform, no doubt formulating some new and sadistic task which he would impose on his prisoner, the now exhausted Hongyang summoned his last remaining drop of energy and lumbered towards him, head lowered, eyes filled with tears. His shoes squelched through the mud and his hair gleamed with rain.

'What are you up to?' Hu Yan asked, stopping. And Hongyang opened both arms wide, rushed at Hu Yan and fell to his knees with a thud, giving a heart-rending cry of 'Dad!' He threw himself body and soul into that cry.

'Dad!' he cried, hurriedly shifting his knees in the rain and closing in on Hu Yan, who retreated and then grabbed Hongyang's head to steady himself. Hongyang gripped his opponent around the back of the knee, pushing his head against it and shouting: 'Dad! I was wrong, Dad!' Tears poured down his face and he wailed and gasped for breath as if he was at his own mother's deathbed. Hongyang's scalding tears dampened Hu Yan's still dry trousers, and the prisoner rubbed himself back and forth against the other man's legs like a devoted guard dog. He would have wagged his tail if he'd had one.

'Dad!' came the cry once more. When Hu Yan tried to pull his leg away, Hongyang banged his head on the muddy ground in a kowtow. He put every bit of feeling he had into this act of repentance and entreaty. 'I've been far far away, a nightmare distance away, and now I've finally come home.'

Eventually, Hu Yan managed to free his leg and thought that it would be hard to rid himself of the taint of this encounter.

'Get back,' he ordered. 'Get back.' He sounded panicky.

9

'And then?' asked Xu Yousheng.

'And then, Hongyang was released.'

10

Hongliang went on with his story.

Hongyang came back a stranger. He wore a pair of jeans that were shiny with grease, leather boots of the sort limekiln workers wore, socks, and a black windcheater with ripped pockets. He sat on the green-painted railings outside the post office, throwing down a fag end every few minutes, pressing his Stetson, which professed to be made of genuine leather, firmly down on his head with his free hand even though there was no wind. He gave off the kind of whiff you often smell on people who keep cats. His gaze flickered from side to side, and he responded briefly to people's greetings.

When we had gone to meet him at the Niujiaolong Reform through Education camp early on the morning of the twenty-seventh, they told us he had already been released. We had worked out that it was not a year to the day since the beginning of his sentence, but a year and a day.

For a couple of days, we kept an eye out for him, without success. Then, a week later, he appeared in Fan township. It was not the long-awaited homecoming we had imagined. He smiled dutifully yet briefly, and the distress behind it made us suspect that he had been tortured; his eyes were dull, his complexion pasty and his frame emaciated. He was grateful that we had gone to meet him but recognised that we could not help him, for which he forgave us. In the intervals when he was not smoking, he kept rubbing his temples and pushing the brim of his cowboy hat higher up on his head while he kicked at the railings with one foot. He sounded hoarse, and seemed as fidgety as a man in love.

Hongyang looked up at us. We understood that expression: he had been in bad trouble and was now dreading the consequences. There was no doubt bad things had happened to him during his absence. Anyone who knew about these things would think he was reacting the way people always did when they had been released from a Reform through Education camp or a labour camp: gloomy, detached, distrustful, on edge, unwilling to engage with anyone. But the majority, including us, figured that Hongyang was waiting for someone, and that if this someone wasn't already in the township, they were about to get there.

Let's not beat around the bush: he was waiting for police chief Yuan Qihai. He was not looking at the police station, but he was listening. And he was gambling on regaining a foothold in the township. He had made his wager, and now he was awaiting the outcome: either he had to win back some of his influence, or he had lost everything.

Yuan Qihai cut the call and set off for the county town, hot on Hongyang's heels. He had felt a spurt of fury when he took the phone because his wife, in his opinion, was lazy and greedy, impulsive and thoughtless, good for nothing except wasting time and food. However, on this matter, he was prepared to support her. The way she described it, the devil had its claws into the family's soft underparts. The devil had turned up without any warning but with the air of having planned this for a long time. Although it had disappeared for now, who knew when it might be back again? Yuan Qihai fetched his gun out of the safe and headed for the county town, still in a foul mood. When he got there, he achieved nothing except venting his temper, because the legendary demon was nowhere to be seen. Finally, he took his wife and children back to Fan township.

Hongyang was still sitting there. When the jeep slowed to a halt in front of the police station, the gravel scrunching under the car tyres, he sat up straighter. The doors slammed open, and one after the other, its occupants hopped out and went up the steps. Yuan Qihai's wife had never wanted to settle in the countryside but now, curious about this new place, she found herself looking around and surveying the street before trailing up the steps behind the others. A second or two later, she halted again and slowly turned. Terrifying images seized her once more: the needle of an insulin pen shooting into a belly, a staple gun stapling together a young boy's drooping foreskin, the knife-sharp edge of an A4 sheet of paper slicing into goggling eyeballs, filthy fingernails scraping across the dark green paint of a blackboard, an infant, arms as soft as lotus roots, its neck dusted with talcum powder, toddling under a nodding guillotine, a turning drill dismembering a doll, a red brick pursuing a fleeing chicken in order to flatten the bedraggled creature onto a specimen slide, or a murderer wielding needle and thread, sewing a child's lips together. She gripped her husband's arm and pointed to Hongyang, who was getting down from the iron railings.

'That's him! I'd recognise him anywhere.' She jabbed her finger fiercely at the approaching figure.

'Ah, you're back.' Hongyang doffed his hat to the police chief, revealing his shaven head. Yuan Qihai let his gaze rest on him, the way a customer who's already settled up might check that they've received everything they've paid for, then reached out and slapped Hongyang's mocking smile. Although Hongyang was not in bad physical shape at all, now he staggered and, when Yuan Qihai followed the slap with a kick, he slumped to the ground. Yuan Qihai sent Hongyang's hat spinning under the wheels of an oncoming car, then placed one knee on Hongyang's abdomen and held down his head. Hongyang struggled to raise it, saying, 'I was only—' But every time he tried to protest, he received a slap on the mouth.

*　　*　　*

'What made the biggest impression on me was . . .'

There was a pause, and Xu Yousheng prompted him: 'What made the biggest impression on you, Uncle . . .?'

It was that as Yuan Qihai clicked off the safety catch, the silvery sound of a song could be heard above the raucous din of a nearby hair salon. The singer was a woman whose age was impossible to work out from the notes rising into the sky like doves released from the hands of young girls. The melody sank into the depths of distant layers of clouds until, just as they were fading, they bubbled up again. Thousands of hands seemed to pull them back to the heavens, and they drifted away. The notes rose and fell, rose and fell. We seemed to be standing in a vast cathedral, but all the while a massacre was taking place in front of our very eyes. The crowd rushed forth, mute like wild cattle, and filled the road; cars swerved into the gutter, first squeezing past and then finding their way blocked completely.

Some of the police officers came out of the station and grabbed the onlookers, saying: 'Go back home, there's nothing to look at.' Others bent over Hongyang in a futile attempt to persuade him to his feet.

Yuan Qihai pushed one bullet after another into his magazine, until he had loaded five. He looked as cool as Arnold Schwarzenegger, but inside he was trying to master the violent urge to execute his opponent with a single shot and make the act look like a delicate surgical operation. He slammed the magazine into his gun, flipped the hammer catch and a moment later smoothly slid the bolt home. 'Don't do it,' his subordinates begged him, surrounding him like a hunter's sack-toting assistants. 'Don't, Chief.'

'Get away from me!' he yelled, cocking his head, his gaze distant and cold like a drunkard's. He shot experimentally into the air. Blue smoke spurted from the gun barrel, and the gun recoiled like a premature ejaculation. A quavering echo reached them from the clouds. The crowd stampeded in all directions like cattle, some jumping on bicycles they had previously flung to the ground, some falling against doors that others slammed in their faces. They were like birds balanced on an electric wire, dropping on take-off before their wings lift them and they rise into the sky. In the hair salon, the cassette tape tangled inside the machine, its guts spilling out like entrails from the abdomen of a road accident victim, and the singer's throat sounded scorched. It emitted a series of helpless squawks before falling silent.

Yuan Qihai had both knees planted on Hongyang's chest, and he took out a handkerchief to wipe first the barrel of his pistol, then Hongyang's sweaty forehead. At this point, the Head of Finance arrived. Speaking as an official and Yuan Qihai's senior, he said: 'Don't do it. Think of your child.'

'I know,' Yuan Qihai answered. 'It's my child I'm thinking of.'

'I was just—' Hongyang began again. Yuan Qihai gripped Hongyang in a chokehold, and his victim turned dark red in the face, purple veins appearing around his temples. His eyeballs looked like they were going to pop out, and his hands drummed on the ground. At the start he had been stuck for words, then, when he urgently wanted to speak, either the gunshots or the roar of the crowd had drowned him out, and now he found himself being choked. Finally Yuan Qihai released his grip, crooked his middle finger and gently rested it on Hongyang's forehead, the way doctors do when they're about to give an infant a transfusion. He placed the cold gun muzzle on the spot where he reckoned the bone was most brittle. Hongyang gasped and went rigid, so rigid that his buttocks left the ground. His eyes rolled back in his head as if he was about to expire. Then he went limp and his breathing and eyes returned to normal. From time to time he shook his head slightly to rid himself of the annoying gun. It wasn't that he was trying to avoid execution, simply that it obstructed his view of the tranquil sky.

I reckon he must have felt some slight regret the instant he stared death in the face. Obviously he had underestimated his opponent's determination to protect his family. Hongyang had wanted to show he was a force to be reckoned with, and had optimistically reckoned that the worst he would get was a beating. He had seriously underestimated how devoted this man was to his daughter.

Hongyang shut his eyes, squeezed out an enormous tear, and became docile, lifting his arm ever so slightly, like a dying man allowing his relatives to dress him in his burial clothes. He shifted his body to make it easier for Yuan Qihai to execute him, like a sick man cooperating with the surgeon who is about to operate.

The onlookers stood a short distance away. At the beginning, they had not grabbed Yuan Qihai by the arms and had only laid their fingers lightly there as an attempt at mediating. Now it looked as if there was no stopping him. He reached his finger through the trigger guard and onto the trigger, regulated his breathing, and squeezed slowly. I learned afterwards that this was called a preparatory squeeze. It did not mean he had any intention of firing. Apparently, that was the correct way to fire that kind of bullet.

Just as it looked as if he was going to fire, he relaxed the pressure on the pad of his finger, pursed his lips and let out a long breath. His forehead was covered in a fine sheen of sweat.

'I just wanted to—' Hongyang began again weakly, and Yuan Qihai again raised the gun he had lowered. The finger he reached through the trigger guard trembled uncontrollably as he fought the desire to shoot. Half of him wanted to shout angrily at the other half: You know, don't you, that your daughter was so terrified she damn well cried till her eyes swelled up like peaches? The other half of him, however, took his more impulsive half in a firm grip: Don't give in, don't give in, don't let him wind you up.

As the action advanced and retreated slowly, millimetre by millimetre, Yuan Qihai's face went from dark, to sallow, to translucent. Every time he sucked in a mouthful of air, his skull showed through his skin. You know, Yousheng, I had no idea until then that it isn't easy to kill someone.

Yuan Qihai shot a distraught look at the onlookers, as if seeking someone in particular. But everyone sent approving looks back. Again Yuan Qihai poked Hongyang in the forehead with the gun, and again he lifted the muzzle away. He looked at the man in front of him, muttering to himself the way an athlete about to take the plunge recites the instructions he has memorised: 'Forget about winning or losing, just remember what you've got to do.'

Just then, as he was repeating the mantra 'Fire, fire, fire,' a bicycle skidded to a halt in front of him and the rider jumped off and pushed Yuan Qihai's arm upwards, knocking the gun to the ground. It was Ho Dongming who prevented the killing. Or rather, it was Yuan Qihai who had waited for Ho Dongming to arrive so he could prevent it.

'What the hell were you thinking of, Yuan?' he yelled at him. But Ho's rebuke was delivered in the affectionate tones of a friend, a brother, a senior who figures that it's no big deal and won't attract retaliation. You could see Yuan twitch ever so slightly as he knelt there. I believe he was on the verge of tears. He had nearly delivered himself to prison.

'That's enough.' Ho Dongming picked up the gun, pushed it back into Yuan Qihai's holster and snapped it shut.

'If I hadn't seen you, Director Ho, if I hadn't wanted you not to lose face . . .' said Yuan Qihai, delivering repeated kicks to

Hongyang's kidneys as the latter lay splayed out, corpse-like, pissing a stream of urine that made a great dark patch on the ground.

'That's enough,' Ho Dongming repeated. Later, people would see the scene as a tragedy born of blind overconfidence. The chief had failed to analyse the situation or his tactics properly, and had allowed himself to be carried away by anger and impetuosity. He was riding a tiger that he couldn't get off, as the expression goes. Finally he had let cowardice overcome him, like a kid.

Hongyang had won. Of course, he acted like the loser at the time. He crawled to his knees, knocked his head repeatedly on the ground in a kowtow, and sobbed.

'I'm just an ignorant peasant.'

'What?' asked Yuan Qihai.

'I just wanted to give you a gift! I wanted us to be on good terms, and I wanted to hang around in Fan township.'

'So that was why you accosted my little Ruirui?'

'Please forgive an ignorant peasant. I knew I wouldn't be able to get close enough to you to give you a gift.'

'Who told you that?'

'Someone in the county town, they told me to go and give the kiddie a present she would like.'

'And now I'm asking you: who told you to give presents?'

'Someone in the county town.'

'Let me tell you one thing,' said Yuan Qihai, grabbing Hongyang by the collar. 'If anything happens to Ruirui from today onwards, you'll have me to answer to, understood?'

'Understood!' Hongyang sang out. Tears of remorse coursed down his cheeks.

Yuan Qihai regarded the tears as a sign that he had wronged Hongyang, who had meant well. He pulled out five hundred yuan, slapped him on the head with the notes, then dropped them on the ground. Hongyang picked up the money and the hat with the sun visor that Squint had given him, now squashed flat, and made his way home, still weeping. Once he was home, he continued to hiccup with sobs like an old woman.

To the end of his days, he regarded the incident that day as the biggest mistake of his life: 'I did the wrong thing for the right reasons! I only wanted to get him on my side.' That was how he put it to Hongbin, to Shuizhi and to his mistress Jin Yan. From then on, he only had to see Chief Yuan reaching for his cigarettes in the streets of Fanzhen and he would rush over and insist on lighting it, holding the quivering flame to the chief's cigarette tip. No one had ever seen such naked fawning before. There were moments when Yuan Qihai would stroke Hongyang's head gently. When this happened, Hongyang not only didn't feel awkward, he actually made sure everyone saw his beaming smile. He was certainly a lot taller than Yuan. Yuan only had to feign aiming a kick at him for Hongyang to act like he really had been hit and to start jumping up and down like a clown, shouting 'Ai-ya! Ai-ya!'

Everyone, including Yuan himself, was well aware that Hongyang's fawning flattery was not heartfelt; it was just a ploy to curry favour. Yuan Qihai, a man who had never feared anyone in his entire life, had a dread of Hongyang, you know. Hongyang had him by the balls, and Yuan had to get something back, to rebalance the scales in a way that everyone could live with. I think that when Hongyang went and fawned on Yuan Qihai, Yuan felt physically sick. But he had no choice: he'd have to put up with his sworn enemy behaving in this creepy, fawning manner. He couldn't shoot him dead, not after the way the previous episode had ended.

'Why didn't Yuan Qihai look for another opportunity to kill Uncle Hongyang?' asked Xu Yousheng.

'I was worried about that too. It wasn't as if he and Yuan had become friends all of a sudden. That's why he put his passbooks in the names of Muxiang and Shuizhi, way back when. I reckon that Yuan Qihai spent every day plotting how to get rid of Hongyang once and for all. As far as Yuan was concerned, his daughter was in danger as long as Hongyang and his cronies remained alive and well. From our point of view, Hongyang and his gang were not worth bothering about, but for Yuan Qihai, they were a bunch of desperate criminals. It has to be said that when Hongyang was alive, they threw their weight around. He was protecting them, after all, so their names became a byword for treachery, cruelty and shameless brutality. Apparently when the provincial government launched its oper-ation against organised crime, Yuan Qihai cooked up a few ideas of his own. That's why Hongyang gave Shuizhi those instructions for after his death.

'In the end, though, Yuan Qihai let it drop. It was unimagina-ble that he should send his daughter away because of Hongyang. He had contemplated sending her to stay with some distant relatives in Ningxia, in Qinghai province on the Tibetan plateau, or asking to be transferred to another job. But taking either of these options would affect his reputation, and he couldn't stand for that. He didn't want to show that he was afraid. As a result, he suffered agonies of anxiety every time he went to work, and had to put up with Hongyang's constant attentions day in, day out. And all because he had to keep up a façade of being in control. When his wife phoned to tell him that Hongyang had given her parents an enormous bribe, Yuan Qihai shut his eyes, feeling that the great ship of life was being dragged under the waves, and that he was powerless to stop it.'

This prickly relationship between the two men went on for many years, until finally the sharp thorns of memory were worn smooth by the passage of time and the two began to take pleasure in each other's company. Gradually they each let down their guard, to the point where they called each other 'mate'. In the end, Hongyang made a substantial gift to Yuan Qihai. Not one that you could see, but nonetheless tangible. It was this that finally extinguished the last scraps of anxiety, wariness and hostility that Yuan Qihai had felt towards Hongyang for so long: your uncle got Yuan Qihai promoted to the position of first deputy chief of the Bureau of Justice, while Zhao Zhongnan was promoted to deputy chief in charge of operations at the Fan township police station, and later to political instructor. By way of farewell, they had three drinking binges, staggering into the back yard to vomit, their arms around each other's shoulders and their eyes bright with tears as they repeated the words over and over: 'It was a misunderstanding, mate, all a misunderstanding,' until all former enmity was dissolved. However, word went around that when the official came to pick up Yuan Qihai and asked him if he was going to say goodbye to Hongyang, he gave a frown of distaste and flapped his hand, the way you might chase away an annoying fly. Maybe all officials are like that.

So, Yousheng, three days after he was almost executed by Yuan Qihai, Hongyang turned up in Fan township with a cartload of illegally felled timber, and looked up Yuan Qihai. But when he offered him a cigarette, Yuan sneered at the brand – it was Double-Ninth – took one and snapped it in half between his fingers, turned on his heel and stalked back inside the station.

'He didn't bother with it?' asked Xu Yousheng.

'That's right. That was the most ingenious part of the whole business. That load of timber was a test. If the police took Hongyang to task over it, Hongyang was going to say that he would voluntarily surrender to the Forestry Police because that was part of their remit. If the police ignored him, then it meant that Yuan Qihai might be turning a blind eye to what Hongyang was up to. So that was that. Hongyang knew what he was doing: he put out more feelers and bribes, just as he had bribed other big players, until he regained and even increased his influence in the township.'

By this time, Xu Yousheng could no longer hide his drowsiness. He squinted sideways at his uncle and his head dropped onto his chest.

Hongliang looked at his nephew. 'You still haven't asked me the most important question, though – what was Uncle Hongyang doing when he disappeared?' But Xu Yousheng was clearly done in, although he still had his mobile clasped in one hand and woke up enough to tighten his grip every time it looked like it was about to fall.

His uncle resumed the story.

The day was growing darker, and Peking opera was being broadcast on the radio, a dan singer trilling an aria in birdlike tones, each syllable drawn out for what felt like a lifetime. Ruirui gripped the iron bars of the gate in both hands, allowing her body to sway with its movement, standing on one leg to show how strong she was, like a seabird perched on the mast of a great ship. It was a game she liked to play.

The alley was only one li in length and just wide enough to fit a truck. The experimental primary school was situated halfway along it, and Hongyang came face to face with little groups of pupils on their way home as he walked in from the southern end. When he got there he looked back, but the alley was deserted now. With a glance at the security guard in his entry box, he put out his hand to stop the kiosk vendor shutting up shop for the night.

Imagine the scene, though I know it's hard to picture Hongyang sweet-talking a kid, tough brute that he was. 'Ruirui, Ruirui,' he says, trying to sound like a kindly uncle or granddad.

'Who are you?' the kid asked.

'What a good girl you are. I bet you're Mummy's special little girl.'

'I am!'

'Daddy's special little girl too?'

'Yes, I am.'

'Come here, Ruirui,' he cooed, as if he were coaxing a stray dog to come to him.

'Who are you?'

'I'm your daddy's friend.'

'What's that mean?'

'It means I'm an uncle.'

'Uncle who?'

'Just an uncle.'

The girl put both feet on the bottom of the iron gate and let herself fall back, swinging with both hands on the railings as she tried to get the gate to move backwards. At the time, Ruirui's mother was four or five li away, playing mah-jong in the farm stores. Although her friends were urging her to go, she just said: 'What's the hurry?' Between quarter past five and six o'clock, they tried to get her on her way three times. She had actually called her younger sister a few times, because her sister lived nearer the alley. 'It's only a few steps from your house, can't you pick her up from school?' she whined. But her sister was either playing mah-jong too, or said she was having a massage and couldn't get away.

Anyway, at six o'clock, half an hour after school finished, Yuan Qihai's wife finally grew anxious. Grabbing the money on the table, she stuffed it in her bag, ran outside, and jumped in the first pedicab she saw. 'Hurry, please hurry,' she begged, swearing at the red lights. Hongyang had worked all this out. He had borrowed a bit of money in the county town, and had sat down opposite the door of the farm stores.

Hongyang tried to grab the girl by the hand, but she pulled away. He smelled a bit musty, the smell of a rat-catcher or someone with only a pile of husks for a bed. She dangled from the gate.

'My mum says I shouldn't go off with strangers, or talk to them either.'

Hongyang fell silent. I'm guessing that he wanted to grab a passer-by and share the joke with them – 'So cute, kids nowadays!' – He went over to the kiosk, with its counter full of gaudily coloured snacks laid out especially to tempt the schoolkids. A moment later, he had bought a great pile and held them out to her.

She looked at them and sniffed. 'My mum says not to take sweets from strangers.'

'What happens if you do?'

'I'll get a bad tummy and have to have an injection.' She was hanging on to the gate but still eyeing the sweets. 'I don't like them,' she said.

'Then what *do* you like?'

'I don't know . . .'

'Come here. Whatever you fancy, Uncle Hongyang will get it for you.'

'No.' She held on to the gate with one hand. It was as if that was her last defence, while the rest of her body leaned in the direction of the kiosk. She giggled.

'What a good little girl our Ruirui is, isn't she?' Hongyang said to the owner. 'Give me a big plastic bag.'

It wasn't long before the girl had forgotten all her parents' admonishments and ran over to him. She rifled through the things in the bag. 'Don't want this, don't want this.'

'Shall we give it back then?' asked Hongyang, kneeling down and pinching her cheek.

'No!'

'Fine, you choose then.' He lifted her up and, like the Empress Dowager, she pointed at this one and that one.

As you can imagine, this was beyond her wildest dreams. From the day they're born, kids are greedy for any kind of food, but their parents keep a tight hold on the purse strings and are always going on about how this and that isn't good for them, so the stuff they dream about day and night, they never actually get to put into their mouths. Children live an existence of monastic discipline, listening to daily exhortations from their parents: eat this, don't eat that, this is good for you, that is bad for you, that's expensive . . . They're fed up to the back teeth with it! They want to eat absolutely everything, everything they've dreamed about, they want to eat as much as they like, whenever they like. The boys want to work in a chocolate factory, the girls want to marry an old candyfloss seller with a magician's touch.

For Ruirui, an uncle had turned up in her cold, lonely life. Anything she wanted, he would give her in the blink of an eye. How could she resist? She kept trying, but she soon discovered that he had no hesitation and no scruples. All grown-ups ought to be as generous and kindly as this, she thought. 'I want that too,' she ventured, pointing at an enormous Transformer in body armour, all shiny and glittering, hanging from the top of the kiosk, its transparent arms full of multicoloured gumdrops. It had never been touched before. He agreed instantly, and asked the owner to get two different ones down. She almost leapt for joy.

'What else would you like?' asked Hongyang. Feeling that this was her last chance, the child hurriedly pointed to the entire shelf. There was nothing much on it any more but she kept pointing, telling him why this or that thing was particularly good, until she finally had to admit that there really was nothing left worth buying.

Finally she stood outside the kiosk with a huge pile of gifts like a bride with her trousseau, waiting for her mum to come and collect her. Hongyang pushed a five hundred-yuan note into her pocket and told her to buy herself something nice to eat. Then, the deed done, he positioned himself a few hundred metres away at the corner. He had his back to them, but he could hear when the mother arrived.

'Where on earth did you get all that from?' she asked, rifling through the pile. She rejected some she thought unsuitable, and her six-year-old burst into tears of rage. Maybe in a few years Ruirui would be able to leave home, but for now she was well and truly under the parental thumb. She pointed at the 'kind uncle' standing a little way away. 'It was him,' she said. And there stood Hongyang, facing a red brick wall, doing something that in his Reform through Education camp he had had to wait to do until the rest of them were sound asleep. As his right arm jerked, his elbow lifted the windcheater slung over his shoulders. He was masturbating furiously.

'Are you awake?' This was Hongliang.

'Where am I?' Xu Yousheng asked.

'In my house, kid.'

'I was sleeping like a log.'

'I thought you township folk didn't like going to bed early. In the countryside it's pitch-black by eight or nine at night at the latest, and there's nothing else to do except sleep. So it's early to bed and early to rise. But tonight I don't much feel like sleeping.'

Of course you don't, but as you say, I've come from the town, Xu Yousheng thought. He put his mobile down on the side table with its screen facing downwards, as if he no longer gave a shit. About ten minutes later he picked it up again, on the pretext of wanting to check the time. He said nothing in answer to his uncle's questions but thought: You've finally found an audience, Uncle, a friend with good manners who's not rushing off anywhere, so you're going to keep talking until dawn.

'I'll carry on with my story, Yousheng.'

'You do that.'

There were a couple of things that struck me when Squint told us his story. The first was when the girl said, 'Someday, someone may tell our story to a person much younger than themselves.'

You can imagine her, wiping her adjustable spanner clean and throwing in a few words now and again to ensure the man wasn't working himself into a rage. She didn't like his silence at all. It wasn't the punishment that she was afraid of, for she knew it must come one day. No, it was the fact that he seemed dead. She finished cleaning the spanner, discarded the paper towel, looked pityingly at him and stroked his shaking head.

'That's just how it is. Better to stop thinking about it,' she said with a sigh. But if he really did something, she would jump to her feet and yell furiously at him. That was her way: she was always totally unreasonable. Their lives had been destroyed in a few short moments. A few minutes ago, they had been doing fine, following the rules of the game of life. And now, a few minutes later, she was mopping up the blood of the man she had killed, the man he had wanted to set free. Their lives felt like a car bouncing uncontrollably along the road, leaping into the air like a pig, hurtling towards the mountain valley. 'They're so relaxed and carefree, brewing up their tea. Hah! They're using our story to pass the long night hours. There's no going back for us now. You know that, don't you?' she said.

'I know.'

'Are you scared?'

'No.'

I get goose pimples when I remember her words. She's been dead for a while, but saying those words out loud, I feel her presence again. I know that she finished talking and glanced upwards, and it's as if I can see her eyes, empty, unfamiliar, tranquil as an animal's. She's holding up the spanner. The 'someday' is now, the 'someone' is me, and the young listener is you. Yousheng, can you pour the water from the kettle into our teacups while it's still hot?

The stranger had come out of a snowstorm. His boots squeaked as he plodded all the way from Tianjiapu. He went first to Fan township, then on to Zhangjiaba, where the Jiuyuan township government offices were – Jiuyuan was still a township then.

From there, he went on to Tianjiapu, where the Xiayuan village committee was based, before finally asking the way to Aiwan. A lot of people did that, using the levels of local government as staging posts, going downwards from provincial capital to city, county, township, village and hamlet. So many pointless journeys. It's like the switchback designed by the railway engineer Zhan Tianyou, with the two wings of each V very close together. Once the train has gone into the point of the V, it's turned in the other direction.

From time to time, he stopped to look back along the road, as if he had taken the wrong turning. As far as possible, he followed the road of his imagination, as if that way he could avoid attracting attention. If anyone had spotted him, he'd have stood out like a sore thumb in the desolate landscape. But everyone was too worn out. Even a leopard could have got as far as the entrance to the village in winter without being stopped.

He bent down to ask Hongqi, who was at his door tipping out spent ashes. Hongqi lifted his head but didn't look at the stranger too closely. Then he carried on towards Hongyang's home. 'An arrow's flight', was what Hongqi had said.

The stranger had been more than three weeks on the road in search of Hongyang. Thoughts of the man had helped to drive fear, boredom and exhaustion from his mind during that life. He'd kept himself occupied by trying to solve life's great mysteries, questions like: was an egg a double-yolker? How many layers of filling did his quilt have? How high was the orange flame?

He'd thought back on tear-jerking, heart-rending scenes of magnificent friendships in films, books and legends. They would pale in comparison to his long-awaited reunion with Hongyang. The only man he could trust, his mate. Now Hongyang's place was also his only refuge. During the long journey, he might even have planned out the conversations he hoped to have with his old friend.

As he walked the last few steps, he felt suddenly as shy as a bride in her new home. He imagined Hongyang shouting out when he pushed open the door, shuffling into his shoes and running over to him, drinking in the sight of him greedily: this precious long-lost friend. Or he imagined him scarcely daring to put one foot in front of the other, as if fearful of using up this instant of happiness, as if it might dissolve too quickly. So when Hongyang completely failed to recognise him, it came as a heavy blow. He thought it would only last a few seconds, but Hongyang carried on looking at him as if he were a stranger. The hostile gleam from Hongyang's pupils felt like a pair of hands stopping him in his tracks at the door.

It was distressing how Hongyang knitted his brows and raised his index finger, moving it back and forth, acutely frustrated at his own inability to remember this person he should know. It was an odd kind of distress, like when you anticipate a sneeze you know will be pleasurable but which takes its time in coming.

The newcomer was wearing an old army greatcoat over a filthy suit, shirt and tie. He wore pointed leather shoes caked with muddy snow. His toes suffered badly after that. Wisps of yellowing grass stuck to his grey face, and the cherry-red birthmark over his left eyebrow had turned dark and wrinkled. His skin was as slack as a Shar Pei's. He smiled awkwardly as he waited for Hongyang to place him. Then he blamed himself: it wasn't surprising that Hongyang didn't recognise him. He'd changed so much that his own mother would struggle to place him, what with being on the run for days and nights without a break. Two police dogs had run themselves to death in an attempt to catch him up. It had been months now since he'd had a proper wash, or even a change of clothes.

All the same, he was obviously disappointed. Hongyang gave a cry of surprise and embraced him, of course, but the affection was slow in coming, so slow it seemed like he was putting on an act. Hongyang's hostility was habitual: he was like that with everyone, except his friends and family. Still, the newcomer wondered what his life would have been like if he hadn't been Hongyang's mate? And what if one day he wasn't any longer? He saw in this unpleasant experience a side of Hongyang that could not be trusted, and decided that, from now on, he would be more circumspect in what he said. He did not talk about the horrendous experiences he had lived through until he was about to take his leave and Hongyang had shown that he was fundamentally a decent man. And after they had downed a fair amount of alcohol.

The snow had not yet melted when Hongyang drove his Buick back from Fan township at night, roused Squint, and took him to a long-abandoned hydroelectric power station. It was situated halfway up a mountain, and the road was overgrown with rank vegetation. When they got out of the truck, they still had to climb another twenty metres up to the station. 'Hard to attack, easy to defend', as they say. Hongyang gave him a new mobile and told him he could use it to dial out but not receive calls. 'You can climb out of an opening in the back wall and cut across the mountains on a steep goat track,' he said. 'And don't ever come back.' Then he added: 'A bunch of police have turned up.'

'Maybe they've not come for me,' said Squint, who had no desire to go rambling any more.

'I heard they're from Anhui province,' Hongyang finally said. And it was those words that led Squint to make a beeline for the hydroelectric power station.

After he'd eaten dried sausage and preserved eggs for a week, Hongyang hauled himself up the mountain on crutches, fetched back his old accomplice and took him to my big brother's house for the night. Everyone said that the police had headed home by then. But the good thing about this new arrangement was that even if they had surrounded Hongyang's house, Squint could leave our place by the back gate and escape back up the mountain.

Hongyang wined and dined us generously. After a few days of that, Squint was overcome with a fit of tears. He'd had too much to drink. Finally he grasped Hongyang's hand and confessed: 'I've done some really bad things.' He had been having sleepless nights and it was time to get it off his chest. Thinking back, I reckon Hongyang had recognised him from the moment he set eyes on him. He just pretended not to because that way he had the upper hand over Squint. That was Hongyang's usual tactic, after all.

Eventually, though, Hongyang gave a shrill cry: 'Squint! My God! What wind blew you here?'

Squint had lost all his composure by this point. 'I don't know whether I should tell you this. If you don't say anything, then I won't.'

'You want to borrow money?

'No . . .'

'Then what?'

'I want you to give me shelter.'

'Shelter?'

'That's right. I need you to take me in, mate.'

'OK. All right then. You can depend on me.'

12

Sometimes as I walk under the branches of this chandelier I am astonished at its silence, or rather, at its impotence. Because it was right here that two conversations took place that even now make my hair stand on end when I think back on them. The chandelier, the house and I are like wooden stakes stuck in the river of time, witnessing what happened and needing to record it: a hardened criminal spilling his secrets before his arrest.

Squint took the leading role during the first conversation. He talked to Hongyang, while I listened in. Before Squint began, Hongyang looked at me then turned to Squint, his eyebrows raised, as if this was a matter for people of their age, for the big boys, to deal with. Squint simply accepted that anyone or anything there that evening must be all right: he was hopelessly trusting by then.

He told the whole story of his friendship with Hongyang in the camp, then told us everything that had happened to him after that. As he talked, he kept swigging and then refilling his cup. He must have downed two or three jin of spirits. He was so drunk that he told us absolutely everything. I suspect every criminal wants nothing more than to find someone to fess up to.

Squint must have kept a lid on it for far too long. He completely forgot that he was wanted by the police and on the run. It was unbearably hot in the room, and pitch-dark outside.

PART III

SQUINT'S STORY

13

Prison. The inmate Wolfdog fell back and banged his head on the bedhead. There was a dull thud. He looked as if he was asleep, both arms dangling, his body sliding down the bed. He opened his eyes with an effort then shut them again. You went over to him and propped his head up straight, Hongyang. I thought you were checking whether he was still breathing, but then you walloped him so hard across one cheek that the other side of his face bulged out as if it was full of thick soup. His servant gave a low cry and fled from the room. You fished out a toothbrush with a sharpened end, a trick you'd learned from watching videos, poked it at their leader's chest and growled: 'You want to die? Come here then.'

After the police arrived, they pulled at their collars and cuffs and shouted all at once: 'This is outrageous! He's dying, or at least he might be, and this one came and punched him. It was a vicious attack!' All this time, Wolfdog lay in bed like a sick woman, groaning to elicit sympathy.

'Are you dead?' you asked. 'Right, so if you are, then keep quiet.'

Young Hongliang, there's something you don't know – that police officer was the most aloof of all the police at the camp, he didn't seem to want to get involved in anything. Hongyang had nothing but contempt for arse-lickers, you know, and back then he couldn't care less what punishment was meted out to him. He regarded every punishment as a challenge rather than a nuisance. Plus he thought it humiliating to be used as a tool by Wolfdog and his cronies. From the moment he'd arrived here, he'd decided to punch anyone he came across.

'What's up?' the officer whispered as he pulled you outside.

'I beat him up.'

'I know you beat him up, I'm asking why.'

'He wanted to kill you all.'

You found out what Wolfdog was planning when you saw my battered face. You had a gun pointed at your head, so you told the police officer you couldn't swim, then I was taken to a corner of the warehouse by Wolfdog and his lot and made to fight a 'boxing match' with someone else who'd offended them, while they placed bets until one of us was beaten to a pulp.

Maybe you don't know, young man, but we had bad flooding, the electricity was cut, it got dark early, and everything was underwater as far as you could see. The Reform through Education camp was like an island, with murky waves slapping against the shore. The rain was still falling in torrents. We were all outside the collapsed perimeter walls. Hongyang, you squatted on the flood defence walls catching the sandbags thrown up from below. The skies went from dark to pitch-black: it was impossible to tell who was who.

Just then, a bunch of men turned up – everyone was running around, no one paying attention to anyone else – and surreptitiously pushed you down into the floodwaters a few metres below. We heard the cry go up:

'Ai Hongyang's done a runner. Ai Hongyang's done a runner!'

I smelled a rat, for three reasons: They didn't shout 'run', they shouted 'done a runner'. They used your surname too: Ai Hongyang. And they shouted in unison.

Obviously this had been carefully orchestrated in advance, but no one was interested in that: the police pulled out their guns and leapt up onto sandbags, looking around for you. Afterwards, you said: 'Mate, these are interesting times, and the bullet doesn't know me and doesn't care if I'm doing a runner or shouting for help.' And you were right. I thought that even if you did get away, you'd drown. I heard the splash and knew you couldn't swim. You have to hand it to Wolfdog, it was a pretty good plan. If he hadn't come after me to settle accounts afterwards, we would never have known he was behind it.

Later on, you called Wolfdog out single-handedly and did him over three times. His reputation was at rock bottom after that, but he never put in a complaint. The last time, you fought for me. I know. Because you wanted to get out before me. You broke his nose for him and said: 'You know if you've got a problem with a mate of mine, you've got a problem with me, don't you? So if my mate's got a problem, then so do you, and your whole family, get it?

'Yes, yes,' said Wolfdog.

And he never dared come after me after that.

When you were leaving, I said: 'Go out looking good, with your head held high.' My clothes may have been shabby, but they were in better nick than the clothes you turned up in.

I told you to sort yourself out. 'Listen up, mate,' I said, 'You're known as being one of a kind nowadays. As soon as people mention your name, it's: "Right, that's him, that's got to be him, Hongyang." '

I got out for a bit, but it wasn't long before I landed in the slammer again. This time it was a Reform through Labour camp, much worse than Reform through Education. I didn't know it at the time, it was all the same to me: detention cell, camp, prison. I had been working as a salesman for a battery factory, then I worked on a newspaper as distributor, proof-reader and probationary reporter. Just when I had hopes of turning my life around, I got caught with a hooker. They said: 'You can pay a fine, or we'll bang you up.'

I gave it some thought and decided on custody.

After that, I couldn't find work any more.

14

The last time I got banged up, I forget what for, they took all my previous convictions into account. The day I was arrested, I already had a bad feeling in my gut as I went into a clothes shop. I even remember the name on the sign: Tong Yulin. I made my choices carefully, but all of a sudden I found myself surrounded by a big posse of police. I went into the station with a suit jacket, trousers and shirt all folded over my arm. I told them if I'd wanted to run away I would have done it ages ago. All the time I was being interrogated my mind was on the garments, as if they were the most important thing there, until they produced a plastic bag and the clothes were placed inside with great care.

'And I've got these shoes too,' I said, taking off the pointy-toed dress shoes I'd kept on after I'd tried the clothes on. They wrapped them in newspaper, then waved the glass tea jar at me.

'Keep this too?'

'Yup,' I said, 'that's worth more than my life to me.'

They unscrewed the lid, tipped out the stones inside and counted them, then swept them back into the jar. They would have had to keep whatever was in there for me even if it was dog shit. A citizen's private property is sacrosanct.

At the start of my time in prison, I kept count of the days to keep my spirits up. Every passing day made it one day fewer, didn't it? But before a month had gone by, I began to feel that the counting was making me feel worse, so I relaxed and decided that it didn't matter whether they kept me longer by design or simply because they had forgotten me. I didn't care one way or the other.

Anyway, one day, once I'd been in prison for a while, I was taken to the prison administration. They asked if I had the receipt for my belongings. I thought for a good while then said: 'What the hell do you mean?' They shook their heads, then brought out the plastic bag, the glass jar and my phone. I remembered that I'd bought the new clothes when I was going straight. I knew no one would be looking after me on the outside, and I needed to make an impressive re-entry into society. The suit still had its price tag on. It had been a bit tight on me when I'd bought it, but now it fit me perfectly. Prison labour certainly keeps a man fit.

They doled me out five hundred yuan.

'Is this my pay?'

'No, the government gives you your fares.'

The inmates were due to get their heads shaved just before I was released, but I told the barber: 'I'm about to get out, and it won't have a chance to grow.' He said nothing, simply got the clippers ready. 'I've got a woman waiting for me with tears running down her cheeks!' I went on. That was a load of bullshit, of course, there wasn't anyone waiting for me.

He sighed, and made a few passes with the clippers in the air above my head – buzz, buzz – then pulled the towel from around my neck. When they let me out and the iron gates opened silently, it was like a grand ceremony, like a pair of theatre curtains parting. Outside, the air, the noises, the thousands of leaves on the trees shimmering with a thousand rays of light all came rushing towards me. I even saw a small boy with a crew cut, wearing maroon sweatpants and riding a bike with stabilisers, his lips pursed in concentration as he pedalled round and round the thousand-year-old scholar tree. All the while, a grey-haired, middle-aged man sat there, his legs twitching spasmodically in a way that somehow made me think of a cotton-carding bow with its strings being twanged by a masked worker.

'Freedom at last! I've been dreaming of this day!' The cry forced its way out of me. But by the time I had stripped to my underpants next to the prison sign with its black lettering and the sentry box, and put on my manager's suit, fastening the leather belt with a snap, I wasn't taking this freedom for granted, I was finding it hateful. Freedom was a bore, just like the sunshine. Neither of them were anything like I'd imagined.

'I'm never coming back, you'll have to chop my legs off,' I had vowed half an hour before, while I was still in prison. But I'd no sooner walked out of the doors to the bus stop than I felt I didn't want to go on. What was I going to do? I had no goal in mind, nothing worth doing, and no one worth going to see. Just a couple of classmates who by now felt that having me as a friend was a burden. My parents were thousands of li away and we'd been out of touch for ten years; they'd told me they wished I'd never been born. I was going out into a huge, hostile world, like a shipwrecked sailor riding a dinghy on an ocean, with nowhere to make a landing, nowhere to anchor myself. Put in the simplest terms, I didn't even have anywhere to stay the night.

I got off at Tugan station, just because the name made me curious. Beside the station signboard was a knoll a bit bigger than a grave mound, and a cement road that might lead to Tugan township. It was still sunny, though rain was drifting in from the south-west. I thought of the short distance that divided life and death, and it was as if, once I spent those five hundred yuan, my task in life was over and done with. I considered suicide. I'd probably go for asphyxiophilia, choking masturbation, something I'd heard about in prison, where you used a rope or a scarf or a tie to hang yourself: the masturbation was exquisitely pleasurable and it was almost always fatal.

I tried to flag down a minibus, jumping onto the highway, but it swerved and raced past me. I had to retreat under the eaves of the lookout post that stood on the knoll and watch the driving rain blow over me. It looked like we were in for a long rainstorm. I felt incredibly lonely, and what I really wanted was to find someone and give them a good slap around the ears.

In the end, I went back to Gui county.

I'd sworn I'd never go back, but in the end it called to me. Like a filthy old whore you can't resist. The nearer I got to it, the lower I sank in my own estimation. I'd once been a petty thief there. Every day, as soon as the sun was up, a stream of minibuses used to arrive from the surrounding townships and pull into the muddy pond of a car park, tyres squealing like a herd of sows. Me and my 'fellows' – that was what we called ourselves – swarmed around them. We got an old newspaper, it didn't matter if it was last year's, or we draped an overcoat over our arms and, as the passengers squeezed their way off, we pushed on board, making it look as if we were expecting someone. They always reminded me of antelopes or zebras on the savanna, their terrified eyes popping out as they let us grope them. And every time I did it, I felt disgust, as if I was ripping off my own mother. We were stealing from loyal citizens, weren't we? We stuffed our ill-gotten gains into the soles of our shoes, or our underpants, but we never dared steal from the townsfolk for fear of getting beaten up. I only ever once got into danger in that car park. He must have been a village Party cadre, and he spotted me about to dip into his pocket. As soon as I realised that he'd seen, I snatched my open fingers back. He gripped my wrist and started to read me the riot act. Although I was a bit scared, I stopped worrying when the fellows made a roll-up and offered him one because he accepted it, dammit, took a light off us and blew a stream of blue-grey smoke heavenwards. I silently trailed him for a whole morning, following him to loads of places: the credit cooperative, the agricultural bureau and the land management office. He was aware that I was following him, and every now and then he turned abruptly and glared at me as if I was a stray dog. I smiled politely back at him and carried right on tailing him again. Finally, he turned into an alley and disappeared. Thinking back on it, I wasn't scared of him; I just wanted something to do.

Not one day went by without me hating that way of life.

Before the minibuses pulled up, I used to prop myself against the wall, looking at my watch and then at my blurry reflection in the dust-coated windows. I was over thirty; in the blink of an eye I'd be forty, fifty or sixty, grey-haired and decrepit. Was I going to be stuck here till the day I died? Every time I asked myself these deep questions, I felt anguished. Over and over, I ordered myself to get out of there: Go! Right now! But I couldn't drag my damned body away. Sometimes I'd bang my back against the wall over and over again as I wept, overcome by inertia. I was going to rot and die here, I thought.

Now I had a different set of excuses to return. Better to have somewhere than nowhere, I told myself. I could do office work or be a doorman. I mean it was work, and anywhere you worked you could call home, surely?

I thought of the fellows I'd been with. It was more a deep-seated cowardice that had kept us together than what we got out of it. To be honest, we were none of us real desperadoes: we were thieves who could do our sums. Most of us had dropped out after lower middle school, but we took a scientific approach to things, like technically trained factory fitters. We set ourselves daily targets for earnings, modest in the off season, higher in the busy season. We wanted to keep our business viable long-term, not kill the goose that laid the golden egg. After we knocked off for the day, we didn't sit around playing mah-jong, chatting, drinking or watching TV all night. It was early to bed and early to rise. And at night it was like we were sharing a sleeper compartment in a train: we ignored each other.

I had sworn once that I'd never contact my fellows again, and in any case they'd disappeared. I searched in the car park, the coach station, the farmers' market, the train station, all the places where we used to do our thieving, and the room we'd rented too, but there was no sign of them. I never even saw any other petty thieves. I asked around, and although people gave it some thought, none of them remembered us. It was as if they'd never ever lost their wallets.

I couldn't think what to do. It was the same kind of feeling I'd had as a kid when we'd had to go and pay our respects to my father's sister, who lived a long way off: when we got there, the place was in ruins. We peeled our red-dyed hard-boiled eggs and ate them one after another. We had no idea what had happened, or what we should do next, and the emptiness hurt.

I found a pocket to pick, but my fingers had gone too stiff. I felt as if I was standing on a cliff top with the wind howling around me. When my target turned around, my shirt ran with sweat. I forced myself to slap him on the shoulder, saying: 'You take good care of that wallet of yours.' He hurriedly patted its hiding place and followed someone else's hastily retreating figure with his eyes.

As I guessed, he was terribly grateful to me. The incident convinced me that combating pickpocketing was a decent job. But I couldn't go to the police and offer to combat pickpocketing. I couldn't imagine them saying: Fine, you do that for us. I knew there were old folk who worked against pickpockets. Anti-pickpocketing and pickpocketing were two sides of the same coin, a way of earning a living. Both of them were much more proactive than the police.

Finally, I wandered into the People's Hospital. The famously accurate fortune teller was still there. 'Point me to the right road,' I said. He used his hand like his eyes, groping as if moving through a dense fog, before finally settling on a westerly direction.

'Will it be good fortune or bad?'

'Don't worry about that.'

'How far away is it?'

'You'll know when you get there.'

I gave him fifty yuan, and he touched the bottom right corner of his Braille board with his finger. As he took out my change, I palmed a hundred yuan from him.

I took a bus going west. One of the other passengers fell asleep, and I couldn't help but notice the money sticking out of his pocket. I took his dozing as an invitation and whipped it off him. I got off in a place called Xinxing. The scurrying passengers always made me think of a maths problem: if there were $3x - y$ people on the bus, and half of them got off during the journey, and some more got on, so that there were $8x - 5y$ people on the bus at that point, then how many people had been on the bus during the journey?

15

The afternoon sun was dazzling, and beautifully warm, like a blanket of translucent silk draped over Xinxing's four little streets, somehow concealing the dog shit, the crumbling bricks, the rotting vegetables and sodden sand, fluttering delicately over the stinking public toilets and the towering mounds of rubbish. If you looked up, however, you could still make out two huge chimneys in the distance, belching out clouds of yellow smoke.

I bought a pair of sunglasses and wore them as I leaned against the wall and watched the world go by. Why did I buy them? Well, it was too early for dinner, so I had to find something to do. I strolled over to the sunglasses stand and found that I couldn't resist the vendor's enthusiastic recommendations. I tried on each pair until I finally felt guilty enough to buy one.

'Thirty yuan, not a cent less,' he told me.

'Ten,' I replied.

'Twenty, and not a cent less.'

'Fifteen.'

He looked like he was going to say something more, but simply said: 'Deal.' Whichever way you looked at it, I had just bought something I didn't need.

A girl appeared at the crossroads. She had startlingly pale skin, even through my sunglasses. It wasn't an unpleasant sickly pallor; it gleamed with the whiteness of snow, or of mutton fat jade: moist, delicate and fresh, brilliant but with nothing showy about it. I completely lost my cool. I found myself daydreaming about having sex with her. Just the thought of whether it could ever happen, the mere idea of it as a possibility, made my heart begin to pound. She held a cigarette between her fingers and kept lifting it to her lips, taking a deep drag and blowing out a cloud of smoke. Her breasts were encased in a tight blue zebra-striped T-shirt which had slipped half off her shoulder so that you could see her black bra strap. She was the image of the goddess I had been yearning for, and she had turned up out of nowhere. I followed her into the Hutong Hotel, hardly realising what I was doing.

I had planned to get a bus out of here as soon as I'd had a meal. It would be easier for me to get a train ticket westwards now that I was in town. But as I watched her retreating figure disappear through the door to the back courtyard, I decided to stay the night.

'Do you have ID?' asked the owner.

'No.'

'Fine,' he said, filling in the form with any old name and ID number. 'Just the one night?'

'If I want to stay longer, I'll tell you.'

'The money . . .' I must have looked like I had a wad of banknotes on me, because he added: 'Perhaps sir would enjoy a visit to the tea room at the back?' It was an obvious hint that they offered 'entertainment for men'. I swallowed. He was wearing a business suit as stiff as cardboard and his hair was slicked down. I noticed that his entire head was covered in specks of white, and realised with disgust that they were probably lice. I thought back to what my gran used to say about poor people using a fine-toothed comb to get nits out: They brushed them into the fire, where they popped and crackled. As he lifted his head to talk to me, his nostril hairs poked out like bayonets.

Once I'd been shown to my room, I had a shower, used dry shampoo on my hair, found a bottle of cologne and splashed it all over my neck, then went down to the tea room. And there she was. The ceiling was quite low, and blue smoke hung motionless above everyone's heads. They were playing mah-jong and a card game called Beat the Landlord. A village cadre who'd blown his hand off dynamiting fish had the cards in his remaining hand while, with his stump of a wrist, he dealt the cards one by one, the way you might peel a mooli into the air. The noisiest table was the one where they were playing Three-Card Brag. The owner was sat at the table, taking a percentage. The woman I'd noticed earlier was taking it in turns with another girl in a zebra-striped T-shirt to be the dealer.

Little Rabbit was what the men called her. And as she got up to deal the cards they reached out and groped her bum, rubbing the back of her T-shirt over and over, the way a cook might give their hands a wipe on a towel hanging up in the kitchen every time they passed back and forth.

'What a good little rabbit.'

She smiled half-heartedly but sometimes lost her temper, for instance when one of the men touched her labia with his middle finger through the crotch of her trousers. This seemed to be exactly what the men wanted. Like servants about to get a whipping from the master, they were getting a kick out of push-ing the limits with their behaviour.

I sat down opposite her and saw her gaze settle on me. I stuck out like a sore thumb among this lot, the way I behaved and was dressed. This was a good start. I felt the vermilion gate of her heart begin to creak open.

I looked down and peeked at my card, then discarded it. I wouldn't make a call, for now. The other men were brandishing their cards, raising them high and then flinging them down, occasionally stamping their feet. As the game ended some shouted and yelled, others sat numb, apparently dumbstruck, not daring to believe the evidence before their eyes. This was the cruellest kind of gambling: the moment when the bayonet tip turned red and all mercy was cast aside, leaving no room for reason, only greed and impulsive urges. A collective madness seemed to overcome them. It was only me who laid down my cards one by one.

My aim was to stake a small amount – five yuan – every round and stick at that. Every now and then I looked at her, and sometimes our eyes met. After a while, we couldn't tear our eyes away from each other. She seemed as obsessed with me as I was with her. I had not even lost a tenth of my money. But I was more than ninety percent certain that I could pull her.

When it was her break time and the other dealer took over, I rapped the table, picked up my money and went out to sit on the edge of the well for a smoke. Not long after, she came out too. I shuffled up and made space for her. We went through the motions: raised a hand in greeting, smiled at one another and each asked how the other was doing. We started to chat. Her voice was hoarse, and she swayed back and forth as she sat. Whenever the conversation was about to dry up and it looked like we would have to part, I thought of something new to talk about. I couldn't bear us to become strangers again. By the end we were chatting freely, like kids who'd learned to ride a bicycle and didn't need anyone to hold the back seat any more.

She crouched on the ground and looked up at me respect-fully. 'You girls . . .' I said, in no hurry to broach the intimacy of the singular 'you'. I would take my time: I wanted to be abso-lutely sure before I made my move. 'You girls . . .'

'You've spent the whole time saying "you girls" this and "you girls" that . . . Give it a break!' she spat at me, before getting to her feet and stalking away. I jumped up too and watched her disappear through the big door into the hotel lobby.

I cringed with embarrassment at the idea that someone might have seen us. I shook my head. It was hard to imagine that I had gone from seeing her for the first time, to feeling sure I'd get her, to then losing her in such a short period.

Around ten minutes later, I followed her in dejectedly. She was standing in a cluster of people, and I could see why she was angry. She wasn't from around here, and there was something about her that seemed more refined than the locals. Yet here she was, accepting orders. She stood in a line with three or four other girls, ramrod straight, neck extended, head tilted to one side, numbering off as if on parade. At a gesture from the supervisor, they all bowed together and chorused: 'Welcome to our guests!'

'Louder,' said the supervisor.

'Welcome to our guests!' they shouted. Their practice over, they marched off to the dining room and sat down in an orderly fashion.

It must have been approaching the busiest time for the waitresses, and they had to have their dinner first. The supervisor, a girl with a moustache whom I later discovered was the owner's daughter, put her elbows on the table and picked up her chopsticks, looking as if she was about to say something to them. They acted attentive, but she simply pointed her chopsticks in the air and said nothing. She put a dried-up morsel of beef in her mouth and chewed it to a mush. It reminded me of a horse, silently munching on its night-time hay. The girls would have to wait for any word from her.

Dinner over, the girls changed into tight qipao dresses and patrolled between the packed dining-room tables. They were at the beck and call of everyone, including old guys who sat there massaging the soles of the girls' feet with their fingers, many of them having a good sniff while they were at it. The girls brought batch after batch of customers into the dining room, pulling out the chairs for them to sit down, pouring tea, bringing out menus and pens, waiting for them to leaf through the menu at a leisurely pace, bringing more tea, pouring wine. The smiles were fixed to their faces like masks. Their qipaos were the garish red of a horror movie. They were all would-be actresses and they'd ended up selling their labour like peasants, selling their beauty by the kilo, sweating as they marketed their talent over and over again.

Even at the beginning of their shift, they couldn't stifle their yawns. They were a good-looking bunch, taller than average and well-nourished, but each one had some obvious flaw. And that was why they'd ended up in this dump. Like a tangerine with a spot of mould, flung out of the basket. These girls had been thrown out of the ballet corps, and now here they were in these bleak city outskirts, their beauty faded like grubby peacocks.

It was the white-skinned one I was in love with, with all her flaws. I couldn't bear the others' thinning hair, fat fingers and sagging buttocks, but her flat chest was an essential part of her, not to be added to or changed. I found them heartbreaking, those lonely nipples of hers concealed inside her padded bra. Then there was her snub nose, her small straight teeth and her occasional coarse laugh, her languid expression, those few grey hairs visible behind her ears, the smoking cigarette she held between her fingers, and her worldly air. As she walked earnestly back and forth, I thought that she looked like a young girl dressing up as a grown woman. Everything made my heart feel as if it was being drenched with rain. Distress, pity and a yearning to protect her: these were feelings I hadn't experienced for many years. Yet now they were surging through me and had found a home in this woman and her beautiful flaws. I guessed she came from an unhappy family background, and that things were not going to get much better for her. I wanted to go up to her and shout: This is what I love about you!

She was climbing wearily up the stairs to the second floor. I stood in her way, my eyes reddening. 'Please stop doing that stuff.'

'What?'

'I said, I'm begging you. Please stop doing that.'

'What's it got to do with you?' She pushed my arm aside once more.

'You'll be tired tomorrow, and the next day,' I yelled at her retreating back. 'And every day!'

'What am I supposed to do?'

'Leave!'

That night we slept together. To start with, she switched off the light. She didn't want it shining on her torso. But as I sucked greedily on those two lonely nipples, I told her that I liked everything about her, especially her pebble-smooth body.

Later, she took over and rode me, and slapped me in the face. 'Call me a slut, quick!'

'What?'

'I'm ordering you, call me a slut!'

'Slut!'

'Again!'

'Slut, slut, you little slut!'

She quickly came to orgasm then flung herself down on me, weeping. I held her trembling body in my arms, feeling protective.

'I really like crying. I don't enjoy it if I don't,' she said. That made me think she'd done it with lots of men here. As I imagined them rolling back their dark foreskins and sticking their ugly penises into her sacred sex organ, soft, white and smooth as a steamed bun, I felt as if a knife was twisting in my gut.

The next morning I set off alone to wait for the bus. Forty minutes later, when I'd all but given up hope, she came running.

We got in the bus and left.

16

At an offerings table on top of a mountain, she spread her arms wide, took a deep breath of the moist air that rose from the dark forests, shut her eyes and yelled: 'My name's Hook-Pinch!'

'What?'

'I said, my name's Hook-Pinch!'

That shout told me everything I needed to know about how much it meant to her to be reclaiming her freedom. It felt like a ceremony. She was elated at finally ridding herself of the servitude of work, she revelled in this liberation. I knew why she was doing it. It was like when the joke's over but everyone pretends they're still enjoying it. The pleasure of telling the hotel owner that she didn't want the deposit back on her room – 'Don't bother, I don't want it, you all spend it . . .' The satisfaction of turning on her heel and stalking out. All that was in the past. Now she was trying to recapture the high of that feeling. Up the mountain, there was no one else around. She lay down and spread her legs, and we did it right there, in the dappled shade of the trees. We felt drowsy afterwards, and fell sound asleep. The truth is, I couldn't tell you how many times we had sex during those heady early days.

Sleeping meant we could put off having to face reality, but things weren't going to be any better when we woke up; the harmony between humans and nature was coming to an end with the fading of the light. Great patches of darkness fell on us from the blue sky, a curtain quietly, inexorably dropping. The night was taking over. We were being driven away by the mountains and the earth: we could hear it. By now we were exhausted, our mouths tasted foul, our throats were parched, and the sight of the endless road ahead was enough to plunge us into despair. We couldn't even muster the energy to end it all.

I'm a con man, I thought as I looked at her. When I said to her: 'I'll give you your freedom,' what I meant was: You give me your body. And she had done that, but I hadn't given her a fine new life that was happy and fulfilled. In my impotence, I had made freedom depressing for her. She must be bitterly disappointed, I thought. By now, she must understand that it wasn't that she'd left of her own accord, it was that the hotel didn't need her any more. She must be upset that she hadn't taken it seriously enough.

Hook-Pinch put on her clothes, pulled down her sleeves over her hands and hunched her shoulders to keep warm. Then she set off without so much as a word to me. We covered at least three or four li that way, the crunching of the gravel under our feet the only sound. I strained my ears, anxious not to miss anything if she spoke. Then, when we were almost down the mountain, she said in a flat voice: 'Burn it.'

'What?'

'Burn the mountain.'

'How do we do that?'

'Are you going to burn the mountain or not?'

I stopped talking, just gathered some dried leaves and pine cones in my hat and pulled twigs off the dark branches, lit them and watched the smoke billow up. We coughed and spluttered, our eyes streamed, but after much effort we succeeded in getting the flames going. Although I had assumed she would want to hang around a bit longer, she broke into a mad run and dragged me away.

'You really made a fire, you idiot, you really made a fire!' she gasped. We ran until we were overcome by thirst, as if we had swallowed a handful of salt. When we got down to the tarmac road, smoke was billowing from the dense pinewoods on the steep mountainside, and we heard shouts and cries and the sound of running feet. She shrieked with laughter. But then as we got on a passing minibus her face fell again, like a grille snapping down when the ticket vendor goes off duty. She started mindlessly banging the headrest of the seat in front.

My original plan had been to take the minibus as far as the county town, but midway there she got off, just like that, so I had to jump down after her. We grabbed something to eat, then looked for a place to stay the night. From nine o'clock that evening, we were stuck there in a strange room. Condensation dripped from the corridor ceiling every few seconds, and we winced at the sound even though we knew it was coming. There was nothing to do except have sex again. We rolled around like two filthy labourers, drenched in sweat. Both of us felt that it was meaningless: an obligation rather than a pleasure. Finally, she pushed me off. That annoyed me. I felt that she had no respect for my needs, even though I hadn't wanted to carry on. I said nothing. She sat cross-legged on the table, then she opened the window. Outside, a street lamp glowed dull yellow and the wind ruffled the white shirt she'd thrown on. She smoked continuously, tapping the ash into a tea mug. Cars drove along the road like ghosts, one every few minutes.

'I don't regret it,' she said.

'Things will get better,' I told her, quietly.

'What's your name?'

'Squint.'

'I'm Hook-Pinch. And I love you.'

'Me too.'

In the morning when I woke up, the door was ajar. The birds were chirping happily, and I could hear ducks quacking some-where in the distance. She had left the impression of her body on the bed, along with a few items of clothing. But she and her bag were gone.

I went to the window. Outside, some dew-soaked bamboo mats lay on the ground, and water gurgled down the guttering. I was furious that she had betrayed me so soon. A few minutes later, though, she pushed open the door with her shoulder and came in, carrying a plastic bag of fried breadsticks, steamed baozi buns and cartons of soya milk.

'Where did you get to? I was sick with worry.' I rushed to her, shouting, frantic. That was the moment I realised I did not want to lose her, not for a single moment.

She stood there, the plastic bag dripping with water in one hand, reaching out to ruffle my hair with the other.

'You got me really worried,' I repeated.

'What about?'

I didn't have the nerve to say I was worried in case she'd been raped, even gang-raped and then killed, and her body dumped in a culvert. I don't know why my imagination was running away with me. 'You were on your own,' I said. She seemed to like that, and planted smacking kisses on my forehead.

She decided that we would take a coach to the provincial capital. We walked along a section of cement road, tarmac road, and a dirt track, then went into a large compound as big as a football ground, where artemisia grew waist-high along the walls. Tyre tracks led in and out, and crates of goods were piled high on every spare inch of ground, some of them covered with dark blue tarpaulin. Hook-Pinch pressed some numbers on her phone and announced into the speaker: 'I'm here.'

A short fat girl ran out of a second-floor apartment and clattered down the stairs. She and Hook-Pinch threw their arms around each other and hugged, then inspected each other closely for any changes. I'd never seen an uglier girl: her face looked as if it had been pickled, her nose was peeling, she had no neck to speak of, and the flesh of her elephantine legs wobbled with every movement she made. I don't know how Hook-Pinch could bear to look at her. But there they were, gazing at each other and kissing.

Around us, work proceeded at a leisurely pace, with frequent breaks. Then, at half past ten, the workers took off their gloves and clustered together for a natter. They soon reckoned that it was time for lunch and a game of cards. Pickle-Face took us for a wander around the upstairs walkways, over sheet-iron floor-ing covered with sand. She told us that she had an elder brother who worked in the Procuratorate. When he'd still been living at home, there was a girl he'd fancied but he'd never told her how he felt, and one day the mother turned up out of the blue with the girl in tow. He brought them home even though he knew it was hopeless. The girl's family was so poor that they only had an old black-and-white TV with coloured cellophane stuck all over it and an enormous old-fashioned wireless set covered in a cloth. Still, he treated their visit as an honour. He followed them around, listening as the mother did her best to explain away their reduced circumstances, not that there was any need to. Their dignity showed in how they dressed: the girl had on a simple skirt. Her mother, by contrast, wore a red velour jumpsuit, the one stylish garment they had between the two of them. This was complemented by black low-heeled shoes, while her hair was permed like the soprano Guan Mucun.

It was obvious why they had come, although neither could bring themselves to put it into words. Finally the older woman spotted the pile of sand in one corner of the corridor. She grabbed a shovel and began to move it, roughly ordering her daughter: 'Why are you standing there like a lemon? Get a dustpan!' Pickle-Face's brother tried to wrest the shovel off his mother, but she was working like an ox and could not be stopped.

'I can't bear to look at it,' she said. She was as stubborn and happy as a peasant who spots a fresh pile of cow dung deposited at the roadside. The brother watched as the goddess of his heart flushed scarlet, then went down the stairs and found a dustpan coated in dust. He said sarcastically, angrily, to the mother: 'You'll never finish clearing up the rubbish, there's too much.' But she retorted: 'Of course I'll finish it.' The incident was enough to put an end to anything there might have been between him and the girl.

Pickle-Face had no particular reason for telling the story – she wasn't sneering at them or hinting anything, she just wanted to please Hook-Pinch. She thought it was hilarious. But we didn't. I felt even more uncomfortable than before. I even hesitated before I sat down on the sofa. Although I felt she could have issued a clear invitation, a 'Please sit down', the two girls were completely engrossed in each other. So I authorised myself to sit down, and stared blankly at the TV screen.

They rushed in and out of the room like the wind, until Hook-Pinch knocked over a porcelain vase as tall as herself on her way out. Pickle-Face looked terrified. It was obvious from the quality of the porcelain that the vase must have been worth well over a hundred thousand yuan. But then Pickle-Face said it was only the crash that had scared her, and I believed her. The two of them carefully picked it up off the carpet and propped it up again. They carried on making a racket as if the accident had never happened.

I went for a wander around the shopping mall. There was money everywhere and you could tell at a glance where the people coming towards you were carrying theirs. It didn't take an idiot to work out that they each had at least ten thousand yuan on them. One group of businessmen had seven or eight bundles of banknotes laid out on top of a cigarette carton as they huddled together playing cards. I didn't dare snatch the money, not because it would have been difficult – far from it, in fact – but because I was scared of the consequences if I got caught: I would lose Hook-Pinch. Just think about it: I was right, wasn't I? Later on, when we were vagrants, and I took up as a thief again so we had a bit of money to live on, and hid it from Hook-Pinch, I felt how tragic it was that that sense of responsibility was making me clumsy. I was no longer footloose and fancy-free, I had a woman. I used to be decisive and quick-witted; now I was hesitant. Sometimes I followed a man for more than a quarter of an hour and still I couldn't bring myself to grab the leather wallet – we called them 'skins' – that was practically sticking out of his pocket. Sometimes, before I left, I would tell Hook-Pinch: 'If I'm not back by the time we agreed, don't stick around for me.'

'Haven't you got a mobile?' she asked.

But I stuck to my line. What I planned to do when the cops got me was hand her back to her family, or to another man. A better man than I was.

It seemed like we could stay in the friend's compound as long as we wanted. The workers and servants were very friendly, and we soon had our feet on the tea table. At some point, the workers, tools in hand, streamed off to their places like ants emerging from a hole in the ground, and began their labours. That was when she – Pickle-Face, that is – suddenly looked flustered and gave Hook-Pinch a shove, saying: 'You two better go.' We were being forcibly ejected, and it felt as rude as if they'd thrown us out while we were having a shower or on the toilet.

She hurried us to the gate just as an Audi drew in. A middle-aged man sat in the passenger seat, a smug, supercilious look on his face. He peered at us as if we were aliens, which made us feel wretched. Clearly we'd been there on borrowed time.

Before we left, Pickle-Face gave Hook-Pinch five thousand yuan. As we said our goodbyes and walked away from the compound, Hook-Pinch began to tell me a story about how she and Pickle-Face had once bunked off school together and looked up the old fortune teller: they wanted some truly diabolical-sounding names because they planned to go off travelling. The fortune teller leafed through an old almanac, closed his eyes, and poked his finger at the words that would become her new name: Hook-Pinch.

17

We went west. 'You'll know how far to go,' Qu the fortune teller had said. I'd paid him with a fifty-yuan note and he'd given me forty in change. Then, of course, I'd picked his pocket for another hundred, which meant he'd really given me ninety for telling my fortune. I figured he'd done a proper job, because I got his predictions before I settled up with him. I had a gut feeling that everything was going to be OK, and Hook-Pinch and I got off the bus in a small township called Liu'an and found a room to rent.

Every day I went out buoyed up with enthusiasm. I took it for granted that I had only to push open the door of an office and the man would get up out of his swivel chair and greet me with a 'Fine, come and do it to me.' Then, as evening drew in, I'd trail wretchedly back to our rented room with the money and food I'd nicked, which I would tell her I'd bought.

Sometimes I'd be afraid of getting back too early and I'd sit on a grassy bank, staring into space. The tarmac road, as ink-black as a bottomless pool, unfurled before my eyes until it reached the horizon, and the cars sped past, growing smaller as they receded. Concrete chimneys of enormous girth reared up at the edge of the road, vomiting one last puff of smoke. Once, a man in uniform came up to me and told me: 'Idleness is the root of all evil.' Looking portentous, he snorted out a lengthy stream of smoke, then patted me on the shoulder and left.

I was well aware of the truth of his statement. It wasn't that I didn't want to change, it was just that I was dragged down by an immense physical inertia. I was dead to the world, as my father used to put it.

Hook-Pinch was always complaining of headaches. The way she slept all day, then watched all those films, it wasn't surprising she had headaches. Soon, time became meaningless to us. First we forgot which month it was, then which day of the week – though sometimes Hook-Pinch could tell that from the TV schedules – until eventually our only indicator of time and date was whether it was light or dark outside. It was as if we were lying in a small boat, being tossed on an endless ocean. Sometimes we didn't say a word all day. Other times we couldn't be bothered to eat. We spent our days dreaming up a concentrated nutrition pill that would mean we were never hungry again. Often I lay on the lawn, almost weeping that my life consisted of nothing more than eating and drinking, pissing and crapping. I felt like I'd been reduced to a mere animal. But then I gave it some more thought and figured that it had nothing to do with that. Human beings were animals by their very nature. Animals were concerned about eating and mating, so obviously human beings were too. But surely we had other, more profound desires? I thought and thought until suddenly I felt a surge of excitement. I would make a serious effort to write down all these ideas.

My thought process went as follows: Every living creature, no matter whether a pig, a rat or a human being, is the unique result of millions of years of tenacious reproduction. The process is fraught with danger, the link can be broken at any moment by famine, disease, war, the political system, even yeast spores in the vagina. All living creatures carry with them a millennial inheritance – their family, their history – and are duty-bound to carry this forward. This being the case, what are we, our ancestors and ourselves, doing it for? Or, put another way, what are we waiting for?

We must have a mission; why else would we tolerate this long, boring wait? Or rather, there must be a conclusion, a climax that makes the long and hugely costly process worthwhile. Surely our lives are more than a repeated cycle of finding ourselves something to eat, then mating and dying, no better than male cicadas? So this great, resplendent mission that we accept so cheerfully, what exactly is it? I spent a whole day gazing up at the blue sky. I figured that in bygone times, there must have been plenty of people doing the same thing. I almost expected a four-horse chariot to come leaping out of the firmament at any moment. My rambling thoughts were meaningless, but wasn't every damned thing meaningless?

Hook-Pinch and I carried on living like this, making something to eat and drink when we felt the need to. As they say about water, 'When it's full to the brim, it must overflow.' Sperm is no different from water, so we had sex constantly, though we often fell asleep, both of us, right in the middle of it. We started to fight tooth and nail to while away the time, much like bullies banged up in prison. Sometimes we were vicious to each other in the spirit of professionalism, as you might say. Finally, one day she began to pace back and forth, hurling anything within reach to the floor, shrieking like a madwoman: 'Enough! I've had enough, dammit!' as if those objects and not me were the source of her anguish. It caused me more distress than if she had yelled at me directly. I've done my best, I thought. I looked up, mortified, and stared after her as she went into the bedroom. I expected her to shove her clothes into her case and slam out of the house. If she did that, it couldn't be helped. That was what I thought. Instead, she came out of the room, and enunciated slowly and clearly: 'We've got to find something to do.' I felt mortified. After a bit, she said to me, sounding like a primary teacher admonishing a child, almost taking me by the hand: 'You do know that, don't you?'

'Yes.'

'What do you know?'

'We've got to find something to do.'

'And? Any luck?'

'No, I'm still looking.'

'Where? You've been at it for ages, what's up?' I looked down again and heard: 'We're almost out of money.'

'I know.'

'You know everything, but do you know what we'll do when we run out of money?

'I'm thinking.'

'We've got to get hold of some money.'

'Right, get hold of some money,' I repeated and spread my hands as if to say: OK, but you tell me how!

'You've got to put your mind to it. It doesn't matter how, but we've got to do it. We can't just rot away here till we die.'

'It's nice here.'

'You're saying it's nice?'

'There must be a way.'

'What way? You tell me.'

I sat up straight, looked her in the eye and said calmly: 'You want it in dribs and drabs, or do we go for the big one?'

'What do you mean?'

'Dribs and drabs means I carry on nicking small stuff every day. Or we go in for armed robbery.'

I thought she'd be appalled. After all, we were such different people that we were never going to agree on a strategy. And she did look taken aback. She digested what I'd said, although she must have suspected I'd been thieving. Now, she had to acknowledge that the man she'd shared bed and board with was a pickpocket. When she opened her mouth again, it was to say very quietly: 'Let me say something.'

'That's what I'm doing.' It was a relief to be open and upfront, but it also risked making me cocky.

'OK,' she said, kneeling down to smooth out the bed sheet then looking up at me again. 'Will we have to use a knife?'

'Maybe not, but we have to use something.'

My only experience of robbery until that point had been as a lookout. On one occasion, my mates had been gone for ages, and I was still on guard outside the door. I only found out the thing was finished when the victim staggered out, pressing his hand to his wound.

'Let's start,' said Hook-Pinch.

'Start what?'

'Robbing people.'

'What do you mean, start?'

'I mean, let's start now.'

I tried to put a dampener on her excitement, but for the whole of the afternoon she was fizzing, wanting to get going straight away. If she wasn't clasping her hands, pressing her index fingers together and taking aim at me, her head cocked on one side, she was holding a bottle of mineral water to my throat pretending it was a knife, or donning sunglasses, hooking her thumbs into the front of her jeans, and looking at herself in the mirror. She made it all into a game, one that was really getting her going. I knew that our game might lead to bloodshed, that it could rip human relationships to shreds. As a petty thief, you could hang on to a last shred of gentleness. Robbery, however, robbed people not just of their property but also of their dignity. So I began to regret ever having raised the idea. To tell the truth, it was she who forced me into it. I had to salvage a bit of self-respect. People often do things they would never otherwise consider for the sake of saving face, and I was no different. She obviously didn't realise that as we were first figuring out how to make some money.

The Law, that implacable merchant, was waiting around the corner to mete out justice. Up until now, I'd been free to gauge the risks and choose what I wanted to do. The reason I liked thieving was that you could steal as much as ten thousand yuan, and even if you were caught you only got a maximum of three years. But the penalty for armed robbery, no matter how small the amount, was always at least three years. And if the victim happened to struggle and you used your knife, well, then it was ten or twenty years. 'If we're going to play, then it's for big stakes,' she said.

I looked at her and thought: It's our lives we're playing with. But what I said was: 'Fine.' I was busy calculating:

1. The minimum penalty for robbery was three years.
2. I did not want to serve upwards of three years.
Conclusion: we had to steer clear of the Law.

There were only a few ways to do that, though. For instance, by committing the crime at night, leaving no footprints, scrupulously removing all evidence linking you to the victim, avoiding being seen at all costs. These were all things to consider. And Hook-Pinch added more extreme steps we might take: if need be, we'd blind the victim, make sure they had no memory of the attack, even kill them and dispose of the body. But no modus operandi was foolproof. Our opponents – who had at their disposal the all-powerful apparatus of the state, all its powers, its intelligence and communications networks – would surely get us once they put their mind to it.

There was another way, said Hook-Pinch. We could buy off the police. But my answer was that if she had the resources to do that, then why would we need to commit armed robberies in the first place? Something was going through my mind, and it was this: the only leeway we had was in our choice of victim. I wanted victims who wouldn't fight back, wouldn't make a noise, and who would want to cover up the crime, just as we did.

Hook-Pinch couldn't see that happening. I kept saying that it was theoretically possible, and quite feasible too. I was thinking the whole thing through, because we could only succeed if we worked it out every step of the way. In fact, we could reproduce it in the future. Once someone created a model, others would follow. But she was not interested. She faced up to her imaginary enemy, a rolled-up magazine – the knife – in one hand and in the other a mobile phone – the hammer. 'When are we going to start?' she demanded. 'We just need the threat of a knife, we say if he dares to go to the police, we'll stab him.' I looked at her. As the one in charge here, I had a responsibility to take control of the situation.

'Let me demonstrate something,' I said. 'Suppose you've ripped someone off.'

'OK.'

'Have you committed a crime?'

'Of course I have.'

'Are you worried you'll get arrested?'

'Yes.'

'Right, now suppose you're being blackmailed. Have you committed a crime?'

She thought this was an intelligence test, and started messing around: 'Yes . . . no . . . yes . . .' until I prompted her that the answer was no. 'No,' she said.

'Are you worried you'll get arrested?'

'No.'

'But you're afraid the police will find out about it.'

'Why?'

'Because if the police find out, then your family will find out too.'

'What's that got to do with anything?'

'You're going with prostitutes.'

'Oh.'

'Would you report it to the police?'

'No.'

'That's why we need someone who's a bit older and married, but not too old – in his fifties, perhaps – and so thick-skinned that he doesn't give a damn about anything. He can even be sixty. A sixty-year-old man is going to be scared to death of having his reputation destroyed.'

'Uh-huh.'

'It's crucial that we find a victim who has a bit of money and appears to have a regular family life. It's easy enough to tell one of them from a man on his own, once you look closely. He needs to be in a steady job, but also weak and keen to keep out of trouble.'

'What you're saying is, you're going out with the knife, not me.'

'Yup.'

'You want me to be the honeytrap?'

'Yup.'

'Fine.'

'That'll make it a bit safer for us.'

Towards evening, we walked into the market. The traders were yawning their heads off by then. They'd been standing there since early morning, some since daybreak. They were run down after playing cat and mouse with by-law enforcement officers the whole day and were planning to stick it out for no more than another twenty minutes or so. The light was dim inside the market, and we nicked lipstick, high-heeled shoes, a purse, face masks, gloves, baijiu spirit and a hammer as easily as if we were invisible. Hook-Pinch was desperate for a small sharp fruit knife, but I stopped her. One, the blade looked like it was going to snap, and two, stealing it would just be showing off.

We wandered around the stalls and discovered that most were selling the same brands of men's outfits and women's skirts, and that was mainly what the locals wore, so we bought an outfit each. Once we had those on, we felt we looked like locals ourselves. We bought a bit of food and took it back to our room. I put a condom into the purse and said: 'Now you're a proper working girl. Do you know how to do it?'

'No.'

'Once we've fixed on our target, you brush up against him and say: "You want it, mister?"'

'Huh.'

'No, in fact, better say: "Mister, you want something to keep you in good health?"'

I remembered those two full breasts resting on top of my head as the salon woman scraped the shampoo suds out of my hair with her sharp nails. She had been nothing special to look at, but my penis had stood to attention all the same. 'Mister, you want something to keep you in good health?' she had asked casually.

I swallowed. 'What do you mean?'

'Well, there's Thai-style, Hong Kong-style, the full service, all different prices.'

'What's the full service?'

'You know what I mean!'

Hongliang here would have said the same: You know what I mean! I told Hook-Pinch: 'So long as the man stops, that means you've hooked him. And a man who's hooked isn't thinking straight, he goes red in the face and his breathing gets heavy, and he'll follow you like a dumb donkey.' We'd had plenty to drink that night and I turned maudlin. 'There's no one in this world who's going to help us except ourselves. We've got to depend on each other.'

'Uh-huh.' She nodded gravely.

'We must never betray each other.'

She grunted again.
'Do you love me?'
'Yes.'
'Are you ready?'
'I'm ready.'

18

We messed around for ages. I had this niggling feeling that there was still something we hadn't prepared properly, or that we hadn't prepared anything properly. We became increasingly pissed off with ourselves as the days dragged by and we had nothing to show for it, until finally we made our move. The evenings rewarded people who'd worked themselves to exhaustion by day, but they were less kind to those who couldn't make up their minds what they wanted. Finally, Hook-Pinch couldn't bear it any more. She put on her high heels and tottered out of the room without a backward glance. I knew as I followed her that there was no going back.

'You know we've only got a hundred yuan left?' she said.

'I know.'

'If we don't get to work soon, we'll starve.'

'Then let's get to work.'

The street lamps were on by now, though it was still very warm. We sweated profusely as we walked along. The paving stones were laid in a zigzag pattern. If you didn't step right in the middle of each one, dirty water splashed up from underneath. It had not rained for ages, so this water must have been the slops that townsfolk tipped out of their houses. I was walking five metres behind Hook-Pinch, watching as she eyed up various men, choosing her prey with care. She was making sure to display her charms. There was one man in a mustard-coloured shirt, hands stuck in his pockets, leaning against the wall, who stared as she went by. The street lights were dim, but I saw him devour her with his eyes. He looked idiotic. He obviously thought he'd hit the jackpot, and was imagining himself boasting to his mates afterwards. She slowed. His face lit up in a foolish smile. He must have decided she was going to ask the way, so he stood up straighter and tried to look like he was pleased to help out a young lady. She reached out with her left arm, the way you'd move an oar. In another moment, it would touch his arm or his belly. This was the bit we'd planned: 'If it looks like a done deal, I'll go straight for his prick and make it stiff,' she'd said. At that instant, I caught up with her, put my arm around her and marched her away. She struggled furiously.

'Let's go,' I said.

'What are you doing?'

'Please! Let's go!' I begged her. I had seen the name of a big local factory sewn on the left breast of his shirt.

The man sighed regretfully, looked as if he was about to say something, but then he appeared to think better of it and simply whistled. 'I had him,' she said in exasperation.

'It just occurred to me that it's got to be someone we're sure is from out of town, right?'

'Is there a difference?'

'If he's a local, we're screwed.'

'You're such a scaredy-cat. If you're so scared, let's just forget it.'

'We just need to be sure. Then nothing can go wrong.'

'I'm telling you, you'll ruin it with your "making sure" about everything. You know that the longer you wait, the more things go wrong, don't you? We'll find an alleyway at night and get hold of someone and do it. Nothing's going to happen! Don't make things so complicated.'

'But if the man's only got a few yuan on him, it's not worth doing it, is it? How do you know how much that man had on him?'

'It was obvious he had money.'

'What I'm saying is, how could you tell exactly how much money he had on him?'

We went back and forth for a while, but we weren't arguing about anything in particular except which of us was going to be in control of our victim. Hook-Pinch got so upset that she started yelling, and then burst into a storm of tears. I was about to walk away, when she said miserably: 'You do love me, don't you? So you should do what I say.'

A crowd of curious onlookers had gathered around us by now, and I quickly hustled her away and back to our room. We lay on the bed as far apart as possible. I hoped my silence would make my message clear: I don't like the way you are now, Hook-Pinch.

Eventually she sat up, scratched my collarbone a few times and whispered: 'I'll do what you say.'

I said nothing.

'Please don't go out stealing any more,' she said.

She sounded so genuine, coaxing me like I was a child, alternately begging and wheedling, testing how I'd react. I remembered that during my time in jail, the others would look down on me for being a pickpocket. They figured that to be a real man, you had to rob and kill. I pushed her off me at that point, but she kept coming back with her teasing. Finally I grabbed her hair and held her down and pushed her face against the wall and fucked her from behind, like she was an animal, a rabbit or a frog, or drunk.

The next day, around midday, I kissed her forehead and headed out to the distribution centre in Liu'an. The centre covered twenty thousand square metres, and the ground was cracked and stained with oil from overloaded lorries driving over it. I felt dizzy from the glare of the sun. There were sheds everywhere. Each had aluminium windows and cream-painted doors with the names of various towns pasted on them. It seemed there wasn't anywhere they didn't distribute their goods; I spotted the names of Pingdingshan, Taiyuan, Tai'an, Jining, Xuzhou . . .

A big sheet of paper stuck to one wall was covered in little red flags, and there was a reddish-brown office table covered in files with sticky labels, an ashtray and name-cards scattered all over. A lorry rolled up, completely empty, then another a minute later. They came to a halt, puffing out clouds of exhaust fumes. The lorry windows were coated in dust, the driver's cabs full of instant noodle cartons, thermoses, ashtrays, toothbrushes black with dirt, toothpaste tubes squeezed flat, shiny black gloves, yellowing magazines and the *Highways Atlas*, the driver's cushion either hand-woven or made of linen, everything bright and glittering. The drivers must have been driving into the sun: sweat dripped from their foreheads and poured down their chests; you only had to open the cab door for their stink to hit you. They got down from their cabs and yawned, chewing with nothing in their mouths, looking bored out of their minds. The drivers drove days and nights at a stretch, and this was their chance to take a break. They chatted among themselves, though it was obvious that there were a few they steered clear of, either because they didn't understand their accents or thought they were suspicious in some way.

After they had registered, they went to the Chengdu Snack Café for something to eat or drink, or they went to stretch their legs, coming back when they were good and ready and the office had arranged their next dispatch. Then, like donkeys, they were off on the road again. Almost all of them wore bumbags, each holding a bundle of notes. As soon as they got out of their lorries, they knew there was nothing to entertain them here. The place was deserted. Hook-Pinch would be a gentle rain falling on them, assuaging their thirst. She would be their mother. Giving them life, then taking it away. I reckoned that there were no easier targets than these sons of the road.

When I got back, Hook-Pinch was outlining her lips in red lipstick. It reminded me of lessons at school, when we had to practise writing by tracing the characters in copybooks. That was another life, back when I was getting an honest education and wrote well.

When she'd finished, she pressed her lips together a few times. Just the line around her lips turned her into a stranger. She looked like a proper hooker, as if she'd been born to do it.

'Shall we get on with it then?' she asked.

'Sure, but first you have something to eat,' I said.

'I don't want anything.'

By this time the sun was going down, though the earth gave off as much heat as before as we walked towards the distribution centre.

She leaned against one side of the wide entrance gate. Hook-Pinch was wearing the skirt we had bought and, carrying the handbag, and she stood with one leg slightly raised, a cigarette between those scarlet lips. Inside the gate, the security office was chained and padlocked. I sat on the kerb opposite, passing the time of day with a fortune teller. Although there were plenty of drivers around, they seemed wary of hookers. Sure, they'd slow down and eye her up, but then they seemed to lose their nerve and drove on past. That happened two or three times. They were probably drivers from the same fleet and looked like workers knocking off their shift, eating out of food containers and getting an eyeful of Hook-Pinch as an added bonus. She was doing her best to offer them what they wanted, yet they were obviously not serious.

'Want a service?'

'What service?'

'Ordinary, special . . .'

'What's the ordinary?'

'A quick handjob.'

'And the special?'

'You know what a special means.'

'I don't know, you tell me!'

'You know perfectly well, why are you asking me?'

'I really don't, you tell me.'

'A fuck.'

'A fuck!' Now they'd got her to say it, they laughed and took the piss out of her accent. 'A fuck!'

Hook-Pinch was furious and bent down to pick up a stone. The men thundered away like a herd of rhinos. I waved at her and she shot me an angry glance, her chest heaving. 'Come back,' I shouted, but she was determined to snag at least one. Finally, a burly man turned up, his lunch box in his hand, and stopped in front of her without saying a word. He was wearing greenish khaki trousers: he might once have been a soldier, or could still have been in the special forces. Although I waved frantically at Hook-Pinch, she ignored me. She began to walk away and he followed, along the east side perimeter wall of the distribution centre and onto a narrow concrete road. He looked perfectly calm, like he was escorting a prisoner. They got to the back wall. I followed, and at the end of the concrete road looked around the corner. I saw he was supporting himself with one hand against the wall, forcing Hook-Pinch backwards, while with his other giant paw he had pulled up her skirt and was gripping her buttocks. Behind them there was a piece of waste ground. I got an erection. At the same time, I felt guilty because I felt like I was using her. Most of all, I was gripped by a fear that rooted me to the spot. When she began to stamp her stiletto heels, I finally slipped along the track after them. Remember, I kept telling myself, you've got to act like you're in charge. You're doing the right thing.

I pressed my left fist against my mouth and gave a cough. The burly man pulled his head back from Hook-Pinch's shoulder, which he had been licking enthusiastically, leaving her ear covered with spittle. He looked over at me coolly. His podgy face was flushed, his head gigantic and his nostrils huge. For some reason, I had a fantasy of red ants crawling in and out of those deep recesses. Judging by the gingery whiskers that framed his lips, he must have been from the far west of China. He sneered at me when he realised why I was there, gave Hook-Pinch a hard shove that caused her to crumple to the floor, and grabbed my arm. He did not put much force behind it but still managed to nearly fracture my upper arm. I yelled in pain and dropped the hammer.

'What did you just say?' he demanded.

'You're messing with my woman,' I recited mechanically.

'She was the one who came on to me.'

I pursed my lips, embarrassed. He was in control of what I did next, I thought. 'I've seen more stuff like this than you've had hot dinners, kid,' he went on. I heaved a sigh of relief at that. He hadn't hit me: that was good news at least. There was no real danger. My head sank lower as I heard him reprimand me: 'If you're going to do it, at least make a proper job of it.'

I retorted silently: You're really no different from me. I waited for him to tell me to get lost, so that Hook-Pinch and I could make our getaway. But a little while later I heard him do up his belt, calmly pick up his lunch box from the ground and disappear, cursing and swearing under his breath. I watched him. It all felt unreal.

'Let's go! This way,' I said.

'To hell with that,' my beloved partner-in-crime replied. 'Why didn't you knock him out with the hammer? What was all that coughing about?'

'I thought we just wanted his money?'

'To hell with his money!'

And then she lost it. All I could do was hang on to the hammer like grim death and beg her to calm down. But she was possessed, yelling at me: 'Gimme that! I'm hungry, get it?' And before I had time to say anything, she flung herself at me again. 'I'm hungry.'

I was hungry too, though that was no reason to throw caution to the wind, was it? She had been wrong from the get-go, and that meant that we were no longer in a position to negotiate with the law. I slowed right down, thinking to myself: Fine, if I can't keep you under control then so be it. We were just two bits of floating duckweed: fate had brought us together, and fate had decreed that we would part. After all, if I hadn't stolen that money on the minibus, if I hadn't got off at Xinxing because I was afraid of being discovered, if I hadn't bought those sunglasses after I got off the minibus, we would never have crossed paths. It might not be today that we would go our separate ways, but all good things came to an end eventually. I looked at the grey hairs behind her ears and thought of the pity I'd felt for her, and the way she'd used that pity, like a young tigress, ripping the self-respect of her protector to shreds. I was devastated. This was my last chance to leave her.

'You know what you're doing?' I asked her. If she answered yes, then I would wave her goodbye and walk fast in the opposite direction.

'Yes, I know what I'm doing,' she said.

I stopped. I was sure that, left to her own devices, her recklessness would get the better of her and she would go ahead and do it. She was incredibly tough. I stood there, hearing the Della Ding song, 'I Never Really Loved You . . .' coming from the street, waiting for it to be over.

But she stopped too.

A man stood in front of her, trembling, looking like he had been dredged up from a well. 'Are you working?' he asked.

There was grease sticking to his hair, the tip of his nose, his shirt front, his sleeves and the adjustable spanner he held that must once have been silver. Even from where I stood, I could feel the tension in him. It was hard to believe that a man well into his forties with such a sour smell to him could be so shy. He was one of the men who had been taking the piss out of Hook-Pinch earlier.

Hook-Pinch perked up immediately. 'Sure, whatever you want.' She could put on an act too. She played hard to get and spent a long time bargaining, until finally he said: 'It's not just me. My mates will be along later.' She agreed impatiently then: 'Fine, fine.'

He led her away. I stood on the corner, and halfway down the track I saw her look back at me to make sure I was following. He looked back too, at Hook-Pinch and at me. He was obviously uneasy. 'Who's that?' he asked, tugging at her sleeve.

'It's all right, he keeps an eye out for me. Safety first, as they say.' Meantime, I walked nearer and stopped just out of sight.

'Get yourself some fags,' he said, and I relaxed. He acted super-confident and pulled twenty yuan out of his pocket. 'Take a break, get yourself something with that.'

I took the money. 'Thanks, mate. You have a good time.' When he was at the corner of the concrete road, he looked round again. I squatted down and waved him away. That must have reassured him because he went.

A few minutes later, we were in the field, having our bit of fun with this man, a stranger from who-knew-where, going who-knew-where. I put on the gloves, and grabbed the end of his belt and brandished it. 'Don't you know . . .?' I began. His trousers were halfway to his ankles, his hands were supporting him on the ground, and he tried to shuffle backwards. 'You really don't know, or you're just pretending?' I said savagely. I saw him try and pull the money out of his back pocket. I thought it would be a few hundred yuan, but he pulled out a big bundle of banknotes.

'I didn't mean to . . .' he said anxiously.

'I know.' I made him get out his ID card and driver's licence and photographed them, then I took a photo of him too. 'If you tell the police what we did, then I'll send these pictures to your family,' I went on.

'Please! Please don't.'

'Now take off your trousers and walk north, towards the river. And don't look back, understood?'

'Understood.'

'If you turn around, I'll kill you.'

'I won't turn around.'

'It's worth spending a bit of money to stay alive, right?'

'Right.'

'You're lucky. If it had been my mates instead of me, they would have killed you stone dead. You know that?'

'Yes, yes, thank you.'

'And remember this too: if you're not a local, don't go with the local hookers. Get it?'

'I got it.'

'You've learned your lesson?'

'I have.'

'Off you go then.'

He took off his trousers and off he went, ID card and driver's licence in one hand, trousers over his arm as he wandered off towards the river. From time to time, he stepped on a stone, which made him pick his feet up gingerly, as if the ground was scalding hot. It would not be long until night fell properly, and the breeze wafted pungent smells towards us. He was bare-arsed and shivering, and later on, when I turned his body over, I would see that his terrified face was covered in tears, his thighs wet with urine.

Hook-Pinch had been fiddling with the adjustable spanner, turning the screw to make the jaws wider or narrower. All of a sudden, she ran up behind him and struck him hard on the head with it. He went down like a slammed door or a felled tree.

'What have you done?' I asked in a whisper.

She refused to look at me, just carried on beating him over the head. The spanner was too narrow and kept slipping to one side. But still she carried on. She did not stop until she had bashed his skull in like a tin can, until he let out a final sigh like a dying ox, the puff of his last breath raising a cloud of brown dust from the ground. Eventually his legs stopped twitching and his blood, ripe and salty, seeped from his head and pooled on the ground. The mountain ranges turned black, the wind caressed the wire grass, the river flowed east in its own unstoppable rhythm. It was that time of night, and to me it felt unreal. All I could see in my mind's eye was the spanner in her hand rising and falling. Mechanical, like a shadow puppet show. She panted, savage as an orangutan baring sharp canines as it slaughtered one of its own.

Finally, she grew tired. 'I just thought: he had a life, and now maybe we do too.' With her left hand, she carefully extracted a paper hanky from her handbag. I was afraid then, afraid that she might murder me too.

A long time later, her face darkened with that familiar pitiful expression. The closer she came to me, the more I wanted to back away. She had wiped the blood from the spanner. I stood in a daze, wishing we could turn back the clock. But things never happened in reverse.

19

'We can never go back, you know that?' she said.

'I know.'

'Afraid?'

'No.'

It took a long time before I saw her and me as 'we' again. She did everything she could to coax and sweet-talk me and eventually convinced me that the reason she had been so violent was that she was desperate for us to stay together. There wouldn't be any more trouble, she promised.

'No way do I want the police turning up and beating the shit out of us,' she said, stroking my head, making it all sound perfectly rational. The corpse lay at our feet, his bare legs clad only in shiny socks. I grabbed his ankle and hauled him into a drainage ditch. His head banged on the ground. We scraped lumps of concrete and clods of earth on top of him and laid a bit of old striped matting on top, anchoring it with stones at each corner. It might be a few days before the smell of putrefaction drew swarms of flies that would alert the people in the distribution centre the other side of the wall. They might assume the stink was from dead rats and wait even longer, by which time Hook-Pinch and I would be far, far away. I stood quietly for a few moments by this makeshift grave, then scooped up some dirt in my hands and sprinkled it over the trail of blood.

I picked up her paper hanky. 'How many did you use?'

'Just one.'

We retraced our steps to the concrete road that ran along the north perimeter wall. We were at the corner when I said: 'Wait a moment.' I trotted back to the murder scene. I was being obsessive, I knew, but I couldn't help it. Slowly, I paced back and forth over the sixty or seventy square metres, checking we hadn't left any evidence behind. I tugged at the matting again and weighed it down with a few more stones, until I was satisfied that everything was more or less OK.

'Nothing's going to happen,' I told her. But then a few moments later I couldn't help asking again: 'Are you sure you only used one hanky?'

'Absolutely.'

'How did you manage to wipe it clean with a single hanky?'

'Why would I lie to you?'

In my mind I recalled every detail of what had happened, from the moment we'd met the man to the moment we buried his corpse. I went over it every which way. Could a passer-by have noticed, I asked myself. Had we thrown any cigarette butts with traces of our saliva onto the rubbish heap by the road? And would the police go through a rubbish heap that far from the corpse? Had we left any fingerprints or hairs at the scene? We had certainly left footprints, but that could not be helped; we would just have to throw away our shoes. The shoes, the spanner and the tissue too. In three different places. And we'd throw away the hammer, of course.

'Did you smoke a cigarette there?' I asked her.

'I already told you, no!'

'That's great,' I said. 'It's not as easy to see in the dark, you know.'

In the quiet hours of the night, my misgivings came to a head. I felt terribly antsy, I wanted to go back to the scene, but I also knew that was how people got caught. I was sure I'd left stuff behind. And those objects would be like a thread, drawing us from the earth or the fog where we'd been hiding, forcing us to hand ourselves in.

'How could there possibly be so many things? And even if there were, you can't do anything about it,' Hook-Pinch told me. She told me my worries were absurd.

'How can you say they're absurd? We've just taken someone's life,' I said. I kept trying to think what we might have left there. To calm myself down I patted my pockets and rifled through my bag, pulling off the sheet and the pillow, then went to check in the toilet. Finally, horrifically, it hit me: my prison release document! That shook me awake. After a while I remembered I was in a sleeper bus and Hook-Pinch was sound asleep at my side. The whole bus was asleep. It was nothing more than a moving hotel that smelled like a pigsty. The world outside was a hellish murky grey. I shut my eyes tight and felt disgusted with myself. I had torn up the document and scattered the bits on the surface of the water a long while back.

At daybreak, we reached Luohou township. The ground was sodden, the place was deserted and the wind whipped through our thin garments. I never thought the temperature could drop so dramatically. Driven by cold, and a hunger that was making us alternately dizzy and clear-headed, we walked over to a café with its lights on and steam billowing from its cooker. On the way, we passed a government office, and I saw from its sign that although we'd been on the road all night, we were still in Anhui province.

Inside the café, Hook-Pinch sat down and rested one foot on the bench as she examined the menu. I took out our money under the table – I didn't want anyone seeing how much we had, or worse, noticing any bloodstains there might be on the notes. Two thousand four hundred, plus some small change. They had gone soft as cotton from being rolled up and folded, and were thicker and darker in colour than new notes. They had clearly been passed around by many sweaty hands. Every day the dead man had slept three or four hours and spent the rest of the time driving with his eyes fixed on the road ahead, sometimes for as much as a week at a time. The monotony of his lifestyle concealed the mortal dangers that lay in wait. And still, this was all he'd earned. The white-aproned owner brought us bowls of eight-treasure rice pudding, preserved egg, and lean meat rice porridge, steamed chicken's feet, steamed chitter-lings, crystal dumplings, dumplings in soup, pigeon soup, fish with pickled vegetables, minced tofu balls, and duck blood and vermicelli soup. Hook-Pinch reached out with her chopsticks and began to tuck in with audible sighs of enjoyment.

I could manage only a little rice porridge. When I tried to pick up a meatball, my hand shook and I dropped the food on the table. 'Eat up!' Hook-Pinch urged, looking exasperated. Then she pulled the meat dishes towards her.

'I can't keep anything down,' I said, and a tear rolled down my cheek.

'What's up with you?'

'I didn't sleep. I'm exhausted.'

It was actually the cost of the meal that was making me cry. We were paying for it with our whole lives, not with four or five years of freedom. Within a few minutes, we'd spent our entire future and our hopes. Maybe it would have been worth it if we'd got twenty-four thousand yuan out of the robbery, but it was only a tenth of that. I was furious at this ungovernable woman, I wanted nothing more than to stand up and scream at her. In the end, all I said was: 'You eat it, Hook-Pinch.'

'Why?'

I rested my forehead on my clasped hands, kneading my temples with my thumbs, on the verge of tears again. My nose was sore. I felt like a dead man, sorrowfully watching another dead person eating. The laws of history dictated that she and I were both dead people, it was just that we had not yet died. But it was only a matter of time. Eat your fill, my darling, I thought, eat your fill, and then we'll use this borrowed time and carry on along the road. I blew my nose on a paper napkin.

Once the sun came up, it quickly warmed one side of the street, though the side that remained in shadow was still chilly. The shops of the old town, selling clothing, tea, local food products, wine, dried fish, malt syrup and handicrafts of every kind, opened their doors and crowds thronged the stone-flagged streets. I put on a face mask, went to an ATM to deposit our money using a card I had registered under a false name, then withdrew some of the money from the ATM next door. At least we weren't using the dead man's money. We wandered around, following a tour group, then chose a farmhouse where we could stay the night, reasoning that they wouldn't ask for ID. There, we watched reruns on TV. 'Nice,' I said.

This is what I made up for our activities the previous evening:

18.30–18.50 Watched the local news
18.55–18.59 Watched the weather forecast
19.00–19.30 Watched the national news
19.33–21.35 Watched TV soaps, three episodes back to back
22.00–22.45 Packed our stuff and ordered a taxi
23.00 Couldn't get a taxi, got on a sleeper bus for a sightsee-
     ing trip to Luohou township

Then I put her through a test. For instance, I asked what one of the TV episodes had been about, what the adverts were about, what the lead story on the local news was, if the weather forecaster was a man or a woman. She mostly got the answers right, but she was a bit vague. If I questioned her more closely, she started to make mistakes. I did my best to drill her in the details I had memorised. Then I said, 'Now I'm going to brain-wash you.' And I proceeded to try and catch her out with

questions like: 'What were you doing at 7.40 p.m. last night?'
She looked at me open-mouthed. 'Watching TV,' I told her. 'All
evening, only watching TV.'

'Right. But what are we doing now?

'Now we're tired from our trip and we're having a nice sleep.'

'You've gone and changed the time without telling me.'

'No I haven't. You've got to keep repeating it to yourself until
you truly believe it. This is just a practice, but if you ever end up
being questioned, if there's the slightest slip-up, the police will
spot it for sure. The best thing is to convince yourself that you
really were watching TV.'

'OK, all right, I was watching TV.'

'The cops are amazing nowadays. When people rattle off a
string of lies about what they were doing, to prove they couldn't
have been at the crime scene, the cops will listen and then ask
the prisoner to repeat all of that backwards. And they end up
completely flustered.'

'That's amazing.'

'You've got to insist you were watching TV, and stick to your
story.'

'But,' she objected, 'honestly, killing that man was such a big
deal I can't get it out of my head.'

'What do you mean, you can't get it out of your head?'

'I know you've been good to me, but I killed that man, and I'm
going to get caught, there's no getting away from it. His mates,
the ones who were winding me up, they'll remember me.'

She was right.

'If I get caught, I'm finished! But hey, I'll live with it.'

'Don't be like that.'

'I've thought it through. If I get caught, then so be it. At least
I've had a good time with you.'

She looked me in the eyes as she said that. I heaved a sigh of
relief. That's right. I felt like a weight had fallen from my

shoulders. For more than twelve hours, I seemed to have been living a nightmare. It had been making me ill, I felt anxious, fearful, panicked. Every so often, my legs would give way under me as I walked. I'd been chain-smoking in desperation, my hand shaking so much I could barely hold the cigarette. Now everything felt better.

'We all have to die,' she went on. 'It's not such a big deal being alive. I don't want to be serving tables until I'm sixty.'

She had a point. We might as well enjoy the time we had left. And because death was politely tagging along behind us like a kindly officer of the law, certain to remind us when the moment of reckoning came, the future stopped being dull and boring and suddenly felt interesting. Thinking about how our flesh would be rotting someday soon was an intense turn-on, and we fucked until it seemed my penis couldn't go any deeper inside her.

20

It was inevitable that it would happen again. Whenever we felt we were in a sticky situation and our victim was being difficult, or we felt like they were going to be, then we did them in. It was like you said to those stooges of Wolfdog, Hongyang: 'Anyone who's not afraid of dying, come at me, it doesn't matter to me if I kill one or I kill ten, I'll die anyway.' Sometimes we offed someone simply because it was easy. Killing just became a habit.

After we'd killed someone, we always made sure to get as far away from the scene of the crime as possible. The cops were like ants or bees: they operated within fixed limits, that is, within their own territory. They knew what the regulations were, and they followed them to the letter. Sometimes two police stations were separated by nothing more than a river, and because the river was the provincial boundary, they had no way of communicating or operating jointly. Sometimes, Hook-Pinch and I were swinging sky-high on our trapeze on one bank of the river while on the other side we could see the forces of law and order – often including armed police – swarming out in force, eager to take on all comers but absolutely failing to follow the right leads.

After a killing, Hook-Pinch wanted to leave, while I always wanted to hang around a bit so that I could decorate the scene of the crime, just to finesse the business a little. Compared to us, most criminals were respectful and took care to remove any evidence. But I'd drop a few of the business cards I'd collected, a few scraps of paper with other people's handwriting on them, or the sort of small ads that people put at the side of the road, deliberately misspelt:

'Zhang the killer'

'Debt reccovery'

'Merderer for hire'

Sometimes I wrote the full names of local officials – which I'd copied from newspaper display stands – and accusations against them, followed by a stream of exclamation marks. Once Hook-Pinch drew four equilateral triangles with six lines. Another time, she wrote the word 'water' in English. Every time before we fled, we'd stand there like artists putting the finishing touches to their work, gazing at the carefully arranged scene. Sometimes we drove off in the victim's car for a little way, if they had one.

Whatever we did, though, the killings did not make us happy. Before each one, we would look at each other and I would see the anxiety, fear and wretchedness in her eyes. She had said that she despised thieving, but here she was, stealing people's lives.

Observing someone's death throes was even more repulsive. Their words, usually in standard Chinese with a rustic country accent, their movements, the pungent smell of cigarettes cling-ing to their bodies . . . I half-expected them to crawl to their feet and brush off the dust or have a feel of their wound and carry on bargaining with us, apologising for the brief pause. But by then they were in some far-off place. In those moments, I used to think vaguely that bamboo shoots stayed lush and lively after you pulled them out of the earth. When you felled trees, their scent could permeate a whole village. Even when the scar on the felled trunk was rotting you could still smell it. Yet when a human died, everything disappeared all at once: the breath, the pulse, the consciousness, the smell, the vigour, the warmth. The corpse just lay there motionless. If you kicked it, it was like kicking a bag of cement. You imagined those hard-working germs invading, pacifying and dissolving it. A human being turned into a frightful bloated waterbed. Then into a series of pus-filled cavities.

The eyes of the victim would always roll up into their head, they would gasp out one last breath, and they would go without even having a chance to shut their mouth, which would remain wide-open, a dark cavern. It was if they were pulling a grotesque face before expiring.

'Are they dead?'

'Yes.'

We always had to make sure. Sometimes that involved kicking the corpse, or using a twig to lift one eyelid. It felt lonely, being left with a corpse, the kind of loneliness you feel when a colleague or classmate or fellow traveller dies, or when natural wastage deprives humanity of one of its kind. This was a feeling that intensified as evening drew in. We would stand there like a doctor who has failed to save a patient on the operating table, tweezers in hand, still dripping blood, staring stupidly as the patient dies under the glare of the theatre lights. When we searched our victim's belongings, we found out what they'd been planning while they were alive, and those plans, whether immediate or long-term, depressed us. It was all much more complicated than simply depriving someone of their life. We were always killing, always on the run, and as time went by it became hard to distinguish reality from nightmare. I looked at disabled beggars and saw one of our victims: it was the gaping mouth, the tongue cut out, the jiggling limbs. I dreamed I was sunk chest-deep in a swamp of thick purplish blood, panting like an old woman, human skulls and broken bones boiling to the surface around me. A red-brown sky was only a metre above my head, and thick clouds rolled across, ravens carelessly brushing the surface of the water as they flew past, the flapping of their wings and their despairing caws close to my ears. Frantically, my feet trod in the deep slime, until a ghostly hand gripped them and pulled them down and down. Every night I woke up, soaked in sweat.

'Let's stop this,' I said one day.

Hook-Pinch merely grunted.

'I'm finding killing these men more and more difficult.'

'It's hard for me too. I'm getting panicky.'

'Me too.'

After a silence, I said: 'So what shall we do?'

'We could find something else to do . . . We could run a snack stall?'

'OK.'

'Get as far away as possible.'

But after a while, we would forget all about our intentions to find another way of life. It was as if we had never had this conversation. We knew well that we could never settle down to a peaceful life. We would be on the run forever; that was the only way to avoid capture. What's more, we were lazy, and it was laziness driving us to repeat this thing we did not like doing, over and over. Our lifestyle suited us, no matter how high the price we had to pay. Besides, hadn't we disqualified ourselves from making new lives a long time before? We put our last energies into heading towards the frontier. She wanted to go abroad at least once before she died, even just to step over the border.

There was an unlicensed cab driver in Luohou township who ought to have been our first victim that day. He almost forced us into his car to take us stargazing at an observatory about seventy kilometres away. The evening was drawing in, so it was the right time. You're asking for this, I thought. The whole journey he was chatting away to someone on his phone, which was tucked between his shoulder and his ear. His voice was rasping, as if his vocal cords had been cut out. But still, every word he spoke was so gentle. The continuous rasping got on my nerves so badly that I wanted to stab him to death. It was like the unending shriek of an electric drill in my ear. Finally, I tapped him on the shoulder and indicated that we needed a toilet. Even while he was braking, he never stopped talking to his lover – I was sure it was his lover. When we got back to the car, he had his mobile wedged against the other shoulder and was saying into it: 'They're back.' There was no way we could kill him. He took us to the observatory, collected every cent of his fare and went over the road to get his dinner. I walked off in a huff, then came back and picked up a stone to throw at the window of a minibus. It hit the wheel.

There was a farm supplies shop at the entrance to the observatory park, with an old guy sitting at an office desk in a corner outside. He had on a pair of thick wire-rimmed optical lenses and was tinkering with a watch that lay open on the table before him. As he worked, he kept repeating emphatically: 'This is worth its weight in gold'. He was about sixty, slack-skinned but decently dressed and dignified, with thinning grey hair neatly combed back over his ruddy pate. Every time someone passed, he would look up and take on the air of a technical whizz, as if that way he could command the kind of respect due to a doctor, a scientist or a laboratory technician. He also hinted that he was a poet: he had a bundle of poetry magazines, rolled up in cardboard tubes like they had just come in the post, sitting on the table in front of him. Probably, if a scholar happened along, he would claim to have had five of his poems published in one issue, the most work that any individual poet had ever had published in the magazine. That made it a special issue: imagine earning such an honour, in a country with nearly a billion inhabitants.

Not that the passers-by paid much attention to him. For his part, he treated them coolly if they looked to be illiterate, unless they picked up one of his crudely printed magazines, unpacked or still in their tube – sometimes they picked it up upside down – and began to leaf through it out of boredom. Then he pricked up his ears and waited for them to ask a question. He was waiting until they reached the page where his poems appeared. But they would politely put the magazine back, seemingly unmoved. You can imagine that this was distressing for him.

I appeared like an angel on a mission of mercy. I only had to ask the simple question 'Are those poems?' for him to pull one of the magazines out of its tube – he must have had twenty or thirty of them – and press one neatly trimmed fingernail down on the thick glass under which he flattened the magazine. He pointed to a dozen or so short poems that he had composed, and began to wax lyrical:

Old King
An eye, an artisan

Borders
The gravedigger returns to the home of his midwife-wife

The Truth
The dyer of hair formulates words of threat.

'We're always looking for meaning in everything. That is, we apply meaning *to* everything. When we write, we keep our language as simple and economical as we can, in an attempt to release for the reader something hugely meaningful that can only be grasped intuitively. As if we only have a quark of uranium and it produces a Big Bang,' he said.

We walked up the hill to the observatory, and when we came down, the watch repair table had been packed away inside the shop. We saw the old man walking down towards the town, a khaki-coloured satchel slung over his shoulder. Night was falling and scraps of paper and dead leaves skittered down the wide tarmac road. With the confidence of a local, the old guy had taken a shortcut, and that was his undoing. We were following behind him, surprised at how old he now seemed. He tottered along, hunched over, his legs wobbling like the pillars of a collapsing house. He leaned to one side, placing his right foot carefully on the next step down, then the left foot. Only when both faltering feet were on the same step did he repeat the procedure, starting with the right foot. There were big sweat patches under his armpits. Sometimes he clung to the wall for support, grunting and groaning like an old woman suffering from constipation. Farts rattled from his buttocks like machine-gun fire or unstoppable firecrackers.

It is only in a deserted landscape like this that human beings can admit to themselves how pitiful and vulnerable they really are. I felt ashamed as we put him to death. First, I clapped him on the shoulder with a hand as heavy as a dictionary, and he lurched to one side. He looked at us the way a beast looks at the butcher's knife before it is slaughtered. It was a look of terror, and he tried to step backwards but couldn't make his limbs move, like in a nightmare. Hook-Pinch took out the spanner, and he trembled violently. He pissed himself three times, the first spurt still beginning to soak through the crotch of his trousers as it was followed by another, darker spurt of urine, like a nozzle opening, closing, opening again. The spanner caught the last, cruel rays of sunlight and glinted silver. The old guy spread his hands, but before he could get the words out, Hook-Pinch had struck him. His gaze was undeviating, like a beam of light, until his body fell backwards and his eyes shifted from Hook-Pinch to the sky above.

Hook-Pinch was startled that her blow had been successful. As the old guy died, he released a stream of warm diarrhoea. We went through his satchel and took just forty-six yuan and an old-fashioned wristwatch. His business could not have been doing at all well. He had died so feebly, it made me feel feeble. In fact, I felt completely limp.

At the Martina Mall not far from the observatory train station, down a dark alley in the early morning, we mugged a traveller on his way home and took his briefcase. He got off with his life by bolting away and not looking back. He lost his leather shoes, and the echoes of his frantic panting ricocheted between the walls and the arched roof. We got a cool one thousand nine hundred yuan from him.

Then, in Xiachen township, the second biggest township thereabouts, we killed a young man by playing a waiting game. We made as if to leave the town: we paid up at the hotel, went to the billiards hall to while away the last bit of time, waved goodbye to the manager and hopped into a minibus that happened to be passing. When we got to a deserted bit of road linking the cement factory to the township, we got down and waited nearly seven hours. Eventually, we saw this man approaching on a Honda motorbike with a remodelled exhaust pipe, its engine roaring. He rode it like a horse, bent forwards, staring intently at the bit of road illuminated by his headlights. I rushed out from behind a transformer and gave him a shove. It was not an accurate shove, but the motorbike reacted like a startled horse and reared onto its back wheel. He fell off.

'What the fuck? Who are you?' he said furiously, pushing up his visor.

I went up to him and held my meat cleaver to his helmet strap. 'Regional champion, that's who I am, get it?'

To my surprise, he crumbled instantly. Like a child, his eyes followed the point of the knife back and forth, and he began to wail: 'What are you going to do?'

'There's a racket . . . don't know if you've heard of it,' I said.

'What racket?' he asked anxiously.

'Cutting someone's kidney out.'

'No, no, don't do it!' he almost sang. He was lying on the ground, trying to scrabble backwards away from us. I brandished the knife and he yelled: 'Don't you want money?'

'We want your kidney.'

'Don't you want to make money from the kidney? I'll give you the money, I will!' He emptied his pockets and his backpack. Wads of banknotes. He almost prised my hands open to stuff the notes into them. 'There's more.' He took out a credit card and told us the PIN. So, it's our birthday, I thought.

That night, I put on a mask, dark glasses and a hat and searched high and low for an ATM in a nearby village. I finally found one, but it turned out that there were only three hundred yuan in the account. The cash he had given us totalled four thousand yuan. I chucked his mobile into the ditch, pressed the knife into his belly and said: 'Let's go.'

He tried to get to his feet, and I poked harder. He seemed puzzled, and said: 'That hurts.'

'Of course it does.' I pressed harder. 'Now it'll be better.'

To start with, he curled up into a ball. Then, when the knife sank into his flesh, he opened out again. He hardly made any sound from start to finish, he was like a patient doing what the doctor told him, as if he expected us to apply ice cubes to the wound. There was no feeling of shame in killing a man like that. If he had been a bit more open to the unpredictable, we might have been too. But then again, maybe we wouldn't. By this stage, I had trouble understanding myself. We drew four characters at the scene, and a dozen or so stab wounds on the body, so that the police would take it as a premeditated crime, settling old scores.

We got on his Honda and rode away down the slip road, Hook-Pinch gripping me hard around the waist, the breeze blowing through our hair.

Like true martial arts warriors, we embraced the creed of gratitude and revenge. Maybe he was the only son of the cement factory's owners, brought up by his mother to think he was better than riff-raff like us, and to steer clear of us. She would have called the people around him country rats, thieves, greedy savages, not to mention unhygienic. And she'd stress the hygiene: I mean, these people go for years without washing their hair, until their heads crawl with lice. Although she might have thought she was educating him, she turned him into a tedious drone. As an adult, he never achieved anything in life, except to hang around the county town and township mocking and humiliating other people, which was the only thing that gave him a sense of identity. His victims were not that bothered, but I was. I was a stranger hereabouts. I still remember how he walked into the billiards hall, shaking out his leather coat, looking around the room, then letting his lids droop and shooting me a sidelong glance. I didn't like the way he looked at me at all, and I had an urge to stick him in the eye. Once that evening, I made a good shot and the owner praised me. I slipped in that I'd been district champion, though I hadn't. The owner whispered that to the cement boss's son. He snorted, nodded, then nodded again, watching as I hit wide at a ball that was harder to miss than to hit. The cue ball fell into the pocket. He repeated in a sarcastic tone of voice: 'Right, district champion.' I looked up and smiled humbly at him. Someone said that you often see odd things on the faces of the dying. But I didn't see anything. I don't even know if he said goodbye to his mother today.

21

As time went by, we learned what it meant to be serial killers. Sometimes we'd be on the run, and our heads would whip round and we'd get a fit of the shakes. It was like being a gambler with a mountain of debts and wondering where on earth they'd all come from. I wrote out a table:

WHEN	WHERE	WHO	WHAT	WIN
20.00	Behind the market	Out-of-town lorry driver	Spanner	¥2,400
19.00	Mountain track	Ret'd farm shop employee	Spanner	¥46 (and a wristwatch)
00.00	Down an alleyway	Young man going for a train	Hammer	¥1,900
01.00	Deserted side street	Son and heir of cement factory owner	Meat cleaver (serrated edge)	¥4,000
13.00	Motorway	Driver of a Liberation lorry	Dagger	¥2,000 (and two gold rings)
19.00	Railway embankment	Convalescent doing keep-fit exercises	Fists	¥740
20.00	Path through the park	Middle-aged woman at an ATM	Dagger	¥30,500 (and a gold chain)
23.00	Quiet side street	Well-off taxi driver	Chopper	¥1,080
06.00	Inside taxi office	Dealer in jade artefacts	Nylon cord	¥20,000 (and jade resold for ¥8,000)
02.00	In department store	Shop assistant	Watermelon knife	¥2,000 (and five cartons Wuyeshen cigs)
00.00	Quiet side street	Man with a white Swift car	Paring knife	¥2,500
14.00	Provincial A-road	Driver of a Polish (Star) lorry	Paring knife	¥800 (plus truck, plus steel resold for ¥20,000)
20.00	Shack yard	Man buying second-hand car	Vegetable knife	¥15,000

01.00	Outside mini-market	Manager coming out for a pee	Brick	¥6,000 (and ten cartons Yuxi cigs)
17.00	Next to a maize field	Man with electric three-wheeler	Fists	¥370 (and three-wheeler, resold for ¥4,700)
16.00	Country road	Man with heavily laden bicycle	Hydraulic pliers	¥190 (and a wristwatch)
12.00	Half-finished building	Middle-aged woman at roadside	Dagger	¥100
13.00	Provincial main road	Owner of a red Buick	Hammer	¥4,500
01.00	Back yard of gold shop	Security guard	Folding knife	¥190 (plus gold chain, plus two bracelets, resold for ¥10,000)
15.00	Dark corner of park	Unemployed coal briquette worker	Steel cable	¥920 (and watch, radio, reading glasses)
16.00	Provincial main road	Driver of a Dayun lorry	Paring knife	¥1,400

One of these, a man who told us he was recovering from lung cancer, and who seemed to think we would give him special privileges as a result, nearly got thrown in the pond and drowned for bellowing at us to fuck off. Before he went in the water, he hawked up a lump of blood as big as a ping-pong ball. I didn't like that one bit, so I told him to get lost. We'd got hold of a handle-less knife, a blade of the sort used for engraving, but we never used it on him.

22

As often as we could, we made them look like revenge killings to cover up the robberies, though, looking back, robbery was clearly our motive. But there was one occasion when the opposite occurred and we used the robbery to cover up the revenge killing.

It had been raining, it was freezing cold, and we were slumped down in the bus seats, trying to keep away from the draught coming in through the broken window. We could hear the surface water being picked up by the churning bus wheels and sprayed over the road. The litter of fallen leaves was being crushed into a sodden mass. The trees retreated behind us and the bus soaked their gnarled, bare branches, leaving them dripping. As the bus sped up, Hook-Pinch became increasingly fidgety. She frowned, clenched her fists, looked down then up again then out of the window, her face the picture of misery. She seemed to feel torn, like when you can't quite remember whether you locked up before you left home and can't make up your mind whether to go back and check and risk having everyone laugh at you. She had always shouted at me for worrying, but now the tables had turned. She clutched my arm and said:

'I'm going to die!'

'What are you talking about?'

'I haven't been to see my mum!'

At that, she burst into tears. She insisted that we get off the bus at the next stop, even after I warned her that there wouldn't be any buses and reminded her that she didn't have any rain gear. But we found a bus to take us back, then a train, and finally arrived in Gujing.

Gujing was on the outskirts of the provincial capital along-side the motorway, and was full of warehouses and single-storey buildings, street lights and T-shaped advertising bill-boards. The last time we'd gone to see Hook-Pinch's school friend at her place behind the mall in Dengyi, we had been within spitting distance of her mother, but Hook-Pinch had never mentioned going home. Now she was insistent.

We walked a long way along a muddy road, passing tarpau-lin roofs slicked black with the rain, and finally arrived at her mother's red-brick house. The iron gate to the yard was padlocked, and so was the house, and there was a cockerel standing on one leg on the moss-covered dirt, lost in lonely thought. Hook-Pinch threw a stone at the bird, and it high-stepped away, leaving a trail of claw prints in its wake before hurrying back to squeeze its plump body into the henhouse.

'This is my stepfather's house,' she said. I began to under-stand where her violence, reclusiveness, laziness and cruelty came from: when she was nine, her parents had divorced. At first, she was left at her father's, where her stepmother and two children lived in the main house, while she was given a shack with a damp floor and a leaky asbestos-covered roof that had previously been reserved for visiting relatives or farm labourers. She felt like a guest in her own home and soon moved out to her mother's place, where she caused her mother no end of trouble. Hook-Pinch was important to her mother, but so was her mother's own happiness, or at least the chance of a good life. Divorced women go cheap, you know, it's hard for them to find a decent home, and she could not afford to jeopardise the new marriage. The mother put up with a lot from her new man, and made Hook-Pinch do the same. Every time Hook-Pinch annoyed her stepfather, her mother automatically laid into the girl and, as she beat her, thumping her with all her might, she looked at her husband until the latter gave the signal to stop. Sometimes, when mother and daughter were alone, the mother would look at Hook-Pinch in a way that was part entreaty, part dislike, a mixture of despair and sadness. Hook-Pinch was frightened of her eyes.

The neighbours could not tell us where her mother had gone, so we headed for Gujing Park. Entrance was free and no one kept it clean; the cracked concrete paths were littered with bits of paper and broken kites; fake mountains made of concrete rocks were glued in place in the muddy pond; and polystyrene food boxes floated on the water's surface.

'My stepfather always comes here every afternoon, come rain or shine,' said Hook-Pinch.

'Because he likes it?'

'No, because he likes to play emperor.' Then she went on, by way of explanation: 'He pretends that all the women he passes are his harem, lined up for inspection.'

We found him in a walled alcove, sitting on a bench covered in faded, chipped paint, behind a banyan tree whose interlaced branches dripped rainwater. It was a concealed nook, from which he could easily see passers-by but not be seen himself. He was lying down, flat out, and as he breathed, bubbles appeared at the corners of his lips, like a fish. We could smell the sour, alcohol tinge of his breath mixed with the scent of rainwater from a long way off. His chest was covered with his jacket, and the crotch of his trousers with a newspaper. A bottle of Gujing spirits lay on the bench beside him. Hook-Pinch indicated that I should creep up from behind and grab it.

Hook-Pinch knelt down and put one hand on the man's legs. He took a long time to come back to his senses and open his eyes. He quivered as he awoke to the coldness of the world. Then he stared blankly at Hook-Pinch until he realised who it was, and it was only then that some warmth entered his eyes.

'Oh, it's you, Huanhuan, you're back!' He wiped the spittle from his lips.

'Yes, Dad, it's me.'

She pulled the newspaper away. Underneath, his zipper was half undone, and you could just about see his dark penis curled inside like a sea cucumber. There was a pungent whiff of spunk, and I spotted a yellowish dribble of it on the tip of his penis. He must have been wanking, fantasising about some passing woman, or more than one. Hook-Pinch pulled his zip all the way down and took hold of his flaccid dick as she talked to him. All completely casual, like any old thing you might grab at home.

'Huanhuan, the first thing for a young person is to study. A young person should make that the most important thing in their lives, and then they should get themselves a good job.' He put his hand on her head, and she began to cry. 'Do you want money?' he asked, delving into his pocket with a trembling hand. 'Studying always needs money.'

'Where's Mum?' Hook-Pinch asked.

'Your mum . . .' He took out a wad of hundred-yuan notes and tried to force them into her hands. When she silently refused them, he scraped them down her arm. 'Take this.'

'I asked where Mum is.'

'She's in the hospital.' He got out the words with difficulty. 'It's back again.'

She stood up, tears streaming like rain down a windowpane. As she turned to leave, I picked up a length of wire and wrapped it quickly around his neck, kneeling down to pull it backwards and downwards. His face flushed red, and the veins bulged to the surface of his skin, as if about to burst out of his forehead and temples. His chest inflated like a ball and his penis stood erect. I'd never seen one so frightfully long and arrogant. His head looked like a gas cylinder about to explode. He kept plucking at the arms of the bench and the wire round his throat, and his feet drummed on the ground till his shoes made scuff marks in the mud. He scraped off his shoes, bent his knees and tried to get a purchase on the ground with one foot. But I was like a barge hauler, turning away and putting my back into pulling on the wire, panting with the effort.

Hook-Pinch came up on one side of him and poked his eyeballs. No reaction. I wanted to be sure he was dead. Finally, she told me he had almost bitten through his protruding tongue and I felt my strength slipping away like a snake. I let go. We stuffed his dick back inside his trousers and pulled up the zip. Then we emptied his pockets.

We went to the mental hospital. It was like a castle in a fairy tale, with high ramparts painted white and topped with broken glass, inside which there were rows of multicoloured pinnacles. An Iveco ambulance stood at the entrance, with a security guard by its door, playing on his phone. Through the locked iron gates we glimpsed five- or six-storey accommodation blocks in dark corners of the compound, and lines of patients' pyjamas drying in the sun. The compound was nice, planted with trees and bushes. One of the patients was yelling her head off, cursing a Japanese banana plant, while a few more stood around, their hands stuck in their sleeves, staring listlessly into the distance. I noticed that many of their eyes and eyebrows were too far apart, and their heads swivelled from side to side as they grinned like puppets as if to indicate how funny they found her. We stayed no more than a couple of minutes, then turned and left. The wire had left red lines on my hands and they were too painful to use for days. It was a long way to come for so little.

The last person we killed brought a heap of trouble on us – though you could also say we brought it on ourselves. When we killed him, I had never felt so disgusted with what we were doing. Hook-Pinch and I both felt the other was responsible, and we despised each other for it. I remembered that after I stabbed him, his head tilted to the right and rested on the steering wheel, his hands relaxing as they slid gradually downwards. There was a rose lying on the dashboard. The windscreen wipers flipped left, right, left, right, in a rapid dance. The windscreen went from steamed up to clear and back again. It was like someone was gesticulating 'no, no, no' at us. But he was dead, and nothing was going to bring him back to life.

We were shrouded in a milky fog, though the ground around us was dark and shiny in the rain. We stared vacantly into space. A couple of cars passed us by, splashing us in their wake like motorboats. We dragged the driver out and flung him to the side of the road. The rain wet our heads and his body. By the time he was found, his skin would be ghastly pale and wrinkled.

We cleaned up the lorry's cab as best we could, covered the blood spatters with the overalls he had given us, threw the rose out of the window and drove off. Perhaps he had the rose to remind him of his absent beloved. Whether she had left him, or had died, he was still loyal to her. 'Whenever it wilts, I get another one.' That was what he had told me when I asked. He was not a talkative man, but he listened politely whenever I spoke. Although his responses were brief, and sometimes I couldn't make out what he was driving at, he was full of sincerity. You felt he was burdened with some beautiful inner tragedy.

He put on some music. A girl singer. It took me a long time to identify what that lazy voice was saying. It was: 'Stay away from it all.'

He was the only one to stop for us that day, and then we killed him. He was driving a blue HGV. Most of the drivers sped on past our outstretched thumbs, though they were polite about it and avoided splashing us. Only this lorry driver pulled up, ten metres past us. A bus had dropped us there; it had broken down and later been towed away. The other passengers cursed and swore, yet eventually made their own arrangements and departed. Then it was just us, standing there in the rain, not knowing where we wanted to go. We hugged our arms around ourselves, shivering from the cold, walking up and down to keep warm, swearing at each other. Finally, he drew up and hooted, and we ran over. He greeted us with a warm smile, pulled out a couple of pairs of overalls and made us take off our wet jackets and wrap ourselves in them. Then he put on the heating. After about twenty minutes, or perhaps half an hour, the heat was making him nod off. His hands clutched the steering wheel, but he drooped a little and his head fell, like gravity pulling a kung fu ball down to earth, then it jerked upright, then nodded again. I only realised what was happening when Hook-Pinch gave me a shove. I held the steering wheel with one hand, and woke him by patting him with the other. He thanked me profusely. Then he felt in the tool compartment for some cigarettes and gave me one. He didn't smoke himself.

We suggested he should park by the side of the road and take a nap. He reckoned this was a good idea, pulled off the main road and fell fast asleep, leaving the headlights on. I took the knife Hook-Pinch passed me and a kind of inertia led me to stab him to death. He had left the headlights on so he could keep the cab warm for us. That was what made me feel I had done something truly evil.

23

'I know you find it hard to listen to, but I actually did these things,' Squint said. He looked at himself, as if unwilling to believe all this had happened to him, and then he started to weep. Finally, he mopped his dripping nose with toilet paper, scrunched it up into a ball and threw it onto the brazier. Hah, when a drunkard starts to cry, it's horrible, yet it has a certain dramatic quality to it. He was trying to show us this great personal tragedy.

'Don't worry, you cry all you want,' Hongyang said, comforting him. As Hongyang patted Squint on the shoulder, his eyes swivelled in their sockets.

'I feel better now I've got it off my chest. You don't know what's been happening . . .' There was another gush of tears. 'I'm so tired, but I feel better now I've told you. I've never felt so physically relaxed.'

Hongyang grunted.

'I've done terrible things. It must be hard just hearing about them.'

'It doesn't matter.'

'What about Hook-Pinch?' I asked.

He looked blank, then said: 'I should have known she was mentally ill. No sane person could have such a brilliant smile and yet be such an imbecile. Her imbecility was bottomless. I should have known no normal person would kill and remain so calm. She was never scared, or if she was, it was only that she was afraid of not getting it right. I should have known from the start.'

24

Whenever I asked her about the phone, she would say: 'I already told you, I threw it away, dammit, I threw it away ages ago.' So I stopped asking. 'It' was a smartphone, 141 mm long, shiny, magical, mysterious, with the most up-to-date apps a traveller needed: camera, video, voice recorder, MP3 player, Wi-Fi, games, chat apps, social media and maps. Just look at that gleaming aluminium case and tempered glass screen! I thought. Change happened so quickly nowadays. It had GPS too, of course – the telecoms man had told me there was no point turning it off. But I remembered how, in the old days, in our prison cell, we had listened to a prisoner griping about how he'd had his phone turned off and had still got caught. So as she was about to swipe the screen, I told her to chuck the phone away.

'In a minute,' she said. A few minutes later, I told her again. I should have watched her do it. But by then I had a painfully stiff neck. I had the dead man's jacket collar gripped between the fingers and thumb of my right hand, holding it up as high as I could, while my left hand was in one of his inner pockets. The blood had soaked through his T-shirt and dripped down to the back of his trousers and his seat cushion, and his neck was a dark gaping wound. I heard her sigh as she dropped it out of the cab window. I imagined the mobile arcing through the air and dropping into the drainage ditch by the side of the road.

'Have you chucked it?' I asked, counting the money I'd pulled from the driver's pocket.

'I'm not some damn kid,' she retorted.

'Have you really chucked it?'

'Yes, dammit, I've really chucked it away.'

'That's good.'

I thought that was the end of it, but to my surprise, she flared up. 'You want to search me? I'm telling you, would they build a satellite costing billions and go to all that trouble to get it up in the sky just to track down some rubbish mobile?' I didn't know what she was talking about.

We got off the bus at Pizhou East station because we were exhausted and hungry, and found ourselves a hotel near the station. It was a Soviet-style building from the fifties or sixties, and the walls were mottled where ugly patches of cement showed through, as if someone had covered them with innumerable small ads and then ripped them off again. The wires that ran along the top floor above the windows were festooned with sheets laundered, year on year, in disinfectant. The guttering had been damaged beyond repair, so that rainwater poured down the walls like piss, leaving rusty streaks. But it was still an impressive structure, monumental. A proper dignified public office, unlike the newer buildings that flanked it, which were painted in an array of garish colours, their pitted walls choked with grit, as dense as mosquitoes on the surface of a pond. They were just a bunch of whores by comparison. It was the kind of hotel that gave face to hotel guests that had a bit of money, or those who wanted other people to think they had a bit of money.

Inside, the concrete floors were freshly mopped and shiny, giving off a smell a bit like a fish market. A woman with green-painted eyebrows, who looked as though she had been working at the hotel reception forever, ordered the couple queuing in front of us: 'ID cards.' They registered and left the desk, clinging to each other like war wounded, and she squinted after their retreating figures. 'What do they think they're playing at?' she snorted scornfully. Then she subjected our ID cards to inspection, holding them up to the light and flicking them with her

fingers. It was what I used to do when I was working in whole-
sale distribution, to see if the light shining through it revealed
anything. It didn't. It was just telling someone with a fake ID
that it took more than that to fool me.

'Off you go,' she said, dismissing us.

The couple queuing in front of us were now in the room next
door to ours. They were husband and wife, or living together at
any rate. They banged against the wall as if they were shaken by
sobs, shoulders trembling, as they waited for one of the cleaners
to bring them the key. The man looked seriously ill, swaying on
his feet: perhaps they both were. A smell of decaying food clung
to them, as if they had festering, unhealed ulcers. When the
cleaner opened their door, they tottered inside, still holding on
to each other, and dropped onto the bed.

I felt like I'd slept for centuries. A dreamless sleep. The first
since we had gone on the run. When I got up and staggered to
the bathroom to wash my hands and face and get rid of the sick
feeling a long sleep gives you, I found her squatting there
fiddling with the driver's mobile phone. She looked up, startled,
as I reached her in a couple of steps and snatched the phone off
her.

'What are you doing?' she protested, getting to her feet. She
must have been there all night: she still had her trousers on.

'What are *you* doing?' I flung back at her. I needed to assert
my dominance quickly and not give her a chance to nag. I
grabbed her by the neck and asked her forcefully: 'How many
times did I tell you to get rid of it?'

'Get away from me!' she said.

'You told me you'd thrown it away. And you fucking kept it!'

'I'm telling you, get away from me!'

'When did you turn it back on?' I smacked her across the face
and repeated: 'I'm talking to you! When did you turn it back
on?'

'I can't remember.'

'Stop taking the piss!'

I banged her up against the wall until she answered: 'A few hours ago.'

'How many hours?'

'Can't remember.'

'You can't remember?'

'One or two hours, no more.'

'And how often did you turn it on when we were coming here?'

'Once.'

'You better tell the truth, or you'll get us killed.'

'Just the once.'

I let go of her, went over to the window, opened the curtains and looked down. Below me, cars shot back and forth over the motorway flyover, but under it there was no movement on the main road or the side roads. The sunlight was bright despite the chill in the air. In the surrounding streets, there was no one to be seen. The wind chased a dead leaf, pinning it to the ground like an arrow.

'Is anyone out there?' she said sourly.

'No.'

'Nothing to get excited about then.'

I pushed her away from me, went to the door and pressed my ear to it. Then I took off the security chain, and whispered to her: 'Get your stuff ready.'

'What stuff?'

'Your things. Just look normal, the way everyone round the station behaves.'

I jabbed my finger in the direction of the floor below. She looked a bit puzzled. I crept outside. In the corridor, there was a trolley on wheels, and the door to one of the rooms was open. One of the cleaners must be in there, or maybe she'd gone downstairs for something. The red carpet was so worn it was full of holes, like a disused running track. I couldn't see a surveillance camera, but I couldn't see there wasn't one either. I stuck my hand in my trouser pocket and gripped that damned phone. I needed to put it in with the mound of dirty sheets on the trolley, or in the rubbish bag by the lift doors, or maybe stick it under the carpet. None of these were ideal, though. Maybe I should open the window at the end of the corridor, fling it out and hope that it landed on the roof of a passing three-wheeler. That way the phone, with its twinkling signal, would lead the police a merry dance all over the city. There was no time for that either, though. Someone was coming slowly along the corridor. It was the woman of the couple next door. I couldn't help being startled by her appearance. Up till then, I had only seen her from behind, and she had looked youthful, with her short hair, narrow shoulders, slim waist, spindly giraffe-like legs and her careless but still fashionable way of dressing. However, what I saw now was someone who must have been over fifty, with lifeless eyes sunk deep in their sockets and a sallow face seamed with wrinkles. She bore all the marks of someone who smoked, drank, stayed up all night gambling and slept around. She must have been to the water boiler along the corridor, because she was tottering along holding a steaming carton of instant noodles in both hands. 'Open the door for me,' she said, her voice expressionless. I could see she was missing at least five teeth.

I turned the handle to her door and pushed it open. She slipped quickly inside and hurriedly put the scalding carton down on the bedside table, slopping a bit over the edge. The man was lying motionless on the bed, muttering to himself, one withered stick-like arm raised in the air. I pulled the door shut and heard the lock click into place. I stood there for a while, running my hands over my hair, then hurried to our room.

Hook-Pinch was sitting cross-legged on a chair. 'What about the mobile?' she asked.

'I chucked it,' I said, going over to the window. 'Hurry up and get ready.'

'There's nothing happening, I've already had a look.'

Lazily, she stubbed out her cigarette in the ashtray. I pulled the curtains back and she moved closer, resting her chin on my shoulder. Then she went limp.

They came out of nowhere. They must have been pursuing us all along, but we'd refused to believe they existed because they had never showed themselves. Fifty security guards and police, some of them armed, had silently rushed the hotel below and surrounded it, cordoning off the outside. Guns at the ready, they sidled in through the main door. At the same time, a bunch of hotel workers and guests rushed outside, came to a sudden halt, and were quickly directed under a tarpaulin-covered rain shelter that had once sold takeaway food. There were two guard dogs too, jumping up on their hind legs, tongues lolling out, jaws working rhythmically, slavering over the task in hand with terrifying eagerness. A man in dark glasses who looked to be in command spoke into a walkie-talkie; the whole hotel seemed to buzz loudly with an electrical current. There were shouts of 'In position!' My Adam's apple dripped sweat. It was more than I'd sweated in weeks, I thought.

Hook-Pinch grabbed hold of me. 'What are we going to do?' I pulled away, grabbed the bag and ran out into the too-quiet corridor with her on my heels, leaving the room scattered with our possessions. She wanted to run down the stairs but I pulled her back. We took another corridor that led to the roof. I leapt up a few steps and hauled her with me. I was moving forwards in leaps and bounds, dragging Hook-Pinch, still limp, behind. I did not stop until we were finally out on the rooftop, with the safety door clanged shut behind us. Then, to be on the safe side,

I found a steel bar lying beside the water tank and pushed it across as an extra bolt.

Then the same thought occurred to us at the same moment: we were trapped.

The rooftop, high in the sky, was like the top deck of a cruise liner, floating lonely in the clouds, or out at sea, like an outlying island. Behind the hotel was the car park; to the right, a flat gravel area and fields; to the left lay the nearest buildings: a low row of shops, with an alleyway five or six metres wide running between for buses to drive through. Unless we had a helicopter – better still, an invisible one – there was nowhere for us to go.

We searched around to see if there was any wire, or cables of any sort. It occurred to me that we might use them to climb down or swing on like baboons. I even considered the possibility of sliding down the plastic guttering. I gripped the rusty railings and looked over and down below a few times. The building was constructed so that it narrowed on its way down. I could not see any windows with anti-burglar screens or sun awnings. No trees either. Nothing for us to land on. In the car park, the police were directing people to stand back. They had occupied the whole area. All they had to do was to fight their way steadily upstairs until they got to our basketball court-size rooftop. Hook-Pinch was crouched by a heap of broken asbestos roofing sheets, hugging her knees and muttering to herself. I turned and looked in her direction. We seemed very far apart.

'Farewell,' I said quietly, then raised one leg. Farewell . . . I was going to free myself of this suffocating situation.

'What are you doing?'

I had made up my mind, several times over, and was about to put my plan into action. I imagined them walking up the stairs, glugging their beer and cracking jokes. They were using their teeth to pull off the bottle tops, and spitting them out in the corridor. One of them toted a heavy electric drill. Soon they would plug it in and drill through the safety locks. Then they would carry us away, like hunters carrying away their prey . . .

But then a mournful cry from Hook-Pinch interrupted my thoughts.

'Nothing,' I said.

'We've still got a bit of time, haven't we?' she said, a sob in her voice. I looked down at myself, feeling embarrassed. I had one knee hooked over the empty pipe, the other leg standing straight, like an old man stretching his muscles on the exercise equipment in the community park. I had been thinking that this was my last chance and I had better grab it before it was gone forever, and now here I was, on hold, as if I'd pressed the pause button.

'We've still got a bit of time, haven't we?' she repeated, now really crying, and crawling towards me. We leaned together with our backs against the ice-cold water tank and looked up at the sky. At that moment, it looked like an enormous mass of liquid composed of innumerable transparent molecules, rising, falling, floating around. Hook-Pinch ran her fingers through my sweat-damp hair, some strands of which had turned white that very minute. 'At least we'll die together, right?' she said, probing my earlobes, eyes and eyelashes with her long tongue.

At some point I heard noises in the building, either the rustling of mice, or the whispering of people who didn't want to be heard, or people thudding up the stairs, or a crack as if something was being split open. I pushed her away and sat up, and then slowly lay back again as the sounds subsided. For a while, I wanted to get up and go downstairs. I imagined holding out my wrists to them and saying: No need to keep on looking for me. And then I no longer wanted to move. I stroked her pubes through her trousers with one finger and said: 'Hook-Pinch, it was me who got you into this.'

'I'm not blaming you,' she said. Then she went on: 'I've never blamed you.'

'Time's up for us.'

'It makes me happy that you're thinking like this, because that means you won't blame me either.'

'I'm not blaming you.'

We embraced each other tenderly and started kissing. Halfway through, I opened my eyes and discovered that Hook-Pinch's were shut tight. Her nostrils were slightly flared, and her face was engorged with desire. She was greedily sucking my saliva, like a piglet. She looked too pale, paler than the whitest milk but she also looked incredibly healthy. No one could have hair that thick unless they were bursting with health and vitality. It seemed unreal to me. Holding back the tears, I kneaded her cheeks. She opened her eyes and stared intently at me, like a mother whose son is about to be taken far away.

Then we heard police sirens wailing down below. They were speeding back to the station, covered in glory. And that was that. Off they went, and everything returned to normal. The fruit sellers, pastry and bean curd vendors, the men touting lottery tickets – 'Three for ten yuan' – all emerged from the corners where they'd been skulking and crowded back onto the streets again. Almost afraid to believe it, I pulled the bar from the door and Hook-Pinch and I scurried downstairs. On our way, we met a security guard, also hurrying along. I stood frozen to the spot. This, surely, was the end of us. And then he told us gleefully: 'Don't worry, it's all been dealt with.' And he trotted on past the other guest room doors, some open, some shut, delivering his news.

Hook-Pinch wanted to go back to our room, but I grabbed her by the hand and pulled her with me downstairs. The lobby was full of people clustered around the reception desk, where I could hear the old bag with green eyebrows explaining, as if the credit was all hers: 'The police broke down the door with a fire-fighter's axe and dragged the wretched couple out. They couldn't believe they were being arrested, they kept looking around them in alarm and confusion. Neither of them weighed much, so the police shouted: "One, two, three . . ." and hurled them into the back of the police van like a sack of potatoes.' Then she finished: 'That's how you end up when you do drugs. People will do anything for drugs. I could see right from the start there was something badly wrong with them.'

We went outside and walked a few metres towards the west, then turned around and went back the other way. I made sure to keep my pace measured and not go too fast, or too slow for that matter. Then we hailed a three-wheeler and squeezed into it, and told it to take us west again.

'What are we doing?' asked Hook-Pinch.

'Just sniffing the air, like a dog.'

'We haven't checked out yet.'

I was looking out of the taxi window at the road, the shops and the buildings we were leaving behind us. I could hardly believe we were sitting in an enclosed three-wheeler. I smiled to myself. When we finally stopped the taxi and got out, I said: 'Do you really think we'd be so lucky if we went back to check out?' I wasn't blaming her, just explaining. 'It was the other couple who got arrested this time, but we can't count on our lucky streak.'

'How did that happen?'

I didn't know how to explain it to her. The fact was, I'd put the mobile phone into the bag of the woman holding the pot of instant noodles. She was standing at the door hopping from one foot to the other because the tub of noodles was scalding her hands, and I quietly slipped the mobile into her bag – it's a lot easier sneaking something into someone's bag than the other way round – while with my left hand I turned the doorknob for her and pushed the door open. 'Thank you,' she'd said, in a voice that was frighteningly detached.

'Hook-Pinch,' I said.

'What?'

'I just want to say, we may die, and we may not be afraid to die, but we shouldn't throw our lives away. Agreed?'

'Agreed.'

'You took the phone. Why didn't you at least throw away the SIM card?'

'I didn't know how to take the cover off the phone.'

'So why didn't you ask me?'

'I thought you'd be angry. If you'd seen the phone, you'd have definitely been angry.'

'But in the end we threw the whole phone away.'

'Are you blaming me?'

'No. No, I'm not.'

We got to the railway and followed the tracks, sometimes at the foot of the embankment, sometimes stepping over the sleepers. Although we were starving hungry, we carried on walking till nightfall, taking each other's hand as it grew dark. On and on we went. The world turned into a huge dark cave. Our footsteps were our eyes. It wouldn't have mattered if a tiger had been strolling towards us along the tracks. We were safer on the railway than anywhere else. The police would eventually discover their mistake and would check all the bus and train stations and set up roadblocks on every road out of town. But I'd never heard of them setting up checkpoints on the track itself.

25

Although I never mentioned the phone again after that, it was like a pair of tweezers left in the body after an operation. You could forget it, forget everything that had happened, but the tweezers didn't see it like that. Sometimes it felt like they'd shackled you so you could hardly walk.

I should have watched her throw it away. I didn't know anything about technology – that was why I respected it so much – but I'd never forgotten what a telecoms engineer once told me: 'Take out the SIM and the battery, and preferably throw the whole phone away, into water.' Hook-Pinch had pressed the button; the window of the cab had descended slowly. Although out of the corner of my eye I'd seen her wave her arm out of the window, she had stealthily pushed the phone under her thigh and turned it off. When she'd seen that I was occupied in pulling the banknotes out of a pile of other stuff, she'd put it away in her bag.

'Did you throw it away?' I had asked.

'Dammit, I'm not a child,' she'd declared. I should have checked her over. I knew well she was capable of this sleight of hand.

Now the incident with the phone had brought the relative predictability of our wanderings to an end. We used to be able to get to point B while the police were still at point A, the location of the victim, that is, giving us a bit of breathing space.

'Yousheng, it was just like Daedalus and his son Icarus fleeing the clutches of the tyrant Minos, daubing feathers with wax to make wings,' interjected Hongliang. 'Daedalus said: "Minos is master of the land and the seas, so we can't flee by land or sea. Going by air is the only way left to us." '

Don't they say necessity is the mother of invention? Whoever would have believed humans could travel through the air? Whoever would have believed two criminals could walk free by plodding along the railway tracks at three miles an hour?

However, we soon found that we had walked into their trap again.

Yan county was a poverty-stricken place where they still built trunk roads by pouring molten asphalt. It belonged to a different province to Pizhou prefecture, separated from it by a mountain that meant the customs and the accent were different, yet here the police were, all ready and waiting for us. As the dawn sky brightened, I saw myself, looking damp, in a Wanted poster stuck to a telegraph pole, the birthmark above my left eyebrow unmistakable. I read my correct height, weight, age, and those habits I was hardly aware of but which existed, and they were offering a reward which anyone would give their eye teeth for. Although there was hardly anything about Hook-Pinch – they didn't even give her name – there was an artist's impression of her that was extremely lifelike. The poster was new. In other words, the police were already offering rewards for information about us as we headed towards Yan county. They had probably plastered posters for hundreds of miles around. For some reason, as I read the poster I felt frightened. Even though the wanted man in the image was me, I found him scary.

By now we had been walking all night, and we were at the end of our tether. Not far off, we saw a stand selling breakfasts, steam billowing from wicker baskets and shiny stainless-steel containers keeping the food warm. We imagined them full of simmering soya milk, squares of silken bean curd and purple rice porridge. We were so close that I could smell it, and a moustachioed waiter carrying some quartered salted duck eggs even came out and asked if we wanted anything, but we could not go any nearer. My stomach rumbled audibly. We were ravenous.

Things could not get any worse than this. We had to avoid the towns. Once we were beyond the tarmac road that led into the country, there was the occasional disused mule track, and we walked along one of those as far as it went, then, when it ended, we crossed into the field. We found an irrigation canal and, pushing aside the weeds on the surface, we chose what we thought was fairly clean water, cupped our hands and drank. And drank some more. It was eight or nine o'clock by this point, and the morning sun gradually warmed us up and gave us some energy. For some reason, I thought of the soft flabby football that lay at the foot of our wall when I was a kid and which inflated to a hard roundness towards midday and then deflated again as the sun sank towards the west. An old woman's breasts are like that too, I thought. Things swell when they warm up, shrink when they cool. I remembered my dad buying that ball, then suddenly turning nasty in a way I couldn't understand, aiming an accurate kick so that the ball flew high above the washing line and landed on the clothes pole, which punctured it. 'That was your birthday present. Don't ever say I didn't give you one,' he'd said.

We were climbing a hill when we met a farmer hauling a stone stele. There were some bags of mooli on his cart too. He came around the bend and pulled on the shafts, stood ramrod straight then let the cart roll down the hill. I gave a loud yell. He couldn't stop, and the shafts slammed right into the wall and sent the farmer flying. Luckily no harm was done. 'Uncle,' I said, 'let us buy some of your mooli, we're starving.'

'Eat as many as you want,' he said.

We stuffed ourselves with the kind old man's mooli. That night we took refuge in a cave and lit a fire with pine needles to

warm ourselves and cook more mooli. I was sorry I hadn't
asked him to put us up as well. He must have had the key to
some house or other. I stirred the white ashes with a twig and
said: 'Whatever happens, we've got to lie low for the moment.'

I'd been on at Hook-Pinch for the whole journey about keeping herself under control. I felt oppressed by the number of
things we had to be mindful of, on edge all the time. It was
pitch-dark outside the cave, there were cries from birds in the
trees and despairing howls from wild animals, and then it would
go silent apart from the rustling of leaves on the ground. She
put her arms around me and held me tight, and I covered her
with my jacket. I dozed off, waking in a panic a few times and
unable to think where I was. When I finally remembered we
were in the depths of the mountains, I was overcome with
sadness. I thought of famous defeats in military history, when
vanquished soldiers tossed their weapons aside in despair and
battled weather, hunger, sickness and depression in remote
wildernesses. They may have nurtured beautiful dreams of
returning home, but most of them fell by the wayside, and in
time gleaming white bones were all that remained of them, like
butchered dogs. Either that, or they simply vanished without
trace. The same thing was going to happen to me soon, I
thought. We'd have to live off raw meat because of the difficulty of finding fuel. I imagined us coming across people, crav-
ing human contact yet fearful, slipping sadly back into the dense
forest. We were only a hair's breadth from that scenario.

I was woken by an ear-splitting shriek. It was broad daylight.
Outside the cave, I could hear Hook-Pinch not far off, yelling at
some madman or perhaps some wild beast. It seemed like she was
too terrified to move from where she was. I rushed out and saw her
in the middle of the trees, shaking like a leaf, clutching a branch in
her hand. Seven or eight metres away a dog, or rather a wolf,
confronted her. It was tan-coloured, with darker patches on its

back and forehead; its ears were pricked and its lips gaped wide, and its muzzle was so pointed it looked like an ink-soaked cork. The markings on its face gave it the look of a clown, but the smile was definitely sinister, and it looked unfazed. It was scrutinising us. Studying us. It was enough to make your hair stand on end.

I made Hook-Pinch stand behind me. She clung to my jacket. The wolf's eyes were a topaz colour and the pupils a mysterious gleaming black. There was no way of telling what thoughts were going through its head. It was a frightful beast. I forced myself to stand still.

At that stage, Hook-Pinch was propping me up rather than hanging on to me. It took every ounce of strength I could muster to stay upright. After a lengthy interval, the wolf finally lowered its head and sniffed around on the dewy ground. It had lost the contest to stare me out. More time passed and it looked up, almost enquiringly, as if to say 'What now?' I threatened it with my fists, and it turned and slipped away. It trotted, its four paws never leaving the ground altogether, so that it moved as smoothly as a horse-drawn cart. It looked as if it had something in its mouth; it was baring its teeth and panting slightly, and its tail hung down behind it. It got to the foot of a gentle slope, paused long enough to scratch at the ground with one hind leg, then leapt into the undergrowth and disappeared.

'Wolves eat humans. Humans may be brutal, but at least we don't do that,' she said accusingly to me, her saviour, as the blood returned to her cheeks. 'I met a wolf, but who's going to believe that? We met a wolf.'

'It was probably a dog.'

'It was a wolf!'

A little while later, I said: 'Well, I didn't expect this either. I just thought we shouldn't deliberately throw our lives away.' As soon as the words were out of my mouth, I was sorry I had said them, even as gently as I had.

She stamped her foot and shouted: 'Well, it would have been better than being eaten alive, wouldn't it? Better than being eaten by a wolf!'

'Let's go down the mountain,' I said.

'No.'

'You'll do as I say!' I grabbed her arm, but she started to jump up and down.

'Get out of my way!' she shouted. 'Let me leave, you can stay here if you want, as long as you want. Get out of my way. You know what? I can't even go to the toilet here. And I'm about to get my period.'

She picked up a branch and snapped it across her knee, then wrapped some item of clothing around it and tried to light it. Over and over, she thumbed the wheel of her lighter, but all she managed to produce was the odd spark. She threw it down. I picked it up and lit it for her. Her theory was that wolves wouldn't dare come near a fire. And, holding her blazing torch aloft, she went off down the mountain.

If I'd known she was going to behave like that, I wouldn't have bothered saving her. I hadn't brought up the subject of the mobile even once. Or that spanner she was so fond of. The one she killed the driver with, whacking him so hard he dropped like a felled tree. And now she was heading right into the trap the police had set because she couldn't be without a bit of soap. Her excuse was the wolf, but who said it was a wolf? There weren't any wolves any more. She did whatever took her fancy without considering the consequences, or anyone's feelings. She was going to die for a tampon. That was what she'd said, you see.

When we came to the first snack stall, we stopped. The owner was cradling a child. Her hands shook sporadically. Hook-Pinch paid over the money and looked scornfully at me, as if to say: See?

I thought the mouldy bread we'd bought must be at least a year past its sell-by, but we gobbled it up greedily, our eyes almost popping out of our heads, we were concentrating so hard.

Outside, everywhere was frost-pale and desolate. We walked towards the main road and from there took a bus to the county town of Zhiliang. When we got off, she headed straight for the archway that was once the old town gate, without looking back at me. That was always the way she made it clear that she was in charge where we were concerned, no ifs or buts.

I stopped and hid behind a small pickup. It would be good if something happened to her the moment she crossed the demarcation line between city and countryside. How many prisoners had told me – and my own experience bore this out – that it was when you were sure nothing would happen and took it for granted that it was safe to cross a line that the cops would descend out of the blue, hold you down and rub your teeth in the dirt, then drag you away. And you had no idea where they had come from: so many of them, and just like that! At this moment, I almost wanted her to be arrested. I wanted her to admit I was right.

You're right to ask why I didn't leave her. I'd had more than enough opportunities to, from when we reached Zhiliang and got a bus to Liusha township, Danqing township, and finally arrived at Shuye Old Town, or even earlier, when we'd been up the mountain lighting a fire: I could have left her then. Splitting up would have been the best for both of us, and the simplest thing in the world, no formalities necessary. She never turned round once, or asked me to go with her. You're certainly right to ask, my friend . . .

'The thought seemed to upset Squint,' said Hongliang, 'and he began to repeat, "Why, why, why?" It was as if this was the first time he'd given serious thought to the whole thing, as if being with Hook-Pinch had been the most natural thing in the world, an unequivocal fact of life.

'It was me who asked him why he hadn't left her. I had no idea my question would give him such a jolt. After a bit, he tried to explain, but he wasn't making any sense, his explanations were so complicated and contradictory, they didn't sound convincing even to himself. All the same, he was making such efforts, I didn't get the impression he was trying to hide anything. He knew I'd read a few books, and he asked me to be his mentor and help him analyse the whole business, begged me, in fact. Yousheng, everything I've told you today is what I heard him say or what I guessed. His story touches on the most secret parts of human nature.

'I managed to persuade him to go back in time, starting from the butchering of his dog, until he saw himself as the thief that he was, desperate to gain control over the helpless, the homeless, and girls, children and dogs unable to stand on their own feet, and he told me how right I was. He needed Hook-Pinch's subservience. And to gain it, he put up with her humiliating and trampling on him, over and over. He acted so generous, but actually he was totting up everything he had invested in their relationship. When the day came that he realised she was no longer willing to acknowledge him as master, then he would demand the capital back with interest, even if it meant destroying her.

'The way he put it, there was no way he could keep that dog. It was old and unsteady on its feet, and it had ringworm. He had never kept a pet in his life and had no experience to go on. His fellow students were against it too because it got into communal spaces, and they blamed the dog when they began to itch. Finally, it developed a tumour and that cost him a lot in vets' bills. It's not like he could rely on his wages doing bag inspections in a car park. And – and this was odd – even though he had the dog, he couldn't stand other dog owners, in much the same way a smoker can't stand other smokers. He developed OCD, washing his hands till he had almost washed them to the bone. It wouldn't be the first time this had happened. Still, the way he described it, when he came across the half-starved mutt by the side of the road, he felt somehow ennobled by the experience; he and the dog were fellow sufferers, he felt euphoric, as if he was being swept up, taken over, by the angelic strains of a heavenly choir. As if a new life was beginning, was how he put it. He provided the dog with everything it could possibly need: food and water, a little jacket, a ball to play with, and a dog bed. Some of the stuff he bought turned out to be completely useless. But one day, he butchered it. For the simple reason that the dog had stopped looking adoringly at him. He watched himself like a shocked observer as he dragged it angrily to a smelly ditch, pulling it by the tail – it had rubbed off most of its coat. There was a spade lying beside the ditch. He picked it up and watched himself beating it on the back, over and over, until its spine caved in. Then he watched himself walking back to the hostel and telling his fellow students that he was getting the spade to dig a nice deep hole for its grave. He would claim that he had buried it with tears in his eyes. What happened, of course, was that he dug a spadeful of stinking mud out of the ditch, shoved the dog's head in, heaped more mud on top and trod it flat, then left.

'He watched himself constantly cracking his finger joints once this was all finished. He told me that the only reason he'd done this was that when he put his hands under the dog's chin in the usual way and lifted its head to look into its eyes, he saw that they were full of gunge, wet like maize pulp or fish eggs, proof that the dog was not long for this world and had lost all its mental faculties. It no longer looked at him, and when it did, it looked pathetic, instinctively wanting to bite him but lacking the strength to do so. He felt that their relationship, that of Heavenly Father and disciple, had changed. He found this unbearable. You see, Yousheng, I've said it myself, and he repeated it often enough: he was a pathetic, self-abasing killer who couldn't bear to be betrayed. I reckon he made Hook-Pinch his quarry from the first time he set eyes on her in Xinxing. To him, she was a lost soul and he had to protect her and teach her how to behave. That's why he never left her. Then, in the end, he killed her too. He told me that when he pressed the pillow down on her head, it was as if he heard himself saying: You're right, and I should have recognised that from the start. I was so blind . . . Those were Squint's words.'

The day before, it was as if Hook-Pinch had a presentiment that she was going to die. She was unusually quiet, letting me wipe the leftover glue from the adhesive plaster at the corner of her lips, pull a woollen hat over her head, right down over her ears, and lead her outside. When I let go of her hand, she stopped and begged me to take it again. Her hand was horribly cold. She acted like someone who's just been released from hospital after a serious illness, looking around feebly yet with curiosity, the breeze chilling her more than it did me, the distance we walked exhausting her, though it was nothing to me, an approaching car scaring her so she retreated to the edge of the road when it was still a long way off, until it crawled past. If passers-by glancing at her were distressed by her appearance, she bravely raised a smile, as if to show they shared a deep understanding of illness and the way it destroyed people. 'Why don't you hire a wheelchair? They've got them over there,' one woman suggested. But Hook-Pinch said no, with an embarrassed smile I had never seen on her before.

'Are you going to make a fuss?' I said when she told me she wanted to go out.

'No.'

'You're not going to tell me to get lost?'

'No.'

'Promise?'

'I promise. Can't you see I've haven't got the strength?'

'What will I do if you kick up a fuss?'

'Just walk away and leave me.'

I looked hard at her. It was hard to believe, but one night's good sleep had restored her to her normal self.

'I promise I'll never kick up a fuss again.'

She sounded so apologetic, it was as if she knew she'd been giving me a lot of trouble lately. Her eyes filled with tears. Only the day before, she'd attacked me three times, chucking stuff around, brandishing an imaginary weapon and yelling at me to get lost. She threw any food and drink I offered her to the floor, accusing me of poisoning it. I scooped handfuls of the rice in soya sauce off the floor, crammed the black mixture into my mouth and swallowed. 'Is this pesticide?' I challenged her. I couldn't control her, though. I was mocking her, but mocking myself too, for my helplessness. I tried doing a count-down, like the calm, determined commander at a satellite launch pad. I kept putting sticky tape across her endlessly blab-bing mouth and tied her arms and legs with a nylon cord, so she could only jump up and down, until she collapsed with exhaustion and went to sleep. 'This is your last chance,' I said, sipping my beer, tipping my armchair backwards and resting my feet on the edge of the bed. 'The last chance. I've had enough.' I felt I needed to deal with her with due ceremony. It was like a TV drama: the moment the other person pisses on your face is the final straw. Up to that point, we could have stuck it out.

Right now, she was mentally ill, just like her mother, who might or might not still have been alive, for all we knew. Our pursuers never let up, day or night, and I reckon that was what tipped Hook-Pinch over the edge. I remember once that a bullet whizzed past us – we could see its trajectory – and embedded itself in a tree trunk without making a sound. Or maybe a little pop, like when you stir-fry peanuts. If it hadn't been such a murky day, no doubt their aim would have been more accurate. We got away because I grabbed the shaft of a handcart parked by the wall and spun it into the middle of the road, where the first police motorbike hit it head on, and a series of cracks filled the alley as if a fire had broken out. The second motorbike smashed into the first and the policeman banged his face on the cart shaft and spat out a mouthful of blood. We ran off with the rest of the crowd and got down into the water. A long time afterwards, when it had all quietened down, we managed to find a dinghy and row away.

Our pursuers were invisible, and even when we did see them, they were completely unmemorable. So I, the one person on our journey who she could see, and who she had come to loathe, as I was getting ever more controlling, came to embody the stress she was under, the weight that bore down on her, the weight she was keenly aware of yet could not see or understand. She couldn't tell truth from fiction any more, and she convinced herself that I was the one who'd taken her virginity, not her stepfather. I was the one who had raped, used and beaten her, hunted her down, starved her, and given her no money, and since he was dead, I was haunting her as his vengeful ghost. Her mind had gone, she could no longer cope with complex ideas, so she simplified things: I represented everyone who meant her harm. She stubbornly believed that whatever thought came into her head must be true. She began to be suspicious and fearful of me; she avoided me and drove me away when I came near. I tried to get her to see sense.

For instance, I said: 'If I was planning to keep you under lock and key, why am I not doing it now?' I tried convincing myself that it was her unhappiness or her stress levels making her ill, but in a couple of days I realised that she was beyond help. When I tried to stop her going out dressed up like a peacock, her response was: 'Now you're keeping me under lock and key, is that it?'

Before I realised she was crazy, I got furious with her one day for picking up a man. I'd been thieving in the city and walking along a back road past a farmhouse when I saw her. I turned around as if I'd just remembered something, and took off my sunglasses so I could see better: there she was leaning against a wall, one knee bent up and her arms around the man's neck, and he was gripping her by the waist. They were completely absorbed in each other, ramping up the enjoyment with whispers and murmurs. I walked up to them and told her: 'Go home.' When the man tried to push his nose into my face, I shoved him out of the way and said: 'This is between her and me,' and thought that after we got back, I would tip my jar of pebbles out on the table and order her to count them. There were thirty-seven of them, and when she asked me why, I'd say I had it in mind to list all her faults one after another. Suddenly that all seemed pointless, though. After I realised she was crazy, I muttered something to the man to make him go. She looked alarmed when I first walked up to them, but he lowered his head and raised his fists. Her acting skills were much better than mine, she seemed to have convinced him I was some sort of monster. What could I do? Spread my hands with a disarming smile and say that I wasn't?

'Come back here.' She stamped her foot and grabbed the man by his jacket.

I turned to go, then stopped and said to the man: 'Did she tell you I was going to kill her?' I put my finger to my temple: 'She's mentally ill, mate. You should have seen that.'

He ran off so fast he nearly tripped over his feet. He must have realised I was right.

Ten days after I realised she was crazy, I killed her. Why wait? Her flare-ups were getting more and more frequent, and she looked increasingly sick, as if something was eating her brain, as if it would soon be an empty shell. I got out some things that were part of the life we had shared, to try and jog her memory, but she completely ignored me. She stared vacantly at me for a long time, then acted all anxious: 'Who are you? What's happening?' She seemed to be trying to figure out if I was a good man or a bad man, and quickly made up her mind that I was a bad man. Otherwise I wouldn't be trying to tie her up all the time.

I decided on the right moment. That last day, she was somehow radiant: back to normal, in fact. Solicitously, I took her arm to escort her outside, like the executioner giving the victim her last meal, I thought. We walked for nearly an hour until we got to a funfair. 'Are you tired?' I asked her. 'Would you like a piggyback?'

'I'm fine walking,' she said.

We walked over to a huge, sad, motionless Ferris wheel suspended between earth and sky. The cabin door was bolted. She gently stroked it and peered in through the window. The manager was a country man with grimy hands and face, wearing a mud-stained tourist's sunhat which must once had been white, and clutched a fistful of low-value notes. He glanced at us, then got on with showing his visitors how to shoot balloons with airguns.

'Hey!' I said, then repeated it, louder, until he finally turned and said: 'I'm not running it for a couple of people.'

'How many do you need?'

'Wait until ten of the cabins are taken, right?'

I went back to Hook-Pinch, who was gazing up at the cables, and thought she must see me as a complete failure. I spread my hands and shook my head. 'We'd better wait then,' she said.

I went back to the manager, who was blowing up balloons. 'I'll pay for ten people,' I said.

'I said ten cabins, that's two people per cabin,' he said.

'No problem.'

He threw down the pump, and was about to tear off the tickets, but I told him not to bother. Although his appearance didn't improve, his manner turned extremely solicitous. He came trotting over and offered his arm to Hook-Pinch as if he was a groom helping a lady into her carriage. Then he unlocked the engine room and fired up the motor. As we rose up into the air, he waved his hat at us. Down below I could see the tin roofs, the dodgems, the merry-go-round, and people getting smaller and smaller.

'Look at where we were,' she said, pointing.

I looked compassionately at this woman I was about to kill.

'Right, yes, that's where we were.' The Ferris wheel creaked and grated slowly round, then we came to a halt at the highest point above the ground, like we had broken down. It felt as if we were suspended in nothingness, weightless, becalmed. I felt a rush of emotions that struck me as pointless. I kneaded her hand. Then the wheel turned mournfully once more.

'Let's go round once more,' she implored me, clutching my sleeve, after we were down. I knew she was faking it. Being too calm was as much a symptom of her illness as being too agitated. But I felt sorry for her.

'OK.'

We had four goes altogether. My eyes were fixed on her face with the anxiety of a peasant checking the sky for rain at harvest time. I never knew when she would flare up. The fact was, when she did, there was nothing I could do, I was screwed. I agreed to everything she said: 'Fine, fine, fine . . .'

We left the funfair and went to a karaoke hall. Although it was still daylight, the interior was barely lit by grease-smeared fluorescent lights, only half of which were working. I couldn't tell if there was a faulty electrical connection or whether they had the lights flicker deliberately, to create an atmosphere. The building was so rickety, it looked like it might collapse at any minute. The rooms were tiny. Screeches and caterwauling could be heard coming from inside. Every singer ought to be made to listen to themselves, like every smoker ought to look at their own lungs. We took a room. The lights seemed to make it darker. It had a sofa with a ripped cover from which springs and foam rubber spewed out. There was a bad smell coming from one corner: it might have been human piss or cat piss, although it was hard to tell which. Hook-Pinch was delighted, this was what she wanted. She held the microphone in one hand, while with the other she stood under the lights and flipped through the song list, then pressed the remote. I lay on the sofa looking around me but there was nothing to see.

'You sing one,' she said.

'I can't sing.'

There was nothing to do except watch her in her dusty clothes, enthroned on her cane stool and belting out her songs. I saw some grey hairs behind her ears. Once, when she had no lines to sing but the music was still playing, she turned to me and bared her spotless white teeth in a genuine smile. I'd never seen such a clean smile. I gave her a wave, feeling unbearable pain in every organ in my body. I reproached myself for never having taken her to gorgeous places, or bought her any jewellery, not so much as a single item of clothing. And I was supposed to be her man! I had drunk a lot. We went back to our room in the courtyard near the tombstones and I played with her hands and looked at her affectionately. She dropped onto the bed and sighed: 'You know, I'm a little in love with you.'

'Me too,' I said.

Then we began to play a game called 'One day . . .' It was nearly New Year and there were firecrackers outside the window, going off with big bangs and then falling through the night sky. Hook-Pinch said one day we'd have loads and loads of children. 'OK,' I said. She came up with a whole lot of names for these non-existent children, each chosen with great care. She figured they should have one of her names and one of mine, so she asked me what my real name was.

'I never asked you before,' she said.

'My surname's Hou and my given name's Fei, the character for "flying".'

'We'll get them piano lessons,' she said, 'and then they'll go to Paris or Pretoria.' I wondered how she kept coming up with these far-flung place names. I took her empty cup and her fingers slipped from mine as she fell happily into an exhausted sleep. I tucked the quilt in, then I got out the meat cleaver, walked past her and threw it out of the window. After that, I sat down and watched her for hours on end. This is good, I thought. It was as if I'd taken her to visit my old home, with its ticking clock, the mouldy smells wafting from the barn, the almanac and the bottles of spirits where they'd always been, those relatives who hadn't moved away dropping in to give their good wishes, watching us fondly. Good to see you back, they'd say. You never forgot your home village, it was the one place worth making your peace with. I reckoned that at about two or three in the morning, she would wake up, well rested, and go and get some water, and we'd sit opposite each other at the table, thinking about nothing in particular. The table would gleam under the oil lamp, the cracks in it filled with dirty old bits of sugar, and an ant would poke out its head and look around. Outside the house, it would look like nothing had changed in years. We would drink spring water from a vat. Life would feel pretty perfect. Then we would go hand in hand to bed, make love when we felt like it, sleep when we felt like it. At daybreak, we would wake up hungry and go out into the courtyard, where the breeze would blow around our bare feet and the bamboo canes would be covered with dewdrops, the world be shrouded in mist, and there would be no one else to be seen. We would collect twigs and branches for fuel and boil up some rice porridge. We might grow mooli and keep a few chickens. Until the day when the police caught up with us, which I knew they would, eventually.

I watched her for a long time. Her face was childishly flushed, robust and round as an apple. The night seemed endless, peaceful. Until the moment when her illness came back and she grew agitated in her sleep. Her face filled with terror once more and then erupted like a volcano, burning, feverish, swollen, and she began to spasm. At my wits' end, I reached out and felt her forehead. In a hate-filled voice, she muttered in her sleep: 'Get off me!'

Everything that had been beautiful was shattered. In a matter of seconds, she would wake up, panting, and grab some weapon or other to drive me out of the room. The whole courtyard – the whole area, even – would hear her terrible cries as they tore through the air around us: Help, help! Or: Murder, murder! And I would pounce on her like a dog and tape up her mouth again to silence her, tying her arms and legs together with nylon cord even as she tore at my flesh with her nails.

No, no, I couldn't go through this again. I climbed on top of her, pulled the pillow from behind her head and pressed it down over her face. I pressed as hard as I could. She arched her body, twisted this way and that. My knuckles went white from the effort of clamping the edges of the pillow over her face. My ring and little fingers hurt like hell, they had no strength left in them. My sweat rained down on the pillow in big drops. Finally, her body relaxed and she lay still. I lifted the pillow away from her face, though it was so stuck to her skin that it was like peeling gauze from a wound.

She was dead.

I scarcely recognised her. There was blood on her lower lip and she had bitten through her tongue; her eyes were wide open and bulging. She had the look of a dumbstruck rag doll, her eyes fixed on the ceiling.

I sat on the edge of the bed. I felt there was a lot I had to do, but at the same time there was nothing I could do. I had to face the remaining time before dawn on my own, I thought.

I found the glass jar in the bedside cupboard and tipped out the pebbles. I said the words I had wanted to humiliate her with, missing nothing out: 'You know I fucked so many women, and you were just one of them, no different from any of the others, little rabbit.'

I took out all her stuff and burned it. From her student card, I learned that her surname was Yu and that she was sixteen years old. I'd thought she was in her mid-twenties.

I left shortly before dawn. She stared vacantly at me as I left.

PART IV

AIWAN, PRESENT DAY

26

Hongliang paused for a moment and Xu Yousheng said, 'He was talking too much, you never knew what Uncle Hongyang was thinking.'

Hongliang agreed: 'Squint was digging himself into a hole he couldn't get out of. He shouldn't have told Hongyang all that stuff. If he was capable of doing away with his woman, as he said, then what was to stop him doing away with one of his mates? As the Good Book says, in the ninth year of the famine in Egypt, Phrasius sought an audience with King Busiris and said he could appease Zeus's anger. All that was needed was to sprinkle a stranger's blood on the altar of the gods. King Busiris answered, "Good, so you can be the first sacrifice to Zeus." Squint had as good as signed his own death warrant. Hongyang wouldn't have got much out of a deal with the Anhui provincial police, so he did one with the local police in Fan township instead. Squint reminds me of young Chen, Shiren's wife: calm on the surface but a real blabbermouth. At heart, he was desperate to get on your good side and to do that, he'd say anything. Even tell lies. I remember that when he had finished talking, he sat there looking sad, like the singer hanging around on stage after the audience has left and the hall's empty.

Squint said this: 'I started to run, with no idea where I was going or what I was hoping for. I began to lose my belongings. One morning I woke up and discovered that the shack by the roadside where I'd huddled for the night had been used as a toilet. The cracked concrete was covered in turds and cigarette paper they'd used to wipe their bums. People turned up almost every day: I was sure because the cigarette butts were all the same make. Still, I was desperate to keep out of the cold, and I hung around for a few days. Sometimes I saw myself in the windows of passing cars and realised that I'd turned into a ragged, unkempt beggar. Actually, I hung out with beggars and passed myself off as one to avoid my pursuers. I missed my woman. If she'd been with me, I wouldn't have been living like this. A woman meant life itself. And I had killed her. Liberty is a noble thing, but I couldn't cope with it on my own. Right now, I would have given a hundred days like this to have even an hour with her.'

In a little while, he gave a quiver, as if he had just finished peeing. And he looked at Hongyang and the rest of us. He seemed to be having difficulty believing what he had done, and did not dare show his panic. We could all see it anyway, if only for a second. There were volumes of information in that second: he had entrusted his deepest secrets to someone who was unfathomable. He'd shared the things he held closest to his soul with her, holding nothing back. It was like he had given away all the family possessions in a moment of confusion, like in *Journey to the West*, when the god-with-one-jewel is holding it tight in his hand and Monkey swipes it, just like that. He felt lost and afraid. For a short while, intoxicated and overwrought, he had shown some remorse, but that soon faded, to be replaced by drunken bravado as he slumped once more into his self-absorption. 'What a terrible business. Who could have known it would end so badly?' He said it several times over, and when Hongyang attempted to cheer him up, he burst into tears.

This was Hongyang's chance to play the villain. The next day, he said to Squint: 'I can see how upset you are. Anyone would feel the same. Hiding out is a scary experience, quite apart from the fact that your whereabouts might leak out, even your smell might carry on the air. I'm not chasing you away, mate, I'd actually like you to stay another two or three days.'

Squint was taken aback and could think of nothing to say. He didn't know whether Hongyang was fed up with him, or whether this whole business had scared Hongyang so much that he wanted nothing more to do with him. Both would have been understandable, but now he was reassured: Hongyang wasn't going to tie him up and deliver him to the police. However, although he could eat and drink as much as he wanted in the village, he was still a man: he couldn't beg Hongyang for protection, the way a woman or a child might. He didn't know what to say. He knew there were limits to human kindness, and he could not blame Hongyang, who had already been kind enough. He choked back the tears, grasped Hongyang's hand in both of his own and said with deep emotion: 'Don't say anything, mate.' You know, Yousheng, Hongyang always chose his words carefully. If he said 'Just do what you like, stay as long as you like' that was exactly what he meant. Hongyang's big-heartedness was in inverse proportion to his education.

During Squint's farewell dinner, Hongyang told Shiren to drive to the county town to buy Squint's train ticket. He managed to grab an unused security guard's uniform from the township's Cooperative shop, thinking that it would make him look similar enough to one of the officials. By the time Shiren came back, the pair of them had finished eating.

'Anything up?' asked Hongyang.

'The police station door's shut, there's no movement inside,' Shiren said.

'And the train station?'

'A ghost town, like always.'

Hongyang sent Shiren to the supermarket to pick up supplies of biscuits and instant noodles, and filled his own stainless-steel thermos with boiling water. Then he gave everything to Squint.

He added more things that he thought Squint might need to the already bulging bag. Squint, feeling like a son being sent away from home, protested: 'Enough! Enough!' and pulled out some of the things.

They were in your uncle Hongxing's house, and by now it was nearly five o'clock. As the lamp cast enormous shadows over the room, Hongyang said: 'Aren't you going to get some sleep?' Then he gave Squint a quick hug and slipped ten thousand yuan into his pocket. It was a perfect bribe: you know you've received the money and at the same time you can pretend to be completely ignorant about it. Ai-ya! Squint didn't know where to put his hand. Should he pull the money out again? Or should he grip Hongyang's arm in an attempt to communicate some of his inexpressible gratitude?

They went outside and Hongyang pushed him into the car. On the way through Fan township, Hongyang urged him to stay out of sight, and Squint ducked down.

'Lights are on at the police station,' Hongyang commented. 'At this time of night they'll all be asleep, though. There's someone on duty, but he'll be asleep too.' At the train station, Hongyang got someone he knew to open up the iron exit gate, and both men hurried inside while Hongyang's buddy looked the other way. Then the man locked up again and exchanged a few words with Hongyang through the silver-painted bars. They crouched in the shadow of a concrete pillar to wait. The rails, worn smooth with use, glimmered in the deathly pale platform lights, although everywhere else was blanketed in darkness. Hongyang asked the station staff about the train a few times, until Squint gently put a hand on his arm.

'It'll come when it comes,' he said.

There was a pervasive smell of engine oil mixed with coal, rubber, timber, salt and shit. In theory, trains could go anywhere in the world: Guiyang, Shaoxing, Yorkshire, Nepal, the North

Atlantic coast . . . I don't know why, but trains always make us think of far-distant places and new lives, and fill us with the fervour of pilgrims. Forty-five minutes late, the train roared into the station, its headlamps blazing. Everything shook as it pulled in: the ground, the windows, and the waist-high weeds growing through cracks in the concrete. The train drew to a halt, snorting and belching out white steam. Passengers laden with bags of all sizes erupted through the ticket gates and crowded on board. Squint waited till they were all inside, and finally strolled up to the train door. Hongyang's parting advice to him was: 'Don't say anything, you're more experienced than me, play it by ear.' Then he waved him off, turned around, and disappeared into the darkness.

'And what were the other words that struck you?' Xu Yousheng asked.

' "Emotional messes." ' Hongliang leaned his head to one side, half-cupped one hand over his mouth and with the other raked the toothpick back and forth between his teeth. Then he chewed as if he had a mouthful of chewing gum, and spat out a wodge of masticated meat. 'You don't know how many of those I've seen, mate,' he said.

Hongliang began to speak again, this time about Police Chief Zhao.

'Should I tell him or not?' Zhao Zhongnan kept asking. The more he insisted, the more I felt he wasn't blaming himself at all. In any anecdote he told, he always ridiculed the person he was talking about, implying they were an arsehole, although at the same time there was a hint of sympathy for the butt of his joke too.

Zhongnan was three years older than me and, like me, had won a place at the area's normal school with his strong exam scores. It was a memorable day for our teacher, Mr Zhu. Most people think normal schools aren't proper educational establishments, and that teacher training doesn't offer good prospects. In those days, though, only the three best of those taking their middle school exams qualified for normal school, and the rest had to go to senior high. We could have decided not to take up our places, but it was put to us that we should go because we were poor. Your maternal grandmother worked it out like this, see? Three years of normal school and you'll be earning a monthly salary. If you go to university, though, that's a total of seven years, with the four years of middle school, as well as a lot of expenses, and if you don't go to university, or you don't get a job at the end of it, then it's all gone to waste.

A normal school education isn't actually all that bad. Nowadays it's the only place where they still nurture the spirit, the soul and the body, where there's still a belief in 'purely ornamental' subjects such as poetry, philosophy, classical music and

theatre, ones that have no market value. Universities, meanwhile, devote all their attention to imparting the kind of skills
and knowledge connected with 'requirements'. It's like the
recruitment slogan goes: 'Providing undergraduate courses
that are immediately applicable to the real world!' They seem
to believe that humans are superior to animals because they can
invent, use and perfect tools, whereas normal schools, which
universities despise as the lowest form of educational institution, admonish their students to excel as people. They believe
mankind ought to aspire to nobility, impose its laws on society,
define the value of their own lives: to be pure and sublime.
They should not waste their energies on this meaningless
human world, abandoning themselves to despair and rolling in
the mire like pigs.

To start with, Zhongnan and I lived like a pair of hermits,
burning the midnight oil, debating who had produced the best
translation of *One Hundred Years of Solitude*, Huang Jinyan or Gao
Changrong, perusing Shelley and Byron, spending our money on
the works of the imperial Hanlin scholars, using the school
photocopier to bring out our own poetry magazine, which we
called *Quantum Poetry* – even though we only brought out seven
issues and only printed ten copies of each issue – and studying
the flora of the seventeen mountains that encircled Fan township. But as soon as Zhongnan got into the police, he changed
into an arse-licker when he was around his bosses, and a bully to
his subordinates. Overnight he became a running dog, devoted
to the interests and petty politics of his little local police department. He picked it all up without the benefit of any teacher until
he was getting along in that world better than men who had
years of experience. Soon enough, he wouldn't acknowledge any
of the villagers, not even his family, let alone his old classmates.

A while later, I had a cosy chat with him one evening – or at
least I sat with him while he talked at me. It was when he was

doing us the honour of a visit. He arrived in Aiwan at the wheel of his huge jeep, his eyes half-closed, one foot on the dashboard and the other on the accelerator. His uniform was unbuttoned and he was sprawled back in his seat, almost lying flat. He'd come to present Hongyang with a commendation recognising his meritorious actions, after which he'd spent all day eating and drinking with low-level officials: the village Party Secretary, head of the village committee, the bookkeeper and the production team leader. He pasted a smile on his face as he listened to their reports, although they were doing nothing more than singing his praises and asking for favours. Occasionally he would drape an arm around the shoulders of one of the officials, as if he were the emperor and they his ministers. He granted none of their requests, just kept refilling their glasses. You should have heard the language: vulgar, corrupt, obscene! Zhongnan sang a raucous song from *Outlaws of the Marsh* . . . And to think that this was the man who once declaimed Shelley's poem for his students:

> Be through my lips to unawakened earth
> The trumpet of a prophecy! O, Wind,
> If Winter comes, can Spring be far behind?

Tears poured down his face all the while. On this evening, when he was paralytically drunk, so Chief of Police Zhao – who has now taken over Yuan Qihai's position, even though he's technically too junior for it – took his leave on the pretext that he had to go and see a fellow student. And take note! It wasn't that he suddenly missed me, it was simply that it had occurred to him that I gave him a good excuse to get away. So the village officials held him upright as he staggered to my house. It was one step forward, two steps back, so badly were his legs shaking. Disgraceful!

When they finally got to my doorstep, they picked him up and manhandled him into the armchair, and he waved them off with the enigmatic words: 'You, home.' Then he plucked at his lips and spluttered and ordered me to make him some tea. He always loved the tea leaves my mother grew. I gave him the teacup filled with boiling water. He blew the tea leaves to one side, put the lid on so the tea could steep, and began to subject me to close examination, his eyes floating over me as if they were defying the forces of gravity. There was a hint of curiosity in his gaze, like with city folk, although it seemed affectionate too. 'Your head needs a shave, mate. If I wasn't a policeman, I'd grow mine as long as yours too, but there's no way they'd allow it, is there? . . . Rules, you know . . . You married? . . . You're no spring chicken, you should get yourself fixed up . . . I've been thinking of getting a car, everyone can do with a car, useful for picking up the kids, you know?'

Fine, I said to myself. We were getting on like a house on fire. Then he started repeating 'Emotional messes, emotional messes, emotional messes, emotional messes, so much mess,' over and over. I took it to mean he was being emphatic, and showing off that he was internet-savvy.

Zhongnan told me: We officers got on the train at Lushan station. The police jeep was on standby at Yangxin station. Hou Fei – that was Squint's real name – was coming from Ruichang. Lushan–Ruichang–Yangxin. We couldn't intercept him until the train arrived at Yangxin station and we could get him off. We were respecting Hongyang's wishes by carrying out the operation like this. He had insisted on it before he reported Hou Fei to us.

The train was a K train, so it had to give way to the T and the D express trains. It was forty minutes late arriving at Lushan station, where for some reason it stopped another five minutes. Chief Yuan called Hongyang's phone, but Hongyang didn't pick up. We had a bad feeling about that. It certainly wouldn't

be the first time we'd had all the officers at the police station
mobilised and someone had made fools of us! Hongyang was a
man you could trust, though. Dongming always stressed that.
If you couldn't trust Hongyang, he used to say, you couldn't
trust anyone.

After the train started moving, I got a text that Hongyang
had asked someone to send for him: *All fixed. Waiting to board
train.* At that point, we had second thoughts. I mean, this was a
Public Security Grade-A Wanted Criminal. We'd never nabbed
such a high-grade criminal before. The passenger platform
between the carriages swayed lightly, the sunlight appeared to
glimmer and dance. Slowly does it, we thought, but the train
was going like greased lightning and in no time at all we had
covered half the distance. Chief Yuan pulled back the curtains.
It was as if a black dragon was following along outside: we
could see its backbone rearing up, then flattening.

'Come and have a drink!' Yuan invited us. His eyes were red-
rimmed, and his hands shook slightly as he took out his hip
flask. He often showed this display of nerves when he appeared
in public in days to come, but that was the time I learned he had
never been on a platform or met the higher-ups. Even though
he squeezed his fingers together, when we chinked glasses, still
they shook as if he had Parkinson's.

After half an hour, we arrived at Ruichang station. As the
train chuntered to a halt, we looked at each other in dismay.
Then Chief Yuan gave a hurried signal with his hand and Xuetao
and Xiaocheng went to either end of the carriage to guard the
doors.

'Handcuffs ready?' Yuan asked quietly.

'Ready,' I responded.

We sat in the corridor seats pretending to chat, like extras on
a film set. With no scripts in our hands, all we could do was
keep our lips moving and force out a few words. Our carriage

was reserved for passengers getting on at Ruichang. They all pushed their way on, and sighed with relief when they found that there were plenty of spare seats. They assumed we'd come from another province, so they treated us with great respect. Chief Yuan had his mobile resting on his left thigh, and he kept glancing down at it. We knew which train it was and which number, and we knew he'd be sitting diagonally across from where we were. But it was a long wait. I was just thinking of getting up for a look when the chief touched my arm and jerked his chin in the direction of the window. Outside, I saw Hongyang walking away, then turning to look back and waving in our direction.

'Get ready,' said Chief Yuan.

'Right,' I said.

Hou Fei got into the carriage, looking around him. He was wearing a security guard's cap, and carried a backpack so tall that for a moment it obscured the overhead light and threw a dark shadow in front of him. I swallowed. I was worried that the noise would give me away, but I was also afraid that if I didn't swallow I'd choke. He looked at us intently, not the way strangers normally look at each other. He was obviously trying to figure out if we were police. Chief Yuan glared back, which seemed to make Hou Fei embarrassed about his suspicions. He found his seat and offloaded the backpack, then got up again and made as if to shove the backpack up into the luggage rack. He was standing in front of us and I noticed that his uniform looked a bit short on him, so that you could see his long johns under his tightly belted trousers as he stood on tiptoe. Then he seemed to change his mind, pulled the pack down and bent to put it under the bunk bed. That done, he patted the dust off his hands, then reached down again, pulled open the bag's zip and rummaged around for something inside.

All this bending down exposed a large expanse of swarthy back and buttocks. We carried on talking, about how supermarkets had forced corner shops out of business, we felt that the key thing was to sound confident, though it has to be said we weren't too confident about speaking in standard Chinese. He took a pack of dried bean curd out of his bag, pulled open the serrated plastic edge and chewed slowly. Then he got out a T-shirt – we saw later that it was a long blue stripy T-shirt – out of his pack, spread it out on his knees, then refolded it gently and put it away. There were big tears in his eyes and he was muttering: 'Slut, slut, slut . . .' over and over. Then he poured some water out of his thermos and sipped slowly, after which, probably because once he was warmed up he started to want other pleasures, he pulled out a pack of cigarettes. Trouble was he couldn't find a lighter, no matter how hard he searched his trouser pockets. He looked at the steamed-up window, trying to remember where he had put it and patting all his pockets.

Just then there was an announcement: they were extremely sorry, but the train would be held at the station another ten minutes. Later, Hongyang said he was furious with us. Although he said he didn't blame us, there was accusation in every sentence he spoke. 'How will I ever hold up my head again?' He was very emotional.

Chief Yuan sounded embarrassed, or perhaps more accurately, injured. 'These operations are a delicate business. I told them to get moving, but you're quite wrong to say that we didn't consider your position before we moved in on him, quite wrong.'

Dongming added: 'For one thing, once a suspect's caught, he's halfway to execution – no escape – and we don't care what a dead man thinks of us. And for another, it was vitally important when and where he was arrested. If we'd arrested him in Yangxin, we might have needed the north Hubei police's cooperation, and if they'd made the arrest, you wouldn't have got the credit for your goodwill gesture, Hongyang.'

'Don't talk to me about goodwill,' said Hongyang. 'I didn't do it out of goodwill.'

'Of course you did it out of goodwill,' said Chief Yuan.

'Yousheng,' Hongliang interrupted Zhongnan's story at this point, 'it was clever of your Uncle Hongyang to put on such a petulant air. He wanted the police to feel less indebted to him, so he played dumb. He was trying to wind them up, because he didn't want them to feel too obliged to him, he knew anyone with a reputation to consider could not allow themselves to accept a peasant's good deed. Hongyang flatly denied any connection with the affair, and he refused to allow us to mention it in his presence. The reasons were simple: he was well known as a scoundrel and he wanted to keep it that way, and he did not want to antagonise the local police.'

'You caught him. It had nothing to do with me,' Hongyang said. How should I put it? At the start, he did hold meetings with us. He kept setting conditions, he wanted to make sure that Hou Fei didn't stumble across the fact that it was he, Hongyang, who'd informed on him. He negotiated with us the time and place of the arrest, even demanded that we should not identify ourselves as being Fan township police and, more broadly, stipulated that our investigations team should not talk in dialect in front of Hou Fei. Hongyang was of course right to be concerned. If we had let the train go on a bit, Hou Fei might not have suffered so much, but because the train was held at the station, we arrested him, and he kept asking if someone had turned him in. It was only when the second announcement came – 'This train is about to depart' – that it dawned on us that we could arrest Hou Fei here.

Why wait another hour? Anything could happen in an hour: he might go for a smoke, or go out to take a piss. He might go and look for boiling water for his instant noodles, or go to ask the train guard something, and disappear from under our noses. He only needed to become the slightest bit wary of us. Hadn't he already managed to evade police capture on countless occasions? If he went off to do any of those things, and we were on his heels all the time, he'd take off straight away, wouldn't he? It would be no problem in a sleeper carriage, but imagine the chaos if he got into a seated carriage, if he took someone hostage. Then we'd be responsible, and we'd have to alert the transport police. How would we explain things to them? Four of us here, and all in plain clothes. If we got out our police ID and showed it to them they'd have to help us, but then we'd have to share some of the credit for the operation's success with them, wouldn't we? And what if the transport police arrested him? They're a separate police force. A railway carriage is their territory, like an American plane flying over China is still in American territory even though the airspace is ours. If they insisted he was theirs, there would be nothing we could do, and if we arrested him on their territory all we'd be able to say was: Fine, fine, we're all one big, happy family, and curse ourselves for being arseholes. And that's without taking into account how dark it was, for the only lights, around the train doors and in the corridors, were dim, and even they would switch off when the train got moving.

He's sitting in the dark, we thought, a dark shadow, and once the train starts off even that shadow will disappear. And we're supposed to sit here for another hour putting on a big act of chatting away, and then we have to settle down on our bunks so he doesn't suspect anything. Even when we're sitting up, we can't see anything he's doing. He might have a knife and stab us with it, and we still wouldn't see anything. All we can go on are our physical sensations; how many things come to grief because people drag their heels, how many people dither because they regret something that's been and gone. Why should we listen to Hongyang? He's not our grandpa! And besides, we'll get a chance to explain it to him now. We should forget about Hongyang and arrest Hou Fei, otherwise he'll do a runner. And this is what we told Hongyang too. 'We're really grateful to you, Hongyang,' we said. But Hongliang, I'm telling you, when there's a lamb gambolling around right in front of your eyes, what wolf's not going to give into temptation, eh?

Chief Yuan tried a few times to give the order, and each time it stuck in his throat. We were watching him. Finally, when the telltale crackle indicated that the announcer was about to start up again, Chief Yuan seemed to be jolted back to his senses. He leapt to his feet and waved his arms mechanically at the officers on either side of him, and I stood up.

'Get him,' the chief ordered, looking as if he was about to collapse.

Hou Fei charged at me, and I felt like he was going to break my body apart. It was only because I happened to be standing between the beds and blocking his exit that I'm here today as head of the station. At the time, I went blank, but the chief squeezed through and banged him savagely about the ears, and we rushed to hold him down. The way we were positioned, it looked like I was fucking Hou Fei and the chief was fucking me. Hou Fei made no sound.

Once the announcement was finished, there was a screech from the train and we bundled Hou Fei outside and pinned him down again on the platform. 'You don't need to sit on me like this. If I'd wanted to escape, I'd be long gone,' said Hou Fei. Under the dim platform lighting, we could see that his face was expressionless and he looked totally relaxed. We pushed him down a few more times and he said: 'What are you doing that for? Cuff me and leave it at that.' I got out the cuffs and he held out his wrists.

The startled train stewardess was watching all this going on, as if being a public servant meant she ought to put a stop to it. As she hesitantly raised the walkie-talkie to her mouth, Xuetao got out his police ID and said arrogantly: 'This is our territory, nothing to do with you.'

The woman backed off a couple of steps, the train doors slammed and the train began to move, so slowly at first that it seemed it was just getting the hang of moving in slow motion. We kicked open the gates of Ruichang station and staggered out as the car the chief had ordered raced up, driven by the chief's brother-in-law. He took us to his establishment, the Bituo Hotel, which had once been a shop and had only a dozen guest rooms. The banisters of the spiral staircase were hung with massage towels from top to bottom, in the belief that airing them would make the lice and the thrush fungus disappear of their own accord, so that the place could legitimately call itself a hotel.

'Out, out, all of this out,' ordered the chief when we got to the large room on the top floor. At first the hotel owner was struck dumb by the order, which came in standard Chinese. But then he jumped to it, hurriedly moving a mah-jong table out of the room and spilling some mah-jong pieces, which the chief kicked away. The chief kept kicking, and the man kept rushing to salvage them from under his feet, and then a mouse shot from under the bed and disappeared outside. Xiaocheng picked up the overturned chairs, while Xuetao wiped the dust from the tabletop with his sleeve. All the while, I kept on gently kicking Hou Fei behind the kneecaps.

'You don't need to do that,' said Hou Fei, and the chief looked at him, then at me, and said: 'No, you don't need to, bring him a chair.' So I brought him a chair and we unplugged the lamp on the bedside cupboard and put it on the table. In the harsh lamplight, we could see every wrinkle and line on his face. I stared hard, but there was nothing unusual about him. He was normal, with nothing to physically mark him out as different from the rest of us. He didn't look like a killer: if anything, he was surprisingly cooperative.

Liu, the chief's worthless brother-in-law, arrived holding a basin of icy water in both hands. He poked his head through the door and caught the chief's eye for permission to come in, then firmly tossed the mix of water and ice over the criminal. 'Out,' ordered the chief, and Liu went out but came back to ask if we wanted noodles. 'Out, I said,' the chief repeated and told us: 'You won't need anything, anything at all, just see how he's going to confess.' And Hou Fei said himself: 'Ask me to my face and I'll tell you whatever you want to know, just ask.' We were annoyed at ourselves for not bringing enough pens and paper, we made him some tea and lit a cigarette for him, and when he got to the end of his account and said, 'That's it,' we believed him. That was enough; what he'd told us was fabulous. The chief gave the head of the bureau a call and woke him to share the good news. He acted like he was standing at the bureau chief's bedside, clasping his mobile, bowing and scraping, saying that yes, this was a unique opportunity for Chief Yuan, yes, this might see him move from junior to senior grade, and when he put the phone down, Yuan stood there for a long time savouring the glory of that moment. 'You did well,' the bureau chief had said.

We grasped the first finger of Hou Fei's right hand, pressed it into the ink, then applied his fingerprint to each page of his statement. Hou Fei used a tissue to wipe his finger clean, and asked with complete assurance, as if he were expecting payment for services rendered, as if he'd thought it all out in advance: 'So now, tell me, who was it shopped me?'

He was astonished when Chief Yuan responded: 'No one did.'

'So how did you know I was on that train and in that carriage?' asked Hou Fei. The chief was silent for a moment, then he said: 'Do you have any idea how infamous you are? Do you know how many people all over the country were out to get you?'

'No, I didn't,' said Hou Fei.

'Did you know how long we've been after you?' said Chief Yuan.

'No, I didn't,' said Hou Fei.

'It's been damned difficult to find you,' said the chief, slapping his head. 'Damned difficult, damned difficult,' he repeated.

We all thought the chief handled it well, but even a pig can tell when something's a bit off, don't you think, Hongliang? And after that, every time Hou Fei saw me, he'd ask: 'Who was it shopped me?'

'No one,' I would reply.

'Really?'

'Really.'

'You guarantee that?'

'I guarantee it.'

'You swear?'

'I swear.'

I think he did the same with other people too. His question was always 'Did anyone shop me?' or 'Who shopped me?' and he never mentioned Hongyang until, one day in court, he tried to inveigle the truth out of us by mentioning the name he had protected so carefully. He was making his confession when he said: 'It was after Ai Hongyang shopped me that . . .' As he spoke he watched our reactions carefully. To check the particulars, we always leafed through the previous day's notes as we listened to the accused give his statement, but simply grunted in response. Hou Fei's eyes flashed and he said in a low voice,

'Now I know.' At this point, the chief stepped in and banged the table. 'Who did you just say? Say that again!' Hou Fei said nothing more, though. Once he had been taken away, we all heaved a long sigh.

In the following days, not one of his interrogators knew who was responsible for turning him in, even though he was to undergo many more interrogations. I thought I wouldn't have anything more to do with this business, but I bumped into him twice more, and these meetings made me feel ashamed of myself, you know, Hongliang? And that's not a good feeling.

The first time was when he was in detention, and he stood in front of me with tears running down his face. 'It doesn't matter, you can tell me now,' he said. 'I'm going to die anyway, you know? I'm going to die.' I hesitated – it was as if this thing he kept talking about, heaven and earth and you and me, we all knew that even if the rules were broken no one would know it was I, Zhao Zhongnan, who had broken them. I could have nodded and that would have been fine, but I shook my head. He stood up with those heavy shackles dragging on his feet, angrily shaking the immovable railings, swearing furiously at me: 'Fuck your mother's cunt, fuck your mother's cunt, I fuck your mother's cunt.'

He could curse with the best of them. By now, his eyes were bloodshot and the sockets were heavily pigmented, the dark folds of the bags under his eyes were covered in pimples as big as rice grains, and his hair had gone completely white. He looked like a ball cactus covered with white prickles. His skin was deadly pale, as if his blood had been sucked dry, probably by the insomnia and constant thinking that plagued him all night long, like a lorry stuck in the mud and out of its last drop of fuel. The prison guards said that once the detainee in question had had a sudden dizzy spell and collapsed on the ground, after which he vomited with the force of an out-of-control fire hose; his head had kept lolling back and forth until the walls were covered with vomit. He suffered terribly. Thinking back on it, our ploy was glaringly obvious, anyone with the least nous would have stumbled upon it, but he was overthinking things, and that brought on anaemia, malnutrition, dizziness and vomiting, and possibly a stroke as well.

A or B, B or A, Yousheng. While in prison, Squint kept picking over the arguments. It was as if he was two different people talking.

Squint One: 'Hongyang was the one who helped me out and beat up Wolfdog and was still concerned about me even when he was about to get out of jail.'

Squint Two: 'That's in the past, and now look at Hongyang, he takes one step and the police come running. And don't forget it was you who came to Hongyang's rescue in the field of the Reform through Education camp.'

Squint One: 'If Hongyang was going to shop me, then why did he take me to the hydroelectric power plant? I could have taken off straight from there, and if I'd gone he wouldn't have got any reward. If he'd wanted to denounce me all he needed to do was call 110, so why bother to make it all so complicated? Once the police had me, I was going to die, and what did he have to fear from a dead man?'

Squint Two: 'You're such a jerk.'

That would reduce Squint One to tears of self-pity, and he would repeat to himself: 'I'm a jerk, such a jerk.'

And so it went on. Squint went over and over these questions day after day. Of course, we also must take into consideration that he knew he was facing death. He only had to close his eyes to see its spectre standing before him like a bloodthirsty butcher.

The condemned men would do anything to get away from Death's baleful stare. They'd spend all day and all night distracting themselves by feeding the ants, the flies and the bugs,

plotting ever more imaginative ways of getting out of jail. They
stared for hours at the prison wall, ordering themselves to get
through that hairline crack and flee, the way the Daoist monks
of Mount Lao once had. They needed to feel part of a cause,
and Squint's was a brain-teaser. A or B, B or A, this was much
more real than their usual games, because every time Squint
went on about whether Hongyang had betrayed him, he was
faced with deciding the ultimate question: was he, Squint, a
noble man or a vile one?

He wavered between feeling guilty and being convinced of
his innocence, between gratitude and blame. In this heightened
state of mind, he recalled every second he and Hongyang had
spent together, subjecting every action and underlying action to
repeated examination, making everything increasingly complicated, and abstruse, and confusing, and incomprehensible. But
when push came to shove, this was just a game, even though he
didn't want to acknowledge it. Wasn't it, Yousheng? It was an
iron-clad fact that he was going to die, and no matter which
conclusion he came to, nothing would change that. We live in a
godless age, and he could not haunt Hongyang to express his
gratitude or wreak revenge.

The second time I saw him was in the prison's press conference room. Photographers were clicking away and I got my
camera out and started clicking too. The moment I lowered the
camera, he looked up and asked me bluntly: 'Did he . . .?'
Everyone turned to look at me. I told him: 'Don't think about it
any more.' He smiled wryly as if he agreed with me. The fruit
and cigarettes on the table had not moved. The fruit was all
imported. I reckon they must have spent hundreds of yuan on
it. Everyone was silent, looking gloomily at him – people often
assume doleful expressions to hide their curiosity.

Soon he was put in an Iveco prison van that looked like a
small white villa. With a lot of clinking, two police guards

undid Squint's handcuffs and bound him tightly with rope, the way a general going into battle might be encased in a suit of armour: with anxious expressions and extreme caution, they bent down and undid his leg shackles, then slapped him on the shoulder. Everybody took a deep breath, then exhaled slowly. Outside the room, the skies were leaden and motionless and peculiarly oppressive.

'Dreadful day,' said Squint as he was about to be escorted away. I hid myself in the background, thinking I would wait until the prison van had driven off and disappeared, and that it would finally be an end to this business, but the head of the city's Public Security Bureau insisted that I get in the prison van with the psychologist.

I don't know why, but Squint always seemed fond of me. He called me 'mate' and looked up to me, even though I was quite a bit younger than him, and according to the police chiefs it was possible that my going with him might produce a miracle, that he might fling himself to his knees and thank the police moments before his execution. Some people did believe that, or maybe it was the prisoner's idea to have me go with him.

During the whole slow journey, I never said a word. The psychologist said the usual comforting things and then lapsed into silence too. Finally, when we were almost there, Squint spoke again, but it was only to repeat himself: 'Dreadful day.'

I forced myself to respond: 'Right, the weather's foul, driving's difficult, and it looks like it's going to rain again.'

'Right,' he said.

Then I followed up with: 'You've only got to go one way – we've got to get back too.' The words come from an anecdote in Proust, the anecdote that Mr Zhu the teacher relished the most: the condemned prisoner on the road to execution complains bitterly that he has to make this appalling journey on such a gloomy day, and the priest, thinking to comfort the prisoner in true Christian spirit, says: 'What are you complaining about, young man, you're only going one way, but I've got to make the return journey in the same weather.'

Squint looked at me and said: 'You can tell me now.'

Hongliang, I swear I wanted to jump to my feet in the prison van and announce: Yes! Yes! He did! But I said nothing. I rubbed one hand against the other. 'Silence is as good as a confession,' he said. I told him that wasn't true. The door to the prison van was pulled open and Squint was dragged out, struggling all the while. He was red in the face with rage and kept spitting in my direction. I stayed stock-still. As the police officers marched him away, he kept turning round, looking vengeful. As he got further away, it was hard to tell whether he was still turning his head or not, though his wretched cries echoed around the execution ground: 'If he did, raise your hand!' I stood where I was, both hands dangling uselessly at my sides.

He carried on walking until he got to a certain point, like someone walking into a lake who finds himself in unexpectedly deep water, and he finally surrendered to the terror of staring death in the eyes. He started to shake all over, his legs gave way, and the guards dragged him forward, his feet scuffing the ground, the tips of his shoes bouncing along the ground as he gasped violently – that's what they said, 'gasping violently'. His eyes were blank, as if the life had already left his body. I gave my camera to the driver and said: 'You just have to press that button.' The driver took some pictures of me, with the prisoner being dragged away in the background.

29

Rain, morning or afternoon, mostly in the morning; croaking frogs, swarming midges, disappearing shadows, and the black shapes of innumerable tanks or fleets seeming to take off and hang motionless in the sky.

Dawn brought the interminable story about Hongyang to a temporary halt, and Hongliang turned off the fan, shut the windows and put a coat over Xu Yousheng, who was slumped asleep over his desk. Xu Yousheng had been leafing through Ovid's *Art of Love*, and had almost got to the end. Hongliang had covered it with notes and underlined keywords.

As Xu Yousheng had earnestly perused his uncle's admonishments and injunctions to himself in his flamboyant script, Hongliang had scratched himself and followed line by line.

'These are all techniques for when a man and woman are in the throes of passion,' Xu Yousheng had said. 'No point in asking me, Uncle.'

Hongliang had let out a long-pent-up sigh. 'It's just for fun, and anything I ask you is just for fun too. It was written for upper-class Romans to read, to teach them how to seduce maids and matrons at the theatre, in colonnades, at the racecourse or banquets. Nothing to do with us country folk, it doesn't supply any techniques for lovemaking in a cowshed or on a field dyke. It doesn't explicitly set out to humiliate people like us, but I feel humiliated by what it doesn't say. Ovid reckoned that neither country people nor beasts had anything to say about love. You should ask: But aren't they the sort of women we long to possess? And then I could answer: Even if it grows wings on its back, a toad can't marry a swan. That's something we have to accept.'

Yilian's name made it obvious that she was from a city family. When she crept in, I was mending a TV that was on the verge of blowing up, and had my back to the entrance gate. I had taken off the screen when some kids came running like the wind, like that gave them the right to broadcast the news all around the village: 'A posh lady's here!' they shouted. That had nothing to do with me. I carried on jabbing at the circuit board with my screwdriver, not really trying to fix it, more like angrily destroying it. A bit like a doctor who doesn't see any chance of the operation succeeding might stick the scalpel into the patient's chest just for the hell of it.

In the midst of this irritating noise I heard something quite different: gauze, or snowflakes settling on the ground. When you've lived a long time in the countryside, you become sensitive to space. Shadows have substance. A shadow slithers to the ground like fine silk, raising a momentary cloud of dust. I heard my neighbour stomping past with a hoe over his shoulder, heard him halt, hold his breath and look in my direction, and I sensed a stranger standing between the two of us. I turned around and saw Yilian, right there in the doorway, in the flesh, her chest rising and falling gently, her lips trembling slightly – she always had an adorable Cupid's bow. A bead of sweat was trickling down her cheek, and one toe poked out of her flat sandals. She pushed it down, but it naughtily, or perhaps bashfully, poked up again.

I went scarlet to my ears. She had materialised out of nowhere, out of the depths of my imagination, and I was dumbstruck. It was as if stones were raining down on me, as if my body was as empty as a ravine in a rainstorm with a torrent roiling down it. I could happily take this punishment: I wanted my life to stop right there, in that very moment. When a warm wave of bliss rushes over us, that's enough. We shouldn't go any further. This girl was still living a lie. She shouldn't have to have her eyes stream with the smell of ammonia in the latrine, or witness the maggots crawling interminably around the edge of the hole; she shouldn't have to know that in the innermost corners of my house, rats died and rotted – the same rats, in fact, that just yesterday leapt merrily onto the table, dived under the muslin cover and ate a third of your leftovers, Yousheng. It wasn't right that she knew that under the mattress there was rice straw, that the cooking pot had a thick layer of rust that would never come off, and that the water always tasted of limescale. Quite different from the bucolic life of your imagination, girl, I thought, where poverty is fresh, clean, exquisitely refined. She must have pictured pines and cypress trees, a vine-clad cottage, stuff like that. You have no idea that that kind of poverty is constructed from prosperity, and all I can offer you is iron-clad, real-life poverty. The sort of grinding poverty revolutionary operas used to be written about. Poverty where you're so poor you won't even pass up a piece of cow dung.

Yilian rode a series of buses to get here from Xiushui county town, without alerting her parents or telling me she was coming, and the way she took charge of her own life told me she was a fundamentalist by nature, that when she was young she had probably read a magazine article that formed her views on love, and that she might never have relinquished these views. We all know that the media back then preached equality in love and kept spreading cruel stories that convinced simple-minded girls that love equalled sacrifice. If they didn't make sacrifices, it wasn't true love, so a lot of them felt duty-bound to marry men with shattered limbs. They probably wanted to marry an idea rather than a real man, and now as Yilian stepped over the threshold of my house I saw the evangelism that blazed in her eyes. She was incredibly naive and superstitious, but at the same time she remained full of self-belief.

It wouldn't take long. It would happen very, very quickly that increasing proximity to reality would make her repent her rash choice. Her parents had predicted from the start that she would not be able to extricate herself from her predicament, that she would wallow helplessly in tearful misery until the end of her days.

Xu Yousheng cried out in his sleep in standard Chinese, not dialect: 'I miss you, of course I miss you, I miss you so much!'

A few days later, I pushed Yilian out of the door, together with her pink leather suitcase. She was obviously upset but she kept walking, firing up and gaining momentum like a car engine needing to be push-started. I felt that I'd done the right thing. The last few days, her expression had never betrayed any dissatisfaction or suffering. It was me who felt that she wasn't for me. I thought of my mum's words: 'Many men have their eye on a girl like that, and you're not strong. They might do away with you.' I also thought of the words of the classic *The Commentary of Zuo*, 'Riches arouse envy in others.'

It was a dream I had that forced me to act. Just like the dream you're having now. Before you drop off you don't know what's going to happen, but when you wake up you can find your mind completely made up. It was a dream and yet wasn't a dream: a wise man beckoned to me and told me what was going to happen sooner or later to this love affair. He was like your maternal grandfather when he was alive, he felt responsible for me, and his teaching was straight down the line: he didn't deceive me, or hide anything or exaggerate. By comparison, my days with Yilian felt like a dream. She was very naive, though she learned quickly, playing her part with a man, me, who was deliberately deceiving himself.

In this dream I had, Yilian and I strolled through the streets of Fan township in glorious sunshine, trailing shadows behind us like dark gauze. Judging by our intertwined fingers, our relationship was on a firm footing and we might even have already been to the registry office. However, that was no protection for me. She was always demanding to be taken into town. I thought this was ominous but couldn't well refuse, so I said, 'Fine, let's go to town,' trying to make it look as if I genuinely wanted to go. In my heart of hearts, though, I was hoping we could get back as soon as possible. The sun shone silver, as if chunks of glass in the hair salon's mirrors had shattered and lay glinting in the street. Before we got to the market, I'd been acting romantic with her, and when she seemed so absent, I started laying it on thick until it got to the point that I was sick of hearing myself.

Who can be bothered to answer questions like 'Do you love me?' when you're getting to the bustling heart of the city? It was gloriously sunny, Yousheng, bright and clear, so that the tiniest things stood out in clear detail, even the individual grains of moist sand in the brown shadows. She was obviously buying stuff for our lives together. She picked up washbowls decorated with double-happiness characters (囍), spittoons, soft cotton pyjamas, and children's clothes with babies embroidered on them. I couldn't help feeling embarrassed, and the more embarrassed I felt, the more my love welled up inside me, until it grew so intense that I nearly cupped her face between my hands and kissed her. Then I watched as she went off to the toilet, leaving me stroking the purchases that were evidence, like an anxious high school graduate caressing his university offer letter with its official stamp. I sat on a stone to wait, feeling secure. Then a man sauntered over to chat. He was casual, but mixed in with the matey language there was a sort of insolence. That worried me.

'Come shopping, have you?' he said.

'Uh-huh.'

'What have you got there? Is she having a baby?' He started pawing the stuff I was holding.

'We're planning one.'

He looked around the market. 'I've never seen your girl, but I've heard she's very pretty.'

I felt like my tongue was trembling. And I was afraid he might see my weakness, the kind of light-headedness that hits when you haven't eaten for days. What a bastard, asking a man about his woman like that. Not that it bothered him; he was known in the area for being an inveterate womaniser. He didn't work on the land and was an idler who spent his whole time planning how to destroy one of the things this town was well known for: the innate chastity of its women. It was like destroying birds' nests. He was bad through and through. He pursued his prey – that is, any woman in the town with the slightest good looks – openly and crudely, flattering them and cajoling them into having 'a bit of fun', with a cold smile. Men like that aren't supposed to be able to win women's hearts, but the fact is that he only had to dangle a few compliments in front of them and they seemed bewitched. Every one of them grew restless, started skulking on street corners, obviously waiting for him to appear again. He pulled loads of women, even though they probably knew before it happened that they'd be booted out of the door first thing the following morning. He was blatant, he'd grab the breast of the woman he was with and say to her: 'I want to come inside you.' And he didn't bother to keep his voice down either. The women didn't seem to mind, though – they fobbed other men off, sure, but him they invited straight in. Sometimes they got into fights with other women about him. The other men in the township were sour about it all. Rumour had it that he had a very long penis and could satisfy any woman's fantasies and desires. He was not a local, not particularly good-looking, pale, short even, but he made sure to present himself well, with his neat haircut and his clothes always neatly ironed, his jewellery and eau de cologne, the way he walked, even down to subtleties like the way he folded his napkin after eating. He wasn't like us. He brought a whiff of the outside world with him. He probably let them mother him too.

Just now, as he followed in the direction Yilian had gone, I hoped the thing I dreaded wasn't going to happen. I told myself that at the rate he was walking he'd be past the toilets before Yilian came out – you know how women are, always spending such a long time in the toilet. And even if they did bump into each other and say hello, he might be able to restrain himself. He had to draw a line somewhere, no matter how bad he was. We were mates, weren't we? He knew she was my wife, and you can't pull your friend's wife, can you? That was how I comforted myself, but still I had my heart in my mouth. I couldn't run and give him a shove to hurry him along, or throw a stone at him, I could only clutch my head in my hands and pray, and sneak a glance every now and then in that direction.

When he reached the toilet, the ground in front of him seemed to be sliding along like the moving belt of a running machine, making him appear to be running on the spot. I looked down in distress. Just from my words, he had sniffed out Yilian, who was a famous beauty. When I looked up again, I nearly gave a cry of pain, even though I'd been expecting it: he was holding her hand. And her hand lay calmly in his like a little bird, its eyes half-closed. The hand that had been in mine until now.

'It doesn't mean anything,' I said out loud. 'It doesn't mean anything.' It's just him taking advantage the way he always does. It's not a big deal, and it's not a small one either, but she doesn't want to make a fuss. Lots of women put up with it, and look, *he's* gripping *her* hand, she's not holding his, it doesn't mean anything.

Sure enough, a few seconds later, he relaxed his grip and she snatched her hand back. He looked taken aback. Apparently he couldn't decide whether to leave his open palm there or put his hand back in his pocket. His hand, raised awkwardly in mid-air, looked like a dead lobster's claw. You did good, I said to myself. She rifled through her handbag, brought out a pocket mirror, and looked at the left side of her face, then the right side, as if he wasn't there. He was still holding his hand aloft, as if it was paralysed and would never straighten. She put the mirror back in her bag and snapped the bag shut with a sharp click. Then her hand reached out blindly, wavered when it received no reaction, and then seemed to say: You take it. Obediently, he took her hand and led her away. Hand in hand, they advanced happily into the shadows. All this time I was sitting on a stone. I felt as if I'd been stabbed silently: I was crying inside.

Some time later, I came to my senses. I spent a long time gazing at Yilian as she slept next to me, then said resentfully: 'I knew this would happen, I always knew it.' I pulled at her trousers. This was my third attempt, and was no more successful the previous two.

She woke up, annoyed. 'Why are you in such a hurry?' she asked. 'I'll give it to you sooner or later.'

I wanted to shake her by the shoulder and say: Well, if you'll give it to me sooner or later, what's wrong with now, eh?

We were on bad terms for a while after that, and when the atmosphere didn't improve, I told her to pack her bags and go. As I watched her virginal figure disappear into the distance, I saw a magical transformation: she was suddenly a woman of the world, flaunting her assets to get what she wanted. Well, it was always going to happen at some point. She was flying from a village trapped in poverty and ignorance. City streets were always paved with gold. Her plumage was too gorgeous for village life. She would bewitch any men she met, and they would pursue her and offer themselves to her, body and soul. We shouldn't regard that as humiliating for her. It absolutely wasn't. It was the poverty that she found humiliating, nothing else.

Later, I went and found a hooker in the township, as if that was a way of wrapping things up. She could have been any age, with her youthful body, but she may as well have been my grandmother in terms of sexual experience. I was terribly tense, even though I'd already been drinking and was still finishing a beer as I walked through the town. My emotions were in turmoil. It wasn't that I was afraid of getting arrested, it was just the realisation that this thing I had longed for was finally about to happen: I was about to push my penis into this woman's vagina.

It was the first time I'd ever done it. The place the hookers used was out in the open countryside. It was once a row of shacks, construction workers' sleeping quarters, probably thrown up in an afternoon and demolished in another, though for some reason one solitary building had been left behind.

Rubble crunched under our feet as we approached. We pushed open the door and a cloud of stale air wafted out. There were no windows and no pillows, just a bed with a tatty cotton coverlet and a dark brown sheet. I felt giddy as I imagined the old men who must have been here, some with hernias, their bodies covered in age spots. You could still smell their tobacco smoke, the tips of their penises white with age, as they knelt over the woman, gripping her around the waist with clawlike fingers.

Distressed now, I looked at this poor woman who was selling herself, struck by the bleakness of the fate that awaited both of us. I was halfway to falling in love with her. I watched as, silhouetted against the sunlight, she turned abruptly and went over to shut the door. Her practised movements after that reminded me why I was here. It was as if her clothes were held together by a single cord and she simply had to give a tug for them to slip off. She lay down and shifted her buttocks to the middle of the bed, then offered her genitals as if they were a bowl of sunflower seeds. I was standing there flustered when I heard her say hoarsely: 'Get 'em off.' I obeyed, and climbed gloomily onto the bed, let her straddle me, push my penis in and ride me. Her cries of 'Ah! Ah! Ah!' were derisive. Heaven knows what was going through her mind, she sounded so dry and detached. When my penis slipped out of her, she carried on rocking back and forth, grinding against my thighs so hard that they hurt. 'Ah! Ah!' Her cries sounded like someone doing throat exercises up the mountain at dawn until she realised it was all over.

She looked at me with a blank stare, then got out a tissue from beside the bed and threw it to me. Dammit, there was no difference between selling sex and selling a bowl of noodles or bean curd, it was just business, I thought. But now I told her sadly: 'You should be at school.'

'I've done that,' she said.

'You could find yourself something else to do. You could settle down and be a housewife.'

'You men, why do you always say stuff like that? You're funny.' I was silent as she went on: 'It's just a slit, isn't it!' I was gobsmacked.

Say it after me, Yousheng, say it aloud, so you can get to the deeper meaning: 'It's just – a – slit – isn't it!' Hongliang gesticulated as he repeated: 'It's just – a – slit – isn't it!' He pushed open the window, gazed up at the sky, and started to prepare some food.

'Red sky in the morning, shepherd's warning,' he muttered to himself.

PART V

THE FUNERAL CEREMONY

30

'It's just – a – slit – isn't it!' Hongliang muttered as he shut the door and headed for the dead man's house. A few dogs followed in his wake, summoned, like him, by a strong smell of breakfast. The animals trotted alongside him, their gait cautious, as if fighting the urge to flee. Every so often they paused at the graves, where they sniffed and scratched at the earth as if they were only there to look for a lost coin. They had been here yesterday evening too, barking. Hongliang glowered at them and went closer, suddenly rose in the air, spun in a circle and lashed out with the point of his shoe, kicking one of the dogs in the muzzle. 'Gotcha!' With both feet firmly back on the ground, he adopted a fighting posture, one palm forward, one drawn back, his eyes cold. The dogs turned tail and fled.

Beneath the glazed tiles the corpses of moths stuck like mud to the bulbs. It was only if you looked carefully that you saw that the tungsten filaments were still fixed, like an appalling wound that has been shielded; like the terrible silent scream of someone who's had their throat cut.

In the house, the emaciated spine of the coffin protruded from a dark corner.

In just an instant
The gilded eaves
Protrude in the darkness
Like the prow of a boat breaking through my window.

That's the poet Bei Dao. And now the coffin, like a fairy boat in mid-river, points at me, Hongliang thought.

The men who had kept watch on their knees all night ate instant noodles and glanced through advertising texts on their phones before falling to the floor into a deep sleep, leaving only the Daoist priest reclining in the rattan chair in which the dead man had previously been seated. He was snoring loudly, his ramrod erection straining against his trouser crotch.

'Sister-in-law!' Hongliang shouted in the direction of the kitchen, and at that moment Hongbin, who had been sleeping soundly with his head cushioned by a pile of brown paper, reached out a trembling hand. He was dreaming: all around was thick with smoke and deathly silent, and when reinforcements arrived they saw a bloodstained hand poking feebly out of a heap of corpses and heard a faint 'Water, water, water!' in English, though you could only make out the word by kneeling close to his mouth.

Hongliang took a carton of Wanglaoji tea from the corner of the room, poked the straw through the hole, put the carton into Hongbin's hand and pushed it towards his mouth so he could take the drinking straw between his cracked lips.

'What's that you say? I haven't had a minute's sleep!' protested Hongbin, who was still arguing with someone in his dream, trying to wake up and open eyes that were shut so tight they might have been superglued. Hongliang went back to the corner of the room and retrieved two more cartons, one of which he shoved into his left trouser pocket and one into his right. Then he heard Hongbin sleeptalking: 'It's what Hongyang himself requested, so what could I do? I never asked to be his cousin.'

Hongbin continued, still talking in his sleep.

The request was like the rhyme of an epic poem, every so often appearing from between Hongyang's lips. Hongyang often made demands, or rather decisions, that involved himself. He rarely demanded things of other people, or even asked their opinions, let alone lobbied them, but on this subject he petitioned everyone insistently.

'Aren't I right? It's been like that for thousands of years, why do they want to abolish it now?'

Hongliang had often wanted to tell Hongyang to do his own thing, to quit hanging around with people who know nothing. Once Hongliang even went and spoke to Honghuai, for no other reason than because he'd come out top in his village's high school graduation exams. Though by then he had Alzheimer's and schizophrenia.

'Aren't I right, mate?' Hongyang asked. And Honghuai, at his lady wife's prompting, nodded two hundred times. The night before at Hongyang's birthday banquet, where he had been forced to cut guest numbers down to one table for reasons to do with the time and the weather and guanxi, he mentioned it to a few of the local bigwigs once more. Although they'd already agreed, he forced them to guarantee it. At the start, they had quibbled and hedged, but once they'd seen he was at boiling point, red-eyed as a bull, they had chorused their agreement. 'All I'm begging you is not to put obstacles in the way when the time comes,' he said, and they responded: 'No, we won't, we won't.'

Old acquaintances like Ho Dongming and Zhao Zhongnan, and new ones like Zhang Nanwei, they all of them agreed.

'You really won't?'

'We really won't.'

'Do I have your word?'

'You do.'

It was a strange game they were playing with Hongyang. Hongyang was implying that he was going to die that evening.

Although they all knew he wasn't going to die in the short term, what they were thinking was: Where are we going to be transferred to when you die? Once he'd toasted each of his guests, Hongyang carried on drinking. And as he drank, the tears came, until his face was wet. They looked at each other, as if to say: It's because he's pissed, so easy to get emotional over something quite ordinary, far away, or even non-existent, but it's like with a small kid, a good night's sleep and he'll be fine, once he's sobered up, he'll probably find some excuse to come around and apologise, that's how it goes, every single time.

But on this occasion Hongyang went to sleep and never woke up, and for that reason his crazy talk stuck in his guests' memories and turned into something terrible and shocking. Jin Yan helped him home, though he looked like he was going to fall on top of her as they tottered along the winding road. Every so often he would reach out behind him and say: 'It's OK, I can make my own way home,' even though there was no one there. Once they were home, he lay down on the bed, set the alarm clock for the next morning, and had a serious conversation with her about the philosophical implications of sleep. Then, after she had gone to sleep, he went and died, just like that.

Hongbin sucked the liquid through the straw as if it was milk, then half-sat up. As far as he was concerned, the ceremony was now, finally, halfway finished and would soon be over and done with. He slurped up the last of the tea, chucked the flattened carton away, and said to Hongliang: ' "Bury me in the earth." That's what Hongyang said to me, and he tugged on my jacket like a child, sounding pitiful and needy. "I want to be buried," he said, and I agreed: "Sure, you want to be buried, I'll bury you." ' Hongbin was still talking with his eyes closed, as he continued his tale.

*   *   *

Hongyang didn't get back till daybreak. Apparently he'd had a nice nap while he was sheltering from the rain, and Hongbin had taken him back to the Cooperative, his trouser legs dripping rainwater all over the concrete stairs. He asked the doctor to put in an IV drip, and after three days Hongyang's temperature finally settled. But the cure was only temporary and the delirium came back, as if every now and then an infection flared up again. Then he would grow agitated and entreat them: 'Bury me! You absolutely must bury me.'

It had all started one morning, when he woke up after a bad dream and discovered that he couldn't move his legs. 'They've gone numb! Numb!' he yelled, and his underlings came running to find out what was wrong. They had barely touched his feet before he started screaming like a frightened pig. Hongyang sat in the doorway for the whole afternoon until the sun went down in the west, and little by little its rays were extinguished, taking with them all aspirations and ambitions. Then at last he leapt to his feet and caught the last bus into the county town.

'If I hadn't gone,' he told Hongbin afterwards, 'I would have felt like a coward . . . a guilt-ridden coward.'

In a fevered dream, Hongyang had seen his uncle, Chen Wangkai, hanging under a grille covering a drainage ditch and doing pull-ups to keep away from a welding torch in the mud at the bottom that threatened to burn his feet. Uncle Chen was not a blood relative – he had been matched up with Hongyang's aunt after they were both widowed, and they lived together without ever acquiring a marriage certificate. After the aunt died, Chen Wangkai arranged a funeral ceremony for her which the folks from Aiwan genuinely appreciated. But as soon as she was buried, it was as if the contract between the families was cancelled out, and they wanted nothing more to do with one another.

'Do you really think that was Chen Wangkai?' asked Hongbin.

'Of course, I saw it clear as daylight, and I saw when he looked at me, begging me, his eyes full of anxiety and sorrow, as if to say: You're my only relative, and you've abandoned me.'

Hongyang said that the last thing he heard in his dream was the spluttering of the flames from the welding torch which lit up the walls of the ditch and then reached Chen Wangkai, and his body was quickly swallowed up in the fireball and he danced like a drunkard in the flames, there was a horrible smell of burning flesh, and when his clothes and hair were all burned up, they turned to ash which rose in the air, and the fat bubbled and began to flow like lava into the bottom of the ditch. Just as Hongyang shut his eyes in horror, his uncle thrust clawlike fingers through the metal grille and gripped Hongyang's ankle. At this, Hongyang had jerked awake, fighting for breath and feeling like he was burning up. There was no doubt that this was a dream, but the sense of unease Hongyang felt was so overwhelming that he decided to go that day to check out Saihu Prison Camp. The camp was situated a mile from the county town. Hongyang had only seen Chen Wangkai in real life on two occasions, and both times he had been surrounded by a crowd of other people. Still, the taciturn and gloomy prisoner had singled Hongyang out on both occasions, led him into his cell and, wristwatch in his hand, had explained his complicated life story to Hongyang. At the start, Hongyang simply sat politely, but then he found himself drawn in.

Hey, he isn't exaggerating, he thought. All these strange things and strange experiences have left their mark on his body, and through these marks we can reconstruct everything that happened, including how he was stripped naked and beaten with electric cable in the mud, how he was hit on the back with the handle of a hoe during a confrontation between two gangs, and how, just when he was taking a piss, he was stabbed by some killer whose name he never found out, and so on and so forth. He came down with an incurable disease because he saved someone's life, and then when he killed the man whose life he'd gone to such pains to save, he was sent to a Reform through Labour camp.

Once Chen had finished his stories, he opened the door and played a tune to a bunch of Aiwan men eating melon seeds outside. Maybe they were his relatives, or maybe not. He played 'The Newspaper Seller's Song', treading heavily on the pedal of the teacher's piano and belting out: 'La, la, la, la, la, la, la, la, I'm a veteran newspaper boy!' The men beat out the time along with him.

Getting off the bus in the county town, Hongyang had taken a taxi that drove him into Saihu Reform through Labour camp along a potholed, treeless, unlit road at the end of which several hundred houses of varying heights had been thrown up by the prisoners. No one had bothered to tile the walls or put in aluminium window frames because at some point the houses might be declared illegal. When Chen and a few other young men had arrived, they threw themselves into learning building skills because they couldn't find any construction workers, and Hongyang went round and round in circles in this maze looking unsuccessfully for his uncle's home. As if he was trying to catch a hen, he grabbed one kid after another and asked them where it might be, but they didn't know where anyone called Chen Wangkai lived. Eventually, however, a mute led him to the Saihu Clinic, and there at the entrance Hongyang saw Chen's Mandarin-speaking daughter teasing a pile of burning ghost money with a twig to make the flames burn more brightly. 'It happened in no time at all,' she told him, putting the twig down; she was shattered and needed a rest. When Hongyang passed over five hundred yuan, she shook her head gently. Perhaps it was the money that spurred her into action again, though, because then she squeezed her nostrils between finger and thumb as if she was choking on wasabi, and burst into tears. 'What's the use of you giving him that money, he can't spend it now!' And that was the first time ever that someone had turned down Hongyang's money.

His uncle had died of a fever because he had been unwilling to spend twelve thousand yuan on an injection. The uncle, who for work reasons had always lived under an assumed name, Chen Wangkai, had gone to Anshun city in South China as a young man, then had found a better job in Guiyang and Chengdu. But his life had changed when he killed a man and was sent to this Reform through Labour camp.

'So where's Uncle now?' Hongyang asked, meaning that he could get lots of the folks from Aiwan to come over and help out, and she said: 'He was cremated this morning.' Hongyang was momentarily taken aback, then he asked: 'So when's the memorial service?' 'There's not going to be one,' she said reproachfully.

Just then, Hongliang heard a rustling. Moments later, a pack of dogs, greedy, shameless and cunning, slipped over the threshold into the room like ghosts in a TV drama. They turned up their noses up at the rice porridge, for they'd had a dozen bones each by the time Hongyang's birthday banquet wrapped up and had come to see what else there was to try. They would taste anything once, even if once they had tasted it they felt it was mediocre and not worth coming all this way for. Still, they felt it their duty to come and taste before they made a contemptuous exit, because it might be that the humans had tucked away a little something. They were certainly cunning enough for that. When Hongliang spotted them, he started waving his arms around like a plane taking off. The dogs all squeezed out of the door and fled.

'So you're here,' said Shuizhi indifferently, and Hongliang grunted in response, grabbed a big bowl, and served himself hot rice porridge without bothering with a ladle. As he dug his bowl into the steaming pan, he thought that there was nothing more cheering or restorative when you've woken up hungry. With some salted vegetables and pickled mustard or mooli in soya paste it would be even better, and he took his breakfast outside the door and used the stone block as a stool.

The burial business was on Hongyang's mind because his uncle's death had seriously upset him. The man had died after nigh on eighty years of travelling from town to town, leading a richly colourful and action-packed life, achieving legendary status, and he had been carted off to the crematorium no more than four hours later, to take his turn and be obliterated, flushed down the toilet like a heap of shit. People in this world were so busy horse-racing, dancing and playing the stock market, grafting away at making their living, that not a single one had come to see what had happened. It was as if the old man had never existed, as if there had never been such a man, like the kind-hearted Miss Henderson from *The Lady Vanishes*, who wakes up one day and discovers that the friend she's just met, Miss Froy, isn't there any more, and that everyone else on the train flatly denies that she ever existed.

Have you seen my friend? she asks.

No, they answer.

The English lady, the elderly English lady, where is she? she asks.

There's no elderly English lady here, they say.

What? she asks.

There's been no elderly English lady here, they repeat emphatically.

But she was sitting in that corner, you all saw her and spoke to her! This is too absurd. She took me to the dining car and then we came back together, didn't we? she says.

You went and came back alone, they respond.

Hongyang was scared out of his mind by this enormous sense of unreality, imagining that the same fate might befall him if he didn't insist on being buried. His corpse might end up in a crematorium as noisy as a food market: the crematorium workers would wait in the hall for a while, dressed in their fire-retardant suits, then come and check the number his family had been given and pull in the wheeled stretcher with his corpse on it. Three-quarters of an hour later he'd be reduced to ashes, and in the middle of all this the temperature of the crematorium oven would rise so high that his corpse might explode with a snap, crackle and pop. This was the way people were used to leaving this world nowadays, the industrialised way, in line with government regulations: die today, cremated tomorrow. Like pulling a vegetable up by its roots, like throwing the circuit breaker to cut off the electricity, like shutting the door, like letting off a fart.

'I expect you think that's the right way to do it,' said Hongyang indignantly to the people who were indifferent to his future and his fate, but he was wasting his breath with all this reasoning.

'He should have come and had a good chat with me.' Hongbin was still sleep-talking. 'I could have told him that humanity advances towards modernisation in the same way that prisoners used to walk into concentration camps: lined up, heads hanging, giving themselves up docilely, completely detached from what was about to happen to them. This collective silence left a huge impression on me, one individual's vulnerability, obedience and grief finding protection – or rather encouragement – in everyone's vulnerability, obedience and grief. They did not utter a word, there wasn't a cough to be heard, just the soles of their shoes hitting the ground in unison, and in their tread there was not the slightest dissatisfaction, subjective or objective. I was stunned by the way they kept themselves strictly in order. I was afraid that Dongming and the others would make problems, wasn't I?'

So that was it, dammit, thought Hongliang. You wanted to carry out Hongyang's deathbed wish, but you were afraid the situation might change if you delayed, so you hurriedly fixed the funeral day for today, because if you left it too long, someone might tell the police what you were planning, and Ho Dongming and the others couldn't allow it. I mean, the government doesn't allow burial, they recently put out a special document. And Hongbin, although you gave a lot of thought to this, if you want my opinion it wasn't clever at all. Why do it all so surreptitiously and give people the impression you're afraid?

31

The morning's business was simple: the coffin with the corpse in was carried outside and friends and family offered libations and were fed in relays. In fact, the whole day's proceedings were simple: once everyone had eaten, clan members processed with the bier on their shoulders, then the out-of-town folk could return home, and by night-time, only Shuizhi remained to reminisce with Hongyang, who had been around just two days ago and seemed still to linger in the dim lamplight.

In this conversation in which his body was absent but his soul present, Hongyang became a silent child and allowed his ex-wife to criticise and admonish him: 'Once you get to the other side, stop being so arrogant. Though we've all put up with you, no one on the other side will, eh, will they? You understand, you've always understood, but I don't know where your understanding's gone these last few years . . .' And so on and so forth.

After the Daoist priest woke up, the three brothers, Hongsha, Hongqi and Hongran, brought in cold water, soap, a towel, herbal tea – 'A stronger brew,' he demanded – and hot rice porridge, fried eggs, preserved eggs, peanuts, shredded fried potato strips, shredded mooli and pickled cabbage, and attended him as he washed his face, rinsed his mouth out and ate his meal. Then the priest made Hongran bang the drums with an urgent roll and Hongbin hurriedly sent someone to call the 'Eight Immortals', that is, Shiren, Shi'en, Shiyi, Shiliang, Shizhong, Shishan, Shiguang and Shican. But just then Shiguang, Shiming, Shitang and Shizhong strode up, bare-chested and all in a line. They had long sticks bound to their naked backs with two strips of turquoise-coloured cloth, which appeared to have been cut from a pair of brand-new Dacron trousers. The sticks, meanwhile, were made by Hongcai from old rosewood, which he had planed into shape little by little, bent over, one leg advancing, the other leg retreating, until the shavings heaped up in a dark corner of the house and crowds of villagers came to collect them to use as kindling.

'Auntie Muxiang, where's Auntie Muxiang?' the bare-chested men cried, a fierce gleam in their eyes. There was no response, so they cried again: 'Auntie Shuizhi, Auntie Shuizhi, where are you?'

Although Hongbin had been planning to take a nap, he was so startled that he went to the door, put one leg over the threshold and paused. He began to step forward with the other leg, but at the last moment he withdrew himself back into the house. As he did so, he felt behind him for something.

'You, stay where you are!' yelled the four.

This bunch of brazen desperadoes are clearly spoiling for a fight. They seem quite unabashed at their ungodly behaviour! Hongliang thought as he got up from his stone stool and moved out of the way, watching as they stepped into the main room of the dead man's house in single file.

'What's this? What are you doing?' cried Hongbin in fright, cowering in terror as if cornered by a Tibetan mastiff.

Then, as light dawned, Hongliang heard a series of bangs and thumps and cursed himself for a damned fool: Of course! I should have known! They were probably struggling to untie their sticks. Before they set off, they had tied them on with great care and had their women check them to make sure they were firmly attached, as if they were going on a long journey. I should have known! he thought again. After all, no one gets into a fight bare-chested, and they had prepared themselves with such ceremony. Bring a bramble and ask for a flogging. He remembered a story from the *Records of the Grand Historian*, in his Chinese language textbook in primary school, called 'The General and the Minister Reconciled'.

The brothers must have been sitting around at home looking at each other in dismay until inspiration struck, just as it had for Hongliang, and they remembered the story that was well known to so many families in China. Re-energised, they had scrambled to find the textbook and turn its pages until they came to the end of the story, which read as follows:

Ling Xiangru saw Lian Bo coming, bringing a bramble and asking for a flogging, and went out to greet him warmly. Only the evening before, Lian Bo's attack on Ling Xiangru had been frenzied, bloody and reckless, treating the law as if it were a plaything. Not only had they boxed themselves into a corner, they were also setting up future generations for conflict. However, after Lian Bo had asked for a flogging, so the story goes, the General and the Minister became good friends, and worked as one to safeguard the Kingdom of Zhao.

Once the four had read that, they were relieved and happy. You see, ever since they had fought with the Zhengtong branch of the family, they'd been overwhelmed by guilt. They scarcely wanted to go on living. What fools they had been: Zhou Ping, Shiming – Zhou Ping's husband – Shiming's elder brother Shiguang, and Shitang and Shizheng too, the whole lot of them. For the sake of a woman who was an avowed troublemaker, they had somehow found themselves declaring furiously that they would no longer lay claim to the twenty thousand yuan inheritance that was their due, nor to the gifts that belonged to the Eight Immortals, which must be worth a fair bit. Impulses were the work of the devil, impulses had cost them dear. As for the distribution of Hongyang's inheritance, they could express their dissatisfaction at any time, but they could not forfeit the twenty thousand yuan they were about to receive in cash because of this dissatisfaction. They could not be so stupid. And what was twenty thousand yuan? It was a hundred hundred-yuan notes, multiplied by two, it was four thousand five-yuan packs of Hongmei cigarettes, it was more than a thousand jin of pork, lean meat at that. And here they were, throwing all this away like a basin of dirty water, cheerfully renouncing four thousand five-yuan packs of Hongmei cigarettes, a thousand jin of lean pork and a hundred hundred-yuan notes, multiplied by two. It would have taken them six months of hard graft to earn that much, and then only if board and lodging was provided. True, they had been cocky about it for a bit, but then they were filled with regret, especially Shiming, who would have liked to kick Zhou Ping to death. 'You petty-minded idiot!' he said. However, Zhou Ping was a crafty woman, and it was she who had thought of a way out.

'It's not true that we've got no room for manoeuvre,' she had said. She vaguely remembered the low-cost remedy in her school textbook and, as soon as she told them, they all remembered too. They leapt into action. They couldn't lay their hands on the 'bramble', but what they did have at home were some smoothly planed sticks. They pulled four out of a bundle and took one each: they would re-enact this Warring Kingdoms story to make Hongbin, Shuizhi and Muxiang weep, and then they would feel (rightly) impelled to hand over the twenty thousand yuan. Thus, brimming with confidence, they had marched into the main room of Hongyang's house.

Hongliang looked inside and saw all four men kneeling in a row, encircling Hongbin and Shuizhi, who had clearly already forgiven them. In unison, they raised their sticks and proffered them in both hands as if they were offering a precious khata. Hongliang remembered the words of the story: Would you please take this bramble and give me a flogging? Sure enough, the four recited: 'Would you please take this stick and give me a flogging?'

'Those fucking bits of dried-up sticks, you've all got your lines off pat!' Hongliang looked at them disdainfully and tut-tutted. However, Hongbin and Shuizhi were oblivious to the brothers' cunning. All they were concerned about was pulling them to their feet.

'You won't miss out on your money,' they said.

'We won't get up if you say that,' they protested.

'What I mean is we're all from the Ai clan, so we can sort it out one way or another,' said Hongbin.

'It's just because we're all one family that we're back, because if we can't help one of our own, then what does that say about us? We have to put ourselves out for family today, otherwise there'll be no one to lend us a hand tomorrow,' Shiguang said. And Shitang echoed his words.

'Dear nephew, it makes me very happy to hear you say that. I'll sort things out,' said Hongbin.

This powerful moment should have reached its climax in tears of joy, but for some reason it fizzled out. To make up for the anticlimax, Shiming mechanically reiterated his imprecations against his absent wife, until Shuizhi – with a generosity almost unheard-of among sisters-in-law – said: 'That's enough, don't blame her.' As the Eight Immortals entered one by one, Hongbin went over to them, muttering to himself, and then made an effort to mollify his nephews, Shiyi and Shiliang.

This is not going to be easy, Hongliang thought. He shook his head and sighed, turned and went out and down the steps. You get people in to fight the fire, and now you send them away again. What are they to think? And on top of that, they're your own family. You make friends of your enemies and enemies of your friends. And you lot, Shiguang, Shiming, Shitang and Shizheng, you're more shameless than those dogs sniffing around outside. Twenty thousand yuan is quite enough, keep your greedy eyes off the Eight Immortals' gifts. You all feel that if you don't do your coffin-carrying duties, then you won't be justified in taking the twenty thousand yuan, I mean, you got into a fight with the Zhengtong branch of the family right in front of the corpse, and were disrespectful to Muxiang and Shuizhi. You're worried that if you're not one of the Immortals you won't get the money, or rather, that it won't be guaranteed, but you underestimate the big-heartedness of the Ai clan. Although you think everyone with the surname Ai is like you, you know what? You make me feel deeply ashamed that I share the same surname with you all. You're banking on the fact that blood's thicker than water, but make no mistake: your behaviour makes me sick.

And Hongliang leapt onto an old grave mound and vomited, after which Shiyi refused to cooperate, not on his own account but because of Shiliang, who removed his head towel and stalked off without a word. This in turn led to Shiren, Shi'en and Shide refusing to cooperate too.

'Why are we doing this for them?' said Hongbin's son, Shide.

And his other son, Shi'en, was even more forceful: 'Fine, I'm not being one of the Eight Immortals any more. You can get them to come and do it.'

Shiren and Shiyi concurred: 'Right, right.'

And Shide added: 'The "filial son" can make them do it,' and got a slap for his pains.

Hongbin felt that was a bit unfair, and administered a slap to Shi'en to even things up. Then he shoved Shiren, Shiyi, Shi'en and Shide in the chest and said: 'I'm telling you once again that you've got to look at the big picture, the big picture! Look at where we're going. What's happened today stops here. I don't want another word from any of you. The next person who disturbs the stability and unity of Aiwan, I'll strike them dead with a hoe.'

That brought tears to the eyes of the four of them. As they lifted the coffin on to their shoulders and went out of the door, Shi'en was overcome, then Shiren and Shide, and their tears flowed like rain and spattered on the ground. Shiguang and Shitang bowed their heads and pretended to be wholly focused on their burden to avoid the embarrassment.

The coffin was laid on three long benches outside the door, where it looked like a pitiful black dragon boat, or a black camphor wood trousseau chest, or a securely bound black sacrifice, berthed in a grey world, ready to begin a lonely voyage in a few hours. When the paper cranes mounted at the head of the coffin fluttered in the wind, it looked even more like it was going on a long journey.

Today's ceremony simply repeated yesterday's: the attendees arrived carrying firecrackers that twisted and turned like the tails of snakes as they crackled, while the family mourners put on a show of alarm and rushed from where they stood a few metres away, slapped their knees in terror and kowtowed on the left side of the coffin, heads on the ground, golden buttocks raised. After this, the congregation also kowtowed to the dead man or clasped their hands in greeting, lifted the family mourners to their feet and, at the appropriate moment, handed over their gifts and money to the accounts office at the back.

Yesterday the congregation had been those living nearby, those with nothing better to do, people who could come on their own, who were not estranged or too lazy to come. Today it was the turn of those who were duty-bound to attend. The whole morning was punctuated with endless bursts of firecrackers. Sometimes two groups of relatives would arrive at the village entrance at the same time, and each felt compelled to give way to the other, the one who gave way stopping for a smoke where they were.

The villagers stood around, some drawing close to observe, others watching from afar, totting up the visitors on their fingers like a housewife counting the chickens returning to the coop, noting who had arrived, who was coming, who had not yet arrived, gauging their feelings by counting, for instance, the number of firecracker pops (1,000, 2,000, 5,000 or 10,000), the number of presents they had brought (two pairs of four items, three pairs of six items, four pairs of eight items or five pairs of ten items, and even whether the blankets were acrylic, polyester or wool), or how much gift money (20 yuan, 50 yuan, 100 yuan, 200 yuan or 500 yuan). It was all recorded on a sheet of paper and stuck on the wall. They commented on how these reflected the favour that Hongyang had bestowed on them when he was alive, as if there existed a conversion formula. 'OK, fine, fine, that's fine' meant that the person had followed the correct etiquette and the gift had passed muster, but most gifts were so-so, showing people's stingy attitude towards the deceased, although that stinginess was easily pardonable because it was never taken to excess. The economic situation of the gift-giver also had to be taken into account. If they were indigent, they were forgiven; if they were well off, then their miserliness made them look petty-minded. The gift could exceed the expected value but not by too much, for that would make it difficult for others to keep up. It was a different matter with those, like Fuzhong, to whom Hongyang had given a new life. Of course, people like that had made endless calculations before they set off, and how people would react to their gift factored heavily in those calculations. In chess, one should always look three moves ahead.

The climax of this parade of the virtuous came when Muxiang, who had left for Tianjiapu at dawn to collect her family, appeared on the opposite bank of the river with her hunchbacked husband, her daughters and her only son, who had contracted polio as a child. Muxiang had the air of an exhausted shepherd or a circus owner down on her luck as she laboriously herded along these pitiful creatures with their four boxes balanced on a carrying pole. From a distance, it looked as if these cumbersome boxes were moving forward under their own steam. When her son and daughters had met her in Tianjiapu, they had no doubt asked: Have you taken your medicine? And Muxiang no doubt had answered: Yes, I got Doctor Han You to give me some painkillers. Then they had set off for Aiwan, with Muxiang struggling to shift her obese, cancer-ridden body along. The consequence of her slowness was that their arrival became the climax of the mourning ceremony.

'Sister! Sister!'

Hongliang and a bunch of other red-eyed mourners trotted over and greeted them, almost snatching the heavy boxes off the family and loading them onto their own shoulders.

'Sister! Sister! Suffering sister!'

When they arrived at the entrance to the village, tears ran down the cheeks of the young female bystanders and, hard as they tried to control themselves, the sight of the solemn, dry-eyed Auntie Muxiang, her white hair fluttering in the breeze like a martyr, was enough to overwhelm them with distress. They all keened in unison. A number of the men wept too.

With Muxiang's arrival, the congregation saw with their own eyes the only remaining branch of Zhengtui's bloodline, which had been broken with Hongyang's death, since there was no one registered as his descendant in his hukou residence certificate. The new arrivals looked like wandering barbarian tribes destined forever to lose all contact with anyone in Aiwan after the funeral.

At this moment, the Shi generation of men – Shide, Shi'en, Shiyi and Shiren – all lined up and fell to their knees. And not only them: those of the Hong generation who were able also knelt down. They waited for Muxiang to stand before the bier and let out her grief-stricken cry:

'Ai! Brother!'

'Ah! Brother!

With perfect timing, just as the weeping Muxiang was about to faint and slump to the ground, her imbecile of a son took up the suona. He was goggle-eyed from curiosity as he looked around him, his hands making meaningless gestures. The instrument was his toy. He had expressed their sorrow beautifully by playing it during their journey.

32

Xu Yousheng approached, laden with bamboo baskets stacked high with bowls and chopsticks, casting occasional glances up at the darkening sky. His maternal grandmother led the way, emitting constipated groans. As soon as he arrived, she had begun to complain vociferously – 'I crapped blood again today!' – in the secret hope that he had told her daughter that the haemorrhoids that had plagued her for half a century had recurred. But her daughter seemed unconcerned, and had actually made her carry the milk, seaweed and silver wood-ear fungus. The old woman gazed greedily at the Naobaijin melatonin supplements that others were receiving as presents.

A leaden grey cloud as big as a basketball court hung in the east. The breeze that had been making the willows shiver for the whole of the morning dropped, while in the distance a swathe of lotus leaves, no longer in flower, covered a pond whose surface was now flat and smooth. The air stilled, and an unnerving silence fell over everything, as if God had died and time had come to an end. The only sound was that of a cricket, which chirped its long-winded complaint, and the noise of a few human beings who now began to shift tables and chairs into place in preparation for the banquet.

Most of the tables were square eight-seaters, although a few were folding tables, and the chairs were an assortment of high-backed dining chairs, armchairs, scissor-leg chairs, plastic chairs and, for convenience, long benches. Xu Yousheng had not been carrying anything heavy, but all the same he felt tired. Sweat soaked every hair on his head and trickled in rivulets down the back of his neck, and he was finding it hard to breathe. Weather like this made him uneasy, as if the dome of the heavens that had previously been so reliably solid had begun to cleave in two. Here, in one corner of the threshing floor, Hongliang leaned against the table, his crossed legs jiggled and he tapped on the tabletop, first with his ring finger then his middle finger.

'It's coming, for sure,' he told his nephew.

No one seemed worried; they still hoped to follow the original plan, perhaps because of their own lazy natures, or rather their urge to gorge themselves once more. The day before yesterday, they had wanted nothing more than to have another great communist feast, knocking back the spirits and gobbling huge chunks of meat. Now their collective prayers were answered: today's meal was all that they desired.

So the tables were put on the threshing floor and the empty space around it. They were even squeezed down the narrow alleyways between the houses, and the tables were set with bowls, chopsticks, plates, spoons, wine drinking cups – though for some, paper cups would have to do – for each of the guests, with six pure white porcelain bowls placed in the centre.

When the banquet began, the serving staff came out with tin buckets and wooden kegs that might yesterday have been in use to carry pigswill or water from the well. They were working in a temporary kitchen which had been put up in the alley on the east side of Hongzhi's house, its roof made from striped plastic sheeting. Inside, a cook who usually worked in the school canteen was armed with a ladle more than a metre long, and stirred enormous steaming pots arranged over four cookers, while assistants fed in fuel or fanned the flames. A white wooden door served as an improvised worktop, while a sawn-off tree trunk did duty as a chopping board and was heaped high with chopped green onions, garlic shoots, chilli peppers, fresh ginger and other condiments. The staff served food to all of the tables, of which there were a total of twenty-two.

The menu today was:

Cold dishes: Fried peanuts, pickled peppered chicken feet, hundred-year-old eggs and bean curd, brined mixed chicken and duck, stewed duck necks, three kinds of shredded vegetables, pork cold cuts, 'husband and wife' sliced beef lungs

Main dishes: Stewed chicken, stewed duck, fish with black beans in broth, steamed pork elbow, best quality lean pork, pork belly with pickled mustard greens, three-flavour soup, ribs, eight-treasure rice pudding, cuttlefish with pork ribs

To finish: Shredded pork with green pepper, pork sliced with Chinese lettuce, shredded pork with garlic shoots, green vegetables in oil, baby Chinese cabbage in broth, steamed egg custard

Drinks and cigarettes: 52% Special Four-Star grain spirit in a ceramic pot, Xuejin beer (one case), big bottles of Coca-Cola and Sprite, best-quality Jinsheng cigarettes, red soft-pack Jinsheng cigarettes

The difference from two days ago was that there was egg custard instead of turtle. Hongbin was blamed for this, and the rumour went round that he was trying to shave a few yuan off the bill. But he protested: 'You can't save money when you lot want to eat animals reared on birth-control hormones.'

The other difference was that two days ago, the deceased had hosted the dinner and invited all the most important local government officials. Jin Yan, Hongyang's mistress, had been there too.

Meat delicacies were brought to Hongyang's house from the Fan Township Hotel in two Wuling Glory vans. To make sure the soup did not spill, the vans were restricted to twenty miles an hour and driven via the flat road through Liangtian, rather than ascending and descending via Tieling Ridge. The convoy was led by a Great Wall pickup truck, festooned with lanterns and blaring out the festive gongs and drums number 'May You Live Forever!' from a speaker mounted on its roof.

The banquet comprised opulent Western dishes: coriander salted Norwegian salmon with sea urchins and caviar, French-style goose liver with apricot jam and beetroot, Australian scallops, beef braised in red wine, and tiramisu with seasonal fruit, all washed down with sherry, burgundy white and red wine, vodka and Evian.

There was a separate Chinese menu which included 'Good fortune first' (lion's head meatballs), 'Good fortune arrives' (stewed premium-quality lamb), 'The phoenix announces glad tidings' (steamed chicken with straw mushrooms), 'The flying emperor arrives at a gallop'(yellow-stewed shark fins), and much more besides.

The plan had been to serve 52% Wuliangye spirit with the meal, but when the hotel staff in white nylon gloves were about to unload it from the van, Hongyang stopped them and ordered Shi'en to bring a case of twenty-four bottles of mineral water which had been filled with pure 72% Wuliangye spirit. Firstly, it had not been blended, and secondly, it didn't go to one's head, he explained to the township head and the rest of the diners. 'Drink it up,' he instructed them, 'otherwise I'll have it taken away.'

We should make it clear that he drank himself to death with a liquor available only to the upper echelons, and even then, it was one that could only be obtained with a special permit. He was one against nine, but it wasn't the nine who annihilated him. No, it was because he overestimated his own abilities and refused to be dissuaded by the others and took them on one after another, in a succession of toasts.

Jin Yan kept gripping his arm and insisting: 'Don't drink so much, please.' Her pleas were noted by the attendant bigwigs, and indeed her real intention was not to stop him drinking, even though she knew he couldn't take much alcohol. She was familiar with the routine that followed his drinking sessions. Each and every time, he would proceed to the wall behind Yangzhi's house, where holes had been dug out for the hens to roost. She would watch as he squatted down, napkin in hand, and stuck his finger down his throat. He'd brace himself with both hands and vomit violently, the next bout arriving before the first was out of his mouth. Then he'd straighten his legs with a jerk so that his buttocks and shoulders levelled out, as if obeying the order 'Get ready, get set . . .'

She had already warned him: 'If you do that any more, you'll turn head over heels next time you vomit,' and when she and Hongyang had gone back inside, Hongzhi would hobble out with a shovelful of ash and use it to cover the heap of vomit that stank of herbal medicine. This evening, though, it wasn't her fear of Hongyang's drunkenness that led her to implore him to stop, but her wish to stress to those present that she was Hongyang's woman.

'Fine, that's enough, don't drink any more. If you keep drinking, you and I are really going to fall out,' she said. Her pouts and frowns infuriated him, though, and he silenced her with a glare of chilling coldness. Then with an evil grin he grasped her head and pushed it down into his lap so that her tongue could reach his zip and her teeth could pull it open, and his penis sprang out. She held it in her hand and licked it, then placed it between her lips and sucked, in, out, in, out, while he gently stroked her hair, alternately pursing his lips to expel a breath, pulling himself upright in his chair and emitting low rhythmic grunts. There was consternation among the other guests; they wanted to say something but nothing appropriate came to mind, so they sat there in silence, bending over to light their cigarettes, until Hongyang proposed another drink and they obediently clinked glasses.

When the storm was almost upon them, a man called Hongpu, who had married into the Zhang family and moved in with them, approached Hongyang – after a moment's hesitation – in order to propose a toast. Hongyang objected that Hongpu was senior to him so there was no need for such ceremony, and then proceeded to down his drink without further ado. At that, the guests of Hongyang's generation and younger felt obliged, out of good manners, to line up and offer the same compliment. To be honest, some of them could not hold their drink and muttered that they had been dragooned into this. When the others heard this they started to feel the same, but they shuffled forward, holding their cups high, some with grain spirit, some with beer, some with soft drinks, some with broth, some with plain water which they made out to be grain spirit. Those drinking water admitted bluntly: 'Look, I can't drink, so I've got plain water here.' As they reached Hongyang, who was clearly extremely drunk despite still making an effort to nod and smile as his guests craned their necks like chickens, they nodded and smiled numbly in turn, then emptied their cups.

At first Hongyang drank half a cup with each one, then a quarter, then finally he swapped his large cup for a tiny one and only changed back to a large one when a good drinker demanded it. In retrospect, they collectively stabbed him in the back: in the feeble lamplight, there was someone from every village family to stick the knife into a tyrant who had lost all ability to resist. At the time, no one was aware that drinking so much could be fatal, just like an elephant could not drink that much, not even if it was plain water. It was only the next day that they realised, when they learned he had died.

The rain began when everyone was sound asleep. Hongyang had been helped home by Jin Yan, leaning on her like an enormous building on the point of collapse or an overloaded truck, so that she emitted painful, ugly groans from the depths of her bones. The officials got into their own cars, turned on the headlights full beam and drove away, muttering all the while that some people drank recklessly – complaining about drunken brawls, crazy behaviour, about Hongyang's insanity or the fact that they were still hungry, despite all the strange things they'd been given to eat. All the furniture was cleared away and on the huge threshing ground only a few tables, chairs and benches were left, as well as heaps of broken bones which failed even to interest the dogs that slunk around on the hunt for leftovers.

Back home, Hongyang set his alarm clock for the following morning and then drank a cup of lemon, grapefruit and wolf-berry tea that sat waiting for him. 'You take your life in your hands when you take a kip,' he said. 'You don't know anything when you're kipping, you know that expression? It means going to sleep – it's like being anaesthetised so you don't feel a thing when the surgeon operates. I've seen people sleep and never wake up. Every time I nod off, I wonder if I'll ever wake up the next morning. I can never guarantee it.'

Hongyang looked immensely proud at his own cleverness. He grasped the sole of Jin Yan's foot and placed it on his crotch, and she gently massaged his flaccid penis. Then she slept. Deep in slumber, she had the impression that her leg was being shifted to the floor, and that he leaned against the door and shouted at her to get him a cup of water, then gave her a kick. The rain-water drove against the window like charging cavalry, stirring up the dust, permeating the air with a pungent smell.

The next day they were able to judge from the footprints Hongyang had left behind and the outer garments he had taken off, on which there were traces of raindrops that looked like bird shit, that he must have woken up parched and gone to the well, where he had drunk all the remaining water in the bucket. Mysteriously, it appeared that he had let the bucket drop into the well then climbed down after it, bracing himself against the walls of the well with his arms and legs. He'd had a good drink and a nice wash at the bottom of the well, then climbed out and dried himself with the electric fan before returning to bed. The proof was a crumpled towel left lying in the reception room, and the fan he had left on. In the morning, when Jin Yan awoke, he was lying on his back, unresponsive, his eyes wide open and his mouth agape, his teeth jutting out.

And now Hongyang lay supine in his coffin, legs bound, toes pointing up, only able to listen silently to the bustle around him. Had he been interested, he might have turned on his side and had a good look: Hongbin, his closest comrade, had hurtled off in pursuit of his maternal uncle from Yaoyingyan while the uncle was busy kicking over the benches, his nostrils flaring with emotion. When Hongbin tried to grab his sleeve, he shook him off and set off straight as a die for the highway going south. I don't know what came over Hongbin – it was all totally improper – but next thing, he caught the uncle and lifted him into the air. The latter pedalled frantically with his legs and finally managed to get down, shouting furiously: 'What the hell are you up to?!'

'Your Uncle Hongbin was going to have to kneel and ask for forgiveness,' said Hongliang to Xu Yousheng. 'As Sun Tzu says on planning offensives: "You will never win battles unless you know your enemy, and yourself."'

The altercations had begun with the seating arrangements, debate raging over who would sit in the highest seats. Hongbin had only thought of the Ai family, leaving Shuizhi out, and had neglected to consider Hongyang's mother's family or the Wens from Yaoyingyan. The uncle was petty-minded and quick to take offence, not a man to cross, while Shuizhi's mother's family were courteous and conciliatory. And besides, if there was an argument, Shuizhi would be able to quell it.

However, it was the Yaoyingyan guests that Hongbin put at the back of the line, and now he was in a real quandary. Just as he was trying to decide what was best, from a far corner of the dining table came Hongliang's reminder: 'Get on your knees, Hongbin.'

Hongbin accordingly lifted the hem of his mourning robes, hurried up to his uncle and knelt and kowtowed. 'Please forgive me, Uncle,' he said.

The latter stepped over him and walked away. Hongbin got up and urgently beckoned to those behind him, some of whom rushed to join him and kneel down before the uncle en masse, chorusing: 'Please, punish us, Uncle.'

The latter simply walked around them and strode away. Again they followed him and blocked his way, with a plea of: 'Please stop, Uncle!'

The only response they received was a loud snort. Hongbin looked crestfallen as he watched his uncle's rapid departure, until a thought occurred to him and, arms akimbo, he burst out laughing. The Aiwan villagers laughed along with him. 'Hungry come, hungry go! You'll be on your own and empty-bellied for all those li on your way home,' he chortled, jabbing his finger at the retreating figure, who then sped up in indignation. 'I gave you a chance to save face, but why did I bother? Good riddance to relatives like you!' And, having vented his spleen, he waved at the rest of the guests and led them back into the house. The man's bicycle stayed right where it was, propped against the mud wall of the old commune meeting room until eventually it was claimed by the smelly waters of the lake.

Hongbin made a point of explaining matters to Muxiang, who simply said: 'Do as you like.'

With the funeral feast officially underway, it started to get rowdy. The air was filled with shouts of 'Ah, here you are, you've arrived!' or 'Have some food!' or 'No, really, I've had enough!'

And from the women admonishing their menfolk: 'Are you still drinking? You'll drink yourself to death!' The answer to this was always: 'Why shouldn't I drink?! I'm going to get plastered. Then let's see if I live to see another day!'

Children pissed on the earth floor and got their bums smacked by their mothers, and some of them wailed when they didn't get what they wanted. Dogs whimpered as they were kicked away. Rain started to fall and the guests grabbed bowls or plates or clothing to cover the food, but it was only a few raindrops. The medley of sounds collected and hovered over their heads, a spiralling entanglement of ten thousand snakes, millions of maggots, in a dense cluster.

Hongbin came over holding a cup of spirits, smelling strongly of alcohol fumes. He looked at his watch. 'Is the grave stone here yet?'

'It should be,' said Hongliang.

'What do you mean, it should be? We've got to get the coffin up the mountain.'

'I'll go, I'll go,' said Hongliang, but what he actually did was make his leisurely way upstairs in the dead man's house, where he plugged in the music system, took a CD from his pocket and brushed off the dust with his sleeve, inserted it into the CD player and chose the track he wanted. Then he reclined on the sofa, pillowed his head on his hands, shut his eyes and draped his legs over the armrest. It was Mozart's *Marriage of Figaro* Act Three, the duettino between the countess and Susanna, 'What a gentle little zephyr'. A unique sound of nature, like a silver spring, the voice reflects the high point of talent and training, and is so glorious that it makes one afraid that imminently, even within the next quarter of an hour, it may be irrevocably damaged.

Hongliang's eyes reddened and his tears began to fall. He spoke from memory a few lines from *The Shawshank Redemption*, where Red, the narrator, reflects on the power of music to go beyond language, to bring hope to the most desolate corners of the world, like a bird swooping through the drab cage of a prison.

Then he got to his feet, clanged the aluminium window open, and turned the volume up to maximum so that it would reach the diners down below. He stood where he was. Unlike the prisoners in the film, who stopped working and stood listening for a long time, no one downstairs evinced the slightest interest. No one even turned their heads. No one paused for so much as a moment, though they had obviously heard the music. Their entire attention was focused on the food in the pots in front of them, while they shovelled the rice and gravy from their bowls into their mouths with their chopsticks. As they chewed, their cheeks bulged as if they were pigs at the trough, while those whose teeth or digestion were not up to the demands of this delicious feast just sat there, picking at shreds of meat stuck between their teeth with fingers or tongue, occasionally emitting loud belches. They were revelling in this great feast, ever so slightly sorry that it was coming to an end, and were certainly very drunk. Creamy yellow mucus oozed from the corners of their eyes and their noses dripped.

Hongliang banged the window shut again. His tears had dried. He felt that his tears were twenty percent genuine, because the music had moved him, while the remaining eighty percent were designed to make himself look 'deeply stirred'.

Why did he have to put on an act for himself, he wondered, as he pushed up his glasses, wiped the tear stains from his face, tore the ring pull from a can of dark beer and took a deep swig.

33

The Eight Immortals had a table to themselves, with Shide pouring the wine and filling Shiguang's and Shitang's cups.

'We can pour our own, no need to treat us with such cere-mony!' they insisted, bowing to him.

'It's just the way we do things,' said Shizhong. Then he made Shide pour some for himself and they clinked cups in a toast. Shide broke open a carton of cigarettes and handed them around, and Shiguang and Shitang got to their feet to accept the gift with both hands, bowing and nodding. Then Shiren and Shi'en clinked their cups with Shiguang and Shitang, though the gesture was somewhat perfunctory. While all this was going on, Hongbin arrived, tore open a box of soft-pack Zhonghua cigarettes and proceeded clockwise round the table, handing out the packs, which everyone stuffed into their inner pockets. Now that they had eaten and drunk their fill, they each drew on a cigarette, their eyes half-closed, then stuck it behind their ears and went to the coffin, where Shuizhi was stroking the wood and making low, unintelligible keening sounds.

'Get away! That's our job,' said Shiren. Shuizhi looked up at him and then down at the bier, heaved a sigh, wiped her tearless eyes, and got to her feet to make way for them. They picked up a pair of dragon poles, fully four metres long and about fifteen centimetres in diameter, and roped them to the base of the coffin on either side. They braced their feet against the poles, pulling as hard as they could to tighten the rope to the maximum.

As they were about to make offerings to the spirit of the dragon, a convoy of nine cars of various makes, led by a three-wheeler highway patrol motorcycle rented from a wedding company, roared into the village from the east and came to a halt at the threshing floor. There was a slamming of car doors as the new arrivals got out, fastened the top buttons of their jackets and brushed themselves down. This posse waited for a skinny fellow with an orange-coloured quiff and a solid-silver ear stud to emerge from their midst, after which they all strode over to the bier.

It was inevitable that Xu Yousheng would come face to face with his one-time friend, Shu Shuang, who was now Hongyang's successor in Fan township. Unlike his predecessor, who had always treated his friends and acquaintances with a degree of coolness, Shu Shuang raised a white-gloved hand in greeting. The posse were all dressed in black suits, white shirts with black ties, sharp black leather shoes and sunglasses, and wore their hair gelled down or tied in a ponytail, as did the women who had come with them. Only Shu Shuang wore a pair of shorts that displayed his hairy legs. They had brought four large funeral wreaths, each with a single character written on it, reading 'Future', 'Life', 'Pure' and 'Land'. Then Shu Shuang led them in kowtowing and lifting burning incense sticks to the spirit tablet.

Once this part of the ceremony was completed, Shu Shuang took off his sunglasses and stared hard at the portrait of the dead man. A full minute passed, and he appeared to concede defeat. He put his sunglasses back on, beamed confidently in the manner of the film star Andy Lau, and walked over to shake the hands of the dead man's family.

'My condolences,' he said.

'What?' said Shuizhi.

'Just keep your mouth shut,' said Hongbin, elbowing her out of the way. Shuizhi fell silent and, amid the expressions of sympathy, allowed people to come up to her and grasp her trembling hands. In the meantime, Shu Shuang went up to Xu Yousheng and neatened his collar. This made Xu Yousheng very proud. Shu Shuang caught a glimpse of Fuzhong, who was standing in the crowd, wiping away the tears with the back of his hand.

'He reckons Hongyang was his benefactor, does he?' Shu Shuang asked.

'That's right,' said Xu Yousheng flatly.

'He certainly seems to be throwing himself into things.'

'Right.'

Although Shu Shuang looked about to say something more, he contented himself with raising an admonishing finger as if to say: You know what I mean. Xu Yousheng did not know, but he nodded anyway. Shu Shuang patted him on the shoulder, then raised his hands in the air and clapped. The whole group proceeded to make a noisy exit, several of them trying to approach Fuzhong on the way, though the mute backed away, shyly. Others tried to catch Xu Yousheng's eye as if to ask whether he was coming with them or not. The latter shook his head. One reason was that his parents were away on a creative industries training course in the Huangshan mountains and had sent instructions that he was not to leave until the coffin had been taken up the mountain; the second reason was that he had no desire to follow behind the grandiose cavalcade of shiny cars on his moped. A moped's something women ride, he thought. He stared blankly as the cars set off along the dirt road going south, then turned east, then north and vanished in the direction they had come from, back east. The roar of the engines seemed to linger in his ears, and he could smell the stink of their exhaust fumes long after the cars had disappeared.

At this point, Xu Yousheng felt a pang of regret about his decision, but he had found the mockery in their eyes unbearable. Their snide expressions implied that there was no difference between his photographic studio and a women's hair salon, that he was one of those timid, fragile girly-boys with the fancy combs stuck in their jacket pockets, flicking their hair back as they walk. Shu Shuang's group saw him as oh-so effeminate.

They, by contrast, were men who had tattoos, went to kara-oke clubs and discos, played pool, got drunk, gambled, fought, took drugs, visited prostitutes, got their girls pregnant, took them to have abortions, then pimped them out in Guangdong and Fujian, stuff like that. They had used to hang around in the streets of Fan township, at Hongyang's beck and call, desperate to be one of his entourage. Hongyang, however, had kept them at arm's length. He had never let them come to the Cooperative in a gang, and had even avoided giving them tasks to do, though they would have laid down their lives for him. Hongyang had been well aware that as soon as they existed as an organised gang, a crime committed by any one of them would be attrib-uted to him, and the guilty individual's punishment would be meted out to him too. The benefits, by contrast, might not land at his doorstep in the same way, and all too soon he might be banged up in prison, awaiting the verdict of the authorities, even facing their bullets. He'd had no intention – none at all – of behaving so altruistically.

After Hongyang died, these young men sprang up overnight, like mushrooms after spring rain, and formed the Eternal Peace Society with Shu Shuang at their head, subdivided into nine branches: the Greats, the Blues, the Changes, the Blacks, the Darks, the Whites, the Reds, the Flames and the Sun. Between them, they controlled the streets of Fan township with an iron fist.

In any case, the rumble of the car engines to the east of the village had scarcely died away before someone else arrived in a cloud of dust from its western end. It was Hongzhi's son Shifei, who liked to call himself Jeff Ai and was insistent that Shide should call himself Snyder Ai. The young man sped into the village on a three-wheeler from the driving school. As he rounded the bend, he tilted his machine so that the sidecar rose into the air and rode right up to the threshing ground on the outside wheels. Then he pivoted on the sidecar wheels so that the bike swung to the right and described another circle, spinning the machine like a gyroscope. The onlookers' mouths gaped in astonishment. His friends seemed more surprised than anyone, and asked him: 'Why didn't you come earlier? That would have given those Fan township folk something to gossip about.'

Jeff (Shifei) dismounted and Hongliang demanded the keys, got on instead and rode down the main road to the south of the village. From there he turned around and drove back, making the three-wheeler buck its back wheels in the air, to cheers from the onlookers. He drove onto the threshing floor and balanced on the saddle on one leg, his palms placed together in prayer. Then he cut the engine, got into the sidecar, one foot resting on the mudguard, and beckoned to his nephew to sit in the pillion seat. At this point, a dozen women, neatly dressed professional mourners, turned up with stools in their hands. Shiren, meanwhile, had made sure he was nowhere to be found, and his wife walked around the bier anxiously looking for him.

The hired mourners surrounded her, laughing and teasing until she was on the verge of tears. Shuizhi and Muxiang were already wailing over the coffin. The mourners arranged their stools, brushed them clean and sat down, heads pillowed on one arm as they beat the coffin with the other and wailed: 'Brother! My poor brother!' or 'Dad! My dearest dad!' Sometimes they came to a sudden halt and calmly blew their noses with finger and thumb. The Daoist priest arrived to chase them away but they simply got up, whirled around and settled down again like a flock of vultures. The priest scratched his crotch with clawlike fingers, then lifted his hands in the air and rubbed his hands together, a signal for Hongsha, Hongqi and Hongran to come and play their music. When the music stopped, the priest dropped the burning ghost money he held in his hands into a bowl, took out a memorial letter that was one hundred and eighty-two characters long, written in ceremonial style in the name of Hongyang's adopted heir, Shide, and began to read:

On 10 July in the year 2012, I, Shide, unworthy as I am, offer these libations and delicacies to the spirit of Hongyang my deceased father, and cry with these words: Alas, what sorrow that you, Father, imbibed so sparingly yet were struck down without apparent illness. I, your unworthy son, wail to the sky and weep blood, my tears wet the dust. Your death is difficult to bear for all who knew you. You were ever helpful, ever busy, always industrious, thrifty and loyal, virtuous and respectful. You nurtured our generation. The virtue of such a man as you will live for centuries. You have abandoned me and now we are separated. Your soul wanders in the darkness and does not hear my laments. My gaze cannot reach you, your voice and your face are far away. My weeping rends my innards apart. I offer up this ceremony to express my filial piety. My father, come from the underworld to enjoy this banquet! Alas! Alas!

Shide, in mourning dress, bowed before the coffin, exhibiting the appropriate appearance of fear and trepidation. The mourning staff was placed to his right. The priest read a few phrases from the scriptures, in increasingly resounding tones, and the children holding aloft the banners and the garlands rushed to the front line. They were closely followed by Hongsha and his two younger brothers, along with a few others who carried small boxes and scattered ghost money. The women continued to beat the coffin with all their might, and keened more despairingly than ever. Tears streamed down their faces and soaked the ground beneath their feet, like water pouring through a leaky roof. A number of other women came over, patted their shoulders and then bent and whispered in their ears: 'OK, OK, that's enough crying now.'

This only made them cry all the harder. They sprawled protectively over the coffin and could not be moved. There was a loud shout from the Eight Immortals: 'Get away!' Then they advanced and grabbed the women, but hauling them off the coffin was like peeling limpets from a rock, and it took some time before they were able to kick the women and their stools out of the way. Then there was a burst of drumming, and Shide picked up the spirit tablet and the mourning staff and hurried off. The Eight Immortals hefted the carrying poles onto their shoulders and kicked over the benches on which the coffin had rested. Although Shuizhi, Muxiang, Wuniang, Siniang, Sanniang, and the younger women like Chen, Zhou, Liu, Zeng and Li, hurled themselves at the swaying coffin on its poles, the onlookers were prepared, and they were tackled, or grabbed around the waist, or tripped up by a long-handled broom. The wails of despair rose to a crescendo. The women did not give up: some, pinned by the ankles, scrabbled on the ground trying to inch their way forwards like army scouts, knocking their foreheads on the ground every now and then. Some fell into a dead faint, eyes glazed, and were only revived after a good deal of pinching.

After some considerable time, they finally emerged from this paroxysm of grief, opened reddened eyes, sniffed, and watched dispiritedly as the bier, with its adornment of paper cranes, sailed into the distance. They seemed utterly enfeebled. But then they brushed the dust off their clothes and went and patted Shuizhi, who was still sobbing prostrate on the ground.

'How will I live without you?' she cried. How will I live all alone?'

The group made arrangements to meet for a game of mah-jong at Sanniang's house, because she was the only one with a magnetic mah-jong set. There were enough of them to make up two tables.

'Will you have the lights on?' asked Chen.

'Of course. Why wouldn't I?' said Sanniang.

'That's OK then. I can't see in the dark,' said Chen.

From Hongyang's house at the west end of the village, the funeral procession crossed the nearby threshing floor and made its way through the village towards the east, accompanied by villagers letting off firecrackers or pouring libations in its path. Muxiang had set up square sacrificial tables along the route, laden with joss sticks, candles and offerings. On the left side of the road, the sons and daughters of Hongyang's sisters kowtowed in the manner prescribed by the ancient *Book of Rites*, and to the right of the bier, Shide knelt to return the greeting. Muxiang asked for music, and Hongsha, Hongqi and Hongran played 'The Good Live a Peaceful Life' and 'Please Tell Us the Way'. Muxiang asked that the offerings be made, and the trio launched into an improvised song, along the lines of 'They give the cigs, they give the fruit, and a case of Special Coke too . . .'

As the procession made its slow way along, there was a loud rumble, accompanied by intermittent flickers of lightning. Still the onlookers were sure that there would be no more rain, because it had rained overnight. But at that moment, black clouds rolled in and covered the earth with the kind of translucent darkness that blankets the road to the underworld. The coffin-bearers halted, unsure what to do. As they hesitated, there was an immense flash of lightning and a shower of sparks, and a bowl-sized hole appeared in the reinforced concrete of a nearby building, revealing the rusted reinforcing bars inside. Everyone scrambled for shelter under the eaves. The rain poured down, mist filled the air, and there was a roaring noise like a river bursting its banks. The effect was pleasantly cool, and the villagers were happy to allow the rain to dampen their clothes, a refreshing experience they had not enjoyed for years.

Then an old woman dashed out onto a patch of bare ground and in an instant the rain plastered her neatly styled hair to her head in half a dozen locks, exposing skin the colour of a fish bladder in between. Her blue jacket was quickly soaked through and turned black, clinging to her shrivelled breasts, which looked like a pair of used condoms, as she wailed in despair. When the rain stopped, she told them that she'd seen all the Aiwan villagers who had died in the last twenty years, in a single flash. She'd tried to catch up with them, but they had vanished in a puff of smoke. She went and told her story to the coffin-bearers, who were crouched down, waiting for the storm to blow over. 'I definitely saw him,' she said. 'I saw shovelfuls of coal slag dropping onto my son's body.'

They asked her: 'Who else did you see? Was Hongyang there?'

'There were too many of them, I can't remember, I was only looking for Hongxing,' she said.

In the days to come, whenever there was a storm, the poor old woman would go outside and stand like a scarecrow watching the flashes of lightning. But now she was pointing at Hongshu, who had been standing a dozen metres away. He was making his way painfully towards them, looking down at the streams of rainwater, his left hand clutching his withered right hand, his right leg flopping loosely as it dragged behind his left. The kids with their banners bounced around, collecting bamboo sticks to put in his path to trip him up. Previously they had been following him, hands over their mouths, imitating his weird way of walking.

'Shall we wait for him to go by?' asked the Eight Immortals.

'That'll take an age,' said Hongbin. But they waited, puffing on their cigarettes.

Hongshu used to go out walking for several hours each day in an attempt to restore his body to its former glory, or at least some way towards 'normal', though everyone knew his efforts were in vain. Every day, the locals saw his inner fury writ large on his eyebrows. He had been badly injured but had been unable to track down his attacker, and physical recovery seemed a distant prospect. In the past, his children used to come back from the county town to help him with his exercises, although eventually they found the endless time it took unendurable. Just imagine, an hour to cover a few hundred metres! So he told them to get lost. Every so often, he would ask Shifei to take him to the township, where he would walk round and round the middle school sports ground, timing himself. Sometimes he went to use their toilets, and students would be startled at the sight of him standing in front of a basin, washing his arse with his left hand, his trousers hanging down to his knees.

The funeral cortège made way for him. He appeared unaware that Hongyang had died and walked on by, his eyes fixed on some point in the distance. Hongliang's mother noticed that the back of Hongshu's khaki shirt was torn. The rain running over his head made his iron-grey hair look sparser than ever, and the muscles beneath his clothing appeared more prominent. The skin on his face was stretched so taut and was so deathly pale that you could see the skull underneath. He looked as if he had not noticed that there was a funeral going on, or that he had been caught in the thunderstorm, though rivulets of water ran down his cheeks and dripped from his trouser cuffs. He was focused only on his slow, ungainly walk. They all knew he was about to die, or perhaps he had already died; a pungent, animal smell filled their nostrils as he came close. Mud squelched out of his trainers with every careful step he took. There was absolute silence, apart from the sound of rainwater running into the drainage ditches and the dripping of water from the roof gutters onto the henhouse roofs.

He walked another four or five metres under everyone's gaze, then came to a wavering halt. He wanted to lift his left leg but could manage no more than a few weak quivers, as if it was glued to the ground. He turned and appealed to one of his Hong cousins for help.

'Are you tense, Hongshu?' asked Hongbin. 'Sometimes it gets like that when you're tense. Try and relax.'

'It's not that. It's that my good leg's losing its strength now.'

Hongshu looked down at it, arms dangling, then raised his head and burst into tears. He seemed unaware of the tears running down his cheeks. All the Hong cousins ran over to him, supporting him as his body threatened to slump to the ground. 'Don't panic, Hongshu, it's nothing,' they said, trying to calm him.

Shiyi eventually came and took him home. He said afterwards it was a bit like carrying an old hen in his arms. It was a long time before Hongshu pulled himself together enough to say: 'Things are going from bad to worse, as quickly as water marks on a stone shrink from the outside inwards.'

That day, his children came and took him back to the county town. Hongshu and Hongyang between them had transformed Aiwan village, or rather emptied it out: the more cultured among them all had followed Hongshu and gone to be traders in the county town, while Hongyang had taken the rougher types off to the township to do his business for him.

When the bier set off again, it was to the accompaniment of more drumming and tooting. The procession took the meandering street to the east end of the village and turned south towards the main road, where it came to a halt. At the turning, a child stood dressed in mourning clothes. He was a little over three feet tall and wore a pair of green wellies clearly belonging to an adult. His head tilted slightly to one side, wedging a shiny umbrella in place to protect himself from the drips that fell sporadically from the cowshed roof. Between his hands he clasped a washbowl, full to the brim with a stew of whole pig's head with chopsticks stuck into it, its ears folded and its eyes shut. The boy was clenching his teeth in an effort to hold the bowl steady, but his hands trembled. Although he was the spitting image of Hongyang, with his stocky build, round face, untameable thatch of hair and gleaming, swarthy skin, he had inherited a single characteristic from his mother: he was cross-eyed, a defect that meant he would never be his natural father's successor. Hongyang had been frigid, boorish and cruel. This kid looked as comical as the man who was nominally his father, the community schoolteacher with a noticeable underbite. When his eyeballs were fixed on you, his mind was elsewhere, and when he appeared to be looking at you sidelong, he was actually looking you straight in the eye.

The boy looked terribly earnest but was also timid and fearful. Having little idea that he was a seed from the testicles of the dead man, oblivious to the significance of today's event and his mother's emotions, he simply waited to fulfil the task he had been given – 'They'll tell you what you have to do,' his mother had said. Hongbin approached with reddened eyes, took the pig's head offering from the boy, ruffled the back of his head and muttered: 'Oh my child . . .' a few times. Then he put the mourning staff in his hand and led him to the coffin where sackcloth had been laid on the ground, and they knelt and kowtowed once, twice, three times . . . The onlookers began to argue between themselves: 'He's a chip off the old block, isn't he? . . . Though I don't know if I'm right in saying that . . . But isn't he just a chip off the old block?'

Hongbin got to his feet and addressed them. 'What do you say, should we let him carry the spirit tablet?'

'Well, he is Hongyang's offspring, so why not?' they answered.

At that moment Shuizhi appeared in the distance, her head-scarf undone and her hair dishevelled as she hurried towards them. 'No, you can't, you can't!' she cried, waving her arms.

The frightened child shrank behind Hongbin, gripping the man's trousers.

'If you let him carry the tablet, it'll kill me.'

As she ran, Shuizhi took a flying leap at the coffin and was only restrained when the onlookers grabbed her and flung her to the ground.

'What's wrong with that?' asked Hongbin.

'It's just wrong!' insisted Shuizhi, screwing up her face.

'Well, you never gave Hongyang a son. If you had, then you wouldn't need my son to come and carry the tablet. And since Hongyang was the boy's natural father, what's wrong with getting him to carry the spirit tablet?' Hongbin was getting thoroughly worked up and looked like he wanted to bite this wretched woman.

'Well, you can't. I'm telling you, you just can't.'

'Sister-in-law, you really mustn't be so rigid. It's time to let it go,' Hongliang interrupted at this point.

'That's right, it is,' the crowd agreed.

Shuizhi looked around at them and took in the situation. Then she staggered and fell upon the bier, flailing her arms as if she was being swept away by a powerful current in a fast-flowing river.

'Are you still here, dead man, are you still here? They're saying I'm rigid, but I'm not at all. They're just like you, protect-ing your bastard child, they got that from you, and that's what they're doing!' she wailed at the coffin. When no one came to comfort her, she lowered herself into the mud and rolled around a few times. The crowd could only watch her performance; it was actually the child, horrified at having provoked such a furore, who burst out crying. Shuizhi clawed the air, glared ferociously at the boy, then darted towards him. The child took shelter again behind Hongbin, dodging to left and right in a blind panic.

Suddenly, Shuizhi reached both hands behind Hongbin and flung herself at the child, who fell on all fours and crawled backwards, not daring to make a sound, before turning to flee. Shuizhi was determined to get him and rushed to the bridge, where she gathered mud and stones and flung them in the direction of the bamboo thicket. When she had flung everything she had, she went back under the bridge for more. She was in such a rush that she slid on her bottom all the way down the track to the riverbank, where she grabbed handfuls of pebbles and pulled up tufts of grass, before bounding up again and launching into a tirade against the boy's mother: 'Come on out if you've got any guts, don't hide yourself away, you sperm-stealer! Come on out if you think you can handle me, you bitch with the unwashed cunt, you slut, you whore, getting your stinking cunt out for men to fuck every day, your cunt that a thousand men have ploughed and ten thousand have tilled, you cheap whore, you bitch, you sluttish cunt, you cunt-hole. If you've got the guts, plant some flowers in your cunt, why don't you? You slutty cunt-hole!' Shuizhi stood on the bridge and heaped vile insults on her rival until she began to vomit with the exertion.

Her insults were so outrageous that the villagers couldn't help smirking to themselves. They found themselves remembering the one and only time that Shuizhi and Zhu Haihua had met face to face, a dozen years ago.

It was early morning and the sunshine was dazzling. When Hongyang brought the painted and perfumed Zhu Haihua home, he felt a little awkward. He had bought her black four-inch stilettos especially for their trip, and the shoes had rubbed her feet raw so that every few steps from the east entrance of Aiwan village to his house, she bent down to wipe off the blood. For a married man to bring home a married woman, even if she had borne him an offspring not long before, was terribly shameful. However, unlikely as it seemed, Shuizhi opened the door to them. With a dog-like devotion, she had cleaned the house until it was spick and span. She had even polished the chamber pot until it shone and heated the charcoal iron so that she could press her outfit stiff and smooth. She looked quite presentable as she took Zhou Haihua by her plump hand and urged her to sit down. Haihua blushed and demurred, until Shuizhi physically pushed her down into a chair.

'Have you eaten?' Shuizhi asked, and before Haihua had had time to decline the implied invitation a thousand times, Shuizhi trotted over to the stove and brought back a bowl of noodles with eggs. Haihua ate every scrap of it. Then Shuizhi brewed some tea for Haihua to wash it down, and the latter diligently drank half a bowlful, then set herself to listening to Shuizhi's chatter. Shuizhi excitedly whispered into Haihua's ear her hitherto never-revealed secrets of making noodles, including how to dry the strands so that they were white and thin and yet still resistant.

'In all of Aiwan, no one makes noodles that don't break, only me,' Shuizhi confided. 'Hongyang likes oily noodles best.'

Zhou Haihua thanked Shuizhi profusely. When Hongyang said he was going to Tianjiapu and asked if she would like to go along, Haihua mumbled something, fell silent for a long minute, then said no, she would rather stay and listen to her new friend. Shuizhi sat down against the south-facing wall, watching Hongyang as he disappeared into the distance, and prattled non-stop. When enough time had passed, she got to her feet. 'Come on, I'll take you to meet a really funny pair of sisters.'

They set out walking. Shuizhi jumped over a puddle and then turned. 'Sister,' she began kindly.

'What?' said Haihua with a sweet smile.

Her skin is so very white, whiter than white, thought Shuizhi, looking enviously at her. Shuizhi herself was skinny, sallow, shaped like a dead log, and there was that goitre she had never got rid of. Then she measured the distance between them and flew at the other woman. Zhou Haihua, sensing that she was about to be struck between her breasts, fended Shuizhi off and took a few steps back. As her centre of gravity wavered, Shuizhi leaned down and grabbed both her legs, slamming her down onto the earth so hard that Zhou Haihua suffered concussion as a result. Shuizhi snatched off the dim-witted girl's high-heeled shoes and threw them violently into the irrigation canal, then straddled her opponent – making her piss herself, so it was said – before reaching out and beginning to twist, pinch, scratch and score that lily-white face until she broke the curved and tapered fingernails she had grown with such diligence over the past six months. If Zhou Haihua had not protected her eyes, she would doubtless have gone blind, but all the same, she was left with bloody, lacerated cheeks. Then Shuizhi turned Haihua over and went for her hair, grabbing a hank with one hand and twisting it round and round, then hefting the weight of it and giving it a tug. When it didn't budge, she braced one foot against a stone and pulled at it with all her strength. She wanted to drag her to Zhengyuan's house and drown her in their brimming privy, but had to reluctantly give up that idea because Haihua was too heavy. Still, she continued to attack her enemy, pulling her silk slacks down to her knees and ripping off her paper knickers. What were paper knickers for, when you gave one tug and they disintegrated?

'Come and look at this!' Shuizhi hollered to the onlookers, and they obediently drew closer. 'Can you see anything special here?'

'No,' they answered.

Zhou Haihua twisted this way and that, frantic with shame, looking as if she might faint at any moment. Shuizhi enjoyed her triumph a little while longer, scooping up some mud and plastering it over Haihua's genitals, then rinsed off her hands in the canal and looked in the direction from which Hongyang would be hurrying back. Her gaze vacant, she took from her pocket a cigarette so crumpled it was about to break, stuck it between her lips, leisurely struck a match, lit the cigarette and took a deep drag on it. She stood there, her right leg a little bent, her head erect and chest thrust out, and puffed on this unfamiliar cigarette. Then she exhaled a cloud of smoke, squinted at it and tapped off the ash. She was enjoying her moment.

When Hongyang returned, Shuizhi glared at him and lifted a bottle of paraquat to her lips. Hongyang slapped her hands down. 'I don't care if you die, but it'll cause me a lot of trouble, see?' Then he tied her up with nylon cord and stuffed her in the hen coop, loaded the coop into the car, drove her to her mother's house and dropped her off. 'She's been trying to kill herself all day, and I haven't got time for a funeral. You've got bottles of the stuff in the house, so keep an eye that she doesn't get her hands on it,' Hongyang said between gritted teeth as he pulled Shuizhi out by her ear and threw the unopened bottle of paraquat at her brother. The end result was that Shuizhi was banished forever to Ruanjiayan, never to return – 'Until the day I die,' Hongyang said – and construction began on a mansion for Zhou Haihua's family.

34

The coffin on its bier turned out of the east end of the village and headed south. On their left was an inlet where a stream rose out of the ground and ran into the Jiuyuan River a couple of hundred metres away. The river flowed west ('All rivers run east, with the sole exception of the Jiuyuan,' Aiwan villagers used to tell newcomers gleefully). Red-brown wavelets threatened to overflow the riverbank, bringing with them rotted tree stumps, upended school desks and naked plastic mannequins that swirled downstream. The run-off from the storm was so great that the musicians stopped playing and the procession turned west along the river bank, then north away from the river, then at the fork hurried west again until they arrived at Ruanjiayan and turned north-west. The rice had not yet been harvested in the paddy fields, and as the funeral procession traipsed through, they left craters of the sort that normally only water buffalo made. The legs of the Eight Immortals were covered in mud. From a distance, the coffin looked like a giant bug being carried along by ants, swaying uncertainly from side to side. It tipped to the right, the bearers hurriedly leaned to the left; it tipped to the left, they leaned to the right, and there was pandemonium as they shouted warnings to each other.

Hongbin led some men armed with machetes and they hacked their way through the dense thorny undergrowth, clearing a wide track up the mountainside. Originally, the side of Mount Shamaochi near Aiwan had been terraced, but cultivation had eventually been abandoned. Between Screwturn and the foot of the mountain there were two crags, one of which had been reduced to a slope by a landslip. The front coffin-bearers climbed up with the carrying poles resting on their shoulders, while the remainder stood behind on tiptoe and pushed the bier upwards and forwards. After this effort, they took a well-earned breather, then Hongbin grabbed the gong from Hongran and began to bang it furiously, a signal for the mourners to redouble their vocal efforts (A-ya-yo!!), the coffin mustn't fall! (A-ya-yo!!). If it falls, his spirit will be lost (A-ya-yo!!). So with a huge effort the bearers hoisted their burden high once more and struggled up the slope for a dozen metres, two steps forward, one step back. The bier started out vertical, then gradually resumed the horizontal and righted itself as the bearers inched forward, but it was taking every ounce of effort they could muster, and gravity was working against them. They reached a stalemate.

'Harder, push harder,' grunted Hongbin, his face puffed and purple with effort.

Some of the bearers pulled their shoes out of the mud and shook off the six-inch-thick layer of mud stuck to them, trying to get a foothold. This was, however, too little too late. They all looked like they had been buried under the mudslide, or frozen to death. Their faces were pasted to the carrying poles, veins bulged from their temples, sweat ran down their cheeks, their nostrils flared, while the muscles in their shoulders and calves bulged as if they had been bitten by some venomous snake or insect. Their legs were coated with mud, each front leg bent, each back leg taut and straight, as they tried with all their might to control the trembling produced by bearing such a great weight. They were getting nowhere. Only the paper cranes on the coffin nodded to left and right as the breeze caressed them, seeming perfectly relaxed and pleased with themselves. There was a long, long silence, finally broken by Shiren and Shi'en, the hindmost bearers:

'Can't you put your back into it?'

Shiguang and Shitang, at the front end of their respective poles, each protested: 'I *am* putting my back into it, aren't I?'

'If you're . . . really putting . . . your back into it, then how come all the weight's at this end?'

'Don't talk such rubbish! Everyone's putting their backs into it, and slackers will be cursed with no sons!'

'Huh! If . . . you really knew how to put your back into it . . . then you wouldn't have put yourselves in front!'

Before the rest of them had a chance to calm things down, Shiren and Shi'en extracted themselves from under the carrying poles and walked away. The whole weight fell on the shoulders of Shizhong and Shishan, who had been sharing the load at the back along with their helpers, and, afraid that their backs would break, they all put the poles down. With the back end of the poles down, the helpers in front had to let go too.

The onlookers leapt out of the way as the newly varnished coffin slipped back down the slope as if it were a children's slide, and the carrying poles embedded themselves vertically in the paddy. The slope was so steep the coffin nearly ended up vertical. There were appalled gasps from the onlookers as the coffin, spattered all over with what looked like manure, settled in the mud. In their mind's eye, inertia was about to propel it into a backflip like an acrobat in Chinese opera or else, now that it was upright, it was going to pace away like a stilt walker.

'If you hadn't nailed it down, it would have shaken apart for sure,' they said to Fuzhong the mute, slapping him on the shoulder. The latter, thus encouraged, beat the grave mound even harder. However, when the coffin that contained Aiwan's erstwhile commander-in-chief landed back in the paddy, Hongbin sank to his knees in distress, putting his hands to his forehead and shaking his head from side to side.

'Oh, Hongyang, will I ever be able to explain this to you?' he muttered. Then, driven by an enormous sense of responsibility and indignation, he got to his feet and shouted at the men's retreating backs: 'Come back! Come back right now!'

But Shiren and Shi'en jumped down from the crag without so much as a by your leave and began walking away along the footpath between the fields.

'Completely disorganised and undisciplined!' Hongbin shouted after them, fuming as he grabbed a handful of mud and hurled it after them. It did not reach the bottom of the crag, which added embarrassment to his anger, so without further ado he picked up some sharp stones, and amid shouts of 'Watch out! Watch out!' he flung those too. Shiren and Shi'en still did not turn around. They merely gave a wave and carried on. Stones as big as teacups flew over their heads and landed at some distance.

'Come back! Come back right now!' Hongbin carried on shouting. As neither his orders nor his pleas were having any effect at all, he finally burst into a tirade of abuse.

'Fuck your mother! Fuck your fucking mother!'

At this, his son finally turned around and said coldly: 'Isn't that my mother you're talking about fucking?'

Hongbin stamped his foot in rage and the onlookers burst out laughing, rocking to and fro, slapping their sides in mirth. Even Hongbin himself let out a bark of mirth. The laughter rose and fell, and just as it seemed about to die away it seemed to start all over again, obviously intended to diffuse the general embarrassment.

Hongbin, however, remained very angry. He announced that the promised allocation of ten thousand yuan to Hongshan's family members was cancelled, and he was fining himself ten thousand yuan too. Then, after some collective deliberation, he announced that, given these circumstances, he might as well distribute the twenty thousand yuan to a different clan who lived at the western end of the village, in return for which those families would permit the bier to pass in front of their houses by chopping down a part of their bamboo groves to make a path.

Such an idea was deeply taboo to the families. They were polite but firm: 'It's not as if you can't get up the crag.' It required the mediation of the chairman of the village committee, Li Honghua, to settle the matter. The families were nothing if not reasonable, although they were not willing to accept the twenty thousand yuan compensation. After much discussion, they finally agreed to accept ten thousand, and a delighted Hongbin issued the IOU. The way Hongbin put it, these negotiations were proof positive of the warmest, most sincere collaborative and neighbourly relations between the two clans for many a long year, and should certainly be entered in the clan records.

Just then, the skies grew overcast, and darkness descended from the skies like a flock of grey and black birds that settled down as if determined never to take flight again.

The grave was already dug, and was longer and wider than the coffin by fifty centimetres to allow it to be lowered in easily. Shiyi and the others had dug with pickaxes and army shovels for a couple of hours without making much progress. Halfway through they had dug up quantities of earthworms which Shiyi regarded as unlucky – as they say, don't bury a body where you find anything hard, soft, alive or dead, and the earthworms were certainly alive. The other brothers and cousins simply stamped on them, ground them underfoot and mixed them in with the mud, with the comment: 'If you haven't seen them, we certainly haven't.'

But then they were joined by Fuzhong, and within half an hour the work was done. The grave was perfectly straight-sided, level and rectangular, as it should be. When the banners and wreaths were all in place, the bier emerged like a python

from the bamboo thicket and wound its way to the graveside,
where the waiting women – who were considerably reduced in
number by that time – lurched forward, choking out the words
'My . . . my . . . my . . .' as if they were on the brink of death.

Before the bier was placed on the ground, firecrackers were
lit and ghost money hurled skywards, and Hongsha's cymbals
clanged with increasing urgency. Then it was put down and the
Eight Immortals made perfunctory bows, shook their arms to
relieve aching muscles and hurriedly lit up their cigarettes. The
women swarmed around the coffin, banging repeatedly on its
lid, until the Immortals finished their break and ordered them
back. They undid the cords binding the coffin to the poles, leaving two lengths that passed underneath. Then, mustering all
their strength, the men manoeuvred the coffin and lowered it
slowly into the hole.

At that point, Hongsha climbed onto a mound, puffed out
his cheeks and began to play 'A Hundred Birds Pay Homage to
the Phoenix'. His suona emitted what sounded like a thin,
wavering, long-drawn-out fart, like a bird beginning with an
exploratory tweet before emitting a crescendo of twitters and
calls, hopping up and down on its branch with joy. The suona
notes multiplied like a gathering of the species, like a flotilla of
boats, their oars rising and falling in unison, now ringing out
clear and melodious, now sounding dark and dull. Then a single
bird flew away from the flock to draw the phoenix down. The
mountains and the valleys resounded with cries of jubilation.
The regal phoenix glided down gently and took up its position
in the midst of the flock, then raised its head and gave a cry that
travelled to the far corners of the sky with the speed and preci-
sion of an arrow. To the onlookers, the suona's treble seemed
ready to go on forever, but Hongsha suddenly flung his instrument down and the sound dissolved, leaving barely a shadow
behind. His audience stood transfixed.

'Bravo! Very good!' Hongliang led the applause.

'Very good?!' exclaimed Hongbin. Everyone looked at him. He was squatting down, slapping the soaking wet stone slab that had just arrived with sheets of yellow offerings paper. 'Tell me, what's good about this?' he repeated.

This was a completely different Hongbin from the helpless, comical figure he had cut that afternoon when the coffin slipped down the crag. Now, he was positively vindictive. Rebuffing all attempts to approach or comfort him, he seemed to have a tight lid on his anger, and it was precisely this self-control that made every movement, every word he spoke, even his stillness and silences, all the more frightening. They all looked at each other, pondering the meaning of his words and bearing, then slowly it dawned on them that Hongbin was not angry with everyone – in other words, not with them – nor was he angry with the trembling Hongsha, who was gently rubbing his hands against his pockets. His anger was entirely directed at Hongliang, the best educated of all the Hong cousins but also the youngest. A wave of sympathy flowed in Hongliang's direction.

Hongliang looked momentarily appalled, then asked in a shaky voice: 'What?'

'Come and look,' said Hongbin, grabbing him and showing him the stone slab. Hongliang saw there was a mistake in the carving of the character for 'yang' in Hongyang's name.

'But I told you exactly what I wanted! Come here,' Hongliang ordered the stonemason. The stonemason, one-eyed and hunchbacked, panted over to them. 'I told you exactly what you were to carve, didn't I? The same yang, 杨, meaning poplar, like in the poem "Poplar and Willow in the Spring Breeze". Not the 阳 yang as in sun!' said Hongliang.

'You told me to carve the 扬 like in "Yangzhou in the Spring Breeze",' said the stonemason.

'How could it possibly be the 扬 in Yangzhou, there's no such poem as "Yangzhou in the Spring Breeze"!' cried Hongliang.

'Don't lie, that's exactly what you told me.'

The stonemason felt in his pocket, brought out a pink plastic lighter, pushed his glasses up his nose, examined it and handed it to Hongliang. The writing on the lighter read *'Yangzhou in the Spring Breeze' Bathing and Recreation Centre. Address: Jigong Ridge.*

'I thought it was because you'd been there and that was why you wanted those characters. Anyway, I want my fee,' the stonemason said, pursuing his argument.

'I know, but what I asked for was "Poplar and Willow in the Spring Breeze".'

'How dare you tell me I misheard!' The stonemason, an honest-to-goodness workman famous for miles around, was incensed at this insult to his reputation. Throwing down his overalls, he stormed off. 'I don't want your money! Go ahead! Put the blame on me!'

Hongbin tried to appease him: 'Meilong, don't be angry, it's not your fault, you go and collect your money from Accounts.' Then, in front of everyone, he grabbed hold of Hongliang's shirt and shook him. 'What do you think about every day?'

Hongliang stood still as a statue, as if his soul had fled and left only his body behind.

'I'm asking you, eh? What do you think about? Well?' When Hongbin received no answer, he crooked his middle and fore-finger and rapped Hongliang on the head. 'You assured me that it was all taken care of.'

Maybe Hongliang's hair was too thick, as the slap did not seem to hurt his head. So Hongbin mussed Hongliang's neatly tied hair until he looked like a Manchu Dynasty Chinese man whose pigtail had just been cut off. 'Take a look at yourself, with your woman's hair,' Hongbin went on. But then he lost interest and crouched down to have a fag. He didn't look up until the filter burned his lips, and he found that Hongliang was still standing there. He delivered his verdict: 'Get lost.'

Hongliang pushed his glasses straight on the bridge of his nose and ambled off down the hill, looking both relieved that the business was over and burdened with lifelong humiliation. He still had the chisel in his hand. He had been thinking of adding a single stroke to the left-hand element of the 扬 character to make it look like the 杨. He might even have told them that in Republican-era textbooks, the 木 element of 杨 had a hook at the base like the left-hand element of 扬, but there was no need for that now; in fact it made no sense.

Although he should have taken the path that led through the bamboo thicket, he was so upset that he got lost and ended up on the slope again. It had been trampled into a quagmire, and with every step he took, the claggy mud stuck to the soles of his shoes. When he finally reached the edge, he stood for a moment and jumped down. He wiped off the mud in the irrigation ditch that ran alongside the field boundary and, still indignant, walked into the twilight. The villagers watched his retreating figure without a word, although they had plenty of silent comments to make. Hongliang is a tree with luxuriant foliage and blossom, but of absolutely no economic value. Imposing but useless. He's unreliable, they thought.

Shide picked up the spirit tablet and headed back the way they had come. There were only two men in front: Hongqi, banging his cymbals, and Hongran, on the drum. Shide walked along all alone, accompanied by Hongyang's spirit. Two strikes of the cymbals, one beat of the drum. Then silence. The women mourners and almost everyone else had gone. There was little left to do on Screwturn. The grave had been filled in and the remaining excavated earth had to be heaped high onto the grave mound. Fuzhong was circling the grave, spade in hand, tamping down the mud so that the crumbly red earth turned hard as iron. Solid as concrete. Solid enough to knock you senseless. Fuzhong was crook-necked and left-handed. His exertions had ripped the seams of his shirtsleeves at the armpit, showing his hairy underarms. When he was finally satisfied with his work, he dropped his spade and fell to his knees, and to the accompaniment of Hongsha's suona-playing he wept and wept.

'What's he crying about?' Shiguang said.

'Probably because he can never pay back Hongyang's generosity,' said Hongbin. He handed out another round of cigarettes and said: 'You know, I've been so busy these last two days that I haven't even had time to take a crap.' He retrieved the remaining offerings paper and now undid the rope and jumped down behind the grave mounds. He let off a pungent fart and said: 'Grandpa, Granny, do excuse me, but this is too urgent for princely manners.' There were a few guffaws.

From further up the mountain came the sounds of rats scrabbling along the steep tracks, the hooting and cawing of birds, and the cracking of tree branches. In the distance, ducks dawdled homewards, streams slowed their flow, children pushed around chairs higher than themselves, daughters-in-law switched back on the dim lamps their mothers-in-law had just turned off. Dusk drew in. A great peace stole over the land.

The death of a man.

It ends there.

This was the excuse for the villagers to eat and drink and enjoy themselves to their hearts' content.

That's the end of Uncle Hongliang, thought Xu Yousheng as he left Aiwan.

It was his uncle who pushed the moped for him to the bridge at the east end of the village. 'Why don't you get yourself a kickstand?' he said as he retrieved the bike which had been leaning against a jujube tree, brushed the flecks of firecracker paper off the seat and walked away with it. After that, he said nothing more. Then, when Xu Yousheng got on the bike, he muttered, 'Take care, Yousheng.' He looked utterly crestfallen as he gave a stiff wave goodbye.

That really was the end of his uncle, Yousheng thought. He looked as pathetic as a single, solitary peacock kept in a hotel garden.

Xu Yousheng watched as Hongliang jumped down from the crag and made his way steadily along the field boundary, vanishing after a dozen paces like a wraith in the thickening twilight. The darkness was as impenetrable as the waters of a lake: dark, turbid, suffocating. The gravediggers took their chance to throw down their spades, borrow a light and have a smoke. Xu Yousheng had never missed his birthplace, Fan township, the way he did now, even though the local government had redrawn the boundaries a few years ago and Aiwan, only a dozen or so li away, was now incorporated into the township. He felt like walking over to the grave and shovelling earth onto the coffin, which lay there like an ox carcass. Starting that morning, he had felt sure several times that the funeral would soon be over, yet here was the coffin, still lying bogged down. He had been in a torment of impatience, like an ant in a hot frying pan. Several times, he'd been on the point of telling his uncle he had stuff to do, and even of going off without a word of goodbye – which wouldn't have mattered – but he couldn't bring himself to do it.

Things in the countryside are endlessly convoluted and mired in procedures, he thought. People dawdle and couldn't care less. They're always dragging things out. The way they drew close to him, a township boy – it made him apprehensive. He was infuriated by the liberties they took with their friendship, and by their desire to keep him here a few more days.

He felt her presence ebbing away little by little.

★   ★   ★

'You've got something on your mind, I can see,' his uncle had said.

'No I haven't.'

'Well, if you haven't, why don't you stay here for a few days while it's flooded, and come fishing with me?' Then Hongliang began muttering to himself some anecdote about Ludwig van Beethoven having arranged to elope with a woman he was madly in love with, but how it had poured with rain and the carriage, to Beethoven's utter mortification, had got bogged down in mud. Later, Beethoven had told a pupil that he had expressed these feelings in one of his compositions, causing the pupil to weep in sympathy. Uncle Hongliang, however, did not press home his advantage on this occasion, and merely said to Xu Yousheng: 'You go home.'

It was only when the gravediggers finally finished their break, took up their shovels and piled the last shovelfuls of earth onto the grave mound that Xu Yousheng felt released, the way a prisoner hears the keys being inserted into the lock at the end of the corridor when they've served their sentence. Fuzhong, however, caused further delays, as he insisted on treading the earth down on the mound then walking round it with his shovel, patting it some more, and then repeating the whole procedure. Then he threw himself to his knees, grief-stricken, and had another good cry. They had no choice but to let him do it. By now, it was so dark that you could only see their dark shapes, blacker than the blackness of night. They were all being eaten alive by insects, and they scratched incessantly.

'What are you still doing here?' asked Hongbin, surprised. Xu Yousheng did not answer. He felt Hongbin's hand gripping the top of his skull and heard him say: 'Kid, you wanted to cry but you didn't, I saw that. I never imagined you felt that way about Hongyang, you stupid kid.' Xu Yousheng let him do it, inwardly rolling his eyes at his uncle's naivety. You idiot, he thought. It was conjunctivitis.

'It's late, why don't you stay the night?' said Hongbin.

'No, no, don't worry about me,' Xu Yousheng replied, resolutely.

After he got back to the village, Xu Yousheng went to say goodbye to his grandmother, and his grandmother made his Uncle Hongliang see him on his way.

'Why does a big grown-up lad like you need seeing on your way?' said Hongliang.

'I don't know,' said Xu Yousheng, but since Xu Yousheng was adamant that he did not want to stay the night, his grandmother insisted that someone see him off. So that was why Uncle Hongliang had pushed the bike to the east end of the village, as if he was sparing his nephew some effort. It was only when Hongliang solemnly handed back the bike with the air of bequeathing something valuable, and waved his arm back and forth like a pendulum gradually coming to rest in mid-air, that Xu Yousheng felt he was truly free to go. He shot off at speed, relying purely on his memory to dodge the dangers in the road that might throw him off: gullies, twists and turns and many other obstacles. In his head, he was already back among the bright lights of Fan township.

I want to be back there, this trip has dragged on so long it's nearly killed me. I need a few drinks. That was his text message to Shu Shuang while the funeral procession was still on its way up the hill. He received no reply. As the gravediggers began to fill in the earth, he sent another text: *I can't stand this damned place any more, I need something to eat.*

In the hotel. They've got it ready for you, Shu Shuang messaged.

Love you, Xu Yousheng texted back.

The younger folk, including Xu Yousheng, who counted as family, had given a sigh of relief at Hongyang's death. Now the territory he had taken over and looted was back in their hands. During Hongyang's rule, joining the gang had been something you had to scheme for. You needed to be physically fit, and have backers and luck. Hongyang had surrounded himself with a few trusted men. The rest he treated like outsiders, and they hung around his door or in the street like scavengers, timorous and ready to betray not only themselves but anyone who stood in their way. It all depended on Hongyang's mood. If he happened to come across whatever shady business you were up to one day and said, 'The apples are ripe for picking,' his favourite slogan, that meant he would be taking all of your earnings. Hongyang had built a high wall between himself and everyone else, making himself as mysterious and remote as a king within his castle. Everyone had to divine his intentions on the basis of rumour and gossip and arrange their own lives accordingly. However, in a single night, after his dramatic demise, Shu Shuang, enthusiastic and generous, had emerged to bestow membership of the brotherhood on any who were so inclined, and the township erupted in joy. Shu Shuang had always been known as a sort of Good Samaritan, helping the poor and rescuing the needy.

As for Xu Yousheng, who was determined to pay his respects, he pedalled back home in the depths of the night, covering the dozen or so li in no time at all. He propped the moped against a wall, pushed open the revolving door and went in.

The private dining rooms all led off a corridor, and over each door hung a wall lamp with a shade made of fake sheepskin that shed an orange glow onto the marble floor. The police, the tax office, the Chamber of Commerce, the offices of finance, land administration, local government, and of forestry, water supplies and mining, all had their reserved dining rooms. There was a separate presidential suite, a premier's suite and of course the chairman's suite.

Xu Yousheng remembered that Hongyang had most often been seen enjoying himself in the office of mining room, and now that Shu Shuang had taken over, it was possible that the hotel had given that room to him. He pushed open the solid black-painted wooden door and found he was right. The room was as brightly lit as day. Shu Shuang was sitting there, one foot resting on the leather sofa, leaning forward and about to hurl the cocktail he held in his hand at the ceiling. Once upon a time, that sofa had been Hongyang's. The waiters had always kept it wiped clean and no one else would have dared touch it. Behind it stood two Hong Kong dragon blood trees, and on the wall hung a calligraphic scroll by Mou Xiangdong, deputy chair of the county-level CPPCC:

> *Black gold chiselled from the chaos*
> *Repository of yang and imbued with meaning*
> *Torches flame at the return of spring*
> *Furnaces illuminate the deepest night*
> *Bronze vessels are the fulcrum of life*
> *Iron and stone are forever perpetuated.*
> *If only the common people had food and shelter*
> *They would not fear to abandon the forests.*

This was the first time Xu Yousheng had entered the lion's den, which had once been a legendary byword for luxury and voluptuousness. Rumour had it that men and women would strip off their clothes when they arrived and get into sex romps.

At this moment, the guests, looking like they were eager to try anything new, were fanned out around Shu Shuang. Xu Yousheng stepped onto the carpet and felt like he was in the clouds.

'Come and sit down,' said Shu Shuang. 'We're on the third sitting. What took you so long, lad?'

'The storm.' Xu Yousheng found a seat. 'It was horrendous. The sky suddenly turned black. It was like being sprayed with fire hoses, the rain churned up the ground, there was flooding, visibility was awful, even the wind was sodden. When you sheltered under the eaves, it was like standing on a pontoon at the water's edge and looking at an ocean in front of you, you couldn't see the horizon. And it went on for ages.'

'Right. We only had a little rain here.'

Shu Shuang raised his glass and the rest of them did the same. He sipped, held the glass stem between his fingers and squinted at it, then put the glass down on the table.

Xu Yousheng got some fried peanuts wrapped in greaseproof paper out of his bag. 'From my grandmother. They're still hot,' he said.

Shu Shuang helped himself to a few, then made a face and dropped them on the table. 'Disgusting. You eat them.'

The others all waved the peanuts away. 'Not for us.' Xu Yousheng looked dismayed and confused but forced a smile.

Then a giant stood up. He must have been at least five foot nine tall, and his complexion was swarthy, with bronzed bloodshot eyes. It emerged that he'd been a mine guard and was older than the other men. Now he lifted his glass and addressed Shu Shuang: 'Brother Coal, let me drink to your good health.'

'Don't talk like that, Babe,' said Shu Shuang, tapping three fingers of his right hand on the table. 'Your good health.' And he drained his glass and beckoned Babe over.

Babe sat next to him and leaned over, eyes fixed on him, listening attentively. 'Yes . . . yes . . . yes,' he muttered. The pair looked so cosy that everyone else felt left out in the cold.

Xu Yousheng found the menu and called the waitress over to order a few of the restaurant specialities, then tapped his chopsticks on the table and began to eat up some of the leftovers. To break the silence in the room, he turned to Li Jun, a man with a round moon face so bloated it looked like it was about to give birth. He might have been on drugs, with his dull eyes, half-open mouth, protruding tongue and rhythmic panting. His knees continually jiggled, as if he was working a loom. And he dribbled. 'Did Chersey win?' Xu Yousheng greeted him.

Chelsea was Shu Shuang's favourite club. Li Jun was Shu Shuang's younger cousin, and Xu Yousheng was a childhood friend of Shu Shuang's. Shu Shuang, still deep in conversation with his new confidant, raised an admonishing finger: 'Chelsea, not Chersey.'

'Right,' Xu Yousheng corrected himself. 'Did Chelsea win?'

After a long moment, when he might have been waiting for his legs to stop jiggling, Li Jun replied: 'What did you say?' Xu Yousheng felt a sudden urge to break Li Jun's legs.

Next, Xu Yousheng raised his glass to Li Jun, who, after a long pause, took his own glass between both hands, though he might just have been going to have a drink. Xu Yousheng would have loved an opportunity to have a heart-to-heart with Shu Shuang, to tell him: You should be on your guard against men who look like they're working like a dog for you. The harder he works for you, the more you trust him and the more you entrust to him, and that makes him ever more powerful while you become less powerful by comparison. One day, even if he doesn't want to supplant you, all these power-hungry young lads might force him to. Outlaws never get to choose their own destiny. Not that I think he'd be unwilling. Men are lazy by nature. The more energetic a man, the more he has an ulterior motive, you better believe it.

'Chelsea were playing Newcastle at home,' Shu Shuang commented, but he didn't mention the result.

'Hang on a moment,' said Xu Yousheng.

Shu Shuang was momentarily taken aback, then burst out laughing.

'I've got something to tell you,' said Xu Yousheng.

'What?'

Xu Yousheng cocked his head slightly.

'These are all my men,' said Shu Shuang.

'Then I'll tell you.'

'You go ahead.'

'You remember the serial killer the local police caught?'

'It rings a bell.'

'It was Hongyang who shopped him.'

'You're kidding!'

'It's true.'

'Well I never!' Shu Shuang nodded and grinned as he took this in. Then he got down to the real business. Xu Yousheng was older than him by a few days, while he was older than Li Jun by a few days. And even though it was just a question of a few days, still, elder was elder and younger was younger. From now on Yousheng, as the eldest, was also the senior. He had a reputation to uphold in and around Fan township, and should understand how best to support his juniors.

'Naturally,' responded Xu Yousheng.

As they talked, Li Jun came over with a glass in his hand. Xu Yousheng raised his own glass, but Li Jun patted him on the shoulder to indicate that he should put it down. Li Jun kicked a chair into position, sat down, rested his brawny arm on the back of Xu Yousheng's neck and panted, open-mouthed, like a dog. He did not chat to Xu Yousheng, merely draped his arm as if Xu Yousheng's back was an armrest, and took in Shu Shuang's words. Shu Shuang was saying: 'Yousheng, from now on, call him Uncle Li.'

'Why?' asked Xu Yousheng.

'We all do, and when "Uncle Li" gets angry, it's a serious matter.'

Then he burst out laughing, although he wasn't joking; it really was no laughing matter. Li Jun panted and refused to comment either way.

Desperately humiliated, Xu Yousheng went into the hotel courtyard, with its artificial mountains and pond, and sat down on a small stone bridge for a smoke. He imagined Shu Shuang passing by his photographic studio one day while he was on patrol. Would he come in and enquire as to whether he had called him 'Uncle Li' today?

Huddled on the damp earth in the bushes was a peacock with the sad expression of a creature that lives only for food. It was always being set upon by the hens and cockerels which regularly scuttled onto its back and scraped and scratched in its feathers in search of insects which they then gobbled at the speed of lightning. As a result, the once beautiful bird had lost at least half of its iridescent tail feathers and ugly dark red patches of ringworm showed through bare patches of skin.

After a while, as the evening breeze rustled the willows and a feeling of desolation crept up on him, Xu Yousheng got out his mobile and tapped in some numbers. He got to thinking:

13 . . . My uncle used to call mobiles 'the cancer of love'. When telecoms split off from the post office, the costs of a call plummeted and people's desire to spy on their fellows increased dramatically. All you have to do is dial eleven digits and you're on someone's tail. There was one man – my uncle called him Hippopotamus – who threatened to break it off with his woman because her phone automatically turned itself off. He yelled at her in fury: 'I topped up the credit on your phone for you just this afternoon!' Then he murdered her, dismembered her body and fled to the south-west, to Guizhou or Yunnan or some-where. Now it looks as if I'm going to be infected by the same cancer, aren't I? Why am I suddenly so anxious, panicky, out of

control? Why do I keep taking my phone out, pretending to look at the time, then stuff it back into my pocket and forget what the time is?

9.00 . . . Everyone has their own rhythm. No two people have the same rhythm. Some have a stride a metre long and others have a stride a foot long. Some are always in a hurry, others like to take their time.

As far as love goes, I'm the impatient sort, but maybe she's the leisurely type. Women like being like that, taking time to digest things or playing hard to get. Women neglect their lovers. Neglect, that's their natural rhythm. Or rather, they secretly like playing games. She thinks that when she needs you, that's your only reason for living, though it doesn't work the other way round. Just because they make a big show of brushing you off, that doesn't mean they've given up on you.

1010 . . . That's the code for Beijing, twice. If she doesn't love me, why does she open her legs for me? Why, when we're half-way through fucking, does she roll over and get on top of me? Why does she stop for a moment when she's riding me, and lie on me and press her breasts into my chest and scratch me with her sharp fingernails? Why does she grip me with her thighs after I've come off? Why does she tell me so urgently: 'Love me, husband!' And then, after our bodies separate, why does she spend all that time licking around my ears, nipples, belly and prick?

30 . . . This is going to prove it, one way or the other.

Xu Yousheng entered the last few digits, thinking that she'd probably be having a midnight snack, or be sleeping, but he didn't care. As it began to ring, he thought of a vital question: what name should he call her? When she spoke, he was flustered.

'Hello?' she said.

('Who is it?' He heard a man's voice.)

Xu Yousheng stood rooted to the spot, as if he'd been slapped by a stranger or had a basin of dirty water emptied over him from the floor above. He said nothing.

'Yes?' she said, then paused for a moment and went on: 'That thing you wanted me to do, I'll ask. But it's not a good time right now. I'm having dinner with a friend.' And she hung up.

Idiot, what an idiot, thought Xu Yousheng, looking at the screen of his phone, which had gone blank. Fucking idiot. She deceives him, she deceives me, and I get in a fluster and . . . 'Yes?' Well, I'll give her sodding yes! What a fool. She was like a frightened rabbit sticking its head in a bush.

A moment later, though, she phoned back and was full of apologies, trying to find ways to explain away her behaviour but ultimately digging herself into a deeper hole. 'Listen to me,' she begged.

Red-faced, trembling with rage, grinding his teeth, Xu Yousheng went back to the private dining room, lifted a bottle, tipped the contents down his throat and banged it down on the table to a round of applause.

Shu Shuang raised a finger. 'I don't want any trouble.'

But the others said: 'What's there to worry about? The walls are made of poured concrete.'

'OK, we'll let it go for today.'

As Xu Yousheng was drinking a second bottle, he looked up for a moment and saw Shu Shuang gazing at him with the soft, docile eyes of a cow. He felt deeply moved and was seized with the desire to go and embrace the man, to break down in tears. He imagined Shu Shuang's comforting words: We're mates, you and I. We're inseparable. Women, they're like clothes. You want them, you can have them, like cabbage, rotting cabbage, cabbage for pig feed, ten-cents-for-several pounds cabbage, flog-it-cheap-because-there's-a-glut cabbage, piled-to-the-ceiling, piled-in-the-courtyard, piled-in-the-streets cabbage, take as many as you want, they're everywhere.

But instead, overwhelmed with emotion, Xu Yousheng put his head down on the table to go to sleep. He sensed Shu Shuang fetching a windcheater from the coat rack and coming over to cover him up, vaguely registered him saying: 'This mate of mine's never been any good at looking after himself!' Xu Yousheng buried his face in his arms and shed silent, bitter tears.

A long time afterwards, or so it seemed to him, he woke up and wondered for a moment where he was. Or, indeed, what time it was. His cheeks were tear-stained. Some disgusting left-overs sat in front of him. Everyone was looking around expect-antly. Xu Yousheng heard high-heeled shoes tapping along the corridor, clicking firmly on the marble tiles. The irregular, unhurried rhythm conjured up the woman's extravagantly swaying hips, as if every step might snap her waist in two. Then the door was pushed open. The heels penetrated the carpet with a soft hushing sound, and Xu Yousheng was immediately, painfully, in love again. She wore a backless, tight-fitting blue silk dress with a pink butterfly bow, and she stepped, then paused, like a model on a catwalk.

Xu Yousheng watched as she approached Shu Shuang, who had opened his arms to her. She flicked back a cascade of immaculately permed hair, put one foot down, extended the other leg, leaned back luxuriously into his embrace, and bestowed a smile on them all. She looked around her. A whiff of perm solution had come in with her. Then, as if she had suddenly realised her father was in the room, she got off Shu Shuang, pulled up a leather chair and sat down, very properly.

'What's up, darling?' Shu Shuang murmured, pressing his lips to her cheek. She smiled stiffly and said nothing. She didn't even glance at Xu Yousheng. It was if she didn't know him, as if they were complete strangers and he was beneath her notice.

When Xu Yousheng raised one hand in greeting, she simply flicked back a lock of dark brown hair and kept her eyes on the floor. Then, to cover up the incident, he picked at a morsel of cold spring roll and chewed it carefully.

Her hair style goes so well with her dainty face and those soft lily-white breasts that I can just see under her dress. She's so beautiful, even if she does have dark shadows under her eyes, thought Xu Yousheng, devouring her with a look. He felt himself smile inwardly, expressive, sorrowful, the way Chow Yun-Fat smiled in his films. He looked up at the sparkling chandelier hanging from the ceiling, and recalled summer afternoons when he used to go to the brick and tile factory, wading barefoot in the warm mud. He remembered the slurry oozing sensuously between his toes, and the obscene squelching noises as he put his feet down over and over again. It was the same intoxicating sound as when he and she had sex. He remembered ramming into her, thrusting in and out, just yesterday. But she had made it clear that she did not know him any more. How fickle she was, to have switched sides so quickly.

A long pause, a very long pause, and Shu Shuang understood. 'I see! Now I see!' he said, lifting a finger in the air. Xu Yousheng suddenly felt that he was not afraid of anything. It really did not matter. Jin Yan was still looking down. Shu Shuang almost dragged her over to Xu Yousheng, and made them sit together. Then he stood behind them.

'You're my mate, and you're Jin Yan . . . Xu Yousheng, she was your uncle's woman before, now you can call her "little sister-in-law".'

'Right,' said Xu Yousheng.

'Now I know why neither of you were talking,' said Shu Shuang. 'But it's OK.'

Xu Yousheng let Shu Shuang clap him heavily on the shoulder. She's got warts on her fanny, two of them, on the left, he thought. That's her left, not the left as you look at her. I hope you've taken note of that.

'Hongyang was like an older brother to me for years, and I respected him even though I had no reason to,' Shu Shuang went on.

'Right,' said Xu Yousheng.

'But he's gone now, he's up and left this world behind. So now she's free. I'd set my woman free too, if I died. I mean, I wouldn't take her with me, you get my meaning? So from her point of view I can't see anything wrong with it.'

'Right,' said Xu Yousheng.

'Hongyang's dead, and she's penniless and alone. She doesn't even have anywhere to live, so she needs someone to look after her, and who's that going to be? When you think about it, can you think of anyone better than me?'

'No,' came Xu Yousheng's monosyllabic reply.

'You're Hongyang's cousin, Hongbin's nephew, so you're one of his family. I hope you can see it from my point of view.'

'Yes, indeed.'

'Good. We're both reasonable men, aren't we?'

'Right.'

Shu Shuang and Xu Yousheng clinked glasses. Every time Shu Shuang said there was nothing wrong with what she'd done, Xu Yousheng had to respond. But he kept thinking about those warts. They must have been sexually transmitted, genital warts. When Shu Shuang demanded the keys to his photographic studio – 'There's an official delegation from Hong Kong being entertained in the hotel right now,' he explained. 'I don't want any problems, we need to find somewhere else tonight' – Xu Yousheng complied. 'It's just for one night,' said Shu Shuang.

The other men began to say their goodbyes. Xu Yousheng dipped his finger in the tea and amused himself writing names on the polished tabletop. He thought back to when he and Shu

Shuang had spent all night watching football, and about their
enthusiasm for *Sports Weekly*. They used to buy one newspaper
between them, split it in two, read half each, then swap. Those
were the days. The names disappeared as soon as he'd written
them: Jimmy Floyd Hasselbaink, Luca Toni, Sebastián Verón,
Rivaldo, Zlatan Ibrahimović, Nicolas Anelka, Christian Vieri.

37

Dreams were cheap and plentiful for the villagers, who went to bed early. Forced to cope with the boundless emptiness of their lives, they took their dreams and the revelations they brought very seriously. They took a forensic interest in the night-time visions that visited their bodies, savoured them, and mulled them over. After the dream machine had run through a number of cycles, a pair or more of matching dreams were miraculously produced.

And so it happened that early in the morning of the day the task force from the township arrived in Aiwan, a stream of villagers dropped in on Hongbin. They claimed to be experiencing a general feeling of unease, an uncomfortable feeling that they wanted to get to the bottom of. On their way to his house they talked, and realised to their astonishment that they had all had the same dream. Every detail coincided. In the dream, they were standing in a dark corner, watching a man strung up from a roof beam, his wrists bound behind his back, being beaten. Every time the man with the whip discovered that it had dried out, he dipped it in a bucket to wet it again. The cracks it made were usually to be heard in the fields, because it was the whip for the plough-oxen, but now it was being used on a human body. The victim's polyester shirt was shredded by the blows, as if someone had taken a knife to it, and his back had been beaten raw. With every thwack, the dreamers in the corner flinched. Although they wanted to sneak out of the dark room, they did not dare move towards the light, could not move their feet. Each one of them felt trapped there, holding their breath and watching that appalling scene.

It'll be my turn next, each of them thought, shrinking back in fear as they watched the victim in the dim light, his tormented flesh stretched taut. After him, it'll be me.

'Did you see it too?' Hongbin asked the growing crowd who had come to commiserate with him. On the verge of tears, he was beginning to believe that this was not a private punishment but a public humiliation. His tormentor had pulled him up by the hair and dragged him in front of the other villagers. At least thirteen people answered: 'Yes!' though at the start each one had believed he or she had been the only observer.

'I don't understand why!' Hongbin said, holding his head between his hands and shaking it. 'He was so angry, he hated my guts, but he never told me why he was so angry.'

In the dream, Hongbin was struggling desperately, his suspended body swaying in the air. But his tormentor did not say a word, just kept raising the whip and beating him. The kerosene lamp sat on a bench. Hongbin was convinced that he had committed no offence, not even in thought, let alone in deed. Everything he had done for his tormentor had been out of loyalty. Hongyang seemed to have reached his own conclusions, though. And when that happened, he would not listen no matter how hard the other man tried to argue his way out of it. He was so stubborn and dogmatic! Still, this was the first time he had treated Hongbin this way.

Hongbin never imagined that Hongyang might beat him. Hongyang was essentially unfathomable, but to beat up someone who had only ever been loyal to you, and on whom you depended, in whom you apparently had absolute confidence, was utterly shocking. It was beyond rhyme or reason, like beating up your own bed, your favourite brand of cigarettes or tea mug. He must have been insane to behave like that. And those who had had the same dream as Hongbin all believed that they could have accepted Hongyang beating up his own parents or teachers – even, if it came to it, beating up his own sister, Muxiang – but it was unthinkable that he should beat up Hongbin, who had devoted himself body and soul to Hongyang for his entire life, like a dog. This was off the bottom of the scale of moral principle, absolutely beyond their ken. Even though it was a dream. Even though this kind of thing only happened in a dream. It was as painful as if he had taken a saw to Hongbin and cut through his skin and flesh. Hongbin felt as if his flesh were being split apart and sweat and salt were flowing out of the wound. The pain at least served to bring him back to consciousness. In his dream, Hongyang seemed to be saying: 'The pain is to bring you back to consciousness.'

'What did I do wrong?' asked Hongbin.

His companion was silent. He just continued to whip him with the assiduity of a craftsman until the ash-coloured whip, as thick as a man's thumb, snapped in two.

They were in an abandoned forester's hut. The building was made of smoke-blackened planks nailed together and it stank of piss, shit and blood. It sat the foot of a cliff, or in a deep gully. The dreamers knew that it was completely isolated, with no trace of human habitation for a dozen li around, dozens of li, hundreds of li around.

Hongyang stepped on the broken whip and pulled the handle off it. Then he bent down and took off one cloth shoe and began to beat Hongbin with that. He seemed to be telling Hongbin: You count the strokes. And so Hongbin counted, until the numbers became entangled like a ball of woollen yarn. Hongbin felt his face puffing up, especially his left eye, which looked like a blood-red plum, the lid so heavy he couldn't open it. Hongbin needed to lift his head to see the man who was beating him. The blood dripped from his nose and the corners of his mouth. Taking a momentary break, Hongyang gave Hongbin's body a shove so it swung like a child's swing, then with a sudden jerk pulled down Hongbin's trousers. They fell to his knees, then to his feet, and wrapped themselves around his ankles. Then Hongyang pulled down his underpants. Hongbin felt the coolness at his crotch and, oddly, his almost-virginal penis stiffened and the tip pushed out of his foreskin. With a contemptuous laugh, Hongyang took off the cover of the kerosene lamp, reached inside with a candle and lit it from the wick, then held the lighted candle upside down. As the molten candle wax began to drip, Hongyang brought it near to Hongbin so that the drops fell on Hongbin's penis. Hongbin doubled up. He felt his penis blister.

Hongyang, a man who exhibited extraordinary patience when tormenting others, finally lifted the lantern and took a long, quiet look at Hongbin. By this time, Hongbin had stopped trying to argue his way out of it. Now he gazed imploringly, pitifully, at Hongyang, like a small, trapped animal. The lamplight only made the surrounding darkness seem more intense. According to all those who shared the dream, the pitch-dark felt like a wild beast staring at them, ready to swallow them in its bottomless gaze. Hongyang looked for a long time, then spat a solid gob of spittle into Hongbin's swollen left eye. It felt painfully hot. Then he took off his gloves, threw them down and left. At that point, the walls and doors that blocked them in seemed not to exist any more, and Hongyang walked straight through them and onto the murky road, which took him to ever-darker places.

'You tell me, what did I do wrong?' asked Hongbin, gingerly feeling his genitals until he was reassured they had suffered no damage.

'Nothing,' they said.

'Then what was he trying to tell me?'

'We don't see it like that. If he wanted anything from you, he wouldn't have done it that way.'

38

'It may be battered, but it's German-made.' That's what they said.

When the Xiayuan Party Secretary and the village committee chairman arrived from Tianjiapu on their bicycles, standing hard on the pedals, first the left, then the right, and pouring sweat, they were brought face-to-face with Ho Dongming, Party committee member and township executive deputy mayor, who was aggrieved that he was always given the worst jobs, never the cushy ones. On this occasion, it was levelling the graves. They had told him: 'We're giving you all the power and all the men you want, you have licence to kill. Act first, report later.' And with all their remaining energy they heaped praises on Ho Dongming's new acquisition, a second-hand Mercedes. With the left hand, they scratched their heads, while with the right, they stroked and rubbed the car's bonnet until they had scratched out all the grease that encrusted the cracks.

It was true that when Hongbin turned up in Tianjiapu to ask permission for a burial on the day of Hongyang's sudden demise, they had not agreed outright. What they actually said was: 'We're fine about it if the township authorities agree.' And Hongbin said: 'I wouldn't be here if they hadn't agreed, would I?' So they repeated: 'If the township authorities agree, then we have no problem with it,' and subsequently they witnessed each other registering the gifts that Hongbin had brought as a bribe. But if the township authorities were to investigate, they could hardly evade responsibility, since their action could be regarded as connivance, or even active involvement in, an illegal action – namely a burial – and this would lead at the very least to a warning, and at worst to dismissal. They could not defend themselves by claiming that the township authorities had agreed to it. No, that would be fatal, even though they had heard a number of the township bigwigs saying to Hongyang at the banquet: 'We don't have any objection, so long as the village doesn't mind.'

Ho Dongming looked at them and nodded, then turned to gaze at the scenery, hands clasped behind his back. 'Pepper Ho' enjoyed the apprehension of people who knew they were skating on thin ice. Although he could be forgiving – and intended to be so now – he had no intention of letting them know straight away. He would wait for today's business to wrap up, and perhaps even a little longer than that, before stating his position. Let them ponder, let them chew it over for a bit. He had come with plenty of reinforcements today, including a total of fourteen local government officials. With the civilian and the military thus represented, there was no need for the village committee to intercede. As soon as he made his grand entrance into the village, leading his posse of eighty people, the village work team leader rushed over like a buzzing housefly, just like the Earth God in *Journey to the West*, pulled a cigarette out of his seven-yuan packet of cheap Jinsheng that were probably left over from the funeral, and offered it to him.

'No,' said Ho Dongming fiercely. Thus rebuffed, the team leader stood miserably at a distance, trembling slightly. Ho Dongming had it in mind to ask him why he had not cleaned the bluish-black dirt from under his fingernails. The ditches had been cleaned, so there was all the more reason for a man's fingernails to be clean too. Instead, he waited while an underling went to fetch Hongyang's next of kin, Shuizhi, who was doing the laundry down by the river.

It was impossible to tell by her appearance that she was newly widowed and would soon be rich. She wore a blue

Dacron army jacket given to her by Shifei when he was de-mobilised, threadbare blue trousers of the sort old people wore, and black wellington boots. Her steel-grey hair was held in place by a cheap clip, and she looked expressionless, vacant and mulish. She wiped her soapy hands on her plastic apron and looked at the threshing floor, where a total of seven cars, two minibuses, a police car, an ambulance, a propaganda van and a truck were parked. The furthest vehicle was parked outside the house of another cousin, Hongbing. There was an excavator loaded onto the truck bed, its orange arm suspended a dozen or so feet in the air, as if ready to carry off or push over the roofs of some of the surrounding houses.

Prior to launching the operation, the township Party Secretary had asked the head of the disciplinary committee, a Mr Wang: 'I'm going to Aiwan to dig up Hongyang's grave. How many people do you think I'll need?' 'About twenty should be fine,' said Wang. But then he asked Ho Dongming, who said: 'At least eighty!' And Wang nodded his approval. Before they went into action, Ho Dongming went personally to the local police to check the household registers and count how many able-bodied young men there were in Aiwan, though in reality, he already knew full well how many there were. As his troops passed the automobile parts workshop, he made them stop and had the entire cavalcade of cars checked over to ensure there would be no mechanical problems.

All Ho Dongming had to do now was go to the widow and announce the prohibition on burials. He did not need to do that, but it was preferable. Later, when she complained, it could not be written into the report that he had never even greeted her.

'Are you the next of kin of the recently deceased Ai Hongyang?' asked young Ma, from the Civil Administration Office.

'I'm Shuizhi.'

'I'm asking you, are you the deceased's widow?'

'The what?'

'Widow, wife . . .'

'I'm Ai Hongyang's family.'

At this point, Shuizhi appeared to remember some previous warnings, and simply answered his questions with an 'Uh.' Even when Ma sighed at the bad weather they were having, she answered as if she was half-asleep, and Ma felt that he, a proper man, was being made a fool of by an idiot. He held up his finger and waved it in front of her eyes. He moved it to the left, her eyes followed. He moved his finger to the right, the same thing happened. The head of the village committee saw what was going on and came running, ready to repeat what Ma was saying, word for word, and adding shouted explanations as if Shuizhi was deaf: 'That is . . .' 'What he means is . . .' Finally, she understood.

'But we haven't done the sevens,' she protested.

'What sevens?'

'It's what we do in the village, because it's only after seven days that the dead man accepts that he's truly dead,' explained the head of the village committee.

'I know, but they're not necessary,' said Ma.

'But I'm not the head of the family, I can't decide,' objected Shuizhi.

'Who can, then?' asked Ma.

'Team head,' muttered Shuizhi, then after a pause, added: 'Family head.'

And so the task force saw practically all the male workers of Aiwan village appear on the threshold to their houses, though they didn't deign to come down the steps, instead leaning on their hoes, or holding a shovel or pole over their shoulders or a plough yoke on their back, or remaining busy at the knife-grinder, or retrieving an axe embedded in a log, as if they were on the point of going to work. They all looked in the same direction, as if they had only this moment noticed the vehicles. As far as the task force were concerned, it was just a look, while for the widow who had given every household ten thousand yuan, it was a stare replete with condemnation, resistance and threat. The men had ways of dealing with matters ambiguously, so that their opponents could not object. Only the children were unequivocally joyful, running madly between the cars, touching first this one then that one, shouting loudly in approval. Now and then, a cry was heard, presumably because one of the children had seen a familiar face among the task force. 'You look so scary!' they yelled. Or: 'Why don't you have a go at the De'an folk, if you're up to it. Why are you charging in here?'

'Who the fuck do you think you're talking to?' There was the plump figure of Li Jun in his camouflage uniform, a veritable tiger of a man, striding unstoppably into the village carrying a red firefighting axe. 'Forget De'an, it's you who'll get taught a lesson today!' Suddenly, even the birds went quiet, only the mountain echoed his shouts. This infuriated the Aiwan men, who ground their teeth and trembled with rage yet seemed unable to extricate themselves from the silence that held them in its grip like boiling waves and rolling thunder. They tried several times – it should not have been that difficult, should it? – but were unable to step forward.

Finally, Li Jun left again with his axe. Shuizhi's sobs and sniffles made everyone feel guilty, as if they owed her something, as if they owed the whole world a favour, as if they were an utter disgrace.

At this point, Hongbin was still trying to separate his dream from reality. He was sitting in the shade slumped forward on a stone, his brows tightly knitted, his cheek propped on his right hand, his knees tucked in a little, sunk in thought, immersed in sorrow deep as a lake. As the task force's thirteen vehicles drove slowly westwards out of the village beeping their horns, making it clear they had come to flatten Hongyang's grave, Hongbin stirred himself from his torpor and moved his stool from the road to allow them to pass. He was still so deep in thought that he'd forgotten where he had put the stool. He thought: If I were really Hongyang's mate, I'd go and stop them because they've gone back on their word. He was the one who decided we weren't mates, though. All those people saw him pull down my trousers and leave me hanging there naked, it's not just me making up fairy tales. And if I'm not his mate, then I'll act how I did in my dream. How can someone act out their dream, anyway? It's embarrassing, ridiculous nonsense. If only that dream could be blown away by the wind, but it's like a demon, reminding me of a fact that I had never previously dared to imagine. That doesn't mean it didn't exist, of course: Hongyang was like a shaggy ram pushing through a flock of white sheep. He humiliated and dishonoured me. If only he were still alive. It's as if he had treated his parents or teachers that way. That's why he did it: he must have wanted to be completely alone. For a moment, Hongbin had the urge to walk into the empty space between the villagers and the task force and embrace someone, anyone, and tell them in all sincerity this hard-won truth: There is no loyalty in this world. He felt something crumble inside him, like a hillside about to collapse.

It was one of his two sons who led him out of the quagmire of his thoughts. 'Dad! We won't have any more graves now!'

It dawned on Hongbin what his duty was, and he made for the enemy lines. It was as if he was back in the time when Hongyang was still alive: there stood the friend he had shared banquets with, a government dignitary, standing with his hands clasped behind his back.

'Dongming! Dongming!' he shouted, with shameless familiarity.

Ho Dongming turned and watched the approach of this unintelligent man, so earnest in his desire to understand before he acted. Some of the young men who were anxious to win the approval of their superiors blocked his way.

Hongbin protested: 'But I know Dongming! I know him. I've known him for years!'

Ho Dongming considered the decade-old 'friendship' between himself and Hongbin, between himself and Hongyang, feeling their admiration, and felt it was a pity to be breaking it off. It's them I feel sorry for, Ho Dongming thought. Then he addressed them: 'And you are . . .?'

Hongbin froze. His limbs trembled a little then went rigid and immobile. The light died in his eyes. Ho Dongming turned away and left his underlings to deal with Hongbin. Breaking up a friendship was straightforward enough, he thought. The void he had felt since he arrived in Aiwan now began to fill a little.

Soon he heard Hongbin's outraged cries behind him. 'I'm an ordinary man, a man of the people!' he yelled, ignoring the men trying to block his way, and flailed furiously as though swimming his way to Ho Dongming. 'I'm a man of the people!' Hongbin repeated, as if asserting his new status and the duties and responsibilities that went with it. He was a countryman at heart and he alternated between childish self-justification, ridiculous threats and a deluded insistence that he was still the township deputy mayor's friend. 'May I be so bold as to ask . . .?' and 'Do excuse me but . . .' issuing from his mouth, these unaccustomed diplomatic phrases acquired a degree of assertiveness.

Ho Dongming recalled his playboy days, when they had loafed around, their sleeves rolled up to expose their tattooed arms, conning their way into the palace of culture and the dance hall, games hall and billiards hall opposite, bored to death but unwilling to give up the freedom of this lifestyle. One day, at a loss for what to do next, they had catalogued the language that could choke the speech out of a living person. These days, he was well prepared. Sometimes he did not even allow the other person to finish the sentence before he hit back with some of the phrases they had garnered back then: Oh, surely not . . . No, I couldn't allow . . . That would be too much . . . Really? . . . Sorry . . . Do you think so? . . . Hey! . . . Oh! . . . Is that right? . . . You're very funny . . . Take your time . . . It's up to you . . . A-yo! . . . Already? . . . Hey . . . Goodbye then . . . Someone like you . . . What can you do? . . . Let me tell you . . . Look how you . . . As for 'Actually', he used it in three different senses:

1. To indicate a brand-new discovery

2. Meaning 'of course', or 'exactly what was wanted'

3. To indicate that the conclusion was obvious, inevitable, and that there was no doubt

As these cutting, sarcastic, mocking phrases tripped fluently off his tongue, Ho Dongming was amazed at his own duplicity, his limitless capacity for despicable behaviour. It was if his lips had been taken over by some demonic presence. His underlings too looked at him in awe, as if he were a travelling magician. Hongbin was able only to repeat a few sentences that sounded quite reasonable to him, but was soon utterly routed. This showed that under pressure, his brain had lost its capacity to function. As the old saying went, he could only ward off the blows, he could not retaliate.

Finally, he stopped arguing, held back the tears and looked at Ho Dongming. In the darkness of his nostrils, the hairs could be seen standing erect like criss-crossed guns, on which the mucus glistened a light green. Ho Dongming felt embarrassed. He felt the urge to go and pat Hongbin on the shoulder and say that he was just teasing. This would be an easy thing for the godlike Ho Dongming to do. Later, the head of water management, who had started out as a village cadre and risen through the ranks and so knew Hongbin, went and gave him a cigarette, put his arm around his shoulders and said a few words to him, and Hongbin seemed to come to terms with it, saying: 'You should have told me this earlier. It would have been better if you'd told me this earlier.'

When the grave was being dug out, the chair of the village committee brought over a high-backed chair and made Deputy Mayor Ho sit in the paddy field at the foot of the crag. The latter had come equipped with a bottle of smelling salts, which he unscrewed straight away and sniffed deeply. Then he crossed his legs and gazed upwards. The task force held their hoes at the ready to begin the excavation. They brought them down to bite the earth, and then flicked it to one side. Soon the handles of their tools came loose, and they knelt and used stones to bang the pegs back into the holes that attached the blade to the handle. They complained that someone had beaten the loose earth so hard that it was harder than stones. The two labourers hired by the civil administration office stood to one side with a brown canvas stretcher, looking earnest.

The village Party Secretary broke the silence: 'Down the ages, the stronger a man, the more grotesque the manner of his death. Some have died laughing, some from mosquito bites, some brandished a hammer to urge on their troops and it dropped on them and killed them. Hongyang died because he was hot and then got cold.'

'Right, but when you're dead it's all the same, as if you've been licked up,' said Ho Dongming.

'Right,' said the Party Secretary. After a while, he added: 'A man as big as Hongyang ... it'll take a lot of firewood to cremate him. We don't want the body to explode. I think the crematorium workers had better stab his corpse all over?'

The godlike Ho Dongming, son of the illustrious Political and Legal Affairs Committee Secretary, did not reply. By this time, a dense mass of villagers had converged on the highway, including those from nearby villages such as Gangbei, Wenfu, Duoshi and Yanwozhou, but as the light faded, they could see little. These men and women who had been reduced to spiritual impotence walked along the dykes to get closer, some of them even standing in front of Deputy Mayor Ho.

Political Instructor Zhao Zhongnan shooed them away as if they were a flock of ducks, pushing them back to what he considered an appropriate distance. 'And not a step closer!' he commanded. But when his back was turned, they crept a few steps forward anyway.

In a little while, rumours reached them that the coffin was visible: stones were being cleared off its lid and flung aside. Because the nails had been driven in so deep, the lid could not be prised off, so the head of civil administration took the decision to hack the coffin open. The wood was quite thin, a dozen blows of the axe were enough. Then they heard: 'Oh my God!' and the man threw down his axe and leapt out of the way. There was pandemonium as the swarm of onlookers fell back in fright before reassembling and pressing forward again to peer avidly into the coffin. Liu Taotao, a seventeen-year-old hanger-on of Shu Shuang's and a loudmouth by nature, glanced at it a few times then hared off downhill, almost flying off the crag.

The news arrived in the village almost immediately, and caused mayhem. The villagers knew they shouldn't go and look, that if they did it would haunt them forever, but they stampeded to get there. Some were even trampled to death. As they scrambled up the crag, pushing and shoving, they churned the earth into a morass. Even though they knew what awaited them, the shock of seeing it with their own eyes would not be reduced in the slightest.

'Terrible! Terrible! Terrible! Unspeakable! Unimaginably awful!' shouted Liu Taotao, still running.

'What?' asked the people coming in the opposite direction.

'Don't ask me to say any more, go and see for yourselves.'

Glossary

The following definitions are intended only to indicate approximate meaning within the context of this novel. The practices described vary in different parts of China, and may have fallen out of use.

adamantine fist: A powerful martial arts technique.

barefoot doctor: Basic healthcare providers in the Chinese countryside, employing both Chinese and Western medicine, widespread during the Cultural Revolution (1966–76).

dan singer: The female role (sung by a man) in traditional Chinese opera.

dragon poles: Long poles sometimes decorated with dragons, which may be used by pall-bearers to support a traditional Chinese coffin.

the Eight Immortals: Legendary Daoist figures who, through cultivating virtue, became godlike, immortal beings. Believed to have been real people born in the Tang or Song dynasties, they were seven men and one woman.

the Empress Dowager: Refers here to the Empress Dowager Cixi (1835–1908), of the Manchu/Qing dynasty. She acted as regent and effectively controlled the Chinese government for forty-seven years, from 1861 until her death in 1908.

fox demon: In Chinese folklore, foxes are depicted as mischievous spirits with magical powers, able to disguise themselves as beautiful women.

ghost money: Also known as funeral money, joss money/paper, or yellow offerings paper. Fake banknotes sometimes burned to ensure that the spirit of the deceased family member has sufficient funds in the afterlife.

guanxi: Refers to a network of personal and social relationships that play an important role in Chinese society.

guqin: A seven-stringed Chinese musical instrument which is played by plucking.

Hanlin scholars: An elite group of scholars who made up the Hanlin Academy, an academic institution founded in eighth-century China.

hired mourners: Professional mourners traditionally hired to accompany family members at a funeral.

hukou residence certificate: The hukou system is the means by which an individual is registered within a household in a specified location in mainland China.

a jin of spirit: A jin is most commonly one pound or five hundred grams in weight, but the jin is also sometimes used to measure liquids, when it equals about five hundred millilitres.

Journey to the West: See 'just like the Earth God in *Journey to the West*'. The novel, published in the sixteenth century during the Ming dynasty and attributed to Wu Cheng'en, is one of the most popular classic Chinese stories. It recounts the adventures of the real-life Buddhist monk Xuanzang, who travelled to India during the Tang dynasty to obtain the Buddhist sutras, and his companions, Monkey, Pigsy and Sandy.

khata: A ceremonial scarf traditionally given as a gift in Tibetan Buddhism.

li: Five hundred metres.

Liberation: Refers to the establishment of the People's Republic of China in 1949.

mantou: Bread buns which are steamed rather than baked.

Mao suit: Type of man's suit with a stand-up collar, originally worn by the early revolutionary figure Sun Yat-Sen, later adopted by officials throughout China, notably Mao himself.

Mount Lao: A mountain situated in Shandong province,

traditionally one of the cradles of Daoism. Numerous monasteries and nunneries have flourished there down the years, and many of the monks practised magical arts.

the mourning staff: Traditionally, the eldest son of the family would lead the funeral procession carrying a mourning staff, a wooden stick with a piece of white fabric attached.

normal school: Teacher-training college.

Procuratorate: The people's procuratorates in China are government offices responsible for the investigation and prosecution of offenders.

qipao dresses: More commonly known as cheongsam, these are tight-fitting dresses with a slit up to the thigh.

Reform through Education camp: A type of prison institution.

the sevens: The forty-nine days after a person's death when Buddhist monks may be hired to chant and perform rituals.

Shanghai-brand watch: A watch from the Shanghai Watch Factory, one of China's oldest watch manufacturers, used to grant its wearer instant prestige.

'Sorry he'd hurt the feelings of his brothers and sisters, the common masses': Possibly a sly allusion to the phrase 'hurting the feelings of the Chinese people'. The latter accusation is often used by the Chinese government when it condemns criticism of China by the foreign media.

spirit tablet: A spirit tablet, memorial tablet or ancestral tablet has the name of the deceased person inscribed on it and is commonly placed in shrines and on household altars.

Suona: The shawm, a musical instrument with a reed.

ONEWORLD FICTION

The Oneworld fiction list has always been committed to publishing the very best writing from around the world – brilliant stories that inspire, provoke, and shine a light on different cultures and ways of living. In the twelve years since the launch of our fiction list, we have published novels in twenty-three languages from over thirty-five countries, and our titles have won numerous prizes from the Man Booker, Women's Prize and Irish Novel of the Year Award to the Goncourt du Premier Roman, the Prix des Cinq Continents, the Leo Tolstoy Yasnaya Polyana Award, as well as the Read Russia Prize, the Finlandia Prize and the Glass Key Award.

Among our translated novels you will find some of the most respected and interesting writers working today – authors like Samanta Schweblin, who was shortlisted for the Man Booker International Prize for her novel, *Fever Dream*, and Ahmed Saadawi, author of *Frankenstein in Baghdad*, winner of the International Prize for Arabic Fiction. We will continue to search out and bring you the very best fiction from around the world, but in the meantime, why not check out the books we have already published: www.oneworld-publications.com.

AVAILABLE AND FORTHCOMING TRANSLATED FICTION

A Perfect Crime by A Yi (Chinese)
Translated by Anna Holmwood

Fever Dream by Samanta
Schweblin (Spanish, Argentina)
Translated by Megan McDowell

Frankenstein in Baghdad by
Ahmed Saadawi (Arabic, Iraq)
Translated by Jonathan Wright

Laurus by Eugene Vodolazkin
(Russian)
Translated by Lisa C. Hayden

Little Eyes by Samanta Schweblin
(Spanish, Argentina)
Translated by Megan McDowell

Sweet Bean Paste by Durian
Sukegawa (Japanese)
Translated by Alison Watts

The Hen Who Dreamed She Could Fly
by Sun-mi Hwang (Korean)
Translated by Chi-young Kim

*The Invisible Life of Euridice
Gusmão* by Martha Batalha
(Portuguese, Brazil)
Translated by Eric M. B. Becker

The Meursault Investigation by
Kamel Daoud (French, Algeria)
Translated by John Cullen

The Unit by Ninni Holmqvist
(Swedish)
Translated by Marlaine Delargy

Things We Left Unsaid by Zoya
Pirzad (Persian)
Translated by Franklin Lewis

Three Apples Fell from the Sky
by Narine Abgaryan (Russian,
Armenia)
Translated by Lisa C. Hayden

Umami by Laia Jufresa (Spanish,
Mexico)
Translated by Sophie Hughes

Voices of the Lost by Hoda Barakat
(Arabic, Lebanon)
Translated by Marilyn Booth

This World Does Not Belong to Us
by Natalia García Freire
(Spanish, Ecuador)
Translated by Victor
Meadowcroft

© Lv Haiqiang

A Yi (阿乙) was born in Ruichang, a city in China's Jiangxi province. He worked as a police officer before becoming editor-in-chief of *Chutzpah*, an avant-garde literary magazine. He is the author of two collections of short stories, and his fiction has appeared in *Granta* and the *Guardian*. In 2010 he was shortlisted for the People's Literature 'Top 20 Literary Giants of the Future'. In 2012, his novel *A Perfect Crime* was published in China (English edition Oneworld, 2015). *Wake Me Up at Nine in the Morning* is his latest work, first published in China in 2018.

Nicky Harman is a literary translator from Chinese. Her work focuses on contemporary fiction, literary non-fiction and occasionally poetry, by a wide range of Chinese authors. Her translations include *Broken Wings* by Jia Pingwa, *The Chilli Bean Paste Clan* by Yan Ge and *Our Story: A Memoir of Love and Life in China* by Rao Pingru. She is a trustee of Paper Republic, a charity which exists to promote Chinese literature in English translation.